THE BEAR AND HIS DAUGHTER
Copyright © 2017 by Peter Fane
All rights reserved.

Published by Silver Goat Media, LLC, Fargo, ND 58108. This publication is protected by copyright, and permission should be obtained from the publisher prior to any reproduction, storage in a retrieval system, or transmission in any form or by any means, electronic, mechanical, photocopying, recording, or likewise. SGM books are available at discounts, regardless of quantity, for K-12 schools, non-profits, or other educational institutions. To obtain permission(s) to use material from this work, or to order in bulk, please submit a written request to Silver Goat Media, LLC, PO Box 2336, Fargo, ND 58108, or contact SGM directly at: info@silvergoatmedia.com.

This book was designed and produced by Silver Goat Media, LLC.
Fargo, ND U.S.A. www.silvergoatmedia.com
SGM and the SGM goat are trademarks of Silver Goat Media, LLC.

Cover art: Kan Liu and Lucia Xiang, *The Last Arrow* © 2017 SGM
Cover design: Travis Klath © 2017 SGM
Author Photo: Tamara Weets © 2016 SGM

This book was typeset in Perpetua Silver by Cady Ann Mittlestadt and Aurora McClain.

ISBN-10: 1-944296-11-5
ISBN-13: 978-1-944296-11-7 (Silver Goat Media)

A portion of the annual proceeds from the sale of this book
is donated to the Longspur Prairie Fund.
www.longspurprairie.org

Started by

  Peter Fane is on Facebook, Twitter, and Instagram. Come visit for maps, art, and stories!

First SGM printing—November 2017, Fargo, ND 1.0—301117
Printed and bound in the United States of America.

The Bear and His Daughter

A Tale from the Canon of Tarn

Peter Fane

The Kingdom of Remain spans all space and memory.

It is the Eternal Kingdom, the Silver Kingdom, an ancient sphere born of our love and our sorrow, our blood and our joy.

The Kingdom of Remain encompasses countless stars and minds. It has served our people for millennia. And we have served it in return.

The Kingdom of Remain is our place. It is our home.

The Kingdom of Remain is our legacy. It is our story.

It is the only tale we have worth telling.

The following events take place in the Twentieth Year of Bellános III, Founding Year 12,032.

Cast of Characters

HOUSE HONE—A FRONTIER FAMILY, LIVING ON
THE EDGE OF AARYN'S CRY ABOVE-THE-TRANGE

DARRO HONE, Branten Hone's brother, killed by Balmás
Dallanar in F.Y. 12,014.

BRANTEN HONE, a trapper, hunter, woodsman, and more.

MARGARET HONE, Branten's wife and confidant.

TEAGAN HONE, a boy of 18 years; injured as a newborn.

EVAN HONE, a boy of 16 years.

ELIZABETH HONE, a girl of 15 years.

SOLDIER, the Hone's 7-year-old rock mastiff.

LITTLE ROSIE AND COMPANY, a pack of hunting
hounds; various ages.

A GREY BEAR CUB, just over six months old.

SOME LOCAL VILLAGERS, HUNTERS, AND FRONTIERSMEN

MR. OTTO JARLUND, a Konungur stockman and loremaster.

MR. AIMO BARNABUS, a merchant; seller of dry goods and tackle.

BELIOS BARNABUS, a boy of 16 years.

BEIRO BARNABUS, a boy of 15 years.

MR. PAAVALI FONHAMMER, a trapper, hunter, and woodsman.

JUREK FONHAMMER, a boy of 19 years.

ANSA FONHAMMER, a girl of 17 years.

INARI FONHAMMER, a girl of 15 years.

MR. SULO TULF, a Konungur trapper, woodsman, and agitator.

LORD TOMAS MODRÓ, a poacher, thief, and killer from the
Duchy of Farák.

CAPTAIN COLJ'S SQUAD

CAPTAIN FELLEN COLJ, an ogre of Jallow, the Tarn's Captain of the Guard.

MASTER BENGAMON ZAR, the Master of Arms of House Dradón; an Anorian veteran.

GREGORY, a messenger dragon of Dávanor, Master Zar's pet and friend, 11 palms long, 399 years old.

NIVAR XEN VARREN, a Targead assassin and arbiter, the 17-year-old son of Varren xen Cenoren, the Grand Master of Assassins, House Targon.

SISTER DARIAN FAER, an Anótean seer, the 14-year-old daughter of High Seer of Anótos, Doron Faer.

OOMA, a Helvanthían air squid.

LORD DORÓMY'S ENTOURAGE

HIGH LORD DORÓMY DALLANAR, High Chancellor of Remain, Brother of Bellános Dallanar, the Silver King, and wielder of the Vordan; also known as "the Iron Lion."

HIGH RANGER GIÁCOMA NORFELL, a bear rider, warden of the Tarn, and Dorómy's adopted daughter; murdered by persons unknown in F.Y. 12,032.

LORD GAREN DALLANAR, Lord Dorómy's 12-year-old nephew, son of Bellános Dallanar; a young prodigy, scholar, and healer unmatched in the Realm.

LORD LAYNE TEVÉSS, a braggart, fool, and Lord of Dávanor, a young man of 21 years.

CAPTAIN ERIK DYER, a dragon knight of Dávanor, Captain of the Sundaggers.

VOIDBANE, a war dragon of Dávanor, Dyer's mount, jet-black, 61 paces long, 99 years old.

"Deception lies at the Heart of Politics, Diplomacy, and War; these cannot exist without Deceit. For this Reason, a wise Prince will study the Falsehoods of his Family, his Friends, and his Enemies as carefully as he studies the Facts he knows to be true. The Ability to know Dishonesty—and to use that Knowledge wisely—is a Mark of true Power. But above all else, there is this: A Prince who would keep his Throne can lie to everyone forever, but he can never lie to himself; Deceit can live everywhere, save his own Heart."

> – Katherine II, *The Canon of Tarn*, "Prolegomena to Imperial Tactics and Diplomacies." F.Y. 189

1

"WHAT'S THAT?!" TEAGAN cried into the freezing wind. "You hear that, Liz?!"

"Yes." Elizabeth Hone nodded calmly. She'd already stopped on the snowy path and cocked her ear at the sound.

Over the mountain's winter wind, through the snow-laden firs, the dogs were barking savagely.

But it wasn't the bay of pursuit.

It was the sound of a fight.

Teagan lifted his furry earflap and tilted his big head in the direction of the dogs' barking. Liz slid her hunting bow from its scabbard. The night sky raced with clouds. The moon was rising white behind the big mountain. When Teagan glanced back at Liz, his eyes were bright with worry.

"That's not right." Teagan looked away, shaking his head, muttering. Liz could barely hear him over the wind. Teagan looked back at her. Snowflakes caked his eyelashes. His cheeks were flushed with cold. "I mean . . . . You *hear* that?!"

"I hear it, Tee," Liz said patiently. She took off her mittens, adjusted her cap, and smoothed a lock of blond hair that had come loose from her braid back behind her ear. Then she bent and strung her bow. Liz was only fifteen years old, but she had an eagle eye and was already an accomplished archer. "Girl can hit a copper sun at fifty paces!" Father would brag to old man Jarlund and the other men down at the village tavern. An icy gust flurried fresh powder from the trees. The moon's hard light made the snow glow.

Another burst of savage barking tore through the wind.

"Come on!" Teagan shouted. He turned off the path, moving between the trees toward the barking dogs, pushing through the knee-high snow up toward the northern ridge. "Come on, Liz!"

Liz followed, walking in her older brother's wake. The

drifts got shallower between the fir trees and the wind was less brutal, but the heavy branches were densely packed with snow and made for hard going.

A yelp of pain ahead of them—then a deeper, more serious barking.

"Soldier!" Teagan shouted, pushing even harder through the drifts, his big, clumsy arms held up as if wading through waist-high water. The ends of his furry cloak brushed the snow crust. "Soldier! What is it, boy?! What is it?!"

Liz slid an iron-tipped arrow from her quiver and nocked it. She understood Teagan's concern. Losing a hound was one thing. *Bad—but ultimately forgivable*. Things went wrong when you were out on the trap lines. But if something happened to their only mastiff, Father would skin them both alive, sure as it was winter.

At the base of the ridge, they pushed into a wide spot between the trees and Teagan stopped short.

Liz edged around him to get a better view—and frowned.

Their rock mastiff, Soldier, and their five hounds had cornered a massive grey bear.

But the bear was dead.

Its left eye was closed peacefully, as if it was sleeping. Its right eye was a bloody squirrel hole, the back of its skull red with gore. Both its front paws had been hacked off at the joint. In the white glow of the moonlight, its silver-grey fur glittered like fresh frost, a frozen statue of a napping bear, the snow 'round it clotted red with blood.

Liz's frown deepened.

Father would be furious.

The hounds edged in at the bear's huge corpse, barked at it like the poor beast was the most dangerous foe they'd ever faced, feinting in and out, stumpy tails poised and alert. Little Rosie's bottom wiggled like mad. Half a palm of snow covered the bear's huge hump. Liz assessed the depth of that snow carefully. *Big guy must've been killed some time ago.* Two, three days at least.

Liz didn't relish the idea of telling Father what they'd found. Father had no patience with poachers, especially those that operated near his trap lines. In fact, the last poach-er Father had caught up here had been sent down to Korfort to turn himself over to the rangers—after he'd received the beating of a lifetime. It had been so horrible. Near the end of it, Liz had actually started feeling sorry for the man.

Teagan had finally realized that the huge bear was dead. He sighed with relief, pushed his furry cap back on his head, and rubbed the scarred depression at his left temple. Tee had been injured as a baby and always touched at his scar when he was confused or nervous or didn't know what to do. Which was often. Then he blinked, looked at the dogs, and cried, "Soldier! Here! Good dog! Leave that *be*! *Leave* it, Soldier! It's *dead*! Soldier! *Soldier*!"

The big mastiff ignored Teagan completely, his attention fixed on the dead bear, huge muscles bunching beneath his smoky fur as he paced behind his hounds, a general directing the action.

But there was something else going on, Liz realized.

In front of the hounds, something she couldn't see . . . .

She made to step closer, but her brother stopped her with a hand on her shoulder. "You ever seen a bear so big?" Teagan asked. "He's a monster! His paws must've been worth something dear! That's a grey bear, right? I mean . . . look at that silvery fur! And look at that shot! *Pow!* Right in his eye! A carbine do that?" He stopped, blinked, then stared at the dead bear. "Father's gonna be real mad. Not at us, though. Right? Right, Liz? Not at us?"

"Right, Tee." Liz nodded, pushing her braid over her shoulder.

The hounds' barking went louder. Liz looked around Teagan, past the pack—and saw something move, something small and grey beside the bear's corpse.

Her eyes widened.

Teagan had been right about Father being mad. And he'd been right about the killing shot. But he was wrong about something else.

The giant, dead bear wasn't a "he." It was a "she."

And it had been a mother.

2

THE HOUNDS WENT quiet and there was a lull in the wind. Then Rosie darted in, yelped, and scuttled back, whimpering, yapping like crazy, her little tail aquiver. Liz pushed past Teagan to get a better look, her bow and arrow held at the ready—but she didn't think she'd need them.

Beside the dead bear, a tiny cub snarled and whimpered.

The little fellow sat with its back against its mother's silver-grey fur, swaying with exhaustion, its skinny rump bumping against the furry wall of its mother's corpse. Its ribs stuck out like a skeleton and its stomach sank like a hollow. A blaze of white fur marked its small chest, just a little left of center, over its heart. When Liz approached, the cub looked at her for a long moment. Its eyes were grey and large. Then it blinked and looked away. There was blood on the cub's muzzle. Fresh blood spattered the snow around it. The cub tried to stand, wobbled, sat back down. Liz frowned. *Having a hard time, aren't you, little guy?*

The wind went still once more and the hounds fell silent. In the sudden quiet, Liz could hear the bear cub's breath: a terrified, wheezing whistle. Liz slid her arrow back into its quiver and unstrung her bow. The hounds started barking again.

Teagan took his furry cap off, scratched his head, touched at his scar. "What do you make of that, eh?" He wiped some snow from his eyes. The sunken white wound along Teagan's temple stood out proudly in the cold. He put his hat back on crookedly, looked at Liz. "Huh? I mean . . . what do you think?"

"Not sure," Liz said. Then she whispered: "Soldier—*here*."

The big rock mastiff immediately turned from the bear cub, leapt back through the snow, and turned at Liz's heel. There, he sat and scooted his bottom down into an accommodating drift, looking up at Liz. Sitting up on the drift like that, their heads were almost at the same height. Liz was tall for her fifteen years, and Soldier was huge for his breed. When Soldier stood on his hind legs, he was taller than Teagan— and Tee was almost nineteen years old. Little Rosie gave another yelp and the pack went nuts.

"I mean . . . . Should we kill it?" Teagan asked. "I don't want to." He eyed the bear cub nervously and adjusted his cap. One mitten went to his horn-handled knife, the other fidgeted with the hem of his furry hunting cloak. "What do we do?"

Again, Liz understood Teagan's worry. If something happened to the dogs, there would be real trouble when they got home, especially if Father's leg was hurting. If something happened to Soldier, Teagan wouldn't sit down right for weeks. *And these days, it might be worse than that . . . .*

"What should we do?" Teagan asked again.

"Don't kill it," Liz said. Then, to Soldier: "Soldier—*bring 'em back.*"

Soldier stood and gave two deep barks from his barrel chest. All the hounds froze, turned, and came back to him, huddling 'round his flanks—all save one: little Rosie, of course. Soldier glanced at Liz, turned back to Rosie, and gave a low growl. As usual, Rosie didn't listen. Instead, she kept worrying at the little bear cub, her butt in the air now, playfully wagging her stumpy tail. The bear cub wobbled to its hind feet. It looked like there was something wrong with one of its rear legs; Liz couldn't tell for sure. Soldier barked again. Rosie paid him no mind. Liz saw Soldier's muscles gather.

"Soldier—*wait*," Liz said. "Rosie—come *here*."

Rosie ignored her.

Soldier looked at Liz. Liz looked back at him, then nodded. Soldier sprang behind Rosie, growling much deeper this time, huge teeth menacing, and gave the little hound a nip on the rump. Rosie yelped and jumped away from Soldier toward the bear cub, who promptly swiped her nose, drawing blood. Rosie scooted back toward Soldier, the big mastiff taking a step back to let her pass, his growl low and deep. Tail down, Rosie's head dropped and she sulked back through the snow to the rest of the pack. Soldier stayed where he was, three paces in front of the bear cub.

"Good girl!" Teagan cried, rubbing Rosie's ribs when she came up to him. She immediately perked up, pink tongue lolling. "Who's the good, best sweetie-girl comes back when she's called? Let's put some snow on your war wound, sweetie. My darling little sweetie-sweetie." Rosie yipped, her stump tail wagging like crazy. She licked Teagan's face, smearing blood along his cheek.

"Don't praise her," Liz said absently. She was staring at the bear cub. So was Soldier.

The cub was still growling in fits and starts. But it was more like a series of desperate gasps and gurgles than any real threat. And the cub was *young*, Liz realized. Maybe six months old? Barely out of the den. And very small. *Runt of the litter, for sure*. Little thing shouldn't have been out here in the first place.

The little bear looked Soldier in the eye, but it was so tired, it could barely keep its head from drooping. Its neck was reed thin. Its paws and head seemed way too large for its body. Its silver-grey fur looked amazingly soft, the white blaze on its chest shining in the bright moonlight. The cub blinked its grey eyes. Then, quite suddenly, it bared its teeth and tried to stand. It bumped against its mother and growled ferociously, raising and lowering its front claws—up and down, up and down. When it stood like that, Liz noticed that the cub's right rear leg was deformed. Not broken, but crooked, the shin slightly bent down and to the side. And there was a weird black claw sprouting off the side of its foot, just above the ankle—like a dog's dewclaw, but much longer, about the length of Liz's palm. *More like a quillcat's spine than a claw.* Liz doubted the cub could stand properly on two legs, even if it wasn't starving. She frowned.

"Soldier—*here*," Liz said. Soldier turned from the cub, walked back to Liz, and sat at her side. Soldier's deep brown eyes were absolutely calm. Liz put her mittened hand on the mastiff's back, pushed her blond braid back over her shoulder, and watched the cub for a moment.

"What do we do, Lizzy?" Teagan asked, rubbing Rosie's side as the little hound licked the underside of his jaw.

Liz unslung her game bag and unhooked her backpack. She fished in the pack for a moment, finally coming up with her leather food pouch. She opened the pouch, broke off a corner of the crusty hardtack she kept inside, then cut off a piece of smoked snow grouse that Mother had given them before they'd left. Liz had hoped to bring some of the meat back home, but this surprise—a grey bear cub, a *live* grey bear cub—would be better, by far.

"What do we do?" Teagan asked again.

Liz grinned. "We're gonna bring it home."

3

ALL THAT EVENING, Liz and Teagan had been keeping their eyes open for game as they completed their real work: checking and resetting Father's traps along the northern line. But they hadn't seen anything at all, barely even any spoor, and the traps had been almost entirely empty. It was as if a new predator had descended upon the forest, pushing everything else away.

This grey bear might explain that, Liz mused.

On the other hand, it also had been a hard winter, cold and relentless. Even for folks down in the village, times were tight. "The King of the Mountain," old man Jarlund had been saying all season, shaking his head. "He's angry. Real angry. Been taking too much timber. Taking too much fur. When you upset the Mountain King, you're in for some long trouble." (Of course, Father thought that kind of talk was pure drivel and he'd remind them of that fact whenever the subject of Jarlund's talk came up.)

Regardless of the reason, if the traps were empty, then you had to improvise. "The mountain way," Father would always say. "Do your best to find what you can, then do your best with what you can find."

Father didn't like nonsense talk. No mountain kings, no stories, no messing around. Just get the work done. Day in, day out. Cycle the traps. Keep your eye out for game. Keep your eye out for spoor. Sharp and tight.

But so far, all that Liz and Teagan had to show for their current outing were three pairs of snow grouse with barely enough meat to justify the effort. Still, you could make a delicious stew from what the grouse did have, and you could sell the feathers for fletching and pillow stuffing down in the village; even the feet could be boiled down for a nice broth. "But you can't do nothing with nothing," Father would always say.

The little bear cub *had* to come home.

No question.

It was worth a hundred times more alive than dead, Liz was sure of it. What else were they supposed to do? Kill the poor thing for its meat? Little guy was barely big enough to be Soldier's dinner.

4

"IS IT WORTH a lot of coin?" Teagan asked, as if reading Liz's mind.

Liz glanced at the near-empty game bag hanging limply from her brother's back and nodded. "He's worth a lot more than what we've taken so far, that's certain."

She put the hardtack and the smoked grouse that she'd pulled from her food pouch into her mouth and chewed on it hard, deliberately.

"If it's worth a lot of coin, that's real good," Teagan said, looking back at the bear cub. It hadn't moved; it just sat there staring at them with its big eyes. "I mean . . . we lost that arrow yesterday morning. Remember that? I figured I'd get strapped for sure." Tee stared at the cub. "How many arrows you think we can buy with him?" Then his voice went a bit lower and he started rubbing at the scar on his sunken temple. "Think I'll get strapped all the same? Evan got strapped last time he lost those arrows couple weeks ago. Think I'll get it?"

"No," Liz said, with her mouth full, still chewing. She spat the soft mass of tack and grouse into the palm of her leather mitten and began shaping the warm lump into a little food ball. She glanced at her older brother. The icy wind shuddered through the trees. Teagan was frowning, worried, still rubbing his scar. Teagan had always been slow, but sometimes he would get himself so worried that he'd just sort of shut down.

Liz patted her older brother's side. "Look there, Tee." She pointed at the cub. "Look. This little one, I bet he's not even off the teat yet, is he? See? Look." She nudged Teagan again. "I'm gonna give it some of this yummy stuff here, see?" She lifted the food ball in front of Teagan's face. "Get some grub into him. Father's going to be happy about this, Tee. *Happy*. I promise you that. Hear me? That's a promise."

"Yeah?" Teagan asked nervously, unconvinced.

"Sure he is." Liz nodded. She lifted her chin at the bear cub. "Look at him. That there's a *grey* bear. Know what a grey bear is worth?" Liz paused, considering. "Don't know for sure if he'll eat this, though." She glanced skeptically at the food ball in her mitten. "But we'll give it a try. And look how tiny he is. Poacher must've found the mother's den, roused her out with his dogs, killed her for her paws . . . ." Liz trailed off, looked around the clearing, studying the peculiar flurry of tracks, the marks not fully covered by snow. "But he only took her front ones. Why'd he leave the back paws? Why leave all that coin?"

"Maybe he got scared?" Teagan shrugged.

Liz nodded. "Rangers have been up here lately. Father's been complaining about it. And there's lots of strange tracks and stuff around here, too. Weird." She looked at all the tracks. "Like some kind of fight. Some blood over there by that boulder—." She stopped. "Look there!"

"What?" Teagan asked, looking around in every direction. "What is it?" The bear cub seemed to sense Teagan's confusion and began looking around too.

Liz grabbed her brother's cloak, pointed at the dead bear's

side, then moved her mitten back and forth up the path, up to the forested ridge above them. "See that other set of tracks? On that path going back there through the trees, up the ridgeline? A *second* set. All different sizes. You can just make 'em out. Almost a kind of path. See? Den's probably up there. Maybe there're more cubs? This little one probably came down after the poacher and his dogs moved off, stayed behind to protect his mom." Liz didn't know if that story made any sense, but it seemed to calm Teagan down a little.

"Your eyes, Liz . . . ." Teagan squinted at the ridge, looking back and forth, clearly not seeing a single thing she was pointing at.

Liz nodded. "The den's gotta be up there, somewhere close. We gotta find it. See if there're other little ones. Bring them back, too. Cut some choice pieces out of the mother's flanks, wrap 'em up to bring home— ."

Liz paused, holding the food ball, suddenly doubtful. "If we can saw through the frozen meat, that is. That'll be tough. And we'd need to do it fast."

She eyed the bear cub, the snow on its mother's huge back. "She's been dead for a couple days, at least. Don't know why the wolves haven't found her yet."

"Wolves?" Teagan asked, looking around, nervous again.

Liz looked again at the sky, the bright moon. "And we've gotta start heading back. Can't risk staying. Father might want us to come back for the bones. Boil 'em down, maybe? Sell the teeth? By tomorrow, next day, she'll be picked clean. Won't be much reason to come back out." But why hadn't the scavengers found the bear already?

"Why'd that hunter leave all that meat?" Teagan scratched his head, staring at the dead bear.

"Trophy hunter," Liz said. "Poacher, for sure. They just want the coin. You sell two grey paws that size, you'd feed me, you, Evan, Mother, and Father for the whole winter and more. Grey bears are hard to find in the wild. See that silver fur?"

"Yeah." Teagan nodded. "Nice and silvery. That means her paws are worth more coin?"

"That's right. You take the paws down to the village, you probably wouldn't get much—they need food more than trophies, just like us. But you start walking down the big mountain—take 'em down through the Trange, to Korfort, say—you could probably get a hundred copper suns, figure. Take 'em all the way down off the big mountain, down to Adara's Hold, you could probably get five hundred."

"Five *hundred* suns?" Teagan stared, his eyes widening.

Liz grinned. "And, if you took 'em all the way down—all the way down to Tarntown—you could probably get a *gold* sun. Long trip, take more than a year to get back, but I bet you could get that much." She paused, looking again at the strange marks around the bear. "The rangers *must* have come. Chased the poacher off—."

"That cub is worth a lot of coin." Teagan nodded, looking at it. "I understand. I should go look for its brothers." He stopped, cocked his cap back on his head, looked up the ridge. "Or maybe it has sisters? I mean . . . what do you think?"

"Dunno," Liz said. "But it's a good idea to go look. Leave Soldier here with me. Don't get lost. Stay warm. Stay on the trail. Come straight back—and don't get bit. If there's another cub up there, if it's alive, try to catch it in your cloak. Wrap it up. It'll be starving, too. We'll give it some more of our food." She held the food ball that she'd made up to remind him. "Rig something out of some branches, something like that. Bring 'em back home."

"Right!" Teagan nodded "Got it! I'll go look! Come on dogs! Soldier, you stay." He immediately pushed his way up the ridge, humming one of his songs. The hounds followed eagerly, little Rosie already out in front, nosing the trail.

Liz turned back to the bear cub, the food ball in one hand, and stepped to the cub's side.

"Alright, little one," Liz said.

And then Teagan screamed bloody murder, yelling at the top of his lungs: "*LIZZY!!*"

Liz snapped her head around, her braid whipping over her shoulder.

Teagan had stopped halfway up the trail.

His face was ghost white.

He was pointing his mitten at something, just off the path.

Liz took a deep breath, then asked patiently, "What is it, Tee?"

"Up here!" he cried. "Here! There's a *lady* up here! She's *dead*!"

5

"Great Sisters," Teagan whispered.

Liz nodded.

Couldn't have said it better herself.

The young woman *was* dead.

That was certain.

Dead and frozen through.

But she most certainly wasn't some random trapper or some lost forager from some lumberjack's crew.

She was a ranger.

Almost certainly.

One of the Tarn's mountain wardens.

Liz could tell by her gear.

Probably all the way up from Adara's Hold.

Or maybe even from farther down the mountain, from the look of her equipment. The ranger wore a finely-made vest of padded leather and a beautiful fur-lined jacket. A handsome wolf-skin cloak was crunched up beneath her shoulders. She wore an antler-handled dagger sheathed crosswise at her belt. Her boots and gloves were fine, too. Dyed dark blue, the Tarn's royal color, made from a soft hide the likes of which Liz had seen only in the best shops down in Korfort; they weren't local made, that was certain. Her leather belt was fastened with a small silver buckle. The buckle was embossed with a six-pointed sigil, an emblem that Liz recognized immediately. Acasius's Star. *The Dallanar Sun*. The high symbol of the overlords of the Tarn.

Somewhere, over the wind, a crow cawed.

Teagan started at the noise, looking around this way and that. "Crow in winter," he muttered, turning back to her, rubbing his scar. "Bad luck."

Liz didn't look up.

Teagan scooted closer. "What happened? Who is she?"

"Dunno." Liz shook her head, fidgeting with the thick end of her braid. "Keep the dogs away from her, Tee."

Teagan tried his best, but the dogs were curious. The woman had short blond hair that she'd worn at chin length; it was much lighter than Liz's, more silvery than blond. Her earrings were unique. Dark blue jewels held in the grip of silver claws, like lizards' claws; Liz could see the individual scales on each talon. *Royal craftsmanship, for sure.* The woman was about ten years younger than Mother, maybe a bit younger. A heart-shaped face, her eyes barely open, one slightly more so than the other, only their whites showing. A single drop of blood marked her cheek. Liz reached down and brushed the snow away from her face.

And there it was. The real giveaway as to the young woman's identity: a small blue tattoo above her right temple. The six-pointed star. The Dallanar Sun, once more.

"Ranger, for sure." Liz nodded to herself.

Teagan looked at her.

Marked for life as a servant of the Tarn.

The crow cawed again.

And then Liz saw the wound.

"Look at this." Liz pointed with her mitten, scooting closer to the body. Teagan leaned over her, eyes wide, trying to hold Soldier back. Liz took off her mitten, put her finger into a small hole in the ranger's fur-lined jacket, high on the left side of her chest. The hole was punched through the leather armor; the material around it was blackened, charred-looking.

A bullet hole.

Fired at close range.

Straight into her heart.

"This was no accident," Liz muttered. And where was the ranger's breastplate? Most of the Tarn's wardens that Liz had seen usually wore a breastplate of high silver. "Ancient, priceless, and indestructible," old man Jarlund had told her when she'd asked about it. "But the high silver ain't just protection. It's another symbol—a symbol of the Tarn's power."

"Wouldn't be dead if you'd worn your gear," Liz muttered under her breath.

"What?" Teagan asked.

Had the ranger been surprised somehow? And where was her war bear?

The dogs sniffed at the warden's cloak with keen interest. Little Rosie pawed at the snow by the ranger's side. When she did, the white crust broke to reveal a dark pool of frozen blood.

The gusting wind went quiet for a moment. Liz looked up and around, suddenly nervous. She was on edge, she realized, the hairs on the back of her neck prickling, the wind reminding her with its sudden silence that they were over two days' hike from home—and that they were completely alone out here. The penalty for interfering with, or attacking, one of the High King's rangers was severe; Liz knew that from both old man Jarlund and from Father.

But to murder a mountain warden?

To kill a servant of the Tarn?

She'd never even heard of such a thing.

Liz glanced back at the dead grey bear, the strange flurry of tracks and markings around them both . . . .

"We need to get outta here." Liz cleared her throat.

"You still want me to look for the den, Liz?" Teagan whispered.

"Yeah," Liz whispered back. "But you need to make it fast. And I mean *fast*, Tee. If you don't find it right away, come straight back. I'll tend to the cub and get him ready to go while you go look. Fast, Tee. Like the bunny."

"What we gonna do about this lady?" Teagan cocked his head at the ranger's body. "I mean . . . she's gonna get all chewed up, we leave her out here."

"Nothing we can do." Liz pushed her braid over her shoulder. "She's frozen solid and we can't carry her. Leave everything. Don't touch *anything*. We'll ask Father what to do when we get back. Now get going." Liz looked again at the dead body. She shivered. "We gotta get home."

6

WHILE TEAGAN MOVED up the trail, Liz and Soldier returned to the dead grey bear and her cub. When Liz approached, she saw that the little bear had moved around to the other side of its mother, apparently to keep an eye on her and Teagan as they'd discussed the dead ranger. Now the cub was watching Teagan and the hounds depart, following them with its gaze as they moved up the ridge. Its eyes were grey, intelligent, and discerning—but its whole body shook. When Teagan disappeared over the ridge, the little cub turned and looked at Liz. Then it blinked. It didn't make a sound. Just looked at her, eyes wide, shivering.

"Here we go," Liz said.

She made sure her mittens were securely fastened, then placed the food ball she'd made in the center of her palm. The mitten's leather wasn't thick, but the shell and its fur lining would provide some protection if her plan didn't work.

"All right, little fella," Liz said. "Let's not do something we'll both regret."

She took three steps forward, then crouched down to the cub's level, holding the food ball far out in front of her, kind of waving it in the cub's direction.

The cub didn't react. It just kept looking at her, straight into her eyes, blinking every now and again.

Liz scooted up another step. Her boots crunched the snow. Soldier was right behind her.

The cub tried to stand, swaying. It tried to raise its paws. Then it sat down abruptly, its bad back leg giving out. Liz could barely hear its breath. The cub looked at Liz for a long moment. Its eyes were smoky grey, the pupils large and soulful. Then it turned away, closed its eyes, and leaned its forehead against its mother's side. It sighed deeply, then stopped moving.

Liz scooted up another step and held out the food ball, waving it back and forth in front of the cub's nose. She didn't know if the smell of the hardtack and smoked grouse would be enough to tempt the cub. Or whether the cub was old enough to understand anything other than mother's milk. The cub didn't stir. It was smaller than she'd first thought. Liz was tall and long-boned, but even so, standing straight up, the cub wouldn't come much past her knee. Curled up like that, it seemed smaller still, especially next to the enormous bulk of its dead mother.

Liz moved a bit closer, reached out, and gently put her mittened hand on the cub's back.

The little bear twitched, but nothing else.

She removed her mitten and put her bare palm against the cub's back. She could feel its bumpy spine through its fur. It scarcely breathed. Its silver-grey fur was thick and incredibly soft. Its paws were enormous.

Liz held the food ball up to the cub's nose.

The cub turned its head, eyes still closed—and sniffed. A long pink tongue flickered out, tentative but most definitely interested. Then—magically, slowly—the cub opened its mouth and took the food ball. Its jaws moved, but it did not chew. Instead, it sucked the ball softly, its eyes still closed.

Then it went completely still.

Liz touched its back again.

No response.

Not good.

She turned her ear to the cub's mouth, holding her hand against its back, ready to push it away if it turned on her.

Nothing.

Liz took off her furry cap and put her ear down until it almost touched the cub's nose, holding her palm firmly against its back. The little guy was too weak to be dangerous, but she still wanted to be careful. Her blond hair brushed against the mother bear's fur. A bit of snow dusted the top of the cub's head. She put her ear even closer to its nose, straining to hear.

Then she smiled.

Over the gusting wind, she could just make out a weak, whispering snore.

7

EVEN THOUGH THEY only stopped to eat and briefly rest it still took them two full days to get home. When they finally did arrive, it was three bells past nightfall. The wind had died and the sky had cleared. The huge moon was rising over the big mountain, a white circle climbing bright past the mountain's black shadow. The stars were thick. The snow glowed blue with winter's light.

Teagan had found the grey bear's den: a cave up among the ridge rocks. He'd also found two more bear cubs. They'd been bigger than their little brother, but both had died from hunger. Teagan had collected them just the same, slinging their poor little bodies over his shoulder in his fur cloak, facing the icy wind home in his hunting jacket alone, despite Liz's protests. Liz herself had hiked back with the little grey cub tucked up under her fur cloak, under her coat, under her shirt, and finally under her long underwear, the little guy nuzzled directly against her chest. The little bear slept the entire way; it didn't seem to weigh anything at all. After a while, its warmth had actually felt pretty nice—when it wasn't pushing its cold nose into her skin.

The entire way home, Teagan had been singing an ancient war song: Hakon's March. For almost two days. Straight. Almost without breaks. Tee sang partly because he liked all the old songs, partly because he was terrified of wolves and he thought the songs kept them away—which they probably did, Teagan was a horrible singer—and partly because he was freezing without his cloak and the singing warmed him. He couldn't hold a tune to save his life and had absolutely no rhythm to speak of, but Liz had joined him whole-heartedly for every chorus. (Or every other chorus, at least.) The hounds had done their part as well, howling to beat all. Only Soldier managed to keep his dignity intact, remaining silent for all but the most exuberant refrains.

As they approached home, brother and sister sang even louder, their voices climbing hoarsely in the cold night air, the hounds spreading down and out in front of them in the moonlight, barking and bounding down the gentle slope into the shallow bowl of their clearing.

"One m-m-more time, lads!" Teagan shouted, shivering, marching down into the clearing with his load over his shoulder, traps clicking, cap halfway off, cocking his big head side to side, not quite with the rhythm:

Across the Silver Realm, high lords! March, march!
Across the stars, through silver doors! March, march!
We will not rest, we will not sleep, 'til all lie dead beneath our feet!
Let our steel strike shield for brother and men, high lords!"

When Teagan stopped singing, little Rosie turned back to him and barked.

Teagan laughed, teeth chattering. "S-see, L-L-Liz? Sh-she

wants us to s-sing it again. D-don't y-y-you think?"

Liz looked at Rosie. Rosie looked at Teagan, not taking her eyes off him.

"Can you blame her?" Liz grinned, shaking her head. "You're quite the singer."

"I th-think she r-really likes that s-song. See how she w-w-wants m-me to sing it again? Don't she w-want me to sing it? I love that s-song."

"Hadn't noticed."

"What's th-that mean? 'S-s-silver doors'?" Teagan asked for maybe the hundredth time.

"Dunno, Tee." Liz laughed.

"Don't m-matter." Teagan shrugged, shivering. Then he grinned, pointing across the clearing. "We m-m-made it!"

8

THEIR HOUSE WAS a low cabin made of heavy fir logs set on a foundation of dark Konish granite. It was nested between two silver spruce trees at the far edge of their clearing, its deep front porch supported by heavy, dressed pines. The porch itself was perfectly swept, the chinking between the logs tight and neat. A thick granite chimney hunkered up the cabin's southeast side, a thin wisp of smoke curling into the night. The small window centered high in the door glowed orange with welcome warmth. The cabin's only other windows were the two facing northwest: the tiny one high up in their sleeping loft and the other one, slightly larger, in Mother and Father's bedroom directly below it. The snow on the roof was piled high, at least ten palms deep. The smell of chimney smoke was home.

"Race?" Liz asked Teagan. "Should probably get you inside."

Teagan didn't reply. Instead, he hoisted his load on his shoulder and took off, running as hard as he could down into the clearing, nose up, cap almost falling off, traps clanking, loaded cloak banging against his back, little Rosie bounding at his heels, her eyes sparkling. Teagan made it to the cabin well ahead of Liz, but just before he reached the porch he stopped short and waited for her. Together they jumped up the porch's two steps, smiling, stamping their boots, cleaning the snow off.

Teagan hung the five empty traps they'd brought home on their proper hooks; none of the five traps had triggered, even though the bait had been taken, so they'd brought them back to Father for inspection. Liz took the oil pot from its cubby beside the door and gave each trap exactly three drops: one on each hinge and one on the spring plate. She returned the oil to its place, pulled the small hand broom off its peg, and brushed Teagan off, top to bottom. When she was done, Teagan did the same for her, careful not to brush too hard over Liz's chest where the bear cub still slept. When they were done taking care of each other, they started with the dogs, cleaning each of the hounds carefully, paying special attention to their paws. Soldier got inspected twice, Liz checking the big mastiff a third time when Teagan wasn't looking. When the dogs were finished, Liz hung the hand broom on its peg and chained the dogs to the iron ring beside the door. Then she took the two snow brooms off their nails and handed one to Teagan. Together, they swept the porch back to front, cleaned the steps, then shook the brooms out. When they were done, Teagan pushed his cap back on his head and looked at Liz, trembling with the cold. Liz inspected the porch carefully, paying special attention to the corners.

Sharp and tight.

Just like Father liked.

Liz nodded and Teagan smiled, shivering. His lips were almost blue. They hung the brooms on their nails and moved together to the front door.

"Dogs—*sit*," Liz said.

As a pack, all six sat together, noses up, looking at her with perfect attention, even little Rosie. Liz unchained them. Then she and Teagan took off their boots, holding them carefully with the soles up. Liz knocked on the door and unfastened her coat a bit so that she could reveal their surprise.

Teagan grinned at her and whispered, "I c-can't wait to see their f-f-faces when we show 'em. He's worth a lot of c-c-coin, right? Father'll l-like that, right? R-r-right? Father'll—it's c-c-cold."

Mother opened the door.

Liz smiled and stepped into the cabin's warmth—and then she saw Mother's face, and stopped mid-step, dead in her tracks.

Mother's eyes were sad and angry—but she was trying hard to smile, trying hard to welcome them home. She clasped her hands in front of her and looked at the floor, almost like she was embarrassed, brushing absently at her worn apron. Liz had always thought Mother was beautiful. Even unhappy and scared and furious, she had this quiet, dignified beauty about her that was hard to describe. Golden blond hair, a brilliant smile, and intelligent blue eyes. She certainly had no equal in the village, not even down in Korfort. "A mountain man would kill for my wife's eyes," Father was always bragging to old man Jarlund and the other men down in the village. Then he'd look over at Liz, who was there in the tavern to make sure he got home properly. "You're gonna look just like her, Lizzy. Taller, for sure. Way taller. But just like her, all the same."

Mother looked at Liz pointedly, then shook her head slightly at Liz's questioning eyes.

Behind Mother, the house was deadly quiet.

Liz swallowed.

Teagan had gone perfectly still, the blood drained from his face. Only his lips quivered.

Mother looked hard at Liz, her eyes telling Liz everything she needed to know.

"That them?" Father's deep voice from inside the cabin, a bear's growl. Soft, slurred with drink, low. And dangerous.

"It's them." Mother gave a slight nod.

But Mother's eyes said something else entirely.

We're counting on you, Liz, her eyes said. *We're counting on your skill and craft. We're counting on your mountain cunning to find a path through the dark pain and the bright drink—a path to your Father's love.*

"They clean th' porch off good 'n proper?" Father asked, the words running together.

Mother made a movement of looking past them at the porch and steps.

"Yes," she said.

"Let 'em in, then," Father said. He cleared his throat. "See what they gotta say for themselves. What they been doin' out there this whole time."

Liz took a deep breath. She realized that her heart was pounding. She tried to calm it.

Breathe. She nodded to herself. *Think.*

"There's a time for war—and there's a time for wits," Father would always say, when he wasn't at his flask. "The mountain way. Hunter's way."

This was the time for wits.

Liz was Father's favorite.

Everyone knew it.

So once again, as it had been for the last couple of years—but so much worse these last six months or so—her family would be counting on her to keep them all safe.

Strange, how the entire trip back she hadn't really thought of the danger that might be waiting for them. Too busy thinking about the dead grey bear, the dead ranger, the grey bear cub, keeping an eye on Teagan. So easy to forget that these days, on some nights, the most terrible thing on the big mountain didn't live in the deep of the woods.

9

MOTHER OPENED THE door and stepped back and aside.

Liz looked at the hounds. They'd heard Father's voice and were sitting completely still. Teagan's face was white. He stared at Mother, his whole body shaking, and not just from the cold. He reached up as if to rub the scar on his temple, then snapped his hand down to his side. Father didn't like it when Teagan rubbed his scar, especially on nights like this. Somewhere outside, the winter crow cawed.

"Dogs—*cage*," Liz whispered.

The hounds stepped silently past Mother in single file, walked to their pine kennel, and immediately curled up in the furs. They made no sound, but looked at Liz sideways, eyes wide. Soldier sat at attention just outside the kennel, his chin high; impassive, but alert.

Liz stepped inside the cabin and carefully placed her boots on their iron stand, soles up. Teagan did the same, his hands shaking. Then they stood next to each other, their shoulders touching in a perfect dress line, their furry caps held in front of them, eyes down, but their backs still at a kind of attention, how Father liked. Teagan was doing everything he could to keep from trembling. Mother shut the door behind them and stayed there.

Father was sitting, like he always did, in front of the fireplace, in his enormous bearskin chair. His massive back was to the flames, so Liz couldn't see his face—only his eyes. His scarred hands rested on the chair's worn arms, his flattened knuckles moving slightly as he tapped his calloused fingers every so often. Father's right leg was held out straight in front of him, resting on a stool, his right knee wrapped in a compress thick as a tree trunk. The compress was the reason that Father had been sending them out to check the traps these last couple weeks. He'd injured his knee a long time ago—Liz didn't know how—and sometimes, when it was very cold, his knee would hurt so bad that he couldn't work. So Father would stay home, the silver flask would come out, and he'd drink pine whiskey for the pain while his kids checked his traps. In the flickering fire shadow, Father's eyes glowed like coals.

And he wasn't alone.

Evan, Liz's sixteen-year-old brother, sat beside Father on a stool. Evan was staring at the ground. He held a blood-stained rag to his nose and face. As if sensing Liz's look, Evan glanced up and their gazes met. Evan's left eye was entirely bloodshot, not a bit of white left in it, the lids and brow already puffy and swollen. With a motion almost too slight to be seen, Evan cocked his head subtly toward the kitchen table. Liz didn't respond. Not even a twitch. Father was staring at her—and Father would detect the slightest movement.

"Who left my axe outside there?" Father asked, his words thick and slurry. He lifted his chin in the direction of the kitchen table. His week-old beard was dense and black, just touched with grey.

Liz looked at the table. Father's hand axe lay there, a thin line of rust marring its edge. The leather wrist thong lay beside the axe's handle, frayed, broken in the middle. The axe's oak handle was entirely plain except for a simple silver leaf inlaid at its end.

"Who left my axe outside?" Father asked again, softer.

Evan cleared his throat. Father swiveled toward him and growled. "Not a word, boy."

Evan bowed his head.

Without pause, Liz said: "Evan left the axe outside, sir."

Father swung his head up from Evan to Liz, his dark eyes glossy, deeply set under heavy brows. "You saw 'im? You know for sure he did that?"

"No, sir. I didn't see him. But he told me right before we left, sir. That is, sir, he asked me if I knew how he should clean it. I told him he was a fool not to remember—and then I told him that he should use a whetstone and oil, just like you do, sir. That's the proper way to take care of a tool, I told him. Fix it up in two moments, good as new, like nothing happened——."

"That one there he didn't forget it?" Father growled and jutted a finger at Teagan, his eyes fixed on Liz's face.

"No, sir." Liz glanced at Teagan, praying her brother wouldn't say a word.

Of course, Evan's look had told Liz everything that she needed to know. And if Liz had known that Teagan had left the axe outside in the first place, then she'd have cleaned it properly before they'd left.

But it was too late for all that. They were all in the lie now—all of them—even Mother.

Father was a different man when his knee was hurting and the flask came out. They all knew that. He could still be decent and kind these days—even gentle, like he used to be. And he worked hard to provide for them; nobody could call him lazy. Liz knew he still loved them. (It was different now, these last couple years—and especially bad these last several months—but it was still true.) It was just when his knee was hurting—when he couldn't work, get out on the line—that things got real bad. Then it was a different story. When the flask was out, he was a different man. A completely different person. Now wasn't the time for truth and honesty. Now was the time for them to protect themselves, to protect each other, and—in a weird way that Liz understood but couldn't fully explain—to protect Father. To protect him from himself. They all knew what kind of words were necessary and what kind of behavior was required. Especially from her, Father's favorite.

Teagan was staring at the floor, his lips pressed tightly together. He shook his head back and forth, his whole body trembling. Then he began rubbing the scar along his sunken temple.

"Stop touchin' your face you," Father said quietly

Teagan rammed his hand to his side, head bowed, eyes shut, squeezing them tight, trying to stand up straight.

Father glanced at Teagan, turned back to Liz—then stopped, looked Teagan up and down. "What kinda boy don't wear his proper cloak out on a night like this, ask you truly. Mountain eat him alive the fool, don't know its ways. Don't know why I bother givin' him one at all. Well?" Father's eyes swung back to Liz. "You *sure* this one didn't leave it out there? Seems like somethin' he'd do—done it enough, reckon. You *sure?*"

"Yes, sir." Liz looked Father in the eye. "Absolutely, sir. Evan left the axe outside, sir."

"Hmm," Father grunted, and gave Liz a long, hard look. It seemed to last forever. Liz returned it, unflinchingly.

"Alright." Father clapped Evan on the shoulder, nearly knocking him off the stool. "I thank you for the honesty, son. Yeah . . . . Takes a man t' admit he done wrong, that's the mountain way, sure." He looked at Evan's swollen eye, frowned—almost like he didn't know how the black eye had happened—then looked at the fire.

"Go put some snow on your eye," he said gruffly to the flames, clearing his throat. "Don't mind if you kids practice throwing your axes or knives back there, shooting and what-not; why we set the range up in the first place, sharp and tight. But you need t' take care of your tools. All you have up in here, understand? And you're lucky t' have 'em. My ol' man? He'd beat us senseless—me and Darro both, *senseless* I tell you—we do something like that. Not no strap on the backside, either. No little tap on the head." He turned, held up his huge fist, and showed it to them. "You're lucky he ain't here, boy." He looked at Evan for a long time, then looked back to the fire. "Anyway, you're gonna give a quarter of your rations to Soldier for a week starting tomorrow breakfast. Seem fair to you?"

"Yes, sir," Evan said, not looking up. He tried to stand, but his legs buckled and he sank to the stool again. His legs were shaky, knees wobbling together. He sat back down and rubbed his thighs to get the blood flowing.

Liz suddenly wondered how long Evan had been sitting on that stool.

Could've been hours.

Maybe longer?

Surely not. There was work to be done.

But they'd been out a long time. And Father's knee had been terrible this past week. Mother had said that the pain was almost unbearable. It had started getting worse about half a year past, and Liz felt like they were getting closer to a dark line, a terrible line that could only be crossed one time—and then only in one direction.

"How were the traps?" Father winced as he stood, his huge frame blocking out the firelight, his weight on his good leg, leaning on his heavy walking stick. When he stood, he seemed to fill the room. The stick thunked the plank floor as he walked. "Eh? How were they?"

Father turned the bearskin chair back around to face the fire, took his iron poker from its hook, stabbed the logs, watched them spark as he speared them. He leaned against the chimney, savoring the fire's heat, then reached inside his vest for his flask, paused—hand in his vest, as if having a second thought. He looked at the fire for a long time. His dark eyes flickered in its orange glow. Then he shook his head, closed his eyes, and tested his weight on his bad leg, flinching immediately. He pulled the flask from his vest, unfastened the steel catch, and drank deeply.

Evan had finally managed to stand up from the stool. He walked unsteadily past Liz, winked his eye that wasn't sealed shut, and gave her the barest hint of a smile. He grabbed his boots off their stand, took his coat off its peg, and stepped to the front door, out into the night. Liz kept her eyes firmly on Father.

"Eh?" Father asked the fire, giving the logs one last poke for good measure. "The traps. I asked you a question. How were they?"

"Not good, sir," Liz said calmly. "But we took almost a half dozen more grouse on the way back in and we found this grey bear cub. Alive. I fed him. A *grey* bear, sir. And we found—."

"Grey cub?" Father swung around, turning with amazing dexterity despite his size and drunkenness. There was a strange look in his eye.

"Yes, sir." Liz swallowed, looking at him directly. "He's been sucking on some of my tack. And grouse. He's alive. Worth coin, sir." As she said this, Liz stepped forward, opened her coat, and took out the cub, cupping its furry rump in the crook of her elbow, holding it out toward Father. The cub still slept. The white blaze on its chest glowed in the firelight.

"And there was something else," Liz began. "We found a dead—."

"Lemme see that here." Father hung the iron poker on its hook and hobbled across the room, walking stick thunking. He plucked the bear cub from Liz's hands by the scruff of its neck and held it up to the kitchen's iron lantern, appraising it by lamplight, wincing slightly with the pain in his knee. The cub's little legs hung straight down. Even his bent leg seemed almost straight. The little thing looked so small dangling there from Father's huge fist. Its black nose gleamed. It didn't wake.

"Get that other lamp over here, Mother," Father grunted.

Mother fetched a clay lamp from the counter and handed it to Father. She eyed the bear cub curiously, then looked at Liz. Liz kept her eyes on Father. It was one of the tricks she'd learned in the last months: never take your eyes off him. *Seek eye contact, seek challenge.* Might not work with every dangerous man—but it had always worked on him. Father was holding the lamp up, giving the cub a close inspection. Then he put his ear to the cub's chest. It didn't stir. Father handed the lamp to Liz. She took it carefully, threading her index finger through the lamp's finger loop.

". . . grey bear," Father said, something different coming into his voice.

Liz had heard that tone a hundred times before, but she knew better than to respond. She kept her chin up, shoulders straight, and her eyes on Father's face. The new voice meant that they were almost through it.

"Near dead," Father said. He gently touched the cub's prominent ribs and sunken stomach. "Starving." He ran his hands over the cub's limbs, pausing at its bent back leg, feeling the bowed bone, assessing the strange black dewclaw sprouting off the ankle. "Never seen anything like this," he said as he fingered the cub's weird claw. "Have to come off."

Without pause, Father drew his bone-handled knife from the small of his back and placed the cub on the kitchen table beside their water pitcher. He set the blade flat against the cub's ankle, then cut away the weird claw where it joined the leg, like he was chopping a radish. There was only a little blood and the cub didn't seem to feel it. Father set his knife down on the table beside his axe. Then he put his hand on the cub's chest, cocked his head as if listening. He grunted to Mother. "Get me a coal outta the fire there. Small little one."

Mother went to the fire, used the poker to prod a small coal into the ash shovel, and came back to the table, bringing along a pair of iron tongs. The coal was dull orange and smoked slightly. Father took it with the tongs, then pushed it hissing against the spot where he'd cut away the cub's strange black claw. The smell of burnt fur was immediate and the cub mewled, but didn't really wake. Father nodded and handed the tongs to Mother.

"Get me that cloth there," Father said. "That clean?"

Mother nodded, handed him the cloth, and then carefully put the other implements back in their places by the fire. Father ripped the cloth in two, folded one torn half over a couple times, then tied it tight 'round the bear cub's furry leg. He picked the cub up by the scruff of the neck, looked it over, put his ear to its chest again. The dewclaw lay on the table. It was long and curved, like the spine of some strange black plant.

"A question, sir?" Liz asked.

"Hmm." Father grunted, looking at the cub. There was a strange look in his eye again. He reached for his silver flask— then stopped and shoved it back into his vest. He cleared his throat. "Make me some tea, will you, Mother?"

"Of course," Mother said, immediately getting to it. Liz saw that the kettle was already on the stove—and that it was already hot. Father's huge clay cup sat next to it, warming up. A tiny canister of precious mint tea waited on the counter. Mother shot Liz a knowing glance.

They were almost home.

They'd been lucky.

One black eye? These days?

Oh yes, they'd been lucky.

"What's the question, girl?" Father asked.

"Yes, sir." Liz nodded, standing tall how she knew Father liked, looking him straight in the eye. "Sorry, sir. I was wondering: Why'd we take that claw off?"

Father grunted and looked at her for a long moment. Then he handed the bear cub back to her and roughly tousled her hair, like she was a boy. It pinched a little, because of her braid, but it didn't really hurt. Even in the worst of it these last months, Father had never hurt her. Or Mother.

"The mountain way, girl." He nodded. "Animal grows up with somethin' wrong like that on him, he'll tear it off himself or he'll catch it on somethin' and pull it off. Same reason we dock dogs' tails. Get torn off and the wound gets infected and there goes all our hard work. That's why we take it off."

Father looked at Mother and cleared his throat. "Clean those up." He pointed at his knife and his axe, then looked at the table where he'd chopped off the cub's claw. He blinked, frowned slightly at the damage that he'd caused to the table. "Yeah, if you clean those up, I'll sand out that scratch there tomorrow. Polish it up. Won't even notice it."

Mother bowed assent and poured hot water over Father's tea; the smell of fresh mint was strong and immediate. Mother bought the tea from a shop down in the village, and that shop ordered it special from another shop down past the Trange, down in Korfort, and that shop, in turn, prob-ably got it from a seller all the way down in Adara's Hold— maybe even from as far away as Tarntown. Very expensive. Very strong. Good stuff. Liz didn't know how they could afford it.

Father was looking at her, waiting for her to say something.

"So." Liz cleared her throat, lifted the bear cub up to look at the bandage on its leg. "You cut it off now so he doesn't hurt himself later. I understand."

Father looked at her for a long moment, then clapped her on the shoulder. Mother brought Father his tea. He drank half of it down in one gulp, set the cup down, turned to Liz, and cocked his head at the bear cub, pointing at its bad leg. "I want you to clean that dressing there in boiling water every mornin', Lizzy. And then you put a fresh dressing back on, just as I did there. Like you saw me. Sharp and tight. Nice and clean. You'll do that for a week, then we'll see where we are."

"Yes, sir." Liz nodded, but she didn't really understand his final objective. Why fix the cub's leg? What was the plan?

Mother was clearing the knife and axe from the table. Father said to her, still looking at the cub in Liz's arms: "When you're done with those, get yourself on down to old man Jarlund's and bring me up ten cups of fresh reindeer milk. Take our pitcher and borrow one off him. Tell him I'll send a kid down for the same ten cups every day for the next six weeks. After that, I'll want twice again as much for another twelve weeks." As he said this, Father reached into his belt and turned out thirteen small copper suns, each one carefully polished. Father placed a coin into Mother's hand. "You tell him this'll cover it for the time being. I'll be down there tomorrow mornin' to work out the rest."

Mother looked at him for a long moment, a strange expression on her face.

"What?" he grunted.

"You want me to go now?" Mother asked. "It's near midnight. He'll be sleeping."

Father stared at her. His face had gone blank again. He took a deep breath. Mother looked him in the eye, like she wasn't afraid of him in the least. But Liz knew it was all a lie—a kind of performance. Mother knew the game. The coin glimmered dully in her open palm.

"You too smart to obey me now?" Father said. Then he chuckled—then frowned at himself, like he was puzzled by his own words—then he shook his head, clapping Liz on the shoulder. Liz looked at Mother. Mother was sad and angry; unlike herself. He never used to talk to her this way. It was as if something had snapped a few months ago——.

"Look there, girl." Father snorted. "Give a woman some coin and all a sudden she's a merchant's wife up from Korfort. Or maybe some high lady from 'Dara's Hold, eh? Ha! She sees six-pointed suns and all a sudden she's down off the big mountain altogether, maybe all the way down in Tarntown thinkin' she's some kind of aristocrat—some kind of high born lady, eh? Ha-ha!" But he said this last part like he was slightly embarrassed, a weird frown on his face, like there was something else behind these particular words that he already wished he could take back. He took up his tea cup, looked into the cup, then drank deeply. Mother stared at him. He didn't meet her gaze.

"I'll go right now," Mother said tonelessly, took the pitcher from the table, and turned toward the door, but Father reached out, grabbed her shoulder, and slowly turned her around.

"You know I'd go myself . . . ." He gestured down at his bad knee. "Maybe it *is* too late."

"No. You're right." Mother looked him in the eye and calmly patted his shoulder. She glanced at the bear cub. "He's weak. He needs care. He's helpless without us. I'll go straight away."

Father made like he was about to say something else—but then he frowned and nodded, almost a little sheepishly. He held Mother by both shoulders and kissed her gently on the forehead. Then he shook his head, like he was confused by himself, released her, and took the bear cub up from Liz's arms, looking it over once more.

Mother placed the knife and axe on the opposite counter.

Then she took her coat from its peg and her boots from their stand. She opened the door. Evan stepped back inside at the same moment, a wad of snow held against his eye. He looked at Mother, then the cub. He raised his good eyebrow at Liz. Liz shook her head once, then cocked her head at the sleeping loft. They'd talk about it up there, later. Evan nodded unnoticeably. Mother stepped out.

"May I go to bed, sir?" Evan asked. He took the snow from his face. His left eye was purple-black and almost completely swollen shut.

"Go on, son," Father grunted. He glanced at Evan, then looked away and shook his head. He held the bear up again, looking it over. He cleared his throat. "How's that eye?"

"Good, sir," Evan said. "Thank you, sir."

"Good boy." Father nodded and took another long sip of his tea. "Put some snow on it tomorrow, too. It'll help . . . ." It looked like Father was going to say something else to Evan—but then he stopped himself. Evan carefully put his coat and boots in their proper place, glanced at Liz, stepped to the ladder and up to the loft.

Father moved the bear closer to the lamp again, then

glanced at Liz. "You did a good job, Lizzy. Real good. We'll start fattenin' it up tomorrow. Pity we can't sell it to a trainer. Or even to the rangers——Great Sisters curse 'em all. That bad back leg . . . . It ain't no good for fighting or war. Nothin' but meat and fur, I'm afraid. Although . . . hmm." He paused for a long moment, as if considering something else entirely. Then he shook his head. "I'll take it down to village when it's nice and fat. Maybe even down through the Trange, to Korfort. I wager ol' Butcher'll give me a couple hundred suns for it, maybe more if we feed it up proper." He paused, blinked, and shook his head. "Imagine what we could do with two, three hundred copper suns up here, girl. Know what we could do?"

"Anything at all, sir," Liz said with a smile. She knew Father liked that. "Anything you wanted."

Father laughed, but it was no cruel chuckle. It was a deep belly laugh, long and true.

In spite of herself, Liz smiled.

"Too right." Father looked down at Liz, squeezed her shoulder gently. He looked at the bear again. But he still had that strange look in his eye. Like he wanted to say something else. Like there was something else going on.

"You think you can take charge of it, Liz? It'll take time, I can tell you that right now. And it'll be hard—especially at the end. You'll have to give it milk eight, nine times a day for another year or so and then whole food for 'nother year at least. Its meat'll be best eating at about two years, I reckon, but it'll be gettin' real expensive to feed then, too. And *big*. We'll have to figure it close . . . figure it real close. A city man, down past Korfort, around Adara's Hold and lower down yet, he'll pay well for the meat of a grey bear. Forbidden delicacy. And there are still places up north, old Konungur strongholds way up past the big mountain, where the mountain way is strong, meat of a proper grey is rightly prized—no matter what those cursed fools in the Tarn say. Ol' Butcher'll see that, sure as it's winter. You got the patience, girl? Can you do it? Big task. Could make fifty times the coin we put into it, maybe more. Eh?"

"Yes, sir." Liz nodded, lifted her chin. "You can count on me, sir."

"Always can, Lizzy." Father grunted, squeezing her shoulder. "Always can."

He handed the bear cub back to Liz, then touched his vest where he kept his flask—but he didn't reach for it. Instead, he took a sip of his tea, almost finishing it off. Liz held the cub next to her chest, in the crook of her arm, and stepped back beside Teagan. Father turned to the table, picked up the cub's black dewclaw, considered it for a moment, then handed it to Liz.

"You keep this," Father said gruffly. "Good luck for a mountain girl. You earned it. We'll drill a hole in the top there tomorrow, thread a cord through, make a nice trophy you can wear. Eh? Like a proper trapper? Can't believe how tall you're getting."

"Thank you, sir," Liz said. She took the claw, leaning the cub on her hip. It was smooth and very sharp. She'd never seen anything like it. She put it in her pocket.

"Now, let's see what this one's got here." Father turned to Teagan, walking stick thunking, staring at the big bundle Tee still carried over his shoulder. Father touched at his flask in his vest, but didn't take it out.

"Eh?" his eyes flashed.

It was the most dangerous moment, the edge.

"You stupid *and* mute? What you got there worth riskin' frost's bite, boy? Didn't I teach you anything 'bout wood lore? Winter? Mountain ways? You understand what 'cold' means? Freeze yourself solid like that, running around out there half naked like a fool."

Teagan kept his head down, kept his teeth locked together, and swung his cloak out in front of him, opening it for Father to see the two dead bear cubs inside. They clung to each other, just as Teagan had found them, two small furry shapes, frozen together, their little heads tucked down into each other's chests. Father leaned forward slightly. Teagan shrank into himself.

"Figures." Father shook his head and squeezed Liz absently on the shoulder. "Lizzy here, she brings home a live grey bear gonna be worth a few hundred suns in time, the big brother brings back a sack of frozen bones." Father stepped up to Teagan, towering over him—then he grabbed his chin, pinching it, lifting Teagan's eyes to his. He looked down into Teagan's face, squeezing the boy's chin 'til it turned white. Teagan clamped his eyes shut. Father's other hand curled into a massive fist.

"Open those eyes," Father growled.

Teagan opened his eyes wide, stared into Father's face, his whole body trembling.

"Great Sisters know why I don't save myself the coin," Father spat. "Cursed free-loader. Know how hard I gotta work to keep your carcass in mash? Eh? Got nothin' to say for yourself? Can't talk without help from your little sister? Near nineteen years I been feedin' your hide. I should strap the life outta your silly skin this very moment——."

"The skins, Dad!" Liz said suddenly, loudly, as if forgetting herself. Father whirled and she shut her mouth with a loud, exaggerated snap, hitching the bear cub up on her hip. "The skins," she repeated softly, looking him straight in the eye.

Father was staring at her, still holding Teagan's chin pinched between his thumb and forefinger. "What you say?"

"With permission, sir," Liz said. She cleared her throat and stared up at him fearlessly. The bear cub was suddenly heavy in her arms.

"Speak." Father blinked and shook his head, like rising from a fog. He let go of Teagan's chin.

"I told him to take the dead cubs, sir. For the skins, sir. I remembered you showing me a cap down in Korfort, sir. That fur cap made from the pelt of a grey? Across the road from the mill when you took me there last time, sir? That cap fetched near ten copper suns, sir—if I remember correctly, sir. On account of it being from a grey." Liz nodded, as if trying to remember. "You told me only a coward would buy grey fur from some worn-out pit fighter instead of taking it for himself up here. I think you told me you could get even more for 'em down in Adara's Hold? If I remember right, sir."

Father looked at her. Then he chuckled, frowned, and nodded. "That's a good idea, girl. Whatever other talents your Mother has—and she's got many, let me tell you—she knows how to pinch a thread and needle." He looked back into Teagan's hunting cloak and nodded. "Probably get one or two good caps out of each of 'em. Maybe more. Doubt the fur is good now, so young, but maybe a little bag or two or something? Just the hide, maybe? Purse kind of thing? Hmm. Have to be real careful who you sold 'em to. Cursed Tarn. Cursed rangers. Always on the look-out . . . . But why not?" He stopped and looked at Teagan. "You walk the whole way back like that? Carryin' those?"

"Y-yes, sir," Teagan stammered, eyes on the floor, trying not to cringe, waiting for it.

Father paused a long moment, looking down at him. "You did right. And you were just doing what Liz told you to do, isn't that so?"

"Yes, sir," Teagan said, not looking up, not sure if the answer he gave was the right one.

"Hmm." Father wiped his mouth with the back of his hand. "Takes strength to walk back in the cold like that." A long pause. "We'll make a mountain man outta you yet."

Father turned and walked back to the fire. Teagan looked up at his back, a huge smile breaking across his face, glancing from Father to Liz, to Father again. And the expression of heartfelt gratitude in her brother's eyes, the honest appreciation for this tiny scrap of praise, nearly broke Liz's heart. She cleared her throat.

"Get on up to your bed," Father said, looking at the fire.

"Yes, sir! Sir! Yes!" Teagan nodded, grinned at Liz, and then all but ran to the loft's ladder, not looking back.

"May I ask a question, sir?" Liz asked.

"Speak up," Father said.

"What's a full-grown bear skin fetch? If it's a grey's?"

"Hmm." Father grunted. He touched his flask through his vest. "Full-grown grey bear pelt? Not too much in the village. Worth something, but nothing like what you could get farther down off the mountain. But you figure down past the Trange, in Korfort those fools, you could take five, six hundred suns for a grey's pelt, maybe more, if you knew the right merchant, if it was big enough. Then you sell the meat, too—on top of that. Gotta be careful with the pelt of a wild grey though, girl. Don't want to draw needless attention."

"Why's that?" Liz asked, already knowing the answer but knowing that Father was still interested in talking, too.

"The Tarn, girl. Tarn's rangers. Always watchin'. Tarn lays claim to every wild grey on the big mountain. Breedin' stock for the war bears. Or so they say, cursed thieves." He looked at the bear cub. "Half the time I think those old Konungur freeholders are right. Take back the big mountain by force, somehow. Make 'em give it back, keep 'em out of here somehow. Damned liars."

He reached for the flask in his vest, then stopped himself and took a little sip of tea instead. "Anyway, you let him get all the way full-grown, you could take his paws and sell his pelt separate, or keep 'em together for maybe double the coin. Plus the meat, like I said. Don't forget the meat, girl. Maybe even head down farther, down the mountain, Adara's Hold, make a lot. At about three, four years old, the fur gets real silvery, worth even more. Twice the time you gotta put in, but maybe three times the money. Maybe more, even. Down in the Hold . . . ." Father frowned, like he was suddenly confused by himself, like he didn't understand his own words. He rubbed his heavy jaw, deep in thought. "Give that cub here."

Liz took the cub from her chest and handed it back to Father. Father held it up by the scruff of the neck and looked it over, top to bottom.

"May I ask another question, sir?"

Father nodded, lost in thought. That strange look was back in his eye. Liz was quite certain she'd never seen that particular look before. She glanced at the bear cub hanging there from his fist, then back to Father. He drank off the last of his tea and set his cup down, still staring at the bear cub.

"Ask," he said.

Liz nodded. "I remember old Jarlund saying once he'd seen some fellow selling grey bear paws down there in Korfort— but that all the claws had been pulled out. Do the paws fetch the same amount like that? With no claws?"

Father shook his head. "Nah. That's the whole point, girl. Gotta keep the claws *in*. In Korfort once—tucked way back in some alley, mind you, illegal—I seen a grey bear paw four palms wide, *with* claws. Average sized one, that. Worth a fortune. What *they* call 'a fortune,' at least." He laughed strangely, then paused. Then cleared his throat. "Forbidden by the Tarn, 'course. Old Konungur families hang a wild grey paw over a baby's bed, keep the chill at bay, fend off the bad luck and cliff ghosts, the winter crows. The way of it up here. Hang a wild grey paw on your front porch, even the King of the Mountain won't come into your clearing. That's the legend. Claws're how you know they ain't been raised up for the trophy, or so they say. Claws is what gives the charm its power. Silly superstition. Fool's talk. But they pay real money. You ain't never seen an adult grey close-up, girl. They're big. I mean *big*. Ain't like no black or brown. Unstoppable."

His eyes shone in that strange way again, the trace of a smile touching his face. "A grey bear is twice again as big as a brown and lives three, maybe four times as long. Grey bear is five times as smart as a black. Ha! Compared to a proper grey, a black bear is like your silly brother up there." Father tilted his head up at the loft, then frowned at himself. "Almost no way to keep a grey in a pen past its third or fourth year. Too big. Too smart. Before the end of the first year, you gotta start training 'em for war or cage 'em up in iron, chain 'em up. We get a good melt this thaw, suppose I could dig a pit." He shook his head. "That'd never work. A good, heavy chain'd do it. Or, maybe . . . ." Then he shook his head suddenly, as if clearing an unwanted thought. "Either way, you kids'll have to work day and night for its food."

He handed the cub back to Liz. She took it, holding it close to her chest. The whole idea of feeding and raising the cub— and then killing it—was starting to make her a bit sick. She was a trapper's daughter. She'd started taking game almost as soon as she could hold a bow. She'd harvested plenty of fur from the big mountain. She knew the life. But, for some reason, this little bear was different. This was a grey bear—the rarest, most prized animal on the mountain, the only animal she knew protected by royal decree, the Tarn's law. It wasn't some snow 'coon that came cheaper by the score. She held the bear cub close to her chest, savoring its furry warmth.

"How do you kill a bear without damaging its coat?" Liz asked casually, trying to make it sound like she didn't really care what happened.

Father nodded. "Put a bullet in its head. Or, if you want to keep the head for the trophy pelt, you can poison it. Starve it for a couple days, then give it a warm pot of mash and honey with a handful of baneberry, string of mooncaps. Burns the stomach out." He frowned, shook his head. "Takes some time and the screamin'll drive you near mad. Almost like a man's scream. Trouble might be worth it. No blood. No damage to the pelt—maybe some vomit. Can hurt the meat, but the coat . . . you do it right, his coat'll shine like silver snow."

Father's frown deepened. He looked at the bear cub in her arms, his face serious. Then that strange look flickered in his eyes once more. "On the other hand . . . ," he began, as if having an entirely different thought. He reached out and rubbed the top of the bear cub's head with one of his huge fingers, stroking the soft, silver-grey fur. Then he felt the cub's bent leg again, ran his hands over its little limbs and spine as she held it—almost like he was looking for something.

The thought of poisoning the little bear made Liz nauseous and sad and angry all at the same time.

And what's he looking for, anyway?

"Hmm?" Father murmured, as if hearing Liz's silent question. But he didn't continue the thought out loud. "Make me a touch more tea, would you, Lizzy?" He shook his head and cleared his throat. "Keep the kettle on, for your Mother? She'd appreciate that."

And that's when Liz realized that she'd completely forgotten to tell Father about the dead ranger.

She'd just forgotten about it entirely.

Liz opened her mouth—mind racing now, thinking about how she'd tell him—then shut it.

Probably best to keep quiet.

She knew how Father felt about the Tarn's rangers. About the Tarn itself.

And with his leg hurting him so bad like it had been lately, with the near miss with Teagan just a few moments ago . . . .

No sense pressing the luck.

So she kept her mouth shut and made Father's tea. And she made it extra strong.

10

LATER THAT NIGHT, up in the sleeping loft, Liz, Evan, and Teagan cuddled around the bear cub. The loft was warm, they all wore homespun pajamas, and Mother and Father always made sure there was plenty of fur for the bed.

Mother had returned from old man Jarlund's with the reindeer milk a bell after she'd been sent. Following Father's instructions, Liz had taken the milk, heated it over the stove, and then filled her leather food pouch with the warm milk. Mother had then pricked a pin hole in the corner of the bag so that the cub could nurse from it. Once Liz had coaxed the cub awake—which had taken some doing—the little guy had sucked the bag's corner with gusto, his eyes shut, silver-grey fur shining in the hearth's warmth, smacking contentedly. Mother had gone to bed, after checking in the loft to be sure they were all tucked in. (Some nights, especially recently, she'd come up to tell them a story, to sing them an old song, or just to cuddle; but not tonight.) Father had stayed up in his chair. The pain had come back and his knee was in absolute agony. So he'd sipped on his pine whisky until he'd fallen asleep. Now he was down there below them, snoring like a great bear by the embers of the dying fire.

In bed, snuggled inside the tent they'd made out of their furs and blankets, the little bear cub slept on its back, breathing softly between Evan and Teagan. Its front paws were extended straight over its head, its back legs pointed straight down, its weird leg bent at an angle. The cub's big head rested in Liz's lap. Its stomach was a furry, round sphere. Liz had placed a broken shard of glazed pottery on the shelf beneath their window to reflect moonlight into the loft. Lit by the moonbeam, the cub's silver-grey fur seemed to glow.

Liz had just finished telling Evan the whole story of how they'd found the cub's dead mother and the dead ranger— with Teagan apologizing continuously for leaving the axe outside, a tempo counterpoint to the entire tale. They kept their voices low, so as not to wake Father. Every so often, Liz would stroke the side of the cub's head with the end of her blond braid.

"I mean . . . I'm *sorry*," Teagan whispered for at least the hundredth time. "I just *forgot*."

"Knock it off with the 'sorries,' already," Evan whispered, punching Teagan softly on the shoulder. Evan's left eye was completely swollen shut. "How many times you gonna make me say it was *my* fault? I should've picked it up when I saw it stuck in the log back there. Or asked you about it, made sure you were done. A wonder Liz could even finish telling the story, with all your cursed *sorries*."

Teagan paused for a moment, looked down at his hands. Then he looked up at them, crossed his eyes, and whispered dramatically: "*Sorry!*"

Evan chortled. Liz stifled a laugh and shook her head.

"What?" Teagan asked simply. "Can't a man say 'sorry' in his own bed?"

Evan groaned and rolled his eyes.

The little bear burped in its sleep—a deep, *long* burp.

They all stopped and stared at each other.

The bear burped again—deeper and longer yet, almost like a full-grown man. And then it was all they could do to keep from laughing their heads off. The fact that they were scared witless of Father hearing them made the giggles even harder to control. The bed creaked softly with their rocking.

The cub rolled its head off Liz's lap, snuffled over onto its stomach, and pushed its little rump into the air. Liz stopped and pointed at the cub's round little butt, one hand clamped firmly over her mouth and nose. They all went quiet. Then the cub's stumpy little tail twitched and a little fart squeaked out and they were snorting into their furs and hands, guts aching, tears of laughter streaming down their faces.

11

"YOU GOTTA NAME it, Liz," Evan whispered a few moments later, after they'd calmed down a bit. "You can't just call it 'bear' 'til he fattens it up and kills it."

Liz stopped smiling. "Don't want to name it," she whispered, looking down at the cub. She stroked its soft back.

"Yeah," Teagan whispered. "Makes it harder when he dies."

Liz nodded. Teagan was slow, but every so often he could touch real wisdom.

"That makes sense, I guess." Evan nodded, but he looked unconvinced.

"If you name him," Teagan whispered, "then he's more like Soldier or Rosie, right? Like he's one of us. I mean . . . isn't that right, Liz?"

Liz nodded again.

"Come on!" Evan groaned. "We've *gotta* name it. You don't think the little guy deserves a name? He's a *grey* bear. He's a born fighter—a *warrior*. The Tarn's lords ride them into battle. And the Tarn's rangers ride them all over the big mountain. If he didn't have this weird, messed-up leg, he'd be worth more coin than all three of us would make if we worked every trap we ever had for every day of our entire *lives*. I say we name him. I see your point, Tee—I do. I get it. But this is a *war bear*, for the Great Sisters' sake! All the great war bears have names. They *all* get named."

"Keep your voice down," Liz whispered, glancing at the loft's ladder. They all went quiet, their heads cocked, listening for any sound. Below, by the fire, Father snorted—then continued snoring.

Teagan looked at Evan, then at Liz. "I mean . . . he *is* a grey bear, after all."

"Exactly," Evan nodded. "He *is* a grey bear, Liz."

Liz rolled her eyes

"What about 'Narmos'?" Teagan whispered.

Evan frowned. "You mean like from the story?"

Liz raised an eyebrow. "Not a bad idea."

"I remember." Teagan nodded, tapped his head. "I remember, see?"

Liz looked at Teagan. "Narmos was the Silver Queen's first grey bear. A gift from the old Konungur kings, way back in the olden times. How'd you think of that, Tee?"

Evan scoffed.

Teagan looked down at the little cub, stroked its soft fur, and shook his head. "Dunno. I mean . . . I was just thinking of how this little guy was guarding his mom from the hounds when we found him, even though she was dead? He even stood up to Soldier, didn't he? I mean, he wasn't afraid at all, was he? He looked Soldier in the eye and growled and tried to scare him away with his little paws, like he was ready for anything, like he was daring Soldier to fight him—and Soldier outweighs him by ten stone, right? So he's a warrior, like he's supposed to be. That reminded me of that story you told me about the other Narmos. Big Narmos, the Silver

Queen's Narmos. That part of the story where Narmos stands in front of the Silver Queen on that, that bridge? When that bad guy—what's that bad guy's name—?"

"'Dodrák?'" Evan snorted disparagingly. "That's all *fake*."

"Yeah!" Teagan's eyes shone, ignoring Evan's cynicism completely. "Dodrák, that's right! And all the White Legions are charging her! Remember that? And the Silver Queen, she's just out there on the Long Bridge with Narmos. Just her and Narmos against two hundred Konungur warriors and their bears. Remember that?"

Liz nodded thoughtfully.

"That is a good story," Evan admitted. "Too bad it's not true."

"Where'd you say that story comes from again, Lizzy?" Teagan asked.

"It's from the Silver Book," Liz whispered. "Old man Jarlund read from it last Middlewinter. Remember? Father was down in Korfort. Mr. Barnabus and his boys were there? Belios and Beiro were there with us."

"Oooh! *Belios!*" Evan mocked her gently, batting his eyelashes. She shoved him with her shoulder, then looked back at Teagan. He was puzzling on her words.

"Remember, Tee?" Liz asked.

Teagan blinked, then his mouth made an o-shape, as he remembered. He nodded. "I like that story."

"That *story* is all made up," Evan hissed. "Don't be such an idiot." He elbowed Teagan. "Dragons and ogre warriors and magical armies and nonsense? That stuff's not *real*. Silver Queen? One lady against two *hundred* trained warriors? Rubbish! It's like a *legend*, Tee. See? There's no such person." Then Evan noticed Liz's look and softened his tone. "That is . . . well. It *is* a good name—I'll give you that—but it's still just a story."

"Well . . . *I* liked that story." Teagan looked away awkwardly. "I really did." He rubbed the scar on his temple.

Liz cocked her head and eyed Evan coolly. "How do you know it's just 'made up'? You know that the Tarn's lords ride grey bears in battle. Said it yourself. Everyone knows that's true." She lifted her chin in the direction of the big mountain. "And how you think that ranger who got herself killed out there got onto the mountain? You think she *walked* all the way out there? Rangers ride 'em, too. Just like *you* said. And we saw those rangers in the village last winter, remember? With their silver armor and carbines and bears? And we've seen 'em down there before, too. You said it yourself. How'd you think that all started? Must've been a first time. Maybe the story of Narmos and the Silver Queen tells it? I dunno. But I do know that there *was* a Silver Queen—the High Lady Aaryn. That was her name. That's why everyone who lives down past the Trange calls the big mountain 'Aaryn's Cry.' High Lady Aaryn was one of the five Great Sisters and she built the Tarn—that's what Jarlund read in his Silver Book. Unless you don't think there's such a thing as 'the Tarn' in the first place—."

"Okay! Okay!" Evan whispered, giving up. He looked at her sideways, then yawned. "Keep forgetting not to get into an argument with someone who remembers every single cursed thing in the whole cursed world!"

Liz shook her head. "I'm not saying the story's true, broth-er. I'm just saying we don't know it's *not* true. I know *he* says all those stories are lies." Liz cocked her head toward the loft's ladder and the fire below, lowering her voice to the barest whisper. "But what does that mean? He doesn't *really* know. He hates anything that has to do with the Tarn. And besides, even if the story *isn't* true, the Silver Queen's bear was still called Narmos in the story and he was still her protector, in the *story*. And it's a good story. Good name."

"So now you want to name him, after all?" Evan winked.

Liz shrugged, almost conceding the point, resting her palm on the little bear's furry back.

"Narmos," Teagan whispered softly. He'd shut his eyes during the last part of their discussion and had put his head beside the cub's shoulder, stroking its little paws, nuzzling down into the furs. "You were so brave when that nasty old Dodrák came to kill your mistress, weren't you? But you showed them, huh? You showed everybody, didn't you? You stood up in front of him, and at the end, all the White Legions, all the old Konungur fighters, bent knee to the Silver Queen. Loyal Narmos. Good Narmos. Brave Narmos. Good little Narmos."

Liz looked at Evan. "Looks like it's decided."

"Guess so," Evan whispered. Then, after a moment: "Maybe you could tell me that story again sometime? I don't think I remember it right."

"Tomorrow night." Liz nodded and yawned. "That's a promise. If I can remember it all."

Evan shook his head and sighed. "You always remember everything, Liz."

Then Evan leaned over and kissed Narmos on the top of the head. "Good night, Narmos." He patted the bear's rump. "Sleep well." The grey cub snorted. Evan smiled.

"Good night, Narmos," Teagan yawned, his eyes still shut, stroking the cub's back.

Gently, Liz scooted down, adjusted her braid, and pulled the cub up onto her stomach, taking special care with his claws. Then she snuggled down on her back between her brothers and pulled the furs and blankets up to her chin, covering herself and Narmos both. Narmos sniffed, adjusted his position, then scooted up and lay flat on Liz's chest, one front paw on either side of her neck. He snored softly against Liz's throat for a moment, then adjusted himself and tucked his nose farther down beside Liz's ear. The smell of his fur was earth and acorns and pine and winter all at once. Liz breathed it deeply.

"Good night, brave Narmos," Liz sighed.

She fell immediately to sleep.

12

THAT NIGHT, LIZ dreamt the big mountain was on fire, a searing nightmare filled with animals of every sort, beasts running and screaming as their hides burned with hellish fury, fleeing flames they carried in their own flesh. There was a dragon on the mountain. Its black scales shone like obsidian, pointed horns curled like gnarled trees. Its rider was a young woman, a screaming demon with a spear of twisted silver, her long dark hair the color of night. In front of the monster, a defiant rider on a silver-white bear, a solitary knight silhouetted against the burning world and the dragon's fire. But then the war bear turned away from the flames, and the rider and the dragon and the fire vanished into mist. The bear sat down on its big rump and looked at Liz. Its eyes were wise and haunted. There was a black-fletched arrow protruding from its back leg, right above the knee; a bad wound. A crow sat in a pine tree behind it.

With Father's deep voice, the bear spoke to her:

"Do you remember when we went down to Korfort a few years ago? At the beginning of that early spring?"

"Yes." Liz smiled. "We found that patch of mountain

prairie, green and completely dry."

"The white clover already up, the smell of clean grass, and that little creek there off to the side, running with the mountain's thaw?"

Liz nodded and swallowed.

She remembered.

"How long did we camp there?" the bear asked. "I can't recall."

"Two weeks." Liz cleared her throat. "We didn't even go to town. 'Let's just stay here,' you said. Remember? At first, we didn't know what you meant. Then we realized that you wanted to stay up there on the prairie in our tents, just stay up there the whole time—instead of going to Korfort— just us, the five of us and Soldier, on the edge of the field. I remember you and Mother made grass crowns and we made those little scepters out of sticks and pine cones and we played every day and had 'royal banquets,' like you called them. You remember that?"

The bear paused. Then it blinked. "I think so."

Liz continued. "We played that game about stories, that storytelling game? Around the fire every night. And then you'd bring out your mandolin and you'd sing to us and to Mother. Do you remember?"

"What did I sing?" The bear frowned.

"Oh, all kinds of things. Songs we'd never heard before. Even some songs in another language. You and Mother, you knew all the words and you sang together and Teagan started crying because it was so beautiful and you cuddled him on your lap and kissed him and told him that everything would be alright, that you'd take care of him. He fell asleep there, while you and Mother sang."

"Was I . . . was I happy?" the bear asked.

Liz nodded, but she was having a hard time speaking, her throat going thick. "I think so," she finally managed.

The bear cocked its head and looked at her. "Were *you* happy?"

Her lips trembled. "Yes," she admitted.

The bear turned away from her, limping, its old eyes terribly sad. The crow cawed.

"Then you'll have to run," the bear said. "Can't hold him back much longer."

"Hold what?" Liz asked. "Who?"

When the bear looked back up at her, its eyes were bloody and savage.

"*RUN!*" it roared, fangs wide.

And then the crow screamed and the mountain burst into flames and Liz woke freezing, her skin sheened with night sweat, laying there in the dark, staring up at the ceiling, her whole body trembling. It took her a few moments to understand where she was, to focus, to push the dream away. When she finally did, she realized that it was still dark, still the middle of the night——.

And Narmos was missing from their bed.

The little bear's furry warmth was gone.

She took a breath. Closed her eyes. *Calm down.* Took another breath. Then quietly, so as not to wake her brothers, she folded back the furs, pushed her braid over her shoulder, and patted the bed, looking for the bear cub.

Nothing.

She looked to the window.

There was Narmos, standing wobbly on a stool on his back legs, looking out the small window, staring up at the moon. His eyes were huge and intelligent. The white blaze on his chest shone in the moon's light. He blinked every so often as he gazed out into the night. Then he looked up to the mountain, to the woods, down to the trees beside the cabin, then back again to the moon. His breath fogged the glass; his little black nose smeared the fog. Liz watched him for a long moment. He looked stronger. As if sensing her gaze, Narmos turned and looked at her. He blinked once, then turned his furry head back to the window, up toward the big mountain, then toward the moon once more.

Liz shook her head.

This is home now, Narmos, she thought. *No more woods, no more snow, no more caves, no more brothers, no more mother. This is where you live now. This is where you live, until you die.*

"I'm sorry, Narmos," Liz whispered. She didn't know why she said it. It just came out. "We thought . . . . I thought we were saving you."

Narmos looked down to the trees beside the cabin again. He blinked, cocked his head, turned to look at Liz. There was a question in his eyes.

"What is it, boy?" Liz frowned.

Narmos blinked, then looked again to the trees beside the

cabin. Cocked his head, as if to say: "Come and see."

Liz rolled out of bed and stepped to the window. The wood floor was cold against her feet. She wiped her hand across the pane and looked out.

Directly below the window, Father was leaning against the woodpile stacked between two fir trees. The bottom limbs of the firs had been cut away so that the cordwood could be placed between the trees for seasoning. Father was getting sick in the snow—vomiting—leaning against the woodpile as he retched. Somewhere, the winter crow cawed.

Liz looked away . . . then looked back.

The sight made her sad and angry. But she was also strangely intrigued and then suddenly embarrassed to be watching him.

You shouldn't see this.

How could you love and fear and hate and care for someone so much—all those things, all at the same time? It had been so different before. She knew that. She remembered. And Mother remembered, too. But when had it started to change? Liz didn't know. It had been slow, so slow. Gradual . . . . Like there had never been any change at all . . . .

Narmos looked down at Father, then up to Liz. His grey

eyes were wide and puzzled. Liz stroked his head. His thick fur was warm and soothing under her fingers; made her feel better. As Liz watched, she realized that Father was talking to himself as he got sick. She couldn't make out the words, but he was muttering about something, wiping at his mouth. Suddenly, he leaned back, took something from his vest, and threw it into the woods. It flashed once, silver in the moonlight, and gone. Father bent his head, wiped his face, and shuddered.

Narmos looked up to Liz, blinked.

"His flask." Liz stroked the cub's thick fur, right behind his ears. She stepped away from the window. "Don't worry—he always finds it. Or one of us does. Happens like this all the time these days."

And then—suddenly, in her mind's eye—Liz saw herself waking her brothers, climbing down together from the loft, gathering Mother and everyone together while he was out back puking. They would leave. Escape. Could they do it without hurting him? Or would they have to knock him unconscious . . . or something?

Then you'll have to run.

She shook her head, clearing the vision.

But the idea stayed.

Sometimes, especially lately, she thought running might be the only way they'd be safe. Father had always taken care of them—even if he was hard on them. But one night, one night very soon, he'd drink too much and something would break, the line would be crossed, and something horrible would happen. And it *was* coming. Liz knew it. Knew it in her bones.

Can't hold him back much longer.

She frowned, shook her head, and crawled back into bed, being careful not to wake her brothers.

Narmos gazed down at Father for a long moment. Then the cub looked up at the moon one last time, turned away, and wobbled his way down off the stool, crawling over to the bed. At its side, he stood up on his back legs, dug his claws into the furs, and tried to pull himself back into the covers, snuffling and grunting. Liz reached down, put her hands under both of the cub's furry arms, and lifted him back into bed. He burrowed down between everyone, finally curling up next to Teagan's side. He looked at Liz, his huge eyes shining. Liz stroked his head, then snuggled down under the covers, her arm thrown over Teagan and Narmos together.

She yawned, stretched her legs under the furs, and immediately fell asleep, Narmos's wet nose whistling in her ear.

She slept like the dead.

13

"LIZ! BOYS!" MOTHER'S voice from below. "Breakfast! C'mon now. Not gonna call again!"

Liz's eyes peeled open, sticky with sleep. From the brightness and shape of the window's light, she could tell it was late. Way later than they'd normally be allowed to sleep. Breakfast smells rose from below. She looked at her brothers. Teagan was snoring, his mouth wide open, his pillow wet with drool as he cuddled Evan's left leg. Evan had managed to get turned around in the middle of the night somehow. He was still lying on his stomach, but his head was hanging off the other end of the bed, his right foot—not exactly the cleanest foot in the world, either—resting on Teagan's cheek, his big toe creeping dangerously close to Teagan's open mouth.

Liz smiled. Narmos was there, too, sitting up against

Teagan's side, quietly looking at her. His big grey eyes were wide and alert. Last night's milk seemed to have done its job: he looked happy and hungry. When Narmos saw that Liz was awake, he gave a little snort, looked around the loft, then lifted his black nose toward the ladder, moving it back and forth in the air, slowly savoring the rising smell of frying boar bacon and hot syrup.

"Morning, Narmos." Liz yawned and scratched Narmos's furry belly.

Narmos blinked, pawed at Liz's hands, then cocked his head at the ladder. Mother was setting the table with just a touch too much enthusiasm, steel utensils rattling pointedly against clay plates. The little bear gave a sniff, then licked his nose with his long pink tongue.

"Hungry, eh?" Liz asked him.

Narmos blinked at her, once, as if to say: "Yes. Yes, I am."

"Let's get you outside to do your business; I'll visit the outhouse, too." Liz nodded. "Then we'll get your milk."

Narmos blinked again and gave a low growl that morphed into a yawn that morphed into a grunt which sounded to Liz very much like: "Well, let's get moving then."

"Boys! Liz!" Mother, from below again. "Only gonna be hot once!"

"We're up, Mom!" Liz called down. She bent forward and gave Narmos a nice long scratch behind his ears. Then, carefully—ever so gently, like a master thief on the prowl—Liz lifted and adjusted Evan's foot so that his big toe rested just inside Teagan's mouth. The tone of Teagan's snore changed, but not its intensity. Evan grunted and his toes wiggled. Teagan snorted and yawned, sucking Evan's toe deeper yet into his mouth.

". . . whatha?" Evan mumbled from under the furs.

"Morning, boys." Liz grinned.

She grabbed her bear and together they slid down the ladder.

14

"You did well last night," Mother told Liz quietly, setting a plate of pancakes at the center of the table, touching her shoulder. "You were perfect." She spoke softly, so the boys couldn't hear, then turned back to the kitchen, her long blond hair swinging behind her, held in a loose ponytail.

Liz nodded. Father must be outside somewhere. Liz sat at

the table and rested Narmos on her lap. The little bear eyed the hot pancakes hungrily, sniffing. But he didn't reach for them. Like he already had manners.

Mother came back, set a pitcher of warm reindeer milk on the table, looked at her, then scratched Narmos behind his ear. "We'll talk when he goes out. Sometime later today."

"Might be time to go," Liz said softly, calmly. It wasn't the first time they'd had this kind of conversation.

"Plans to make." Mother nodded, then put her finger to her lips and cocked her head at the sleeping loft, a thousand words communicated between mother and daughter in half a moment. Then she leaned forward, kissed Liz on the forehead, and whispered. "You are better than I could have ever dreamed. Better than I deserve."

15

FATHER FINALLY CAME back in from outside while they were finishing up their breakfast—as the kids literally licked their plates clean. Narmos had drunk another two cups of reindeer's milk from Liz's improvised nursing bag. Now the little bear was busy helping Liz clean the last film of syrup from her plate.

Hot pancakes, hot boar bacon, hot syrup. And they'd each had a small glass of reindeer milk with fresh honey, too. A delicious breakfast. A royal breakfast. A breakfast fit for kings. Sometimes Liz wondered where Mother came up with the coin for these celebratory feasts, but the questions didn't last long when there were hot pancakes in front of her. These pancakes were shaped like bears' heads. Two round ears, a big round head, and a little nose. Or maybe they were supposed to be mice? Liz looked at Mother; Mother winked at her and glanced at Narmos. Liz knew the little bear was part of the reason for the special breakfast. The other part was that Father usually felt sorry the morning after a bad night. He was always a different man, the day after. And last night had been pretty bad. Evan's swollen eye—horrible, puckered, and purple-black—was the testament.

"Morning," Father said heartily as he opened the front door, leaning on his walking stick.

"Morning, Father!" they all replied in unison.

Father shut the door behind him, gave the scene a careful inspection, but didn't take off his boots. "Good breakfast?"

"Yes, Father!" they all said. Narmos nodded, burped, and made a kind of wet little gurgle.

"And you, little bear?" Father asked. "How are *you* feeling?"

Narmos blinked at him, licked his chops, then blinked again, as if to say: "Never better. Can I have more pancakes?"

"Good," Father grunted. "Another cup of tea, Mother?"

"Already ready." She handed him his big ceramic cup. He took it, set it on the counter, grabbed her hand, kissed it, then brought a small carved box out from one of his coat pockets and handed it to her.

"Just brought this up from Jarlund's. Had him order it special a couple weeks ago. Thought you'd like it."

She looked at the box, then said gently, "You shouldn't be walking down there with your leg as it is."

"You're right." Father shrugged, picked up his cup, and drank.

Mother opened the box, looked inside, looked at Father wonderingly, then smiled. Her face lit the room. Father looked down, kind of bashful. Liz wanted to know what was in there, but she knew it'd never happen. Father was always finding these little things to please Mother. Liz didn't know where he found them, or where he found the money, but

Mother clearly loved them all. She kept them in the bedroom and the kids were never allowed in there.

Mother stepped up to him, stood on her tippy toes, pulled him down, and kissed him on the cheek. Liz knew that Mother was still furious with Father for last night, but this was all part of the ritual. Later on, she'd try to talk to him and it would go well. Or it would go poorly. And then around sunset, Father's leg would start hurting again, and they'd start all over again . . . . But they still had the morning.

Father smiled at Mother, then looked up to find that the kids were all watching his performance as they finished their breakfast. Even little Narmos seemed intrigued.

"Alright." Father cleared his throat. "Big day today. Big day on the big mountain. Jarlund's got Fonhammer and Barnabus up at his place. One of his reindeer has a tumor on his leg that they're helping with. Anyway—it's gonna be a big day, all around. Evan, how're you feeling?"

"Good, Father," Evan said.

Father nodded. "I did your early work this morning, so you could rest up. Big day. You'll take your brother and the hounds up the eastern line for a quick pass. Leave Soldier here with Mother and Liz. Want you back before twilight, understood? We're gonna have to re-space the traps and move the whole line three bells closer in so we can run the cycle more often. Sharp and tight now."

"Yes, Father!" Evan said. "Right away!" He started cleaning up his dishes immediately.

"Teagan," Father said sternly.

Teagan looked up, reached automatically for his temple, then put his hands in his lap and looked back at his plate. "Yes, sir," he said, not looking up.

"I've got something for you."

Teagan looked up, worried. From his cloak, Father brought forth an axe identical to his own. It even had that small silver leaf in the wooden handle. Father set it on the counter beside him. Teagan stared at it, then looked at Father, even more worried than before.

"We're gonna try something else, son," Father said seriously. "You're gonna have your own axe from now on. You're almost nineteen years old and you need to learn how to take care of your tools. So this is yours." He touched the axe. "*Yours*. And you need to take care of it properly. Got a scabbard for it for your belt, too. Think you can do that?"

Teagan looked from Father, to the axe, to Father again, nodding, his mouth slightly open, speechless.

"Alright." Father nodded. "Now, finish up and get to your work."

Teagan nodded quickly, several times, and immediately started cleaning up. He glanced once at Liz and smiled beautifully.

"Liz," Father said, "suit up and bring your bear out back to the shed. Had an idea last night. We're gonna take care of him right now. His leg isn't as bent this morning, is it?"

"—yes, Father," Liz stammered. "I mean, no sir."

But her stomach turned in on itself and her fingers went to ice.

At exactly the same time, Evan and Teagan each shot her a covert glance. Then they looked at little Narmos. Narmos looked back at them calmly—then burped.

"*Take care*" *of Narmos now?* Liz shook her head.

That hadn't been the plan.

And if you don't like it, what exactly are you gonna do about it?

Cursed bears and Silver Queens and Narmos. Why

did they have to name him? Liz looked back at Evan and Teagan. Teagan was staring at the table now and Evan kind of eyed the floor, both of them looking miserable. Liz glared back at them. *All in agreement on the naming issue now, aren't we?*

"Mother, fetch my skinning kit?" Father asked. "Throw a couple of smaller bits in there, too? With the drill? Already put the other stuff I need in there earlier." He made a sheepish kind of gesture at the floor, as if to say that he'd like to get his gear himself but that he didn't want to take off his boots, or track snow into the house.

Mother nodded, left the stove, and stepped past him—then she stopped suddenly, got up on her tiptoes again, pulled him down, and kissed him on the cheek once more. Then she continued on to their bedroom door. There, she unlocked the iron lock with the key from her apron, opened and shut the door behind her.

"Make it quick, Liz," Father grunted gruffly. "Lots to show you. And don't forget to change the dressing on his leg. That's important. This won't be like anything you've done before."

"Yes, Father." Liz nodded, trying to look him in the eye.

But there was a sinking stone in her gut and her hands were frozen.

Why bother to change the dressing if we're just gonna kill him?

And why couldn't the thrice-cursed voice inside her head just shut up once in a while?

Beside Liz at the table, Narmos burped again, made a funny little squeak, and looked up at her. Time for some adventures?

"Yes," she whispered, sick to her stomach.

She stroked his head, marveling at the softness of his thick fur.

Never should've named you, bear.

16

LIZ PUT ON her furs and gear. With Narmos on her hip, she pushed her blond braid over her shoulder and stepped out onto the porch. She was halfway down the front steps before she realized that Father wasn't alone outside. He was standing just off the porch, leaning on his walking stick, talking in a low voice to Mr. Tulf, an old hunter from the other side of the valley who came 'round every once in a while.

Tulf was tall, shorter than Father of course, but still a big man. He wore wooden snowshoes and carried a long, expensive carbine slung over his shoulder in a leather scabbard. His hunting cloak was made of wolf pelts, its hood the top of a white wolf's scalp. His beard was dark grey, his hair worn in the old Konungur style, a series of tight braids on the top and back of his head. He sported a necklace of bear teeth. A wide belt of brown leather circled his waist. The belt was hung with a trio of curved daggers with handles of horn.

Upon seeing Tulf, Liz immediately backed into the house on her tiptoes, carrying Narmos with her, but Father turned and stopped her.

"No need, Liz." He inclined his head, his face serious, appreciating her concern in keeping the bear cub hidden. "Tulf here knows our little secret."

Tulf stared at her impassively. He rarely had much of an expression on his face, but his eyes were sharp.

"Bring him out, girl," Tulf said. "Let's have a look at him."

Liz stepped out onto the porch, holding Narmos on her hip.

Tulf whistled, but didn't smile. "Grey bear, alright."

Father inclined his head, but didn't say anything.

"Rangers catch wind of this, gonna be trouble for you, Hone."

"You gonna tell 'em?" Father didn't smile.

Tulf snorted. "Day I rat a mountain man to those dogs is the day I start diggin' my own grave. They been all over the place these last weeks. Something's up. Cursed Tarn. You hear they're callin' another meeting on fur and timber rights north of the Trange? They want to renegotiate the treaty, again."

"Heard something about that."

"Never ends. Give 'em a toe, take your whole cursed leg."

"You and yours gonna sit still for that?"

Tulf gave Father a cool look, scratched at his dark beard, tucked a thumb into his leather belt. "No."

He looked at Father for a long moment. "Kind of what I come up here to talk to you about, Hone."

"Long hike for a chat."

Father's eyes were dark. He didn't say anything else.

Neither did Tulf.

That went on for some time, both of them looking at each other. Narmos squirmed in Liz's arms, trying to get loose.

Finally, Tulf broke the silence. "We ain't gonna do this no more. We're workin' on somethin'. Some new supplies.

Some new leverage."

Father raised an eyebrow.

Tulf shook his head. "These 'treaties'—just a bunch of lies dressed up in Tarn fancy talk. We got rights, too. Ancient rights. My people been up here on the big mountain since the beginning, since before the Tarn and all of 'em. Hundred generations, at least. Got some special help comin' in. Thought you might want to know about it. Thought you might like to take part. Things are in motion. Could be what we've been waitin' for."

Father looked at him calmly, then nodded. "Alright." But he didn't invite Tulf into the house, nor did he ask Liz to bring out the chairs.

Tulf looked at him. Father returned his gaze.

"So, you wanna hear about it?" Tulf asked finally.

"Maybe some other time." Father inclined his head. "I've got something to do now." He glanced over at Liz and Narmos, then lifted his chin in the direction of the village. "Next time you're over, we can talk."

Tulf stared at him. "You don't got the time now? That's what you're sayin'?"

Father looked down at him, not saying a word. There must've been something in Father's gaze, because after a long moment Tulf looked away and cleared his throat, then glanced up at the big mountain like he was checking the weather.

"I'm off." Tulf stepped up and down a couple times in his snowshoes. "You think old Jarlund'll wanna hear this?"

"Maybe." Father shrugged. "Probably knows about it already. Safe journey."

Tulf frowned, then nodded. Without another word, he turned away and snowshoed down the path to the village.

Father looked at Liz, his face grave. He winced when he took a step, leaning hard on his walking stick. He looked at Narmos. Tulf had disappeared around the bend. Narmos was really squirming now, making funny little grunting sounds.

"What did he want?" Liz lifted her chin in the direction Tulf had gone. She hadn't really understood the conversation.

"Trouble." Father shook his head. "Some of these boys up here need a good, hard schooling every thirty years or so. Get it through their skulls. I got no love for the Tarn—but that's 'cause I understand what it is; what it *truly* is. Tulf's alright. He and his people are gonna bite off more than they can chew, that's all. Maybe good for 'em. See if I can talk 'em down a bit."

Liz nodded, but she still didn't understand.

Father sighed. His breath steamed in the cold. In Liz's arms, Narmos was going nuts, grunting and pawing and squirming.

"Just put him down, honey." Father grinned. "He'll follow us to the shed. Promise you that. He thinks he's part of the family. And grab me another cup of tea, eh? Gotta be clear for this."

17

"C'MON, YOU." LIZ cleared her throat and pushed her braid over her shoulder. Narmos was following them along the snowy trail down to the skinning shed. He had this funny way of running: slightly sideways, his hips and rear paws not quite following the lead of his shoulders. And he'd only run in these weird little spurts. He'd run up ahead of them. Then he'd sit down. Or sniff at a pine cone. Or sniff at the fresh dressing on his back leg. Or just look at Liz and blink. Then, when they'd walked past him, he'd follow again—get out in front of them, tumble into the snow, roll around, then get up and do it all again, huge grey eyes blinking, looking up to them as if he wanted approval or direction.

"Feeling better after all that milk, eh?" Father nodded. He had his long steel tool box—his skinning kit—in one hand, his walking stick in the other. They were going slowly and carefully down the path, but his knee did seem to be feeling a little better; that was a blessing. And there was no sign of his flask. Probably still out in the woods where he'd thrown it last night.

Liz hunched her shoulders in her cloak. She was carrying Father's tea with two mittened hands. She knew they had work to do this morning. But she also knew that she had to tell Father the rest of the story about the dead mother bear and the dead ranger . . . . Or did she?

Liz paused on the trail.

Could she use the story of the dead ranger to keep Narmos alive somehow?

Think! Think, you silly thing!

But how would she explain not telling Father last night, right when they'd gotten home?

Liz didn't know.

On the other hand, if Liz *didn't* tell Father about the ranger, then how would Father even find out? Liz hadn't mentioned where they'd found Narmos, hadn't mentioned any of the details, and the dogs had pulled them north, well off the trail and trap line, toward the northern ridge.

Should she just stay quiet?

Liz shook her head. She already knew the answer. Teagan would blurt something out. Or Father would simply ask her today or tomorrow about the details and she wouldn't be able to hide them. When his knee wasn't hurting, Father had a keen ear for the particulars. Scary keen.

But is it worth the risk to tell him now?

It was, actually.

Safest place, really. Away from everyone. And his leg wasn't hurting that bad and he didn't have his flask. She looked into his tea and nodded to herself. She had to tell him now. Besides, Father always knew everything anyway. Did any of this help Narmos? No, it didn't.

Your brothers think you're so clever.

But she couldn't think of anything and her brains were just running in circles now. The dead bear, the dead ranger, the soon-to-be-dead Narmos. And crying never worked on Father. Ever. She'd tried it once before, a long time ago, and he'd told her, flat out: "Liz, little girl tears don't work on me. Want to change my mind? Then try a calm look in the eye. A measured plan. An argument."

Where did that leave her, then?

Up ahead, Narmos looked back, yawned, then suddenly charged back up the snowy path and jumped on her leg, hugged it with all four of his paws, and looked up at her with his soulful, grey eyes, as if asking her the same question: "So where does that leave us, Liz?"

18

THE SKINNING SHED was about fifty paces away from the cabin proper, nestled at the bottom of the trail in a stand of huge fir trees. In the heart of the summer, if they got a good melt, the smell could be a little strong; Mother insisted on keeping the work away from the house.

As they turned the path's last bend, Liz saw the tight stacks of neatly piled stretching boards that surrounded the shed. Each stack of boards was covered by a roof of tarred pine and set on a raised platform to keep it off the ground. The small boards closest to the shed were the ones they used to stretch marten, mink, and smaller snow 'coon. Bigger snow 'coon, winter foxes, and smaller cliff lynx would get stretched on the medium-sized boards in the next stack. The largest stretching boards in the last stack, each about three paces long, were for big lynx and wolves. Each board was tapered to a point at one end, well-oiled, and meticulously cleaned. Sharp and tight, just how Father liked it.

They walked around the side of the shed to the door. Father unlocked and opened it. Inside, the stretched pelts of two score 'coon and marten greeted Liz with their dead smiles and empty eye slits. They'd already been cleaned, of course, pinned to their stretching boards. About half the pelts were ready to be turned; the other half were ready to be taken off their boards and brushed out. Narmos waddled right into the middle of the place and curiously started sniffing at everything, especially the skins. Above Father's workbench, a well-organized shelf of s-hooks, pliers, and clamps waited. Beside them were several clay jars filled with stretching pins. All the expensive gear and tools—the steel scalpels, the fine steel brushes and combs, the broad fleshing knives—were in Father's skinning kit. Narmos growled at a marten's lifeless face.

"Father——," Liz began.

"Where's that claw we took off him last night?" Father asked. "You got my tea there?"

Liz nodded, handed Father his tea, and took off her mittens. She dug the black claw out of her pocket.

"Let's see here." Father took a sip of his tea and set the cup on the worktable. He placed his kit on the workbench and opened it. From inside, he took out a pair of steel drill bits. He held each bit up to the wide end of the black claw, assessing. "This'll do fine," he said to himself. He took an iron spring clip from the kit, clamped the claw to the workbench, then took a small awl from a sheath in his kit's upper lid.

"Gotta mark the spot and get a little pilot hole started here, otherwise the drill'll just slip away and we'll scratch up your trophy, eh?" He set the awl against the thick of the claw and tapped the back of it with a small pin hammer. "Like so." He took his hand drill out of the kit, tightly chucked the steel bit into its jaws, then put the bit into the pilot hole he'd just made. Very gently, he drilled a small hole through the top of the black claw. When he was done, he unclamped the claw from the bench, blew through the hole, then turned to the light from the door and peered through the little hole, squinting one eye shut. Narmos watched this entire process with keen interest.

"I need to tell you something, Father," Liz said. She was shivering and her stomach ached. She wasn't scared for herself; not really. She was nervous about not telling him sooner. And she was sick for Narmos.

Father nodded, but didn't look at her. "Hand me that cord there. Not that cotton one, the leather one on that nail there by the door, girl. Not that one, that one—the little longer— that's it."

He threaded the thong through the black claw, tied it, then clipped off the tattered ends with a clipper. He held the black claw out to Liz, dangling it on the end of its cord. "There you are."

Liz took the claw and hung it around her neck. "Thank you, Father." She swallowed.

"What's wrong?" He looked at her closely, then glanced at the strange claw. "Don't like it?"

Liz held the claw in her palm, looking down at it. It was

long, black, and very sharp. Just a touch shorter than her whole hand. She hadn't realized how long it was when it had been attached to Narmos.

A weird thing. A wrong thing.

She looked up at Father. "Something happened on the line when we were out. I couldn't tell you last night——."

Father turned to face her, giving her his full attention at last. He was a huge man. Just huge. And his presence was like standing beneath the big mountain itself. But it wasn't just his size. The force of Father's gaze was even more potent than his enormous bulk. Liz felt herself shrinking into her own skin.

"Tell me now, Liz," Father said gently.

So she told him everything. All of it.

19

WHEN LIZ HAD finished, Father was quiet for a long time.

He'd listened intently as Liz had told her story, listened to her with that quiet, gentle look he got sometimes when his knee wasn't hurting, when it was just the two of them alone together. Liz had told him the whole tale from start to finish, leaving nothing out. Father's eyes were dark and penetrating; they became even more so when Liz described the dead mother bear, the dead ranger, the wounds that had killed them both. And now her story was done and she was waiting, looking at Father, waiting for whatever came next.

After another long moment, Father said, "You did right to tell me, Lizzy."

She nodded.

He sipped his tea. Then he took Liz's small hands in his own giant ones. "I've been thinking all night about this little bear." He cocked his head at Narmos, who was sniffing at something or other over in the corner. "Told Mother the same thing this morning. Had to be more to it. You don't find a grey bear cub wandering around in the woods, alone and unprotected. A mother grey bear? The most ferocious protector there is. Here, on the big mountain, anywhere. No way a cub would be out of the den on its own, not unless something happened."

"Did we do right to bring it back?" Liz asked.

"Absolutely." Father squeezed her hands. "Now, I want to ask you some questions about this dead ranger, Liz. And I want you to think hard about your answers. I want you to give them your most careful and thoughtful consideration. It's important. Do you understand me?"

There was something in Father's eyes and voice that Liz had never seen or heard before. It was subtle, to be sure. But it was there. A kind of seriousness. A kind of intensity. And there was something different about the *way* he was speaking, too. The way his sentences . . . well, the way everything he said fit together. That was even more disconcerting. These days, the morning after a bad night, he was always very careful with all of them, very gentle with his words. But this was different.

Completely different.

When he spoke now, he didn't sound like a trapper on the brink of the wild. He sounded like a businessman from down in Korfort—like he'd be more comfortable in a big library in the city than in a little skinning shack at the mountain's edge. As if something in her story had somehow done something to his voice, to his words.

"Do you understand me, Liz?" he repeated gently.

Liz nodded. But she was confused. She fidgeted with the end of her braid. "Yes, Father."

"Of course you do. Now: How old would you say this ranger was? You said in her thirties or so. Closer to her twenties or to her forties?"

"In the middle . . . I think." Liz hesitated. "Maybe ten years younger than Mother?" She shook her head. "I don't know. The snow and dark. We only had the moon. I don't know if I can be certain . . . ."

Father squeezed her hands again. "Your best guess is all I need, Liz."

"Middle thirties, I guess."

"Alright." He nodded. "You said she had blond hair. How did she wear it? Shaved? Ponytail, like Mother? Long? A long braid, like you? What?"

"Short." Liz made a kind of gesture, brushing the back of her fingernails along her jaw from earlobe to chin. "Like right below her ears, here kind of."

"Short blond hair. Dark blond? Light blond?"

"Very light. Like silver-blonde. Not grey, but silvery."

Father nodded, but his gaze went darker still.

"And her gear? You said it was quality?"

"Yes. Highest grade."

"Did you see any jewelry? A ring? Or a necklace? A pendant, maybe? Something in the high silver. You said she didn't wear her breastplate. Something else like that?"

What kind of questions are these? It was almost as if Father was asking about a specific person. But how could that be?

"No, Father." Liz shook her head. "She was wearing riding gloves. I didn't think to check for rings or a necklace—or anything else. I was worried that whoever did it would come back. I mean, who would leave all that gear out there? It was getting late, too. Teagan was getting nervous—you know how he is. And I didn't want to take anything. Didn't want to make it seem like we were involved, somehow."

Father nodded approvingly and seemed to relax, just a bit.

Then Liz remembered the ranger's unique earrings.

"She was wearing earrings. Very elegant, but simple. They were studs. Blue jewels—dark blue—held in silver claws. Like lizards' claws, kind of? Some kind of scaly thing, with talons—."

"Like this?" He held his hand out, like he was gripping an invisible apple. "Small, matching sapphires? Held in claws of silver?"

"I—yes, sir—," she began.

"The claws of a dragon," he said. His eyes flashed. He was still staring at her, like he'd never looked at her in her entire life. His eyes had gone black with something that looked like rage—but wasn't. She didn't know what it was. She didn't know what was going on at all. The whole conversation, the questions, were so sudden, so bizarre. And she'd never heard him talk like this. Then he shook his head, cleared his throat, and took a deep breath, patting his vest as if looking for his flask, shaking his head again. When he finally spoke, he muttered something that Liz didn't understand: "Of all the homes in all the Realm—of all the Kingdom's infinite places—she dies on my doorstep."

"Sir?" Liz asked, completely bewildered.

Father looked at Narmos, then looked back to Liz. "Is there anything else that you can remember, Lizzy? Any detail. Anything at all? It's important."

"No, sir."

"You sure?"

"Yes, Father."

"Very well." Father nodded. "Let's get this bear taken care

of. Then we need to get in. I need to talk to Mother."

"Father, I——."

"Bring him over here. Quickly now."

And Father's eyes and tone were so earnest, so sober, so deadly serious that all the tricks she'd been working on to keep Narmos safe, all the arguments that she'd been trying to prepare, all the ploys to save the little bear—they all simply vanished.

20

NARMOS WAS SNUFFLING in the corner, utterly engrossed in whatever it was that he'd found. His little bottom was wobbling and bobbing in the air, his stumpy tail moving side to side every so often, almost like he was doing a little dance. Liz went to him while Father took a tray out of his kit and set it down on the workbench. Liz grabbed Narmos beneath his furry arms and brought him over to Father.

"We're not going to sell him, Liz," Father said, laying the little bear down on his back on the bench. His voice had gone back to normal . . . but not really.

"We're not?" Liz stared. And in spite of herself, a smile

crept onto her face. "We're going to keep him?"

Father shook his head, still messing with something in his kit. "We're going to fix his leg and then we're going to take him down to Korfort, turn him over to the rangers at the garrison down there. There's a reward for this kind of thing. Won't be as much as what his pelt would be worth . . . but that wasn't right anyway. Didn't want to have anything to do with them—but that's unavoidable now. Mountain will be crawling with them any moment. Surprised they're not here already." Then he paused, as if considering something.

"Who's that dead girl, Father?" Liz asked, throwing caution to the wind, so happy with the news about Narmos, so curious about the dead ranger, about Father's questions, her head spinning, all restraint gone. "You know who she is? How do you know? Who is she?"

"Hold both his front paws in one of your hands, Liz," he said. "Make sure his pads are touching, so he doesn't claw you. Then hold him down—here—with your other hand." He touched the center of Narmos's chest, right next to the white blaze over his heart. "You're going to have to hold him tight. He won't like this. Hurry it up."

Liz nodded and did as she was told.

There was her answer. And the answer was this: She'd get no answers now. Father's tone made that clear. But her mind raced in a thousand directions at once. She held Narmos's front paws together with one hand, just like Father had told her, and pushed the little bear flat to the workbench with the other.

"Good." Father grunted.

"See, Narmos?" Liz said. "Everything's gonna be just fine."

"Narmos, eh?" Father raised an eyebrow.

Liz nodded.

"Good name," Father said.

Narmos didn't struggle. Or even pretend to struggle. He just looked up at her, sighed, and gave a little yawn, like: "This isn't that interesting of a game, but if you need me to play like this, if this is what you need—then, alright."

"No sense pretending that 'crooked' is 'straight,' Narmos," Father said to the cub, as he proficiently laid out the tackle from his skinning kit. "And this'll be easy to fix. Seen this kind of thing before, many times. Especially at this stage, when a cub's growing fast, still only on milk, but out of the den. I should have—." He shook his head, then continued.

"We're going to have to take him off pure milk, Liz. He can still drink it, but we'll need to get him some river oyster from down in the village, or old man Jarlund. Some berries, too. Did you notice that his leg was better or worse this morning? Better, right?" He'd taken out a flat, straight piece of wood from his kit. It was about two palms long.

"Yes, Father." Liz nodded. "It looked better."

"As I thought." Father took the flat piece of wood and held it against Narmos's bent leg. "Looks about right. Now hold him tight, Liz."

Liz did so. Quickly, with what seemed to Liz a very practiced hand, Father wrapped a soft piece of cloth around Narmos's bent leg, then placed the piece of wood on top of it. With his other hand, he looped a leather thong around both the wood and leg, tightened it, then began wrapping the thong around Narmos's leg, adjusting the bent bone to conform to the wood with each pass. Narmos squeaked, not so happy with the "game" anymore, and tried to move, but Liz held him fast.

"This's for your own good," she said soothingly, and kissed him on his wet nose. Narmos stopped moving, looked at her for a long moment, then went quiet. His huge grey eyes did not leave hers. The white fur on his chest seemed to glow.

"Bone is soft, that's all." Father nodded as he splinted the leg. "And he's walking upright on it a lot. Straightens out at night, but a day of jumping around on soft bone will make it bend even worse. He's going to grow fast. This here's just a basic splint. Have to rub some pepper and mink oil over the binding, make sure he doesn't spend all day gnawing on it. If we get his food fixed and if we keep this tight, his leg'll be as good as new within a month. A month and a half, tops. You'll still be in charge of him, though. Right?"

"Right," she said, suddenly smiling like a fool, even in spite of everything that was happening.

He looked up at her, saw her huge smile—and smiled back at her. It was a rare and wondrous sight, especially these days. Then he went back to work.

"A question, sir?" Liz cleared her throat.

"Hmm." Father grunted as he continued to wrap Narmos's leg.

"How'd you learn so much about grey bear cubs?"

Father paused, looked at Narmos. Narmos looked back

up at him and blinked. Then Father shook his head, absently patted at his vest, wiped at his mouth, and went back to his work. "That's a long story. For another time, girl."

Liz nodded and kept quiet.

But she knew—she knew in her guts—that there was more going on here than a "long story."

21

Up FROM THE skinning shed and back at the cabin, Liz and Narmos sat together by the fire. Soldier was there too, basking in the hearth's heat, his tail thumping every so often with the pleasure of some agreeable dream. Teagan, Evan, and the hounds were still out on the eastern line; they wouldn't be back until sunset. Mother and Father had been in their bedroom, the door shut, talking in hushed voices for the last half bell. "Wait here, Liz," Father had said. So Liz waited.

Narmos kept sniffing, then biting, at his splint. Every time he did so, however, Liz gave him a stern "No," and pinched his ear. At first, Narmos had thought it was another game. He'd sit up on his furry bottom, almost like a little human, rocking back and forth. Then he'd look at Liz sideways for a moment, making sure he had her attention, and reach slowly down to his leg and the splint wrapped there, as if daring Liz to go for him when he went for it. It was a short-lived game, however. As the force of Liz's ear pinches increased, Narmos began to realize that he shouldn't mess with the splint.

"Don't do it," Liz warned as Narmos started looking at her sideways. "I know it bugs you. But it's for your own good. We want you to get better."

Discipline is love.

She'd heard Mother say that before. Liz realized that she was beginning to understand what the phrase meant. Narmos stopped mid-reach and instead of clawing at his splint, rolled over onto his side, looked up at Liz, his huge grey eyes blinking.

"Good," Liz nodded. It was kind of like training a dog, she realized. Although Narmos seemed way smarter than any dog she'd ever trained. Smarter than Soldier, even. They'd have to treat the splint's binding with oil and pepper again, before bedtime. Otherwise, Narmos might be up all night fussing with it. But the little bear seemed to be getting used to the new arrangement.

The bedroom latch clicked and the door opened. Liz got to her feet. Soldier's tail twitched. Narmos looked from Liz to the bedroom door. Father came out and Mother followed. Her face was pale, but she was composed and as beautiful as ever, her blue eyes bright.

Liz looked to her, but Mother shook her head. *Later*, Mother's eyes said.

Narmos ran to Father and wrapped his front paws—and then his back legs—around his ankle. Father leaned down, wincing, one hand on his walking stick, then picked the bear up by the scruff of the neck, holding him to his chest, cradling his bottom with one huge arm. Narmos looked up at him, blinking. Father stroked his soft head.

"Liz," Father said. "I'm going to head up to the northern line first thing next morning—."

"I can show you where she was, sir," Liz interrupted. "I can help you with—."

Father looked at her pointedly. Liz shut her mouth.

"You *are* going to help, Liz," Mother said kindly. But her eyes were deadly serious. She stood beside Father in a way that Liz had not seen in what seemed like ages.

"That's right." Father nodded. "You are going to help. I'm not going to overdo it. I'll take my time. Go real slow. I'll be out for about four days. I'll take Soldier and the sled with me. You'll stay here with Mother and look after things. Understand?"

"Yes, Father." Liz nodded.

"You found her about five hundred paces north of the northern trap line, that right? The dogs, they nosed something up off the trail, up under the north ridge? Do I remember correctly?"

"Yes, Father."

He nodded. "I think I know the cave you kids found." He turned to Mother. "Four, five days, tops. I'll take it easy. I'll stop and camp if there's a problem." He cocked his head at the big mastiff by the fire. "And I'll have Soldier and the sled." Soldier's eyes opened at his name; he yawned and went back to sleep.

Mother nodded, looked at Liz. Her voice was gentle, but stern. "The most important thing," she said, "is that nobody can know anything about this. Is that clear, Liz? If Tulf or Fonhammer or Barnabus or even old Jarlund, someone else from the village, asks for your Father, you're to say that he's gone on the line. That's all."

"Especially Tulf." Father frowned. "He and his people can't know about this. Not a word. And keep little Narmos in the house." He stroked the little bear's head. "Take him outside to do his business, but carry him out back by the outhouse, not up front in the clearing. No tracks. Out back, cover it up, then straight back inside. And I don't want you or the boys leaving the clearing until I return. Understand me, Liz?" He looked at Mother. Mother inclined her head in agreement. Their faces were calm, yet deadly earnest.

Liz nodded.

But something had changed between them.

And once again, Liz was struck by the *way* Father was speaking. The subtle difference. His voice was steady and serious, like he usually was when he wasn't at his flask. But it was the *manner* of his phrases. Something had changed. The tone, the cadence, the words themselves; all just slightly . . . *off*. She'd heard a similar shift in the words of old man Jarlund sometimes when they were down past the village. Kind of reminded Liz of the merchants' talk down in Korfort, even though she'd only been down there a dozen times. And Mother didn't seem to notice anything different at all.

Or at least, she was pretending not to notice.

And now that Liz thought about it, she didn't sound quite right, either. It was a *small* difference—but it was still there. Liz frowned and looked at Father, then Mother.

And then she put a concrete thought to the hazy feeling:

It was as if she was listening to the words of altogether different people.

Like listening to people that she didn't know.

22

"WHAT DID FATHER do for work, before he was a trapper?" Liz asked Mother, as they packed Father's rucksack for the next day's trip. Father was in the bedroom with the door shut, getting some things ready. "Did he always live on the big mountain? Did you meet him up here?"

They were working together in the kitchen, smearing some cold grouse breast with the grease from breakfast. The grease would keep the meat moist and made for good hiking fuel. Some cold pancakes, boar bacon, and other food also went into Father's pack.

"Mother?" Liz asked again. "Did he always do this kind of thing for a living? Trapping and such?"

It suddenly seemed quite strange to Liz that she didn't already know the answers to the questions she was asking. People on the big mountain kept to themselves, that was certain. "The mountain way," Father would always say. But, as Liz reflected on it, she realized that the past was the one thing that Mother and Father never really talked about.

In fact, now that Liz thought on it, she couldn't remember Mother or Father ever saying *anything* about life before they'd had Teagan. There was always a pile of work to be done. Work to be done now. Today. This moment. And it was the same work, every single day. So work was what they talked about: Should they run a new trap line farther north, above the old one? Did the handle on the new fleshing knife need to be replaced already and, if so, who was the cursed fool who made such a piece of junk? Did Soldier hurt his foot that last time out? And then more recently, if it was really cold and Father's leg was hurting and the flask came out, then there would be that hell to contend with, too. Liz did have a vague memory of Evan asking Mother about her parents once. But the answer had been something elusive and non-committal, like they'd died a long time ago, weren't mountain people, something like that . . . .

"He always run trap lines, Mother?" Liz asked again. "He learn the trade from *his* Dad? Like we do?"

Mother's eyes flickered, but they did not tell more. "Pass me that cooking pot and tripod," she said. "Then run outside and bring me three nice, dry bundles of kindling. We'll wrap it up good and proper, keep him warm. We'll talk about those other things when he gets back." She looked up, saw Liz's skeptical frown. "That's a promise."

Liz's frown deepened.

They'd never needed "promises" before.

Ever.

Liz looked at her for a long moment. Mother finally looked back and cocked her head meaningfully at the front door. Liz nodded, handed Mother the pot and tripod, and did what she was told.

But obviously something else was going on. Something

bigger. Something that went beyond a poacher, a dead bear, a dead ranger in the woods.

And she was going to find out what it was.

23

TEAGAN AND EVAN came home just after sundown, tired and worn out from a long day on the line, but happy. It had been a good haul of fur. Liz, Mother, and Father had finished most of the preparations for the next day and had already eaten dinner, but they'd saved two big plates of leftovers for the boys. Mother had completely ignored Father's decree from yesterday—that Evan give a quarter of his rations to Soldier—and Father hadn't reminded her, if he even remembered.

When the brothers arrived out front, Liz heard them laughing, cleaning off the tackle, the hounds, and the porch, Evan gently correcting Teagan's work. Father was in the bedroom, getting his last things ready, triple checking his gear. He'd taken the silver flask in there with him; Liz hadn't seen him go find it. She, Mother, and Narmos were working on the dishes, making small talk—but they both knew the flask was out, so there was a kind of unspoken tension hovering in the kitchen, a silent predator. Soldier slept by the fire after a double portion of dinner, fuel for the long hike tomorrow.

The front door opened and the boys came in with the dogs, red-faced, cold, but smiling, their boots held upside down. Narmos immediately jumped all over little Rosie, who scampered like a demon to get away from the well-fed and fully energized bear cub.

"How was it?" Mother asked.

"Good stuff." Teagan grinned, touching his new axe proudly. He looked from Mother to Liz to Evan and back again. "Good stuff."

"Yeah." Evan smiled, his black eye crusty and gross. "Pretty decent out there. It's all down in the shed. Good haul." He set his boots on their stand. "Where's Father?"

Mother inclined her head at the bedroom door. "He'll be pleased to hear it. Your dinners are on the stove there. Wash up, get to it. Then I want you all in bed early. Liz will tell you what's going on."

"What's going on, Liz?" Evan grinned, his black eye crinkling.

"Yeah, Liz," Teagan repeated. "What's going on?"

24

SHE TOLD THEM everything as they ate, the dogs playing in front of the fire, on and around the sleeping Soldier, Narmos seemingly now an honorary member of the pack, all of them tumbling and rolling around in a giant heap of dogs and bear. Mother and Father were in the bedroom, talking in hushed voices.

"So," Evan said, sopping the last of his gravy up with a corner of dried bread, popping it into his mouth, "Dad's going out tomorrow and we're gonna stay down and work the lines. He's gonna bring her body back here?"

Liz nodded. "That's the idea."

"Why?" Teagan asked.

Teagan had been confused through most of the conversation, and Liz hadn't had any answers for his innumerable questions.

"Who is she?" Evan asked. "She's a ranger, like you said last night. We got that. We know that. Probably rich. But *who* is she?"

Liz shrugged. "Dunno who she is." Then much more softly, "That's what I'm trying to tell you." She cocked her head

146

at the bedroom door. "I think *they* do."

Evan shook his head skeptically. "How'd they ever know someone like that?"

"I don't——."

The bedroom door opened quickly and Mother stepped out, shutting it softly behind her. She had something in her hand, something shiny and silver. Liz couldn't see what it was. It wasn't Father's flask, that was certain; wrong shape. Mother tucked whatever it was into the wide pocket at the front of her apron and smoothed her hand over it.

"Everyone to bed," Mother said. She caught Liz's eye, cocked her head up at the sleeping loft.

Behind the bedroom door, Father muttered something that Liz couldn't understand.

But she didn't have to.

She knew the pattern, the dangerous way the words sloshed together.

"I'll pick up." Mother glanced at the kitchen table, back to Liz. She was calm, as always. But a mix of distress and determination shimmered in her eyes.

"I'm still hungry," Teagan said, his mouth full. "I'm still——."

But Evan and Liz were already scraping their chairs back, holding Teagan's elbows, guiding him smoothly up and out of his chair, toward the ladder. Narmos and the dogs had stopped playing. Soldier's head was up, his ears cocked and alert. Narmos stared at the bedroom door, his grey eyes wide and discerning.

Behind the door, Father muttered something again that Liz couldn't understand. Then louder. "We dunno if it's even *her* out there for sure, no." A pair of shuffling steps, the heavy thunk of the walking stick, closer to the door now. "Ain't nothing wrong with a sip before a long trip out. You tell me I'm wrong about that . . . cursed thing."

The latch rattled.

Teagan had realized what was happening and silently crawled up the ladder, hand over hand, looking straight up, careful so that he didn't miss a step. Evan was close behind him, Liz bringing up the rear.

At the top of the ladder, Liz looked down over her shoulder. "Mother?"

Mother stared at the bedroom door, a strange mix of fear, sadness, and anger playing across her face. Liz could hear the bedroom's iron latch catch and stick, as if Father again had somehow forgotten how to work the mechanism.

The door rattled.

Rattled again, even louder.

BANG!

A huge fist smashing against wood.

Little Rosie whimpered and crawled into the kennel.

BANG! BANG!

Soldier was up and alert, a low rumble in his chest, Narmos at his side, a weird little growl coming from his throat.

The door shuddered again. Mother touched her apron pocket. Without looking up at Liz, she said: "Don't come down here. No matter what you hear."

Liz stopped at the top of the ladder. Her blood went to ice. She stared down at Mother.

"Mother? What—?" Liz began.

"Do as I say." Mother didn't look up. "And pull the ladder up after you."

"No," Liz said, and started to climb back down.

"Elizabeth." The steel in Mother's tone stopped Liz cold. "Do as I say."

One leg on the ladder's top step, Liz looked to Evan. His face was white, his black eye standing out proudly against his pale skin. Then he nodded, leapt across the bed, and together they pulled the ladder up into the loft, setting it across their bed. Teagan was sitting cross-legged on the furs, rocking back and forth, rubbing his scar, his eyes shut, whispering something to himself. Soldier hadn't moved from the fire, but little Narmos had taken two steps toward the bedroom door.

BANG! BANG!

Mother went to the bedroom door and opened it. Narmos was walking slowly away from the fire, toward the bedroom door now, sometimes on all fours, sometimes on his hind legs, that weird little growl building, louder and louder. He was about a dozen paces from the door now.

"Narmos!" Liz hissed from the loft, Evan at her side.

"No! Narmos!" Evan whispered.

The little bear ignored them.

"Let me get you something else to eat," Mother said gently, into the bedroom.

Father mumbled something that Liz couldn't hear. His walking stick thunked hard against the wooden floor. Then he spoke again, lower. Liz couldn't hear his words.

"No," Mother said, calmly.

Another slurred growl.

"Enough," Mother whispered, and stepped into the bedroom.

There was a deadly quiet. Mother said something, but again Liz couldn't hear what it was. Father growled, his voice soft with menace. An extra loud thunk of the walking stick—and then a blinding flash of silver light—CRASH!

The house seemed to shake.

Breaking things, then a heavy, bone-crunching thud.

Narmos charged the door just as Liz heard the bedroom latch snick shut, the little bear growling, banging into the door with his head, scratching at the wood with his front claws, that weird little roar coming out of him, surprisingly loud.

CRASH!—the noise like a body being hurled across a room, shattering glass, splintering wood . . . then a low groan.

"Put the ladder down!" Liz cried, heart hammering. "Put it *down*! Evan! *Help* me!" She touched the knife at her belt, reached for the ladder, pulled it toward the loft's edge. Soldier gave a deep bark, huge and loud in the confined space of the cabin. The hounds' eyes rolled white in their kennel, little Rosie's whimper almost a cry.

Narmos was banging his little head against the bedroom door, that weird little roar of his coming louder than ever. On the bed, Teagan was on his side, curled entirely into a ball, his hands clamped over his ears, eyes smashed shut. Evan helped Liz drag the ladder across the bed, sliding it down—then it slipped halfway and crashed to the floor, Liz already on it, sliding down the sides, Evan right behind her.

The bedroom door opened and Mother stepped out calmly, scooped Narmos up to her hip, shut the door behind her, and walked past Liz and Evan to the kitchen.

There was no noise from the bedroom.

At the stove, Mother deftly opened Father's tea while swinging Narmos over to her other hip, setting the pot to boil, all in one smooth movement.

She turned to Liz and Evan. Her eyes glowed. She was unscathed. Completely untouched.

Liz's mouth opened to speak.

"Wha—?" Evan began.

Mother cut them both off.

"I told you to stay up there and to keep the ladder up." Her voice was totally calm and utterly commanding. Her eyes flashed.

Liz's mouth closed with a soft click. Narmos was staring up at Mother from her hip.

"When I give an order," Mother continued, "I expect to be obeyed. Instantly and absolutely. Is that clear?"

"Yes, ma'am." Liz managed. She couldn't have said otherwise, even if she'd wanted to.

"Yes, Mother." Evan nodded, swallowing.

"You still hungry?" Mother asked.

They both shook their heads without a word.

Mother took a little pack of leftovers from inside the stove's warming box and handed it to Liz.

"For Teagan," Mother said. "He wanted more."

Liz nodded silently. The hounds made not a peep. Soldier had sat down, alert but calm.

"Now," Mother said. "Take your bear, go to the loft, and go to sleep. Father will be out in a while." She cocked her head at the huge bearskin chair. "He has a long trip tomorrow and he needs his rest. From you, there will be *no* noise. Not a peep. Nothing. Now get moving."

Without another word—without even the thought of another word—Liz took Narmos from her, went to the ladder, and crawled up into the loft.

25

Liz LISTENED TO Mother tidy the kitchen a bit. Then, after some time, Mother went back into the bedroom. About half a bell later, Father came out with her and Mother sat him down in his chair by the fire, placed a pair of logs on the hearth, stoked it for the night, whispering a few words to Father and Soldier. Father slurred and grumbled a little bit, then immediately set to snoring. Mother went into the bedroom and quietly shut the door behind her.

Evan was looking at Liz. Liz had her ear cocked to the fire. Father's low snore was steady and even. Teagan and Narmos both stared at her, their eyes wide, bits of food on both of their chins.

"What happened!?" Evan hissed. "What the heck *was* that?"

"Shh!" Liz shushed.

Evan shut his mouth and they all scooted back close

together under the covers, cuddling Narmos between them.

"Clean your face," Liz said to Teagan.

Tee wiped at his chin. "What did Father do?" he whispered. "What happened to Mother? What happened—?"

"Nothing," Liz said. "I don't know. I don't know what happened."

And that was the Sisters' honest truth.

"But what was all that *noise?*" Teagan asked, whispering as quietly as he could. "That loud noise?"

Liz looked at Evan. Evan shrugged. Liz shook her head. "I don't know, Tee. Truly, I don't."

"Did you see Narmos charge the door?" Evan asked, petting the little bear's stomach, picking a little piece of leftover out of his silver-grey fur. "He was trying to get in there, trying to protect Mother."

"Just like the story," Teagan said.

Evan looked at him, then nodded.

Narmos yawned, his long pink tongue lolling, and shut his eyes.

Liz rubbed his furry stomach with the end of her braid.

"Brave Narmos," Teagan mused, stroking the little bear's

soft head. "Brave little Narmos."

"You *were* brave, Narmos." Liz patted the white blaze on the cub's chest.

"*Brave?*" Evan whispered. "He was *fierce*! He just ran straight at him! If the door had been open, he'd have gotten in there to fight—!"

"And he'd be dead," Liz said.

"Brave Narmos," Teagan repeated. "*Brave* Narmos."

"No kidding." Evan nodded. "Brave Narmos."

And then, from the darkness below, by the dying fire, a low snuffling noise came.

"Brave Narmos, eh?" Father slurred slowly, almost like he was talking to himself, his voice still thick with whiskey.

Liz's head shot up and she looked at Teagan and Evan. None of them breathed.

"Good little Narmos . . . brave Narmos," Father slurred again. "Brave, brave Narmos." His voice was low and dangerous, the words all smashed together. Teagan's face had gone white. He rubbed his scar nervously. Evan didn't move; he was listening, staring at Liz.

"What do we do?" Evan mouthed silently.

Liz put her finger to her lips.

"Brave . . . ," Father said, his voice soft, the words sloppy. "Tell you 'bout *brave*. Lemme tell you . . . . Might not want to hear 'bout it . . . but you're gonna hear it. Was the night of the big fire, way back durin' the Long Summer. Far side of the big mountain. Near thirty years ago it was now, your Uncle Darro and me, and old man Jarlund, some others from up in here . . . back when I was . . . when I was with . . . back before I left. First time I met Jarlund, too. Just a kid. That night. We were all over there on the Tarn's order, see? There on the cursed Tarn's order. To fight the big fire. Hunter was there, too, my old Pa's mastiff—you kids didn't know Hunter. Was a good dog, strong. *Brave*. Ol' Hunter, he'd burnt his feet up bad in the fire, see, but that dog wouldn't leave my side, no he wouldn't—."

Father cleared his throat roughly. Liz heard the rattle of his silver flask's cap, heard him take a sip.

"We was all sittin' there on that weird night, lookin' over our boots, checkin' 'em out, the big fire glowin' off there, over the hillside like a giant's forge. Had to re-sole our boots durin' the fire, see? Ground so hot it'd burn right through the soles. So every night we'd pull back from the big ditch we was makin' and cut the old soles off the boots and stitch new ones on—had to do it. Under the Tarn's order, I was. Back when I was . . . . Thrice cursed Tarn tellin' us what to do. Your Uncle Darro was there, sittin' and talkin' about the big fire to some of the fellas from some nearby village and there was a crew of big Konungur boys there too from way up high on the big mountain, sittin' around their own little fire. They wouldn't sit with us, see. Hated the Tarn. Still do. Blamed the Tarn for the fire. Damn liars. Everyone worked all day fightin' the cursed blaze, but those Konungur boys, they'd lost two of their number, see. Cursed Tarn put 'em right up front. Had to. Still—they weren't too bad off. The King—Balmás, that silly fool—had finally given 'em leave to hunt the south side of the big mountain—given 'em permission to hunt their *own land*—so there was plenty of meat for everyone. We'd seen to . . . that is, the Tarn'd seen to that.

"So everyone was restin' and talkin' in that tired way you do. I was sittin' there on a stump lookin' at my boots and wondering if they'd hold up for next day's work and Hunter was there, lyin' in front of me lickin' at one of his burned paws, when—all of a sudden—I seen Hunter's head snap up and his whole body set up hard and stiff, like he was listenin' or gettin' ready to fight. Then—Hunter, see?—he gets up and walks off some ten paces and stands at the edge of our fire, just at the edge of the light, starin' out into the night, down the slope of the big mountain, down toward the big fire's glow. I get up and walk out there with him and everybody—even those old Konungur boys—they go quiet. They all knew to pay heed when Hunter was on the alert."

Father stopped. Liz heard him take another sip from his flask.

"Ah. Right, well. At first . . . at first we didn't hear nothin'. But then that first howl came. That's what Hunter had heard, see? Crag wolves. Whole pack. Huge and hungry and mean as they come. Big fire stirred 'em up. Rip you to shreds in half a moment. Then there was another howl, this one from a different direction, opposite side. Hunter's head snapped that way, growlin' in that deep way of his. Then there was another howl, farther back on the other ridge, and Hunter looked *that* way, too.

"Now, there ain't nothin' strange about a pack of crag

wolves howlin' in the night, we'd all heard that before. A thousand times. It was the *way* they was howlin'. *That's* what made it odd. It was comin' from different places—this way, then that way, then this way again, almost like they was talkin' to each other. The Konungur boys looked at each other, talkin' in that barking mountain gutter talk of theirs, and old man Jarlund, he asks them what they thought about it all 'cause he knew their Konungur language. He didn't have no respect for the Tarn, either. Didn't give us . . . . Well, there was no respect. Dunno . . . .

"Anyway, the leader of those big Konungur boys—big, tall guy—says the wolves were on the hunt and that they was callin' to each other, showin' the direction of the chase, so that the wolves in front might turn the prey. The mountain way . . . that's how he called it—'turning the prey.' A crag wolf pack, see, when it gets real hungry, it keeps its prey in a circle and lets the fresh wolves jump in from time to time, runnin' the prey hard and constant so eventually they wear the poor beast down—that's the way of the crag wolves' pack. Find one animal, cut it outta the herd, then follow that one, that one, *lone* animal—with their crazy patience . . .

160

their invincible patience . . . ."

Father's voice trailed off.

Liz glanced at Evan and Teagan. They were both listening intently.

"*Invincible patience.*" Father cleared his throat. "That's what your Uncle Darro called it. Invincible patience. Those wolves, see, they begin the hunt *knowing* it'll last for a long time. They *know* that in speed, they've got no chance—not against a reindeer or a fast young moose. So a pair of wolves or two'll take up the chase with a slow run to keep the prey goin', givin' it no time for breath or rest—all the while givin' this weird, short howl—those howls that we heard, yeah?— lettin' the pack know up front when to take up the chase. Those wolves at the front—the fresh ones, see?—they'll howl and 'turn the prey,' while the first ones take a rest, droppin' back and followin' 'round 'round and 'round and so on. There's a cruel darkness in those wolves, I tell you— dark minds at work. Once they've chosen you, ya ain't got no chance . . . ."

Father gave a long, deep sigh.

Liz realized that she was holding her breath.

Father took another sip from his flask.

"So the howlin' went on 'round and 'round for some time, the big fire glowin' red in the night's distance. Sometimes those wolves come close enough so that you'd hear their panting breath—sometimes so far away, that for a while you didn't hear nothin' at all and we all thought the hunt was finished. Old Hunter though, he didn't sit down, he was up and movin' from spot to spot along the campfire's light, always watchin', always listenin'. This went on for at least a full bell's time, or it seemed to me that long.

"All of a sudden, the wolves seemed to come closer still, from high above on the big mountain, see? There was a certain sound in their howl that even *we* could understand. Whatever they hunted, it was done for. A matter of moments, those wolves would feast on blood. There wasn't no single howls now, no widely spaced little barks, eh? Just that single dark voice, the voice of the pack. It was 'bout five hundred paces out from us now—but up on the big mountain, hard to be sure of the distance. There was a pause and then the howls picked up again, closer still. And then it seemed like they was comin' straight down at us—right at us, I tell ya——*straight* at us."

He took another drink. Liz could hear him swallow. The silver flask's cap rattled.

"Your Uncle Darro, he says to me and the rest of us, real calm-like: 'Better get ready, boys.' They were almost on top of us now. We took up our axes and the shovels and I called Hunter back to the fire. He didn't want to come at first, but then he came back. And then the howlin' pack come out of that night like an avalanche, you could hear the crashin' through the dirt and the burnt up brush, gasps of the prey in front and the wolves pantin' in back. The hunt came at us like a storm, and then——BAM!——outta nowhere a young reindeer buck came bustin' into our fire circle, haunted, gasping, eyes rollin' white and ears spread wide, legs all weak and wobbly. He ran straight to the center of the circle and just kind of collapsed——and before I knew what was happenin' one of those Konungur boys jumps up with his axe to brain the little buck——for food, you know?——but your Uncle Darro——just like a night lynx, he was——jumps in front of that Konungur boy and drops the man with a blow to the jaw like nothin' I'd ever seen. Then Darro, he goes to one knee beside the young buck, and he throws one arm around it, starin' into the night and out at the wolves and then back at that pack of old Konungur boys, back and forth at all of 'em like he would kill every last one of 'em *and* kill every last wolf, too—like he would kill them *all* . . . . And he could've done it, too, let me tell you.

"Right at that moment, the biggest wolf I've ever seen— huge brute of a crag wolf, maybe fifteen stone—jumps straight into our circle, lookin' at its prey: the little buck Darro was protecting. Nobody moved. They couldn't believe it. Nobody had ever seen anything like it. The monster pauses a moment, then walks slowly up to Darro and that little buck. You could almost understand that wolf's language. 'You got somethin' of mine there, Man. Hand it over, or me and my Brothers will come in here—and we'll take it.'

"Now, your Uncle Darro, he doesn't blink—not once, I tell ya. Instead, the moment that wolf got close enough, Darro jumped straight at *him* and split the wolf's skull clean open with his axe, like a log. Darro and me, we both trained down there at the . . . . Well, we did some training when we was younger kids, signed up back when Balmás first took the throne . . . . Darro knew how to use an axe—but then *another* wolf jumped into the circle, and then another—and there were more of them wolves behind them, outside in the circle, eyes shinin' in the firelight, eyes movin' 'round the edges. Must've been near a score more wolves out there. Anyway, those next two that came in, they stop and look at Darro and the young buck beside him, then they look at the rest of us, and then they look at their dead brother.

"We were all standin' up now, our axes and tools ready, but that was all we had—we didn't have a bow or sling in the entire crew, and we sure as spit didn't have no guns. Then those two wolves, they just *went* for Darro. No call, no signal, they just *went* for him, one goin' for his throat, the other goin' for that little reindeer Darro was holdin' in his arms. And what does Darro do? Darro, he kills 'em *both*, faster than you could blink—CRACK! CRACK!—goes the axe. Then, without so much as a pause, he holds out his hand like a cup and pours some water into his palm from his canteen and the little reindeer, that little buck, he *drinks*. He *drinks* from Darro's *hand*, his little hooves in wolf's blood.

Again and again that reindeer drinks from Darro's hand like that, then it lays down and actually rests its head in Darro's lap. Darro . . . he starts strokin' it gently, talkin' to it like he were talkin' to his own child. And all those wolves, they go away. The entire pack just ups and leaves.

"After about half a bell, that little reindeer buck, he stands up beside Darro, like he wasn't tired no more. Then he looks out into the dark, up toward the big mountain. Everyone was watchin' him. The little buck walks away from Darro, looks at our faces, looks at the fire, looks out into the dark— as if he was tryin' to understand what had happened—how he'd been saved. He walked around like that for a while, just stepping around our fire, looking at us. Everyone went real quiet and still. I tell you true: It seemed to me like a scene in some story, some story where some kind of spell held us all in its sorcery while that little buck stepped around the circle. Then, a few paces from the center, the buck stops for a moment, his back toward us and the fire. Everyone abso-lutely quiet. Not a sound. Just the popping of the fire and the little buck standing there like that, eyes and ears turned out to the big mountain, the night, and all its dangers. Then he looked 'round, gave us all one good look, and then his eyes stopped on Darro for a moment, almost as if to say 'Farewell,' or 'My thanks to you,' or some other thing. And then he walked out of the circle into the dark.

"Darro loved that little thing, see? Fell in love the moment it came into the circle. That's how he was. Had to protect it. Darro, he was brutal and savage, but with a huge heart. *He* was brave."

Father cleared his throat, his voice going thick. "Always protected me, too. So brave. Just like that night. Darro, he wasn't never afraid. Ever. He would've killed those old Konungur boys, every last one—if they would've touched his little reindeer. And he would've killed all those wolves too. Just to save that little buck. And he *could* have done it, too. Can't tell you how many times Darro done saved *my* carcass from my ol' man's strap. My ol' man makes me look like a sissy. You have no idea . . . no idea at all what he'd do to us. But good ol' Darro, he always stood up for me. Never once even said a mean word to me in his life . . . so brave. Killed by the cursed Tarn . . . . He tried to protect you, Teagan. He tried . . . . I love you kids.

Know I'm no good at showing it . . . but I want to make you good—good on your *own* without the coin and court and everything—'s why I'm so hard on you. You grow up with money, it ruins you. Makes you *weak*. Mountain way is better. But my brother Darro—he was never afraid. *He* was brave. Just like that little bear . . . little Narmos. 'Specially if we train him up . . . . Trained bear is priceless. Know that for a fact . . . ."

Then, as abruptly as he'd started talking, Father went silent.

After a long moment, that drunken bear-like snore rose again from below.

Liz looked at Evan and Teagan.

Both of them were staring at her, cocking their ears toward the fire.

Teagan's face was pale, but he wasn't scared anymore. Evan grinned, his swollen eye puckering, and melodramatically wiped his brow as if to say: "Whew! *Another* close one."

There was no other sound from below.

But there were clues in that story, Liz knew.

She was so tired.

Too tired to think about it.

She looked at her brothers for a moment. Then, as if on some silent cue, they all sighed, cuddled together around little Narmos, and closed their eyes.

"Crazy couple days," Teagan muttered sleepily.

"And the prize for understatement of the year goes to Teagan Hone," Evan murmured.

Liz smiled.

And then she slept.

26

THE FIRST RANGER arrived at their clearing later the next day, just before sunset.

Father had left early that morning without a word to anyone, right after he'd finished packing and triple-checking his supplies. As had been the plan, Father had taken Soldier and the sled. Teagan, Evan, and all the hounds except Rosie were out again, finishing the work on the eastern line, moving it closer to the house so they could cycle the traps faster.

When the ranger arrived, Liz, Mother, Rosie, and Narmos were alone at the house.

27

BEFORE THE RANGER showed up, the entire day had been as close to perfect as Liz could remember. She was anxious about Father and what he'd discover, and her curiosity about everything else was making her crazy. But the gorgeous weather, the clean mountain, and the morning's beauty had almost made her forget the last couple days' craziness.

And Narmos would live!

Liz still couldn't believe it. He'd go to the garrison in Korfort. It felt like a miracle. She'd miss the little bear—they all loved spending time with him—but she was happy for him, too.

The whole day had been like that. One of those rare moments on the big mountain when the southern winds had pushed the clouds from the sky, leaving the mountain rising clear and huge above them, a colossal tower of snowy white crags cut against a blue eternity. Mother had re-braided her hair, but she'd given her no answers as to what had happened the night before. And now, with dusk coming on, the sky and snow had taken a lavender glow. Through the pines, up on the far side of the clearing, a pair of snow grouse set to calling, their soothing murmurs floating over the snow like friendly ghosts.

On the southeastern side of the cabin, Liz was chopping firewood. Her favorite time to think things over. She stacked the wood neatly, filling the storage eave next to the chimney. Little Rosie was with her, sitting on the porch, scanning the clearing every once in a while, then leaving to go snuffle 'round the cabin, looking for trouble to get into. Mother was inside with Narmos, feeding the cub for the ninth time that day. Mother had been working on a project in the bedroom since Father had left; she'd ignored each of Liz's subtle—and not so subtle—questions. When Liz started pestering her nonstop, Mother had sent her outside with Rosie to chop wood.

"But we're almost completely full up out there," Liz had protested.

Mother glanced up from Narmos. "The *first* eave is full up. Isn't that what you mean to say? Fill the second. Let's have it stocked and stacked with a nice split cord by the time Father gets back. And take Rosie with you, she keeps nibbling Narmos's splint. Narmos is encouraging her, somehow. She doesn't seem to mind that peppered mink oil. They're in it together. Aren't you? Aren't you, little clever one?" She rubbed Narmos's furry grey tummy, stroked the white blaze on his chest. The little bear barely opened his eyes, so content he was, sucking his milk sack.

So Liz and Rosie had gone outside to chop wood, alone.

And two bells into the job, the ranger appeared.

28

"Ho there! In the freehold!" a strong voice called out from across the clearing. Rosie turned, ears perking up, but she didn't bark—which surprised Liz. Instead, the little hound gave a soft growl.

There, at the northeastern edge of their clearing, at the top of the path down to old man Jarlund's, a tall ranger in armor, furs, and riding leathers waited respectfully astride an enormous grey war bear. Liz was certain that Mother had heard his call, so she waited a moment before answering so that Mother could hide the bear cub and get situated inside. Hospitality would demand they extend an invitation.

"Ho! To the freehold!" the ranger called out again.

"Ho! To the forest!" Liz shouted back. She dropped her wood and walked around to the front, tapping the butt of her axe against the cabin wall to alert Mother again, if by some chance she wasn't already aware.

Rosie came with Liz, that soft growl still grumbling in her chest. She looked up at Liz, as if to ask: "Who is that?"

"Tarn's Ranger, Rosie," Liz said soothingly. "On patrol. Nothing to worry about."

But that wasn't true.

In fact, the last time they'd seen a ranger in their clearing had been a year ago; and that guy had just been passing through. Liz had seen rangers down in the village from time to time, of course. But unless there was trouble, they were careful to leave the mountain's settlers and homesteads alone, especially the old Konungur freeholds where the Tarn's authority was resented. Rosie looked out across the clearing and gave another soft growl. The little hound didn't seem convinced by Liz's words.

"Not much else to do," Liz said to her. "Can't leave him standing there." She stepped onto the front porch, pushed her braid over her shoulder, and waved her mittened hand.

"Approach, rider!"

The ranger whispered something to his bear and the giant beast leapt forward, lumbering powerfully down the clearing's slope, plowing through the snow, its huge hump and shoulders bunching beneath thick silver-grey fur. When it ran, it ran slightly sideways, its hips not fully in line with its shoulders, grunting steamy plumes that broke against its massive chest, wispy clouds against a mountainside. The ranger carried a short lance flagged with a blue pennant at its tip. The lance's butt-spike was held by a brass ring fixed to his stirrup. The pennant snapped in the wind. It was high blue, the color of the sky, a silvery, six-pointed emblem at its center. *The Dallanar Sun*, Liz thought. Acasius's Star. The high symbol of the Tarn. The pennant's meaning was clear: The ranger was here on special business. Royal business.

Liz cleared her throat as the ranger stopped a few paces from the front porch. There, he leapt lightly from his bear to the snow, planted his lance in a snowbank, clapped his bear on its huge shoulder, and stepped toward the porch—but he did not make to ascend the steps.

"Good evening, young miss." The ranger took off his

fur-lined helmet and bowed politely to Liz.

Liz returned the gesture. "Good evening, sir."

The ranger made for an interesting—and intimidating—sight. He was tall. Not as tall as Father, of course, but still taller than most men in the village. Probably in his early thirties, or thereabouts. His shoulders were broad, an effect amplified by the shoulder pads of his armor. He was clean-shaven and had dark blond hair that he wore tied at the nape of his neck in a kind of bun. Two steel spikes were shoved through this bun. *Could probably kill an entire pack of wolves with just one of them*, Liz thought. He wore a high silver breastplate under a fur-lined jacket. A wolf-skin cloak hung from his shoulders, several bushy tails brushing the backs of his ankles. His heavy hunting breeches were fur-lined and dyed deep blue, the Tarn's lordly color. His wide belt was fastened with a silver buckle. The buckle was exactly like the buckle worn by the dead woman they'd found, but bigger and slightly less ornate. And just like that buckle, this one was embossed with the six-pointed star, the royal sigil of the Tarn and House Dallanar.

The ranger was also armed to the teeth. Two horn-handled

daggers were sheathed crosswise at his belt, so that he could draw them with his left hand. He also carried an expensive sidearm, a revolver. It was strapped to his hip at an angle that suggested frequent and professional use. Its handle was made of a silver-white wood, the likes of which Liz had never seen.

As for the ranger's grey bear . . . . Well, the bear was something else entirely. Liz had never seen a war bear so close before. And she most certainly had never seen one standing off her front porch.

The war bear was huge. Its massive hump towered over its rider. *Must be twenty-five palms at the shoulder.* Its giant paws were at least five palms wide, the claws longer still. Its jaws were enormous. It looked like it could swallow little Rosie whole—without even chewing. The bear wore a protective collar of studded leather and a beautifully-made saddle of soft hide. Its harness and reins were dyed dark blue and studded with small silver stars. Of course, the bear didn't wear a bit in its mouth like a mule or a reindeer might. Instead, its reins were clipped to the side of its leather collar, so that the rider could signal his wishes without interfering with the bear's lethal fangs. Behind the saddle, two finely-crafted saddlebags—leather, dyed blue, and fastened with engraved silver buckles—framed a bedroll and camping kit. Right in front of the bear's huge hump, slung from the saddle within easy reach, a blue leather scabbard held yet another expensive firearm: a priceless long carbine, oiled and clean and deadly. The other side of the saddle held the ranger's sheathed sword. The blade was nearly twelve palms long. Its pommel, hilt, and grip were made of grey steel, the grip wrapped with worn blue leather. The pommel was the shape of a bear's head, its mouth wide, its fangs bared as if it was roaring at an enemy. The scabbard itself was made of soft hide, dyed dark blue. The point chape and locket were that same smoky steel. It was not a thin dueling rapier or a long sword, like Liz had seen in the weapons shops down in Korfort. Rather, it was a kind of thick saber, curved and broad at its end, exactly what you'd want for slicing a man's head off from bearback. Liz could only imagine what the great bear and his rider would look like in full dress armor. They were absolutely magnificent.

"Beauty, isn't he?" The rider grinned, noticing Liz's gaze. He clapped his bear on its massive shoulder again. The bear grunted and nudged the rider with the side of its huge head, its breath pluming, the throaty grunt low and impossibly deep. The rider stroked the bear's huge head fondly, sinking his fingers into its fur. "Tharos, he's called. From a long line of warriors. A fierce and loyal friend."

Liz nodded and stared. Rosie had retreated to the front door but still stood on alert, as if taking up a second line of defense. She was brave, but not *that* brave.

"Amazing," Liz said. And she meant it.

The ranger smiled. "He is indeed." His teeth were straight and very white.

Then Liz remembered herself. "Can I offer you food and drink, sir?" she asked politely. She cocked her head at the big mountain, the darkening sky. "Near night soon. We have meat and bread. You're more than welcome to what we have."

The ranger looked at her closely, and Liz was suddenly embarrassed by the plain, patched coat she wore. The leather laces of her boots had been broken and retied so many times that they looked like a snarl of overlapping thongs rather than the fasteners for proper footwear. And she was wearing a pair of Evan's pants, so they sagged everywhere. And her belt was Teagan's, so it was too long, too.

"I thank you, miss." The ranger nodded. "But I'm afraid I can't linger."

He reached inside his cloak and took from it a bone-colored message tube. The ranger popped the cap open, removed two sheets of parchment, both rectangular and of identical size.

"I'm looking for these people," the ranger said.

He handed the sheets to Liz.

Liz unrolled them.

The picture on the first parchment was printed with black ink. The parchment itself looked old. The image on the page was a portrait of a man. Below the portrait were some words in a language that Liz couldn't read. The man in the picture was older than Father, perhaps in his late fifties or early sixties. He had a scar that started along the left side of his head, cut through his left eyebrow, past his left eye socket, then ran along his nose, through his lips, to his chin. His nose looked like it had been broken and badly set. His left nostril had been sealed by the same wound that had made the scar; the side of his mouth and his scraggly moustache cleft in a permanent sneer. His eyes were widely spaced, lurking under deep, shaggy brows.

"Has a gold tooth, right here," the ranger said.

Liz looked up. The ranger was touching the pointy tooth on the right side of his mouth. "Can't mistake him. You seen anybody like that, miss? Around here? Down in the village? Maybe down farther when you all are selling your fur? Wears a lot of black leather. Heavily armed. Rides a huge, white bear. Albino bear. Almost pure white, touch of yellow 'round the neck. Enormous white bear, very old. Bear's even bigger than him." The ranger patted Tharos.

"No, sir." Liz shook her head honestly. "Never. Is he a criminal?"

"Yes," the ranger said plainly, but gave no further information. "What about her?"

But Liz was already looking at the second parchment, trying to keep her expression blank.

It was her.

Of course it was.

It was the dead ranger, the young woman whose body they'd discovered.

But she was alive in this picture. And in this picture, she

wore entirely different clothing, clothes like the daughter of a rich merchant. It was almost as if the picture had been based on some other picture. The technique of the printing was the same as that used for the portrait of the nasty old man, but the style of the illustration was completely different. The parchment was new and bright white. The young woman had short blond hair, worn at about chin length. Her face was heart-shaped, with a smallish chin. From the picture, she smiled out at Liz; a breathtaking smile. She looked younger in the picture, too. Her eyes were very bright—they seemed to shine. And there were her earrings: two blue stones held in silver claws, small in the picture, but clearly rendered in every detail. There was one thing missing, though: the tattoo of the Dallanar Sun on her temple. The mark of the Tarn. It wasn't there.

Liz started and glanced up. How long had she been staring at the picture? The ranger was looking at her closely. He had a slight smile on his face, but his eyes were deadly serious. His bear grunted and shifted beside him. Liz pushed her blond braid over her shoulder and looked back at the picture.

"You've seen her," the ranger said matter-of-factly.

He knows!

It was at this point that the skills Liz had developed in the last half year—the hiding and lying and pretending in front of Father, especially when the flask was out—came to the fore.

"No, sir." Liz looked the ranger in the eye and shook her head. "She's beautiful, that's all. I'd never forget that face. Never in my life." She said it simply, directly, then looked back down at the paper as if to assess the girl's beauty once more.

The ranger said nothing, but Liz could feel his eyes on her. After another long moment, Liz looked back up to him. "I could show these to my Mother, sir." She lifted the parchments and gestured with them to the front door. "She goes to the village more than I do."

As if on cue, the front door opened and Mother stepped onto the front porch. She had fixed her hair and she looked lovely. She carried a steaming cup of mint tea in front of her. She patted Rosie on the side, held the door open for the hound to enter the cabin, then walked out onto the step.

"Have we offered you food and drink, sir?" she asked the ranger with a heart-stopping smile. She handed him the tea.

"Yes, ma'am." The ranger nodded politely as he accepted

it. But Liz could tell that he was taken off guard by Mother's beauty. He cleared his throat. "Your daughter was kind enough to extend the courtesy. Alas, I'm due in the village tonight. I'm late as it is."

"A pity," Mother said, moving behind Liz, placing her hands on her shoulders. "What brings you up this far? Don't normally see the Tarn's riders on the edge unless there's something about."

Liz handed the picture of the dead young woman up to Mother. Mother took it and looked at it carefully. A slight frown touched the corners of her mouth, and Liz thought she saw recognition there. Mother looked back up with a quizzical, slightly vacant expression on her face.

"Looking for her." The ranger lifted his chin at the parchment. "She was supposed to report down to Korfort about a week ago. She's never late."

"Never seen her before," Mother said simply. "Have you been to the village with this?"

"Yes, ma'am." He bent his head and sipped the hot tea gratefully. "Mmm." He nodded, lifting the cup slightly. "That's good. Couple folks saw her a few weeks ago, not since. She's part of a larger group. We're looking for that old guy there." The ranger made a gesture to Liz and Liz handed the other picture to Mother. He took another long drink of his tea and scratched his war bear between its huge ears.

Mother took the parchment, unrolled it, and looked at the image of the old man for a moment. Then she shook her head, handed the parchment back to him. "Can't help you, I'm afraid. Never seen him either."

The ranger nodded. "Very well. If you do see either of them—or if you see anything unusual up here—we'll be basing a squad down in the village in the next couple of weeks. Using it as a base camp. We think he's around here—."

CRASH!

Behind them, inside the house, a smashing clatter of breaking pottery. Rosie began barking like it was the end of the world.

"That dog of yours," Mother said, shaking her head, squeezing Liz's shoulder. She smiled at the ranger. The ranger smiled back. Mother glanced at Liz. "Why don't you get her out of whatever she's into? Clean up for me?"

"Yes, ma'am," Liz said. She turned to go inside, but then

she paused, looked back at the ranger with a slightly wistful expression, and asked: "May I have permission to touch your bear, sir? Is it allowed?"

"Sure." The ranger smiled as he rolled up the parchments, slid them back in their tube. He handed his cup to Mother, trying not to stare at her. "He's gentle as a lamb—with the right people." He slipped the tube back into his cloak, grabbed his lance from where he'd planted it in the snow bank, and moved to his bear's side. He stroked its soft fur.

"C'mon." He nodded to Liz.

Liz looked to Mother, as if asking for her permission. Mother's eyebrow lifted ever so slightly, then she nodded. Liz stepped up to the war bear—and that's when her performance ended. This close, it was simply impossible not to be awed by the animal's sheer, gorgeous enormity. It was like standing next to a shifting, breathing wall of fur.

Narmos will be this big someday. Liz shook her head. Hard to imagine.

Liz put her hand on the bear's enormous head, buried her fingers in his soft fur. The bear's skull was huge, the muscles enormous. Feeling his fur was like running your hand through a thick, luxuriant forest. The bear cocked his head slightly toward her and grunted.

"You're sure it's safe?" Mother asked, feigning alarm.

"Yes, ma'am," the ranger answered, his chest puffing out. "Like I said, with the right sort of people, he's cuddly as a kitten."

"And with the *wrong* sort?" Mother asked, giving him the impression that she was impressed, nervous, and curious all at the same time.

The ranger looked up at her and grinned proudly. "A man's worst nightmare."

29

BACK INSIDE, AFTER the ranger departed, Mother looked at Liz closely. "That line about wanting to pet his bear was a nice touch."

"Thanks," Liz said, sitting on the ground, scratching Narmos on the tummy. The bear looked up at her, then grabbed her arm and tried to gnaw it. "Rarrr!" Liz whispered, and went on the attack herself, squeezing and rubbing Narmos's furry body, wrestling and rolling him to the ground. His splint clicked and ticked against the wooden floor.

Mother turned to the washtub, cleaning the cup that the ranger had used.

"Looks and wits and guts are many things, Elizabeth," Mother said, as she washed the cup. "But they're also weapons. Countless books tell of great kings brought to heel by the right girl's glance—storied warnings to men, encouragement to women." Mother set the cup down and turned to look at her. "Beauty and brains and gumption *are* powerful. Individually, they're potent, of course. Together? Unstoppable. And it's resolve that binds them together—the conscious readiness for a woman to own her strengths, whatever they be. *Resolve*. A trait the great queens of antiquity cultivated and mastered. There's no shame in having it—in *using* it. A woman's power can be the greatest power there is."

Liz didn't know where her next words came from, but they were out of her mouth before she could stop them. "If that's true, then why does Evan have a black eye? If that's so, why can't you tell me what's happening? What happened last night? *That's* our power? Lying? Keeping secrets? Father at his flask all the time—getting worse and worse every day—and we can't do anything about it? What are we gonna do when he gets drunk one night and beats Teagan senseless? And it'll happen—you know it—the way he's going."

She said these things plainly, without thought, as she petted Narmos, rubbing his soft fur, pulling on his ears, being careful of his splinted leg. It took her a moment to realize what she'd said, and that Mother hadn't replied. Liz looked up. Mother was staring at her. Her cheeks were slightly flushed, her eyes alight.

"Have you ever been hit?" Mother said. Her voice was calm. "You ever seen me get hit?"

"Mother, I'm sorry. I—," Liz started. "No. Of course not—. I only meant that—."

"No." Mother blinked and shook her head as if shaking away a bad dream. She took a deep breath. "*I'm* sorry." She smoothed her apron, tried to smile, lifted her chin. She came to Liz and kissed her on the forehead. "You're right, of course. I—. It wasn't always like this." She frowned, as if annoyed by her own words. "It wasn't. You know that."

Liz nodded. "But we have to do *something*. Before something happens." She paused. "Maybe it's time for us to leave."

Mother looked at her for a long moment, then shook her head. "A day ago, I would have agreed. But things will be different now. This dead girl you found. She changes everything. We'll talk when Father gets home. You'll understand. That's a promise. Look." She pointed at Father's flask. It lay there, dull silver flat on the counter. "He didn't take it with him." She picked it up and put it in the cupboard.

"Like that's going to stop him?" Liz snorted scornfully, with unaccustomed boldness.

Mother shot her a hard glance. "The past can earn the man you love a lot of credit."

"How's that help us now?" Liz asked simply, pulling on one of Narmos's ears.

Mother looked at her for a long moment. Then she shook her head and turned back to the washtub, starting in on the dishes. "You'll see." And then—as an afterthought, almost to herself—she said: "And you'll see that the past has a way of catching up with you."

30

THAT NIGHT——UP in the loft, the fire crackling warm and orange below, with Narmos tucked safely into his accustomed spot under the furs, between them all——Liz led her brothers down the wild and winding road of rampant speculation.

"I mean . . . maybe Father and Mother are *outlaws* or something," Teagan said, rubbing Narmos's soft tummy. Narmos looked up at him, batted at Tee's hand with his paws. "Like criminals or robbers or someone dangerous like that?"

"Bootleggers?" Evan grinned. His black eye was purple and crusty. He tipped his thumb back against his bottom lip. "That'd make sense. The cause of all our problems, under our nose the entire time——too much of his own wares?" They all chuckled——but a bit uneasily. *Too close to the truth,* Liz supposed. Regardless, the whole conversation was interesting in its own right; the sleeping loft was a different place when Father wasn't home.

"Yeah." Liz nodded. "Like I said, I thought of something like that. Some kind of fugitives? Like they were hiding out here from the law? But you didn't hear Father talk when we were down in the shed. The *way* he was talking. It wasn't how he normally is the morning after. He was nice and looked kind of guilty, like he does, but—I dunno. It was like each word sounded out of place. Like he was *educated*. And what about what happened last night? How would them being outlaws explain that? And how would they know a ranger from the Tarn? Because I'm *sure* they know who that dead girl is."

"He hates the Tarn," Evan added. "And what *did* happen last night? That flash and a crash and——."

"Maybe Father knows her from his time in jail or something," Teagan piped in. He stroked the white blaze on Narmos's chest. "I mean . . . you know? Like that lady arrested him or something. She threw him in the Tarn's jail?"

"'Dungeon,' you call it," Evan said sagely.

Liz shook her head. "She was *young*, Tee. Younger than Mother. I don't think she arrested him when she was a little kid." She patted Narmos's good leg. The little bear was adapting to the splint nicely, and his bad leg was straightening right up. It looked hilarious when he ran—more lopsided than ever—but it was working exactly as Father had said it would.

Evan cocked his head. "But something like that would explain why he hates the Tarn so much. Wouldn't it? They locked him up. Maybe it wasn't her. But maybe he was in the Tarn's dungeon? Mother, too? Maybe? What kind of crime do you think they did? Rebels? Or poachers or something?"

"Father? A poacher?" Liz shook her head. "No way. What if they're not outlaws, though? Think about all those stories Father's always telling us when his leg is hurting, when he's into his flask. Just think on it for a moment. Always something to do with his brother Darro, right? See what I mean? Whenever he tells one of those crazy stories, he's always drunk, it's always him, Darro, and they're always doing some crazy thing, and the Tarn is *always* involved—some way or another. Isn't that right?"

"I guess so." Evan shrugged. "You're the one with the wicked memory."

"He hates the Tarn," Teagan said, looking from Evan to Liz for approval for his remark.

Evan nodded. "That's right."

Teagan smiled.

"And how did Father hurt his leg in the first place?" Liz continued. "How did Darro get killed? How does Father know so much about grey bears? How did he buy this land we got here? You ever think about *that*? Where'd he meet Mother? You ever seen a woman like *her* in the village? *That* pretty? And smart? And what about those books she reads? Some of those lessons we do. You ever seen anything like *that* in the village? And how did *she* learn? And where's the rest of our family?"

"And what happened last night?" Evan added again.

"Exactly." Liz nodded. "What was that? And if we were from up here, wouldn't we have aunts and uncles and cousins and stuff—like *everyone* else in the village? And think about Fonhammer, Barnabus, and even Tulf, those guys. They'll drink with Father in the tavern when he's buying, but do they really spend a lot of time talking to him? Ever notice that? Always business: drop off the fur, pick up the supplies, check on repairs for this or that, maybe go to the tavern if the leg is hurting—all polite and cordial, but then straight back home. Every time. Business associates—but not friends. We're half a bell from old man Jarlund and Jarlund is a half day up from the village. We're completely alone up here. We don't even really go down for the festivals anymore, unless he's not here. The only reason we went down last Middlewinter was 'cause he was in Korfort. 'Member that?"

"What are you saying, Liz?" Evan asked.

"I'm saying that we don't know *anything* about who they really are except what *they* tell us."

"I only remember being up here." Teagan nodded, rubbing the scar on his temple. "I mean . . . I'm the oldest." Evan nodded at this. Narmos growled and tried to chew Liz's hand.

Liz nodded. "Yeah. But they never talk about *anything* that happened before. It's like they've just always been here. But that *can't* be."

"Alright, smarty-pants," Evan said with a yawn. "This has been going on all night. I'm tired. I can't explain it. We've covered all kinds of nutty possibilities and I want to get some sleep. Not everyone gets to sit around the house talking to rangers and cutting wood. Some of us have to go out, work for a living. What's your final word?"

"I'll tell you," Liz said neatly, with a nod. "It's simple. He used to be a ranger himself. That's where he met Mother. Something happened during his service and he and Mother left Korfort—or wherever. He resigned his position and they moved out here onto the big mountain to put the past behind them. They had enough coin to buy this land, to build this house, to set Father up in a job where he wouldn't have to see anybody or talk to anyone from the old life, but where he could still make a good wage: trapping."

She paused. "But now, after all those years, the plan is falling apart. He knows that dead ranger somehow, probably from when she was younger. He recognized her earrings. And I'm sure Mother knew her picture. They know who she is and they know who's looking for her—they probably even know who killed her. Mother and Father aren't from here. They're from down *there*. All the way down off the mountain, past the village, past the Trange, Korfort, or maybe even Adara's Hold. And mark my words, in the next couple days you're gonna find out that what I'm telling you is true."

Teagan and Evan both stared at her.

Teagan's eyes were wide.

Then Evan laughed uncomfortably. "Good one, Liz. Your best yet."

But Liz knew—knew in her bones—that she wasn't far off.

31

FATHER CAME BACK five days later, a couple bells past sunrise. Liz was outside chopping and stacking wood. The sky was grey, but every so often the morning sun would break through in a blinding dazzle of white frost and glistening icicles before falling back into gloom. The air smelled of snow. The winter crow was back, cawing lonely somewhere in the trees.

Liz glanced at the sky. For sure they'd get some flurries later in the day. And then Father hollered from the clearing's edge and Liz thunked her axe into the chopping stump and everyone piled out of the house onto the porch, pulling on their coats and boots, Narmos and little Rosie out first, charging, growling, and falling over each other to get down the front steps, claws scraping against wood, charging into the snow and across the clearing, Narmos's splint dragging behind him.

At the forest's edge, Father was leaning heavily against his walking stick, wincing with every step he took. His face looked bloodless, shiny beneath his furs and gear. Soldier walked slowly at Father's side, impassively pulling the loaded sled behind him.

There was a body-shaped bundle in the sled, wrapped tight, bound in fur and cord.

They met Father halfway across the clearing, the kids asking a flurry of questions to which he gave no answer. Teagan, way too excited, made some thoughtless remark about a squad of rangers coming to take them all away to the Tarn's "dungeon." The withering look that Father gave him shut his mouth immediately. Mother said not a word, but instead watched Father closely, one eyebrow raised. He looked at her, winced, and gave a short nod— as if his suspicions had been confirmed. Mother nodded, her face pale.

"Everyone inside," Mother ordered, clearing her throat. "Liz, tend to your bear."

Narmos was standing on his hind legs, his front paws around Soldier's neck, trying to push his nose into the big mastiff's ear. Soldier was eternally patient, especially when he had work to do, but Liz could tell that the mastiff was reaching his limit. Liz pulled Narmos off Soldier and lifted the cub to her hip, pulling a little piece of reindeer tack from her pocket for the cub to suck on. The binding had come loose on his splint.

"Evan," Mother continued, "put the stew on. Tee, you go on ahead and bring the night's wood in."

"Yes, ma'am!" they answered in unison, and got moving to their tasks. Evan looked pointedly over his shoulder at Liz as he left. Liz gave a slight nod in return. She'd keep her eyes and ears wide open.

The moment the boys were out of earshot, Mother stopped Father with a hand on his arm. The winter crow cawed.

"It's her?"

Father nodded with a grimace. He leaned heavily against his walking stick. His face was sheened and his eyes looked slightly wild. He blinked, took off his furry cap, and wiped his forehead. "Took me most of half a day to get her out of the snow. Frozen solid. But she hadn't been touched. Neither had the little one's mother." Father cocked his head at Narmos. "Made no sense 'til I started looking around. The whole clearing had been marked—piss and tufts of white fur and probably something else that I couldn't smell. But Soldier could smell it, and he didn't like it. Deliberately marked to warn off scavengers. Don't know when it was marked, 'course. But whoever did it was planning on coming back. Strange tracks and markings all around there, once I started looking, brushing things off. And I found another body. Dead war bear on the other side of the ridge. Big—from a royal line, without doubt. Full kit, saddle, pack, harness—everything but her carbine—everything was there, untouched. That bear was hers. Bullet through the head." Father touched his temple. "One shot."

"Great Sisters," Mother said. She cleared her throat. "We must send word, Hone. Now. The rangers are up here already. We were visited the day you left. But *we* must send word. *Ourselves*. No question."

Liz looked back and forth between them. It was starting to feel like she was listening to strangers again.

"Agreed." Father nodded, shifting his weight, flinching with the pain. "Absolutely. I'll leave for Korfort tomorrow. Send a message from the relay there. Can't tell these rangers direct, they don't know the whole story."

He paused, took a deep breath, and looked Mother in the eye. "This will destroy him, you know. He loved her like she was his own flesh and blood. More than that."

Liz stared uncomprehendingly. She didn't understand a word.

Mother nodded. Her eyes were dark, but her voice was absolutely composed. "This will destroy more than him."

32

"Lizzy," Father said through clenched teeth, his voice a bit hoarse, "after you hang the sled up, I want you to fetch my flask. Take Soldier and Narmos with you. How's his leg doing?"

Mother had gone back to the cabin. Father and Liz had gone down to the skinning shed, making room for the ranger's body. They'd keep it in the cold.

The pain in Father's knee must've been terrible. He'd undone his scarf and unbuttoned the top buttons of his coat. He'd left his cloak on the front steps of the porch. His face was dampish and green; his pupils large and slightly glazed— almost crazy. There was a smell, too. Something not right. Something *off*. A stink of cold sweat and fever. Narmos was busy harassing Soldier, growling and rolling around in front of him.

"You hear me, girl!?" Father snapped. "How's the bear's leg?"

"Yes, Father!" Liz started, looking him in the eye. "It's better, sir. Just as you said it would be. We could stay down here, and I could help you——."

Father raised his hand and stopped her mid-sentence. "Hang that up." He lifted his chin at the sled sitting in the snow outside the shed's door. "Then take that bear and the dog. And go get my flask."

33

LIZ LEFT THE shed, carrying Narmos on her hip, and walked up the snowy path to the cabin.

"He wants his flask," she said flatly, when she'd gotten inside. "Where is it?"

All their eyes went to her. Evan frowned and shook his head slightly. The blood drained from Teagan's face; he reached for his scar, then stopped himself. Mother glanced at her, a strange look in her eye. Then she paused, nodded, opened the cupboard, and took the silver flask from the dark.

"Mother——," Evan began.

"Be silent," Mother said. She opened the flask, poured half its contents into the washtub, then refilled the rest with water from the pitcher. "He will have it one way or another, and he'll be gone tomorrow. And everything will be different when he comes back. Count on it."

"Right." Liz snorted with disgust and undisguised sarcasm. "Don't know what I was thinking. Of course he'll be 'different now.' Things are always changing up here. Every day, a new adventure. And now Dad doesn't like his whiskey. Just like that."

Mother shot her an icy glance that chilled her to the core, but Liz didn't look away. Mother continued: "Teagan, Evan, when you're done cleaning Father's gear, I want you to go straight up to bed. Not a sound, understand me?"

"Yes, Mother," Evan said.

Teagan nodded.

Mother turned to Liz, wiped the flask with a clean cloth, and handed it to her with an imperious look that dared no refusal.

"Take it to him."

34

OUTSIDE NOW, BACK on the path leading down to the skinning shed, Liz pushed her braid over her shoulder and looked up at the sky. The sun was still out, but the snow would be there any moment.

She looked at the silver flask. Odd, but she'd never really examined the cursed thing. Flat, silver, and worn.

Simple thing to cause so much misery, she mused.

The lid and cap looked newer, like they'd been replaced. Probably more than once. She frowned. A couple years ago, she'd sniffed at it and tasted it when nobody was looking, and it had been horrible—just totally revolting. Resinous and burning, like the hard smell of pine needles cutting the back of your throat. The flask was larger than her hand, big for what it was, broad and flat. She'd seen other flasks down in the village, but they'd always been smaller and made of leather or corked clay. Not silver. She'd never really thought much about *that* difference, either.

She looked down the path, toward the skinning shed. The flask had a kind of weight to it, heavier than it looked, the terrible contents sloshing slightly as she moved it back and forth, back and forth. And the thing really was worn, wasn't it? Had she ever seen him carry another? Drink from another? She didn't think so. Must be older than Teagan.

Better get moving.

No sense delaying the inevitable.

Maybe she could keep him talking down in the shed? Keep him out of the house altogether?

That'd be good.

Either way, they were counting on her—again.

The sun came out suddenly and the snow went from grey to that crazy, unbearable white.

Liz closed her eyes and used the flask to reflect the sun up into her face, the radiance warm and red against the inside of her eyelids, taking her to another place, a place that was warm and safe—and then it too was gone.

She opened her eyes.

She was still standing on the path, of course. She hadn't moved. She looked at the flask.

Could she say that she'd lost it in the snow? And then what? He'd just drink from the wooden barrel behind the house and it would be worse.

Did anyone else out there know what it was like to feel like this? To be scared out of your wits by the person who was supposed to protect you? The hate and the love and the fear and the respect, and above all, the endless need for their approval and acknowledgment that you don't really want— but that you *need*—all at the same moment?

Liz realized that she was starting to understand the trap that Mother had fallen into. And then, for some reason, she thought of all that fur stretching down in the shed. All those empty eyes, slitted in the dark. A snow marten stepping on an iron spring plate. SNAP! "A trap kills two ways," Father would say. "Two ways only: *fast* or *slow*." That's why they set their traps like they did, why they took such good care of the gear. A fast kill was always better, for lots of reasons. And it usually *was* fast. Fast and painless and true. It was the slow trap, the one that malfunctioned, the one that you knew, the one that you saw and understood and fought against, the one you had to maim yourself to escape—that was the horror.

Liz looked down the path. The winter crow cawed.

"Bad luck," she whispered to the silver flask.

At that same moment, a single snowflake landed in the

flask's center and stuck there. She looked at the snowflake for a moment, then lifted the flask to her mouth and breathed on it, the heat of her breath vanishing the flake immediately, its unique, crystalline patterns melting against the shining silver——*but what's that?*

It was an engraved design.

There, in the steam of her breath——and gone.

She breathed on the flask again and tilted it slightly to the light.

She looked at it.

Unmistakable.

The engraved design had been rubbed and buffed away to almost nothing. Worn by use and polish and the habit of years, nothing more than the faintest edges left, the barest trace, smooth to the touch, the shape of the inscribed mark invisible unless you caught the light and the angle *just* right. As she had, just now.

The Dallanar Sun.

Acasius's Star.

The symbol of the Tarn.

It was inscribed on Father's flask.

And, for some reason, it made all the sense in the world.

35

LIZ OPENED THE door to the skinning shed. Father looked up, his forehead glimmering with sweat. His teeth were clenched, hot breath steaming in the cold. The dead faces of the fur stared at her, countless eye slits creased in silent smiles. The wrapped body of the dead ranger lay flat atop the far workbench, a tight bundle of fur and leather, another mute witness.

In her absence, Father had cut his pants leg up the side seam with his bone-handled knife. His right leg was propped up on a stool. He was icing his bare knee with a handful of snow. He'd pulled another workbench up beside him and set an empty clay cup on it. Wet boot prints marked the plank floor, little clods of snow spattered and melting beneath his stretched-out leg.

And his knee . . . .

His knee looked horrible: a mottled and purple mess, puffy and veiny, almost black in certain places, a deep cleft of scar tissue running a raw and puckered curl above the kneecap. It stank, too. That was at least part of the feverish smell. Liz didn't see how Father's pants leg could fit over the swollen mass.

She made to speak, but then swallowed. It was hard not to

look at his knee—she'd never seen it exposed like this. She'd never seen anything like it.

Father winced and grunted, noticing her gaze. "Pretty nice, eh Lizzy? Some sight?"

"Yes, Father." Liz nodded. Her hands were cold.

And then she realized what she had to do.

"Give it here." Father motioned with his free hand. "Give it. Or pour it in there." He cocked his head at the clay cup on the workbench beside him, wiped at his mouth.

Liz stepped into the shed, but she didn't get closer to him, and she didn't hand him the flask. There was no way he could reach her, not with his knee like that.

Instead, she looked him in the eye.

"I know you're not who you say." She raised the flask in front of her deliberately, her gaze steady. "I know you're someone else."

He looked at her for a long moment, sighed, and closed his eyes.

"This is who you are," she continued, lifting the flask. "You're my Father—but *this* is who you are. Who you *really* are. I know you're not—."

His eyes still shut, Father held up his hand and Liz stopped. The snow in his hand dripped on the floor. The horrible smell was everywhere. He sat like that for a few moments. Then he opened his eyes and looked at her. His eyes were bloodshot, bright with pain and need.

"You're right, Lizzy." He nodded and cleared his throat. The words surprised her. "I didn't know how much I missed it, how much I needed it, until now. That's my fault. Mine alone. But the things that'll come in the next days—they'll change everything. You don't understand now, Lizzy, but you will—."

"I don't *believe* you!" she spat suddenly, all restraint gone, her face going hot.

She wasn't crying, but she was so sad and scared and angry, head spinning, her cheeks flushed, and everything was trying to come out at once.

"I don't *believe* you! How can you do this to us? *How*—?" She was shaking. "We just want you to—to *take care* of us! How it was before!"

She choked and coughed a little and cleared her throat. And then she looked him in the eye, her chin up, barely knowing what she was saying but knowing that it was now or never. "I don't know what they did to you, or how this happened." She gestured at his knee and lifted the flask, waving it at him. "But this isn't *right*, Dad! You're hurting us! It's worse and worse! I won't let you do it!"

And then—without really thinking—she pulled her hunting knife from its sheath and got ready. For what? She didn't really know. But she had to do something.

"I'm not afraid of you," she whispered. The knife shook in her hand. "I'm not."

He looked at her, his eyes softening.

"I know, Liz," he said gently. "I know."

"I won't let you do this. I have to stop it."

"Yes." He nodded, something tender and resigned and terrible coming into his face, their eyes locked together, seeing into each other. "I've been where you are now," he said. "Exactly where you are. I know how you feel. But—."

She shook her head, lifted her chin. "If you do something to Teagan or Evan—anything again—I'll take them away. If you touch them again—at *all*, one thing—I'll take them from you. We'll run." She pointed her knife at his ruined

210

knee. "We'll run away and you won't be able to catch up. You'll *never* find us. Ever. You'll be *here* and we'll be *gone*. We'll never come back."

She had moved closer to him as she said this, unconsciously, not realizing that she was now within his reach.

He snatched her wrist, lightning quick, twisted it, took the knife away from her in one smooth movement, spun her around, and pulled her to his chest, one huge arm around her waist. His skin was hot with fever. She punched at his enormous arm, screaming now, but she might as well have been hitting the side of a mountain. And now she *was* crying—but not just crying, sobbing with grief and rage and frustration. "You can't *do* this! You *can't* do this! It keeps getting worse! I won't let you. I won't *let* you! I won't!" She squirmed, trying to get away, clawing at the flesh on his arm, but her nails were dull and short and his huge arm felt not like flesh but warm iron. And then he was holding her knife out in front of her in his other hand, showing her the well-oiled blade, turning it slightly, as if showing it to the ranger's corpse, to all the dead animals watching with their slitted eye holes.

"Put the flask on the bench, Lizzy," Father said.

His voice was absolutely calm, his command irresistible. She moaned, went limp, and set the flask down flat on the bench. The light from the door caught the silver just right, and she saw the traces of the six-pointed star. And she hated it. And then she spat at it—but she had no spit. She could feel Father's chin on the top of her head, heavy and coarse. She could feel his hot breath in her hair. That horrible, strange smell.

"Do what you want to me," she said softly, vacantly, staring at the open door. "Do what you want. But if you hurt Teagan again, or Evan . . . ." She swallowed. "I'll take them. When you're sleeping. We'll run. Mother will come with us. She already wants to."

He squeezed her hard and she suddenly realized that he was shuddering. Shaking. His whole huge body shaking, a strange, thick noise coming from his throat. He held her tight to his chest and then, in a single, swift movement, he reversed his grip on her knife and drove it straight down into the flask, the blade punching through silver and wood, clear fluid hiss bursting, burying the blade hilt deep in the dead center of the symbol of the Tarn. He squeezed her again, then cleared his throat.

"I want you to go on up home now, Lizzy," Father

whispered over her head. She could feel his deep voice through her whole body. "I'll stay down here tonight. I'll get the little stove going here. Have your mother bring me some of that stew. I'll be down here. Need to be clear for what's coming. Totally clear. No choice now. We're dead otherwise. Should've done it before—but I didn't . . . . I wasn't—." He shook his head, his beard rasping the top of her head. "You go on. You're fine. You just go on now."

Then he let her go and gently pushed her toward the door. She stumbled a little and opened the door and walked back up to the cabin and did what he'd told her to do.

36

FATHER STAYED DOWN in the skinning shed the rest of the day, all that night, and for the rest of the next three days. Mother had gone down there when Liz had come back up; she'd spoken with Father for some time and then they'd set up a schedule for his meals and what Mother called his "treatment." Mother would go down to the shed three times a day with food, clean linen, and plenty of tea. Evan and Liz would bring wood for the little iron stove. Mother had sent Teagan

213

to old man Jarlund with a note and Teagan had returned with a sack filled with three jars of various sizes, each packed with dried herbs of some sort. Liz had asked Mother about the herbs and Jarlund's note, but received only the vague answer that they'd help Father's leg. (All of Liz's other questions had received similar short replies—factual, but no more.) That night, up in the loft, Liz told her brothers about what had happened in the skinning shed. They stared at her with open disbelief until she showed them her empty sheath.

"Left my knife where he stuck it through his flask," she said. "Mother hasn't brought it back, not sure she knows. Didn't want to mention it."

Tucked in between them all, little Narmos listened to her with great interest as he sucked his paws, something calm and wise in his huge grey eyes.

37

IN THE EARLY evening of the third night, Father came back up to the house and sat them down around the kitchen table. They all took some tea and Mother set two lamps on the table top.

Father looked different, indeed. He was still using his

walking stick, but he didn't wince with each step. He looked gaunt, kind of hollowed out, but his eyes were clear. He was wearing clean clothes, and he'd shaved. Mother had given him a haircut, too. Liz looked at him skeptically when she sat down. He returned her gaze, his look calm and lucid.

He really does *look different*, Liz thought.

And so what? Was a haircut supposed to erase everything? She'd believe it after ten full years of proper behavior. She looked away from him. The hounds were in their kennel and Narmos and Soldier were lying beside the fire, the little bear cub sprawled over the big mastiff's back, both of them snoring away to beat all.

"I'm going down to Korfort tomorrow morning," Father said, cupping his tea in his massive hands. "I'll be taking Evan, Soldier, and the sled with me. The plan is to hire a sleigh in the village, but if we can't do that, it'll be a good four weeks for us to get down and back—unless we can hire a sleigh down there for the return. Liz, Teagan, you two will tend the trap lines and bring the catch straight to Jarlund. We've made arrangements with him to clean it and bring it to the village when it's ready. That should free up enough time for you two to keep the lines open without worrying about stretching. That clear?"

"Yes, Father," Liz said, a little impatiently, waiting for the rest of it.

"Yes, sir," Evan said.

Teagan nodded, staring at the table top.

Father looked at them earnestly. "The most important thing, however, is this: You're not to mention anything that's happened up here. Just like we said before. Not to anyone. Not a whisper. No dead bears. No dead rangers. Nothing. Just a regular winter, trapping on the mountain. That's it. And you're not to go down to the village, for any reason."

Father looked at Teagan, his eyes kind. "Teagan, you must not speak a word of this to anyone. Not Barnabus's boys. Not Fonhammer's kids. Nobody. Someone comes by, you're not to say anything. Do you understand, son?"

In spite of himself, Teagan looked up at these words and nodded. "Yes, Father."

"Good." Father sipped his tea. "Lizzy, in addition to your other tasks, you'll keep working on Narmos's leg. It's straightening out nicely and the new food is helping, but I want us to finish strong. Keep tightening that binding, keep him from chewing on it, and we should be able to take it off a week or so after I get back. Alright?"

"Yes, sir," Liz said with a frown.

That's it?

What was this?

There *had* to be more.

"Very well," Father said, and made to scoot his chair back.

"May I ask a question, sir?" Liz asked.

"No," Mother said simply. Her gaze was direct. "You may not. There's plenty of work to do. We'll talk about all this after Father returns."

"You promised," Liz said bluntly.

"We need to wait," Mother said. "To be sure."

"And meanwhile," Liz said brashly, her impatience making her bold, "a dead ranger lies strapped to a board down in the shed? Just another part of the grand, mysterious 'plan'? A ranger that you both know, and we don't get to understand what's going on—."

"Lizzy," Father interrupted her, his tone stopping her cold. But it wasn't like before, not the scary tone of an angry drunk.

It was something else. "*We* don't know what's happening yet. That's the truth. Do your chores and carry on, and when I get back, after I have a better picture, I'll tell you everything we know and explain what we think happened. You have my word." His eyes were plain, serious, and absolutely command-ing. It was as if all the authority of his huge size had somehow crystallized behind his gaze and voice—as if he was accustomed to giving commands and having them obeyed to the letter. And not just commands to his children, but also to . . . to . . . .

To what? To whom?

"You have my word, Liz," he repeated.

And for the first time in a long while, Liz actually believed him. She nodded, grudging affirmation, and pushed her braid over her shoulder. A slight smile touched his lips. He scraped his chair back from the table. They all did the same.

"Oh yeah," Father said, as if he'd just remembered some-thing. He pulled Liz's knife from behind his back, flipped it in the air, caught it deftly by the point, and held it across the table, the antler handle extended toward her. One of Mother's eyebrows went up. The blade's oiled edge gleamed wickedly in the lamplight. "Sharpened it for you."

38

EARLY THE NEXT morning, Father, Evan, and Soldier packed up and left.

And then the waiting began.

And it was a little bit like torture, Liz realized.

All the crazy waiting. This stupid, silly, endless waiting for days on end with Mother unwilling to say a word about anything. Liz knew that she was right about Father and the Tarn. The flask had proved it. (At least she thought that it had.) But that was just a general connection. The specifics, the details—*that's* what she wanted to know about. *And what does Mother gain by not telling me?* What was *she* hiding? And *why* was she hiding it? It was enough to drive a person crazy . . . .

So when Liz wasn't working the trap lines, doing her chores, or taking care of Narmos—who was getting bigger and smarter by the day—she was talking with Teagan about everything that had happened over the last week, compiling all the information. Teagan was more than happy to oblige. And Tee looked different, too. Not all hunched over and scared. Somehow, his instincts were telling him that he didn't have to be as frightened. Or that he didn't have to be scared in the same way, at least. He'd stopped rubbing his scar almost entirely and he seemed more articulate, especially when they talked about Narmos. He actually seemed . . . well, he actually seemed *happy*. Liz realized that it had been a long time since she'd seen him like that.

"He's gonna be a war bear, Tee," Liz said one night as they played with the cub by the fire. Narmos looked up at her words, stood up on his back legs, and attacked her hand as if to emphasize the point she was making, then dropped and rolled around with his funny little growl, rump pointed at the ceiling, keeping his eyes on her all the while.

"Yeah." Teagan nodded. "He's gonna be a great fighter. I mean . . . *look* at him. And all those tricks you taught him? He'll be just like the real Narmos, from the story. Right, Lizzy?"

Liz nodded. "Watch this." She paused. "Narmos—*sit*."

The little bear, his mouth wide open to gnaw on her sleeved arm, stopped immediately in mid-chomp, closed his mouth, then sat back on his silver-grey haunches, grey eyes wide. He cocked his head at her and blinked as if to say: "Go ahead. I'm listening."

"You showed me that three days ago," Teagan said, equally

unimpressed.

"Yeah?" Liz grinned. "Watch this. Narmos—*lie down*."

Narmos dropped flat to his stomach, his little legs tucked up beneath him, his splinted leg held just slightly away from his body. Teagan nodded again, as if getting ready to say, "So what?"

Liz raised her hand for patience.

"Narmos—*hide*," she whispered.

Without waiting, the little bear scooted on his tummy straight under Father's massive chair, his legs going flat as he dug with his front paws underneath along the plank floor. Both his rear paws—pads up, black and slightly shiny—still stuck out from beneath the chair, but he clearly understood the command.

Teagan laughed, pointed at Narmos's feet, and shook his head.

Liz laughed, too. "You've got some kind of crazy smile going, Tee."

Teagan looked up, gave her another huge grin. "What's not to smile about?"

39

THE DARK RIDER arrived in their clearing eighteen days later, in the early morning, just after dawn. They'd had nothing but snow for the last week and the morning was grey and foggy. A cold army of clouds had marched down from the big mountain the night prior, bringing with it a freezing mist. There was no wind; a sheen of ice covered everything like a hard glaze. Liz was chopping firewood with Teagan beside the cabin, stacking it in the storage eaves next to the chimney. Rosie was with them, snuffling around the cabin's foundations as had become her favorite pastime, hunting for snow voles and mice.

Then Rosie stopped short, went stock still, and gave a little growl.

Teagan turned to the little hound. "What is it girl?"

Then, at the edge of their clearing, Liz saw the huge white bear and its rider appear out of the fog. The pair was just a shadow at first, lumbering smoothly through the mist and the snow. And then they were in the clearing's center, coming straight down at the cabin from the tree line with neither call nor signal. Five huge rock mastiffs followed noiselessly at the white bear's heels. All the dogs were as big as Soldier, smoky black, wearing leather snow booties and collars of spiked leather. The bear's harness and tackle were wrapped in heavy fur, the dogs expertly trained to silence; there was no sound as they approached. Rosie growled again, then barked once. It was loud in the fog, as if the bark couldn't penetrate the mist. She lifted her nose again at the clearing, then growled with unusual ferocity.

"What's gotten into you, sweetie?" Teagan asked. He'd not looked up to see the bear and its rider.

Inside the cabin, the rest of the hounds began to howl and bay.

"I'll go look," Mother said from inside. "Good dogs. Shush-shush, now. Narmos, leave him *alone*."

"Rosie—*easy*," Liz whispered. Rosie stopped growling, but her hackles bristled.

Teagan glanced at Liz, a quizzical expression on his face. Liz looked over his shoulder, toward the clearing and the rider. Teagan turned and said immediately, "I'll get our bows." He dropped the wood he was carrying with a clatter and made to step toward the front of the house, axe held at the ready.

"No." Liz shook her head. "Look at him. Look at that bear.

If he wants something, he'll just take it. And we'll lose Rosie for no reason. Keep your hand behind you with your axe, don't let him see it. Keep your face totally blank. Alright? No matter *what* he says, Tee. Don't even twitch. Not a muscle."

"Alright, Lizzy. Alright. Not a twitch."

Liz nodded. "I'll talk to him—if he'll talk. Come on. Rosie—*heel*."

And to her surprise, Rosie obeyed her command perfectly. Together, the three of them walked around to the front of the cabin and stood on the top step, right in front of their door. Liz faced the rider directly as he approached. Her left hand hung at her side; she kept her right hand on Rosie's back. Teagan held his axe hidden behind him. His face a flat mask, his eyes determined. He ran his thumb over the silver leaf in the axe's handle.

The rider didn't pause when he got closer to the cabin. Rather, he kept moving straight across the clearing, his huge white bear plowing a deep furrow through the crusted drifts.

The rider was tall, bundled head to foot in dark, mismatched furs and pelts. A thick woolen wrap covered his face entirely. His seat was perfect, his shoulders and torso didn't sway at all with his bear's lumbering run; rather, he seemed to float above his mount effortlessly, like he'd been born to it. His headgear was distinct. It was more of a helmet than a cap, the sides adorned with the curled black horns of a snow ram, spiraled and sharp, the top plumed with a high crest of black eagle feathers. His hunting cloak was a dark patchwork of 'coon, wolf, and snow possum. Two huge bear paws capped each shoulder. The knuckles of his leather gloves were studded with well-oiled slugs of dark iron. A hunting horn made of black metal hung from his belt. He held his bear's reins loosely, with complete control. A short, broad-bladed sword hung from his saddle. A case of oiled leather was slung behind him; to Liz's eyes the case could only hold a crossbow. A long scabbard hung over the bear's front shoulder hump within the rider's easy reach. A carbine, for sure.

The bear itself was massive. Its fur was white, with a band of slightly yellowish fur running 'round the neck and shoulders. Now that it was coming right at them, Liz realized that she'd never seen a bear so big. The bear was enormous—far bigger than the ranger's bear had been—standing maybe thirty palms at the shoulder, hulking but somehow smooth, its immense white shoulder hump sloping down toward its huge rear haunches. Its eyes were red, sad, and intelligent; they glittered with an old wisdom. The bear's nose was red-brown and there was a ring of iron punched through the soft cartilage of his nostrils—a cruel means to control him, a last resort. His scarred muzzle was the color of old bone.

The bear and rider stopped five paces from the front porch, the bear's breath steaming in the cold. The rider's dogs, his black rock mastiffs, stopped behind them, perfectly disciplined, their eyes sharp and alert.

"How can we serve, my Lord?" Liz said calmly, wasting no time. She kept her shoulders square and her chin up. Even on the top step, she had to look up to meet the rider's eyes.

The rider turned in his saddle and whispered to his mastiffs. They sat immediately, their dark eyes on Rosie. Then the rider swung his leg over the saddle, dropped to the snow, and stepped forward toward their steps. Rosie growled. Beside her, Teagan shifted from one foot to another and cleared his throat. The rider was broad and tall. Not as tall as Father, but a big man.

Then he pulled the thick wrap from his face and she was

ready for it.

It was the old man.

The scarred criminal from the ranger's parchment.

Almost exactly as he'd been shown there.

She kept her face absolutely calm.

And he was *old*. Much older than Liz would've guessed from watching him ride, older than he'd seemed in the picture, too. The long, pale scar on his face started beneath his horned helmet and fissured down through his left eyebrow, down past the corner of his left eye, through his nose and top lip. His left nostril had been sealed by the scar, just like in the picture, the side of his mouth and white moustache cleft in a sneer. His eyes were widely spaced, pale blue set under deep, shaggy brows.

The eyes of a lunatic.

The thought came to her unbidden, almost automatically. She swallowed and raised her chin. The artist hadn't done him justice. He was nastier and more horrible in real life.

"Get your pa," the rider said bluntly. His voice was a growling rasp. He talked like a mountain man, or at least like a man from above Korfort and the Trange, but there was a strange, foreign note in his voice that Liz didn't recognize. Yet familiar, somehow. When he spoke, one of his front teeth flashed dull gold. His breath steamed in the mist. He spat into the snow and looked at Liz with his strange, pale eyes, waiting for her to comply.

"Father's just now coming back up from the village, sir," Liz lied. "With my brother, a few others, and the rest of our dogs. He should be here shortly, any moment. You're welcome to come inside and wait, sir. We've tea and a grouse stew on. Mother makes the best stew on the big mountain."

The rider looked at her closely. Liz kept her own eyes straight and steady. The rider stared at her, like he was trying to see through her. His pale blue eyes didn't blink. They were utterly unnerving. The ghost eyes of a dead man.

"Mother makes a fine stew, sir." Liz cleared her throat.

"No time," the rider said finally. "Looking for three bear cubs. Greys. You seen three little greys, girl?"

Liz kept her eyes locked on the rider's face, but let her face go puzzled, like she was trying to understand something. The rider stared back at her, not hiding the fact that he searched for the lie in Liz's expression. Liz didn't risk a glance at

Teagan, but from the rider's reaction it seemed clear that her brother's face remained a stone wall. The rider continued to stare at her. His pale blue eyes were ruthless and horrible. Behind him, the albino bear grunted deeply, shifting in the snow. Liz glanced at the bear and when she did, the bear looked back at her with its sad red eyes, cocking its head, as if to say: "I'm sorry I brought him here." The iron ring in the bear's nose was crusted with old blood. Abused.

"I'm looking for three grey bear cubs, girl," the old rider repeated.

Liz looked back to him and shook her head. "Ain't seen no bear cubs, sir. And we trap most of this area—we'd know it if there was a grey den around."

"That so?"

"Yes, sir." Liz cocked her head in assent. "You should wait and ask Father. He's got a keen interest in the people riding on his land. When we tell him you've been here, he'll find you anyway. Might as well just stay and wait."

"That right?" The rider's scarred mouth kinked into what passed for a smile, but his dead eyes didn't twitch.

"That's right." Liz lifted her chin, pushed her blond braid

behind her shoulder, and rested her hand on her knife's antler-horned handle. "And there aren't any bear fights up here, either. No breeders and no fighting pits—not on this side of the mountain anyway. The old Konungur freeholds run that kind of thing on the other side. And they have a small pit in Korfort—but I've never seen it. Father doesn't like it. That's about two weeks down by foot? Three days by post sleigh. Perhaps you should go look down there."

"Not looking for someone else's property, girl. Cubs are wild. They're mine, by rights. Lost 'em few weeks or so back. You seen my three little greys, girl?"

Liz shook her head. And again his lifeless pale eyes stared right through her. If she hadn't been looking into ever-more-dangerous eyes for the last year, Liz might've been nervous. But she wasn't—not really. She was wary. She was alert. But she wasn't really afraid. And the great white bear and pack of huge dogs didn't unnerve her either. In the bear's sad eyes, Liz could see its deep wisdom, the tricks of the ancient forest and high mountains, the loyalty to rider and pack, loyalty inspired in part by cruelty but also by hard winters and brutal necessity; a good bear, like Narmos—even though his rider was a madman. The rock mastiffs were just dogs. Big, well-trained, huge teeth—but just dogs. They'd mind whoever was in charge.

"What about you, boy? You seen my bears?"

Teagan gave him a blank expression, then shook his head.

"Who else can I ask around here?" The rider asked. "Where's the next closest freehold?"

"Old man Jarlund is half a bell's walk down the mountain, sir. Down that trail there. Not much else above us. Then there's the village, about half a day's walk on foot." There was no point lying about either. The rider would find them both soon enough, if he didn't know it already—which he probably did.

"This Jarlund, he a trapper like you all?" The rider glanced at the iron traps hanging freshly oiled from their hooks under the cabin's porch.

"No," Liz said. "He does reindeer and some other stock. Trades in herbs and lore, too. Knows the area as well as Father, though. Probably better. His people been here a long time."

"Old Konungur freehold, eh?" the old rider asked. Something wicked in his eyes.

"That's right." Liz nodded.

"You said something about the best stew on the moun-tain," the rider said suddenly. He didn't step forward, but he pulled one of his gloves off by the fingers. The iron slugs on the knuckles shone. His hands were scarred and calloused. "I'm hungry."

"Of course, sir." Liz blinked. Narmos would be sleeping by the fire after his milk. "Best stew there is. That's a promise. Have to brush you off first, though. Father's rules, sir. And you'll have to leave your boots at the door." Liz glanced at Teagan. "Go inside and tell Mother we've a guest—."

"No." The rider shook his head.

Teagan stopped in mid-turn, dead in his tracks.

"But—," Liz started.

"My dogs need their feet worked on now." The rider's pale eyes didn't blink. Then he shook his head and made a vague gesture at the big mountain, the dead mist. "Frozen fog, water in the air. Bad for dogs' paws, gets down in the leathers." He looked away from Liz, straight at Teagan. "You'll take their leathers off here on the porch, clean the ice from 'tween their toes, then take the leathers inside to dry a touch at the fire.

Got some mink salve here you can rub on their pads. You'll do the same for the leathers. Want you to start work on it now. Got five dogs and it'll take time. Got some coin for you, 'course." He cocked his head at Liz, his eyes still on Teagan. "Your sister here can show me inside straight away."

The rider took off his ram-horned helmet, turned it upside down, and shoved his studded gloves inside it. His white hair was long and yellowish, bound at the nape of his neck with an iron clamp. Teagan looked at Liz.

"I'll pay for it, girl," the rider said. "I'm no thief. Never take what's not mine, by rights."

The rider gave Liz a nasty, false smile. His scarred lip curled. The gold tooth shone lifelessly.

"Of course, sir," Liz said with a slight bow. "Teagan, see to the sir's dogs right away. And make sure that the porch is perfectly clean before Father returns. Should be here any moment."

"Alright, Liz," Teagan said. His voice was calm, but she could see the worry in his eyes.

"Here," the rider said as he passed Teagan, holding his fist out toward him. Automatically, Teagan put his hand out.

The rider dropped a copper sun into his palm. "My thanks," the rider said. He cocked his head at the mastiffs and continued, "They'll give you no trouble. Get started. Want to see this Jarlund before noon."

Teagan didn't seem to hear him. He'd pushed his cap back on his head and was staring at the copper sun in his palm, cupping the coin as if he held a snowflake of glass.

The rider stopped. He was staring at the scar on Teagan's temple. "Where'd you get that scar, boy?"

Teagan looked up sharply, then down at the ground. "Accident," he mumbled, pushing his rabbit skin hat firmly down on his head.

"Hmm," the rider said. He stared at Teagan for a moment, then snorted. "Buy yourself some food and some decent clothes. New hat maybe."

"Yes, sir." Teagan frowned, not looking up.

"*Dogs*," the rider said softly. He pointed at the porch. Silently, the huge rock mastiffs streamed up the two steps on either side of Liz and Rosie. Rosie shook, scared out of her wits, but she didn't back down—not even a little. The big dogs sat together to the right of the door. Teagan turned without looking up, sat down in front of the biggest mastiff, and began removing the leather bootie from its front paw. The rock mastiff sat at perfect attention while it was serviced, its eyes on its master.

The rider looked at Liz, motioned to the door with his horned helmet. "Shall we?"

Liz turned with Rosie, took the hand broom off its hook, and carefully brushed the rider from waist to boots, taking her time. Then she handed the rider the broom so that he could take care of his own chest and shoulders. Liz worked on Rosie's feet for a few moments, brushed herself off— still stalling for time—then knocked on the door. Mother's shadow blocked the warm glow of the door's window. The iron latch clinked. Liz looked up at the rider. "And how shall I introduce you, sir?"

"Modró," the rider said plainly. "Tom Modró."

40

MOTHER OPENED THE door and Modró stepped into the cabin. Liz followed. The house was in perfect order and Mother herself was radiant. Her blond hair was pulled back

235

in a functional ponytail and she'd put on a clean dress accent-
ed with little blue flowers, the one she usually wore during
the Middlewinter festivals, the little petals picking up the
color of her eyes. Liz immediately felt better. Mother had
everything well in hand.

But what about Narmos?

Mother had set the kitchen table with a clay bowl and cup.
A large wooden spoon rested beside the bowl, on top of one
of their best cotton napkins. The bowl was filled with grouse
stew. The cup was filled with hot mint tea. The fire was built
up and crackling. The hounds were in their kennel. Not a
trace of Narmos or his milk. Liz wondered where Mother
had hidden him—and if he'd keep quiet. Liz was suddenly
quite certain that the little bear's life depended on his silence.

"Mother," Liz said as they entered, with just the right touch
of respect, "this is Mr. Tom Modró."

Modró gave Mother a slight bow. "Just Tom will do, ma'am."

"At your service, sir." Mother bowed formally. "I am
Margaret Hone. Welcome."

Modró bowed again slightly, but at their family name, Liz
saw something flicker in his eyes.

"May I take your hat, sir?" Liz asked, clearing her throat. Mother gave him her most charming smile.

"'Course," Modró said, his voice softening a touch. There wasn't a man on the big mountain who could resist the power of Mother's smile. He handed Liz his helmet. She placed it on a hook by the door.

"Please, come and sit," Mother said.

Modró nodded, stepped to the table, and sat.

"We just finished breakfast not half a bell past, or we'd join you," Mother said, hands clasped in front of her.

"Grateful." Modró nodded, took up the spoon, immediately digging into the stew with relish. "Mmm." He nodded, his accent shifting slightly. "First rate." He sucked up the stew, staring at the table as he did so, grunting and nodding with the taste of it. Then he stopped suddenly, still staring at the table top—then shook his head with evident pleasure.

Mother glanced at Liz, then cocked her head to the front door, lifting her chin. Liz frowned at her gesture.

"Jarlund," Mother mouthed silently.

Of course!

They had to warn him, too. Mother had been listening at

the door and knew that old man Jarlund's place would be
Modró's next stop.

Liz nodded.

"I'll go help Teagan with your dogs, sir," Liz said. "Be
faster. And I've got that other work for Father, too. We'll be
right outside, Mother."

Mother tilted her head in agreement.

Modró nodded, not looking up, slurping at his stew. "My
thanks," he said with his mouth full, stew running into his
yellowish-white beard. Then he cocked his head and looked
up at Mother. "She was right. Best stew I've had in recent
memory, ma'am. Your girl, she doesn't lie."

41

OUTSIDE, ON THE front porch, Teagan was busy with Modró's
dogs. He looked up as Liz came out. The dogs were sitting
there patiently as Teagan worked on them. A pile of leather
booties surrounded Teagan's feet. When Liz shut the door,
Modró's huge white bear looked up with its sad, ancient eyes.
It was sitting in the snow, gnawing on something that Modró
had given it. Looked like the leg bone of a large animal.

"Good bear," Liz said. The bear looked up at her, blinked its red eyes unhappily, then went back to gnawing its bone. It looked hungry.

"What's happening, Lizzy?" Teagan whispered, but not soft enough.

Liz put her finger to her lips. Then, in her softest whisper: "You need to slow down this work, Tee. Pretend you're stupid, that you don't know what you're doing." She cocked her head at the door. "Put the booties on backward and make him show you how to put them on properly. Drop one of 'em off the side of the porch, lose it in the snow. You understand?"

Teagan blinked, then rubbed his temple, started muttering something under his breath.

Liz grabbed him by the coat and shook him gently. He looked at her. His eyes were scared. He looked over her shoulder, at the closed door. "Who's that man, Lizzy? I mean . . . Father wouldn't like this."

"Doesn't matter," Liz hissed, trying to be patient, but not doing a very good job. "You need to give me some extra time so I can get down to old man Jarlund's." She stopped.

Maybe Teagan should go?

239

No. That would never work. He'd never be able to explain it properly.

She shook her head. "Even if I take the short cut, if that guy leaves right after he finishes his stew—and by the way he's snorting it down that could be in half a moment—he'll beat me down there. See? You've *got* to pretend that you don't know the work. That you don't know how to do it properly. You have to give me *time* to get down there. Do you understand what I'm saying, Tee? You have to give me time."

Teagan nodded, but he was starting to shake.

"Teagan!" She shook him again, harder. She knew it wasn't the right thing to do, but she had to do something— she half expected Modró to come out on the porch any moment. Teagan looked at her. His lip quivered.

"Can you give me more time?" Liz asked. "Father's not here, so *you* have to help me. You've gotta give me time to get to Jarlund's. You've got to pretend you don't know what to do. Slow him down. Can you do it?"

He nodded dumbly—and then he blinked, as if waking up. His eyes cleared. "I understand, Lizzy. I mean . . . I know what you want me to do."

Liz squeezed his shoulder. "Good. Don't make it obvious. Just pretend like you're dumb. When he comes out, you tell him that I'm down at the shed working the fur."

Teagan nodded. "I'll keep him here. Pretend I don't know what to do. Drop a boot under the porch. Take half a bell to get it out."

Liz nodded. "That's right."

Teagan smiled suddenly and crossed his eyes. "I'll pretend I'm a dummy."

In spite of herself, Liz laughed out loud and threw her arms around him, squeezing him tight.

And then she ran.

42

FLYING DOWN THE mountainside, fog thick in the black trees, snow slipping and crunching beneath her furry boots. She knew the path by heart, of course, but she realized immediately that she'd have to slow down. "Slow is smooth and smooth is fast," Father would always say. "Especially in the deep woods. The mountain way." She nodded, slowed her pace, took a deep breath. If she tripped in the fog, sprained her ankle, got hit in the eye with a newly fallen branch, then Jarlund would be left without warning. Old Jarlund was a clever coot—the smartest around, even Father had to give him that—but all the wits in the world wouldn't be able to explain the fur-lined crates of reindeer milk stacked and load-ed on a sled pointed at the Hone cabin—the only freehold up that way. Which was exactly how deliveries ran these days. Modró would know instantly that Father was buying milk. And he'd know why.

If he doesn't know already.

Liz shuddered at the thought.

There was something truly mad in the rider's pale eyes.

Modró talked a good game, sure. But his eyes told the truth in a word: *killer*.

43

JARLUND'S PLACE WAS an ancient heap of stone, two stories high with a small observation tower built into its northern corner. The house proper was roofed with local slate and backed up against the cliff side. A couple of its back rooms had been dug straight into the bedrock by the earliest Konungur homesteaders. "Some of the rocks in this shack were placed ten thousand years ago," Jarlund would tell her proudly. Several long outbuildings were situated on the edge of his clearing, sheds to keep his reindeer warm during the coldest months of deep winter. The herd was out in the fenced paddock now. A curl of smoke rose from the heavy chimney.

Liz dashed across the clearing, past the sled loaded with milk, and pounded on the iron-banded door.

"Hold on, hold on," came Jarlund's voice. There was a long pause. Then he opened the window set in the center of the door, saw that it was her, and let her in.

Old man Jarlund wasn't really that old. Probably only twenty or so years older than Father. But he wore a huge white beard and expensive reading spectacles that he'd ordered up from Tarntown; they made him seem older than he was. He had a nice round belly and a nose that was always a bit red, especially when it was cold. When he stood aside to let her in, Liz saw that he wore his reading slippers and his dark green robe. He was holding a thick book with gilt pages, his finger stuck in the middle to mark his spot.

"Liz?" he asked, looking over his reading spectacles. He glanced past her, looked outside, his eyes concerned. "What's going on?"

44

As Liz caught her breath, she quickly told Jarlund what had happened. Modró was coming. What he looked like. The giant white bear he rode. His dogs. He wanted to take Narmos. The rangers were looking for him. A criminal. A murderer. And he'd be there any minute. Father was due back soon, anytime, but only if he'd hired a sleigh down in Korfort.

Jarlund nodded seriously at all of it and, when she was finished, got busy at once. "Let me pull the milk sled 'round back, brush out your tracks, then you can tell me more about it. For now, just sit down and have a cup of tea. Water's on there. You know where." Jarlund stepped into his work boots and pulled the door shut behind him.

45

H<small>E CAME BACK</small> a few moments later. Liz was sipping some lemony tea, mostly out of politeness. She'd never wanted tea less in her life. Jarlund walked through the front door, went into his back bedroom, and came out wearing his leather work pants, a white work shirt rolled up at the elbows, and a broad leather belt. Liz knew he wore a horn-handled blade sheathed across the small of his back. She was glad to be there with him.

"How long it take you to get down here?" Jarlund asked.

"Just under half a bell," Liz said, taking another sip of tea for Jarlund's benefit. "But maybe he'll just go down to the village. He looks crazy. A criminal, the ranger said. I keep expecting him any moment——."

"Sooner than that, I'm afraid," Jarlund interrupted her, looking over her head, through the window in the center of the front door.

Liz got up from the table, peeked out the window.

Modró was at the edge of the clearing, a huge, dark shape just barely visible in the fog. But he wasn't moving. He was carefully checking out the place. Or so it seemed. He didn't move, not even a little. Liz could picture his lifeless blue eyes scanning the outbuildings, the paddock, the house proper, the woods and cliffs around. Not saying a word, just looking, dark in the mist. The huge albino bear took a few steps forward. Modró looked some more. The breath of the bear and mastiffs steamed in the cold. Modró's black-horned helmet turned slightly, toward the house. Even at this distance, Liz could feel his eyes. Could he see her through the window? The white bear took another careful step. The fog curled around them, like something out of a child's nightmare.

Softly, almost like he was worried Modró would hear, Jarlund said, "You need to hide."

46

"HO THERE! IN the freehold!" Modró's voice rang out over the clearing. "In the freehold, there!"

"Where?" Liz asked. Her voice was calm. She looked around, her long braid swinging behind her.

Jarlund nodded, folded his reading spectacles, and put them in his shirt pocket. He pointed to a large, iron-bound chest in the near corner of the main room and walked over to it.

"Here," Jarlund whispered. "The side latch is torn out. You'll be able to breathe and you can look out a bit, too. But not a sound, Liz. Understand?" Jarlund touched his back, adjusting the blade sheathed there. "This knife's sharp as they come, but I don't want to try him. Not if he's like you say. Better use the wits and live, eh?"

Liz nodded. Jarlund didn't seem nervous, but his expression was serious. He opened the chest, took out five fur blankets, leaving one blanket on the bottom. Liz stepped over the chest's edge and crouched down inside. It smelled of fur and clean cedar.

"In the freehold! Ho there!" Modró's voice hallooed again from outside.

"Not a sound," Jarlund said. Liz realized that she'd never seen his face so grave.

She looked at him, grinned reassuringly, and patted the chest behind her. "First time in my life I'm sad to be tall."

"Good girl," Jarlund said. But he didn't smile. He put his finger to his lips and closed the lid over her. Liz heard him place the blankets back on top of the chest.

"In the freehold!" Again, Modró's voice from outside. It

seemed closer.

Liz sat cross-legged and bent over. She could see the kitchen table from the small hole where the chest's side latch had been. Jarlund walked back across the room and cracked the front door a palm's width. He stood there with his boot against the door's bottom corner, his left palm flat against the wood. With his right hand, he loosened the big knife sheathed horizontally across the small of his back.

"What you want, foreigner?" Jarlund asked flatly.

"Heading to the village below." Modró's voice, from outside. "Thought I might be able to buy a meal for me and my animals. I've coin, both copper and silver; good suns both, and pure."

"What you want for your bear?" Jarlund asked.

"Heard you do reindeer."

"That's right."

"Do any milk?"

"No," Jarlund answered flatly. "Just horn, hide, and meat."

"Hmm. How much you want for two whole? One for the bear, one for the dogs."

"Won't sell 'em to you live," Jarlund said, "but you can

take two whole after I put 'em down. Thirty copper or three silver, don't much care which, long as they're suns."

There was a pause. Then: "Sounds fair. How much for me?"

"You pay for the two whole, you come in as a guest."

"Very well."

Jarlund nodded, took an iron lantern from the counter, and pulled his coat off its peg. He opened the door, cast a quick glance at the chest, then stepped outside.

"What brings you all the way up here?" Jarlund asked. He shut the door behind him. Modró answered something and Jarlund grunted back something Liz couldn't hear. Their voices faded as they walked toward the shed.

47

AFTER WHAT SEEMED like forever, they returned, Jarlund chatting with a bit too much enthusiasm as he opened the door. "— is some tale, to be sure," he was saying. "Never heard nothing quite like it. Hope you find your property. Grey bear cubs, they're worth good coin, even up here. 'Specially if you know the old Konungur freeholds. I can sure keep my eyes open, too." Jarlund stamped his feet outside and stepped into the house. "Here, gimme your coat. Just pouring myself a cup of warmth. Know it's early. Take a taste? I'll fetch your breakfast."

Modró stood outside. His pale eyes scanned the kitchen, the main room, the chest where Liz hid, taking it all in. He didn't blink. Then he looked at Jarlund, smoothed the jagged scar in his moustache, and nodded, removing his gloves and horned helmet. He hung the helmet on a peg and shrugged his coat off. He kept both his gloves, holding them together in one hand. Jarlund hung the coat and motioned to the table. Modró sat, smoothing his gloves beside him, adjusting the hunting horn on his belt so that it didn't pinch. The iron slugs on the knuckles glimmered with fresh oil. Jarlund lit a pair of lamps, then took two clay cups from his cupboard and set them on the warmer above the iron stove, poking the wood inside. Then he went to his pantry under the stairs and returned with a glass jug filled with clear pine whiskey. The drink sloshed as Jarlund walked, glossing the jug's sides.

"Take it with a little honey?" Jarlund asked. "I do. Comes up from below the Trange, below Korfort. Good southern clover."

Modró grunted and nodded.

Jarlund fetched a tiny clay pot from the cupboard, stood by the stove for a moment, then took the cups off the warmer. He set a cup in front of Modró, poured it half full from the jug, then opened the tiny pot and followed the liquor with a line of golden honey. He fixed the same for himself, cleaning the honey pot's edge with his finger, licking the finger clean. He placed the jug carefully on the warmer and sat down across from Modró.

Modró took a sip from his cup. His eyebrows went up and his face brightened. "Well, that's a fine surprise."

Jarlund chuckled. "My own. Boiled down from spruce resin. Aged in my pa's oak barrel from the other side of the big mountain. Barrel's 'bout a hundred years old."

"How long you keep it in there?"

"Least ten years."

"Long time."

Jarlund nodded. "On the big mountain, we think in decades."

Modró grunted and took another sip. His pale eyes glowed. He smoothed his bedraggled moustache, ran a finger along the jagged scar at his lip, and settled into his chair. They sipped their drinks for some time in silence.

After a while, Modró scooted his chair up to the table, cradling his hands around the warm cup. "There's a family back up the ridge there," Modró cocked his head at the door. "Cabin up there. You know the freehold I mean?"

"Up on the far side over? Little cabin flanked by two big spruce?"

Modró nodded.

"The Hones." Jarlund cleared his throat. "Two lads, pretty tall girl always wears a long braid. The parents."

"That's them. They buy any extra food from you of late? Any giblets or innards? Milk? Last weeks here?"

Jarlund shook his head. "They don't have your cubs. And they don't have no coin neither. I give 'em what I can, but Hone, he's a proud man. Don't take charity from nobody on this mountain. Keeps to himself, mostly."

Modró stared at Jarlund, his hands laced around his cup. He leaned forward a bit, pale eyes staring. "You gonna answer me?"

Jarlund looked at the table and coughed into his fist. "Thought I had—."

"Those people buy milk or soft scrap from you the last few

weeks or so? Maybe some river oysters? Something like that."

"Course not. Like I said, they don't have no coin. They ain't feeding no grey bears. Couldn't afford it, even if they wanted to. I don't do milk, anyways."

Modró looked at Jarlund for a moment. Then he nodded, apparently satisfied. He leaned back in his chair and grinned. His gold tooth flashed. "How old are the kids up there?" He took a long sip of his drink, looked at Jarlund over the cup's brim.

Jarlund nodded. "Liz, she's fifteen. Teagan, got a scar on the side of his face? He's almost nineteen. Evan's about two year younger than him. Why you ask?"

"Need to hire a guide. Don't know this side of the mountain well as I should. Spent near my whole life on the other side. There's one more grey I need to kill and he's over here now. Closer than he's ever been. Need a pathfinder for a month or so, to hire."

"Well, 'bout that, meant to ask outside. Don't all this worry you a bit? Account of the Tarn? Last I heard, every grey line not owned by a local house was property of the Silver Throne."

Modró sneered. "Adara was a grand ruler, that much is true. But Tomas was a bureaucrat. And Balmás? A pathetic weakling. Bellános now . . . . Well, they may call him the 'Silver Fox,' but he's got problems of his own. If it was his brother Dorómy—well, that'd be another thing altogether. That man's strong as a bear and his word counts. The 'Iron Lion.' Good name for that one. But it's *Bellános*—not Dorómy—who sits the Silver Throne. And he'll be years upon it, unless something changes. Law's only as strong as the king who enforces it, old man. Bellános, he's distracted. Spends a lot of time away from here, on Paráden, other duchies. Hmm."

He paused, and took a sip of his drink. "Been nine centuries since Hakon first claimed the remaining grey bears for the Tarn. In *his* day . . . well, his word was harder than granite, sharper than steel. But times change. Old minor houses won't obey just anyone—the only language they understand is *this*." Modró clenched his fist in front of him. "Near four decades now, I've sold wild stock to old Konungur families. They've been training and fighting greys forever, since before the Founding. A royal order with no force behind it? Just a bunch of empty words. And the old families are getting strong again. Stronger than they've been in a long time. How you stand on that? This place of yours seems old. You have the look of Konungur nobility. You loyal to the Tarn?"

Jarlund gave him a long look. "The Dallanar got nothing to do with us out here. They leave us be."

"So, you just bend knee and keep quiet, eh?"

Jarlund leaned back in his seat and yawned. "Don't know nothing about all that. And I'd steer clear if I did. Look, why not hire Hone to help you look? Had some trouble with his knee these last years, but Hone knows the high country here good as anyone, I suspect."

Modró looked at him for a moment, as if considering their family name.

Jarlund looked back at him.

Then Modró nodded and sipped his drink. "Don't know if he'll take kindly to me crossing his land. The girl, she seemed sharp. Made mention that her pa might have some words for me. Bold kid."

Jarlund snorted in mid-sip.

Modró frowned. "That funny?"

"No, that's *true*," Jarlund said, chuckling. "But I'd never tell her that to her face. Ruin her for good. Only thing worse than a bold kid up here is a bold kid who *thinks* she's bold. Understand me?"

Modró grunted.

"But it makes no difference," Jarlund continued. "Hone would never let the girl go. Any of 'em. They run his traps and he cares for 'em, in his way."

"What about you? I have coin."

"I'd be no good to you. I know the big mountain, sure. But I could never keep up. Too old. Maybe you'll have some luck down in the village, find some young buck looking for a challenge. There's a Mr. Barnabus down there, runs tackle and some trade. Rents a sled every now and then. His two sons—Belios and Beiro—they might be of good service. Both good boys, and strong. Village only a day from here on foot—hmm." Jarlund stopped and shook his head. "Strange."

Modró stared at him, waiting for him to continue.

"Now," Jarlund said, clearing his throat, "I don't claim to know much about grey bears, but ain't it odd how close she was? This mother bear you telling me about? If what you was saying 'bout her spot on the ridge was right? Why'd she den

256

so close to settlement? Only two days out or so? Never heard of such a thing. Not with a grey, at least."

"She was a tricky sow, that one," Modró said, nodding. He took a long sip of his drink, savored it with his eyes shut. He stayed like that for a moment. "Like I said, been after her particular near six years now. She knew me and she knew my old bear. She knew we were after her. Last year, she made like she was gonna head far north, way up over the mountain. But she doubled back during thaw, used the streams, knew I was after her, moved down as close as she dared. She thought I'd never think to look so close here. Tricky old mother." Modró grinned, and his gold tooth flashed. "She was almost right. Need her cubs, though. Gonna set a trap for the monster. Need his sons to do it right. You want to catch a king, you gotta threaten his young."

Jarlund frowned. Then he stood, fetched the glass jug from the warmer, and filled Modró's cup. Then he made to fill his own, but stopped and poured only a finger's worth for himself. He dripped honey into both drinks, returned the jug to the warmer, and sat back down at the table. Modró took a long sip, smoothed the jagged whiskers around his scar, and sighed. They sat there in silence for some time. Then Modró leaned forward over the table and said softly, "It seems mad, I know. Sometimes I wonder if they're in it together." He drained his cup in one swallow and tapped its bottom twice on the table. "More," he said, cocking his head at the jug.

"Who's in it together with what?" Jarlund asked gently. He stood and refilled Modró's mug.

Modró shook his head. "That tricky sow," he said, "the cursed beast who gave me this." He pointed two fingers at the start of the scar on his forehead, followed it down across his brow, past his eye and nose, to his moustache and mouth. He took a deep sip of his fresh drink. "I know for a fact that she mated the cursed monster, and that more than once. Same cursed beast killed my brother, Great Sisters sing his praise. Dear Konnor." He touched his scar. His pale eyes seemed to burn. "Something else to remember him by." He stopped and gazed into his cup.

Jarlund sipped his drink quietly, waiting for him to continue.

"Out hunting reindeer," Modró said. "We were guests of the Tarn, some forty years past. Twentieth Year of Tomas the Second. My mother and High King Tomas, they were 'friends,' see?" He shook his head. "Doesn't seem possible. So long ago. So long to wait for justice . . . . "

He trailed off, but Liz noticed that the strange, foreign tone in his voice—that tone that she had noticed before— was more pronounced.

"I've never seen such a creature. We were deep in the high country—too high, I know now. We must've wandered into his range. Didn't see spore nor mark. Although, to tell you true, I didn't know what to look for back then." Modró scratched his scar. "I used to wonder sometime if the High King's scouts didn't lead us up there on purpose. A wicked thought, no? Our families were close, but the lies of the Silver Court run deep, eh? How can you claim murder, how can you cry foul, when the killer is the wild itself? I didn't believe it at first, but as the years passed, the proof mounted and I stopped wondering. It was true. That bear did the killing—but it was the Tarn that made it so. The Dallanar killed my brother. But my time is coming soon. . . . Oh yes, it's coming." He paused for a moment, closed his eyes, as if to better remember.

"We'd seen a good herd of reindeer three days prior and

we'd come up on them again. They were led by a handsome old buck and we all wanted to try for it. Konnor missed his shot, but the herd must've roused the monster as they ran to cover. Or maybe it was the noise of the shot itself? Dunno. Maybe the beast knew we wanted *his* reindeer. Maybe he had a mate around. Whatever the reason, he came. We heard him before we saw him. Dogs were going crazy, Konungur scouts looking around, eyes bugging out like they'd go mad. 'The King of the Mountain!' Scouts kept shouting. 'The King of the Mountain!' We didn't know what that meant. There was this deep grunting coming from everywhere and—I tell you true—the ground shook as he came. And then he was in the middle of us. Just like that. White and silver-grey, broad as a glacier, sixty hands high at the shoulder, roaring like an avalanche. Didn't even bother with the men, at first. One passing swipe with the side of his paw, glancing blow, and I was down, trying to see through the blood. He wanted the dogs, see? Must've had two dozen good mastiffs with us. Big dogs too, top lines. Royal lines—and by the Sisters, did they go at him with all they had. Didn't make a bit of difference. He tossed 'em against the trees like they were toys, broke their backs, and if the throw didn't kill 'em, he'd rake 'em once down the chest, like pulling open a coat down the middle, and it was over. No time, snow 'round twenty paces was pure red. Everyone else had run while the dogs fought him, but Konnor . . . good Konnor stood his ground, Great Sisters praise him, firing as fast as he could. Must've hit the beast five times, didn't make a difference. Trying to save *me*, you see? I couldn't get up. I couldn't see. All the blood." He pointed at his scar. "The monster tore the last dog's head off, ran straight at my brother, knocked him down, tore his throat out like it was nothing, kept on chasing the others without a blink, like it was nothing but the greatest sport in the world. Killed every-one in the party save me and one scout, a little Konungur boy who'd been back doing his business in the trees."

Modró shook his head. "Never went home after that. Glad for it, too. Taken me forever, near a whole lifetime, but I'm closer than I've ever been to having some justice. I'll take his cursed skin home to Farák, give it to my nieces. They'll burn it in memory of their father. And I'll kill the kin of those who sent him. Those Dallanar liars——." Modró stopped short. "What's that? You *smile* at my brother's death?"

Modró stared at Jarlund, his knuckles suddenly white around his cup. Liz swallowed.

"I'm not smiling." Jarlund shook his head carefully. "No, sir. Any man's death is cause to mourn."

Modró grunted.

"But if that big grey you hunt is the Mountain King," Jarlund continued, "you ain't never gonna find him. And if you do, you won't live to tell it. You know as well as I that a male grey lives about a hundred fifty years, if he don't die in the pits or get himself killed by some hunter, some freak accident. But the King of the Mountain ain't no regular grey. He's *old*. He knows the whole range, the whole top of the world, watches all the rivers and forests, keeps all the animals and shepherds, protects 'em. He'll kill whatever pleases him, whenever it suits, to keep the mountain at peace, to keep his realm free of mens' poison. Every Middlewinter up here, we dance the bear dance for him and leave him his due out over on Flat Rock. The old Konungur up there been paying him honor since 'fore the Silver Queen came—and never once has he come into their villages. Not in all that time, if you believe it. His father was the big mountain itself and his mother was the moon. That's why his coat's so silvery, why your brother—

Great Sisters sing his praise—shot him with no harm. You

might as well hunt the rocks atop the bluffs, the boulders in

the passes. Might as well try an' shoot the moon from the

sky. You've seen the great lord of the high country and lived,

sir. You've been blessed and marked. If he'd wanted to kill

you, you'd be dead. The only trophy you're ever gonna take

from him, he already gave you." Jarlund pointed two fingers

at his own forehead, slashed them down his own face. "Try

for him again and he'll end you. Mark my words."

Modró had gone still. He didn't blink, but his face had

flushed, and there was something truly crazy in his flat eyes—

the drink bringing it out. Jarlund stared straight back at him.

Liz saw him scratch his back and loosen the dagger in its sheath.

And then Modró tipped his head back, adjusted the hunting

horn at his belt, and laughed.

It was a cruel and mirthless sound.

Modró stopped and looked at Jarlund.

Then he laughed again, louder still, pounding the table top

with his fist.

Then his face went blank, he drew a short dagger from his

boot, and spiked the center of Jarlund's forearm to the table faster than Liz could blink, the sound like a single chop in a wet log. Jarlund cried out, pulled back, but Modró kept his fist around the dagger's handle, took his gloves off the table, and slapped them hard across Jarlund's face. Liz stared, her heart in her throat. Modró's eyes were shiny coins, the scar across his face a white fissure. Liz could see the point of the blade through the bottom of the table. A single drop of blood clung to its tip. Jarlund moaned, his face pale. Liz was frozen in place, petrified.

Modró reached into one of his shirt pockets and pulled out something Liz couldn't see. He held it, pinched before him, like he was holding a tuft of air, then he set whatever it was on the table between them.

"Know what *that* is, old man?" Modró asked, tilting his head at the table. When he spoke, he didn't sound like the same man. The strange, foreign tone in his voice was so strong now that Liz had a hard time understanding him. Jarlund didn't respond. Modró slapped his gloves across Jarlund's face. Jarlund raised his eyes.

"Shall I tell you? It is the fur of a grey bear cub. I found it in the Hones' kitchen, stuck in a crack in the kitchen table while I supped. The whole hovel reeked of bear and rein-deer milk. They fed me stew with a touch of my own cubs in it. Grouse sure, in a broth of boiled *bear* bone. Can you believe such a thing? The finest grey stock on the mountain, finest blood in the Realm, and you ignorant peasants *eat* it. I understand. You have it all planned. You think that you know what my prize is worth to the right family. You think to transform your frozen pile of worthless shacks into some-thing grand, no? Look at me when I am talking to you, sir!" Modró slapped Jarlund across the face with his gloves. "You could have taken part in my vengeance, but now—I think *not*." He slapped him again. Jarlund moaned and tried to lift his chin. Liz could only see the side of Jarlund's face, but blood flecked his eyes, the iron studs of Modró's gloves. "I know at least one of my cubs still lives. Is that not true? How many still live? One or two? Or three?"

Jarlund shook his head. Modró tilted the dagger forward in Jarlund's arm.

Jarlund screamed.

Blood dripped under the table.

Modró screamed with him, screamed in his face like a madman.

Liz felt dizzy. Warm. The chest was getting hot.

Modró leaned back and took a deep breath.

"One or two or three?" he asked. His voice was calm once more, but his eyes flashed.

"One," Jarlund groaned. He sank into his chair.

"Good. I shall find it. There is no question of that. Do they hide it up there in their shack, old man? Where do they keep it? I thought for a moment that it might be down here."

"The mountain take your cursed hide, outlander," Jarlund said weakly. Then he lunged forward and spat into Modró's face.

Modró didn't wipe the bloody spittle from his beard. Instead, he tilted the dagger back and forth, back and forth, rocking it further into the wound. Jarlund screamed and reached for Modró's dagger. Modró slapped him three times, hard, with his gloves. The knuckles' iron slugs glimmered bloody.

"I do not think you understand my commitment," Modró said. "I do not think you understand what this is." He shook his head. "How could you? This is *real*. Near four decades

I've been on this cursed world—and I'll not stop now. Your 'mountain king' cannot save you. The cursed beast I seek is no spirit, no ghost. It is a great grey bear with a giant white mark on its chest, a mark that he passed in flesh and blood down to his three sons. And he is the key to my *true* retribution. My justice on the high family who summoned him. Now, where do they keep my cub?"

Modró made to tilt the dagger forward again, but Jarlund stopped him with a loud gasp. "It's gone!"

Modró looked straight at him. "Where?"

"Hone . . . he took it down to Korfort about two weeks or so past," Jarlund moaned. "Took the bear down to Korfort. It's gone."

"Why?"

"Sell it. They couldn't take coin for it . . . not up here at the village, too many rangers around. Couldn't go farther down to Adara's Hold neither. Too far down . . . . And they can't afford to raise it. Had to be Korfort."

"What of the other two cubs?"

"They was dead when they brought 'em back. I didn't see 'em but that's what he told me."

"The girl said her Father was 'at the village.' Are you suggesting that she lied? You suggest that her Father is *not* gone to the village? I doubt it. Unless she's an exceptional liar. I think *you* are lying, old man." Modró slapped him again with his gloves. "Are you lying?" He slapped him again. "Eh?" And again, harder still. Liz swallowed. The inside of the chest was stifling, really hot now. She was having a hard time breathing. It was as if the air in the chest had suddenly gone bad. And she was terrified. She wanted to help somehow, but what could she do? It was like her body was locked in stone. If she revealed herself, the madman would kill them both. She'd never been more certain of anything.

Jarlund shook his head and mumbled something. Modró slapped him again.

"Speak out, old man!"

". . . I ain't lyin'," Jarlund whispered. A thread of blood leaked from his broken lips.

Modró cocked his head, looked at him closely. Then he nodded. "Korfort is about two weeks away by foot, through the Trange."

Jarlund said nothing. Modró watched him for a long moment.

"I shall let you live, old man," Modró said finally. "I shall either meet Hone on his return from the village or on his return from Korfort. If you are lying—if Hone is indeed at the village—I shall come back tonight, belt your leg above the knee, and burn your leg to the leather before feeding you to my dogs. If he returns from Korfort—or if I find him there, or on the way back—you shall never see me again and I'll leave you in peace. I offer one last chance for the truth."

"It's true," Jarlund said thickly. "Hone's . . . down the mountain. He went to Korfort. Took the little bear . . . with him. Should be back any moment. But the bear cub . . . the little bear is gone."

"Very well," Modró said. He stood, pulled his dagger from Jarlund's arm, then lightly slapped him across the face with his gloves, almost playfully. Jarlund leaned back in his chair, gasping, like he would fall out of it. When Modró spoke next, his voice had changed again. Gone was any trace of his strange accent.

"Sure's good of you to feed me an' my animals, shepherd." Modró grinned. "You're good people up here. Fine people.

Next time I'm through, I'll stop by for 'nother drink, sure as it's winter."

Modró turned, put on his coat and gloves, took his horned helmet, and opened the door. Then he stopped and walked back to the table. "I'm gonna take another two of your reindeer with me. Take the coin I gave you outta your pocket."

Jarlund looked up at him.

"Take that coin out."

Jarlund's head bobbed. A line of blood ran down his temple and jaw.

Modró looked at him. "I need to take my gloves off again, old man?"

Jarlund leaned over, dug in his pocket, and placed a handful of copper suns on the table. His hands trembled.

"Lying thief," Jarlund muttered.

"Ha!" Modró snorted. "I ain't no 'thief,' fool! This is *my* property." He patted the pile of coins. "I never take what ain't mine, by *rights*. You think of a better 'right' than a blade? The strong take from the weak. The strong do what they want. Always been that way—always will be. Nature, my friend. That's all we have. Mine and yours. Scholars spend millennia trying to prove otherwise—'til a man with a sword teaches 'em the truth."

Modró swept the coins off the table into his hand, dumped them into his pouch. Then he turned without a word and left, leaving the front door swinging behind him.

48

LIZ WAITED IN the chest for a long moment, for what seemed like an eternity, before she dared move. The air in the cramped space was furnace-hot, suffocating. Her heart raced, she could barely breathe, and she was starting to feel numb.

"He's gone . . . he's gone," Jarlund muttered, almost to himself. When he wiped at his nose, his fingers came away bloody.

Liz opened the chest lid, took a breath of cool air, leapt over the chest's edge and ran to him. His face was puffy, streaked with blood. In one of his eyes, all the white was gone.

"Tried, Lizzy," he mumbled. "I tried."

"Let me bind this, you're bleeding," Liz said, looking at his arm, trying to be calm. But it was hard. She cast around, braid swinging, looking for a cloth she could use. And Father was where now? A day away, if he'd found a sled down in Korfort? *Too far.* She didn't know what to do.

"You've gotta stay here." Jarlund shook his head. "Pass me a rag from that drawer there. I can do it. Didn't cut nothing vital. Knew exactly where to hit."

He closed his eyes, then looked up at her. "He didn't believe me. He knows."

Liz stopped cold, her blood running to ice.

"What do you mean?" she asked. The nape of her neck snaked with frozen claws.

They were alone up here.

There was nobody else.

"He didn't believe me. He knows little Narmos is up there with your Mom and Teagan. He knows."

Her throat clenched.

Breathe! She swore at herself. *Think!*

Easier said than done.

He closed his eyes. "He's going back up there now, this moment. Sure of it. Just came down here to be certain we're alone."

"How can you know——?" Liz started, looked up toward home,

an unconscious gesture. She blinked. Then her body shook and her hand went automatically to her horn-handled knife.

Jarlund shook his head.

"You can't, Liz. He'll kill you. He's insane."

But Liz was already running, at and out the open door before she could even remember deciding, running up the shortcut path as fast as her legs could carry her.

49

SPEED. HER BRAID streaming flat behind her like a meteor's tail. Sprinting up the path. The fog hadn't cleared and she could barely see the way, but she didn't care. A tree flashed past, thorn slashing her cheek. Uphill was so much slower than coming down. But she held nothing back. Her lungs were on fire, her legs burned. She sprinted uphill, faster than she'd ever run in her life—and faster still. Jumping a downed tree, boot skidding on the ice-slick bark, and she almost went down, caught herself by some miracle and kept going, pushing harder.

A shrieking yelp tore the mountain's stillness.

A dog's scream.

Followed immediately by a single gunshot, far away—
echoing through the quiet—yet right there, as if the discharge
had taken place in front of her.

Then nothing but silence and dead fog.

50

SHE RAN PAST the skinning shed, still going as fast as she
could, but so tired now, slowing down, feeling like she was
running through water. Her legs ached, her throat was raw,
she could barely see. The shed's door was ajar. As she passed,
it opened slowly—then shut with a lifeless thump. The lock
had been broken, hanging mangled from a bent nail. As she
passed, the door creaked opened again, and the curing pelts
smiled at her with their lifeless eye slits. The wisdom of the
dead, quiet in the dark.

Up ahead, a noise from their house.

A low, throaty moan.

Liz broke through the trees into their clearing.

Into a nightmare.

51

LIZ TOOK IT all in at once, with perfect clarity. The glimmering shards of icicles hanging dagger-like from the porch edge. The piney smell of amber sap frozen in pine bark. And the blood—the red blood against the snow. Up in front of her, three paces in front of their porch, Liz saw Rosie—or what was left of her. The little hound's throat had been torn out; tattered flesh, brown fur. The snow a riot of bloody spatters. Rosie's eyes were wide open, her little pink tongue protruding slightly between soft teeth. Her black nose looked wet. Beside Rosie, Mother knelt on the ground. Her back was to Liz. She held Teagan in front of her, rocking, rocking slowly, kissing the top of his head, kissing his scar, her hand pressed against his chest. More blood. Blood welling between Mother's fingers. Teagan lying on his back, his legs straight in the snow, boots pointed outward slightly, like he was taking a nap. Mother kissing his forehead and whispering something. *How can there be so much blood?* Then Liz was at Mother's side. Teagan looked up at her. His eyelashes were caked with snowflakes, his eyes calm, slightly glazed. He clutched his axe in his right hand, the leather thong wrapped around his wrist, holding the axe like a talisman. The silver leaf on the handle shone, by some strange chance the only thing not smeared with gore.

". . . I did a good job." Teagan nodded at her, but it was as if he was talking to himself. "I know I'm . . . not smart like you, Lizzie, but I know I did right . . . . Even he'll have to see . . . . "

Liz grabbed Teagan's hand, squeezed it, looked around. Mother shuddered, pushing the spot high on the left side of Teagan's chest. The scar along Teagan's temple shone proudly in the cold. There were flecks of blood on his lips. Blood pulsed between Mother's fingers, a slow spring.

"Old Jarlund!" Liz made to stand. "He'll help!" She cast around, braid swinging, not knowing what she was looking for, but knowing she had to act, to go, to do . . . to do *something*. Mother looked at her and there was something in her eyes that stopped Liz cold. She dropped back to her knees.

Teagan smiled in that crooked way of his. "I can be . . . brave, too. He'll see it now, sure as it's . . . . I *know* he'll see I did a good job. I did right. We did good, didn't we Rosie sweetie girl? Good dog . . . . Brave Rosie, just like his dog was . . . . Brave like his dog Hunter was . . . ." Teagan looked up at her. His eyes seemed suddenly clear, as if focusing on her, and her alone. His voice was soft. "Thank you, Lizzy. Thank you for you, for so much everything."

And then he just stopped breathing. His eyes were open, slightly crossed; his lips slightly parted. But he just wasn't breathing. Mother groaned and folded over Teagan's chest. She clutched his jacket with bloody hands. Liz looked around. Blood everywhere. *I can't* . . . . Rosie's dark little eyes stared at her, her soft pink tongue paused in a hound's smile. Somewhere, a crow cawed. *Crow in winter.* Bad luck.

"He came so quiet," Mother moaned. "I couldn't . . . ."

But then there was something *else*.

A feeling behind Liz's heart.

A presence. An image.

Something *different*.

It was hard to understand, at first.

Liz wasn't crying anymore.

Or was she?

Had she been crying at all?

That clarity of vision was still with her, but it had somehow *sharpened*. She was desolate—her throat constricted, nose clogged, she was barely breathing—but she still saw everything with mineral precision. Yes, she was crying. But there was something else happening, too. Somewhere, somewhere down in her chest, beneath her heart, something seemed to open. The door was warm and dark and merciless. *You know me now, don't you, Elizabeth?* She looked around in the trampled, bloody snow. Unsteady. Dizzy. The innumerable paw prints made by a pack of black mastiffs. *You know me now.* The huge claws of the sad, albino bear. Boot prints, heel sharp edges. Blood. *You know me.* Her brother, standing with his small woodsman's axe in his hand, the axe Father had given him, the silver leaf shining on the handle, standing on the porch before their home, standing in front of the snow brooms and the traps on their hooks, protecting the door with his little axe and his little hound, two bright sparks set against a black surge of fangs and guns and savagery. She saw it happen. She saw his fear, his defiance, his courage, his certainty. She saw her brother and his little dog go down in a blinding rush of light and blood. Silver radiance devoured by darkness. And then the door in her heart opened and revealed a deeper hole, deeper and darker and ageless——an eternal place, as old as time itself. Something was crawling out of it. A shape. A presence. A person. Yes. And here it is. The thing from the hole looked just like her. It *was* her. But it was skinnier, lankier, whipcord muscle honed by hunger and rage, its eyes like lightless moons, eyes that saw everything—saw everything not as she *wanted* things to be, but as they *were*. And she knew the thing.

Knew it by name.

Fury, it was called.

And I will show you the way.

52

AFTER WHAT SEEMED like hours, Liz stood up and said tonelessly, "Shouldn't we cover them, Mother? Shouldn't we do something?"

"No," Mother said simply. And when she looked up at Liz, her eyes were hollow and wild, but Liz didn't look away. Instead, she stared down at her, as if seeing her clearly for the first time. Beauty and kindness and fear and frailty and sorrow and power—all of them lived in Mother's face. But Liz felt nothing. Nothing except a vague kind of sadness, a distant sadness, as if feeling it from the other side of the world. Liz stared back at her, and in the end it was Mother who looked away.

"We need to do something," Liz repeated.

"No." Mother cocked her head at the trail down to the village, not looking at Liz. "Because he'll be home soon." She nodded. "Tomorrow probably. Maybe today. And he's going to see this." She made a gesture at the clearing, the carnage, not looking at Liz. "He's going to see all of it. Exactly as it is. *Exactly* as it is, right here. I'll stand watch. Until he returns."

That was fair. Liz nodded and pushed her braid back behind her shoulder. "Where's Narmos?" she asked, already knowing the answer.

"Gone," Mother said, waving her hand loosely up at the clearing, at the big mountain; her eyes were haunted. "Taken. Reason he came back. The reason he came in the first place. And he will know that, too." Mother glanced down the trail toward the village, touched Teagan's smooth cheek. "He'll know his boy died protecting his home. His bear."

And then, dreamlike, Liz heard the high jingling of sleigh bells, turned to the trail—suddenly exhausted, so tired, tired deep in her bones—and saw four reindeer pulling a sled, the driver with his whip in front alongside Soldier, Evan and Father on the sled's back bench. Evan's smile dropping off his face the moment they came 'round the bend and saw the scene, Father's face going pale and rigid. Soldier and Father leaping from the sleigh in slow motion, the driver's eyes wide with bewilderment and dreadful curiosity, looking at the snow and the blood. Father there now, falling to his knees beside them, white knuckles gripping his walking stick like it would break. Gentle Soldier nosing little Rosie's savaged corpse, a weird sound coming from his mastiff throat. Evan coming up behind Father, confused and staring and casting about and finally looking to Liz, a million desperate questions on his face. Liz looked back at him and Evan must have seen something awful in her eyes because he looked away, falling to his knees beside Father, Mother, and Teagan.

"What——?" Evan began.

"You did this," Mother said plainly, holding Evan close to her, kissing his head, staring at Father. "You, Hone. *You*—— and nobody else. We trusted you. And see? See what we have?" Mother stroked Teagan's temple absently, brushing his bloody hair from his face—and Liz saw that her words cut

Father to the bone. He stared speechless at Teagan, at Mother, his face a mask of rage, confusion, sorrow; he seemed unsteady on his knees, wavering, squeezing his walking stick.

"Oh, what a man you are," Mother said, blinking up at him. "Thrice-cursed coward. Here we are, chasing your 'honest country life' and 'peace' . . . our lone boy and his dog defend your hearth and home. You're no man . . . ." She sobbed, her voice thick, and she folded again over Teagan's body, shuddering, her face hidden by her hair as she cradled his face in her hands. "You're not who I married," she whispered, her tears dropping onto Teagan's cheek. "You used to be . . . . Great Sisters save us, Hone—you *used* to be . . . . And now our boy is dead." Her back convulsed and she sobbed into Teagan's hair.

Liz stood there staring down at them, listening, recording it all, but it was like she watched the entire scene from another place.

Evan looked up at her again, his knees crunching in the snow, as if looking at her would help somehow. Liz looked back at him. She wanted to go to him, to hold him, to hold them all—but she couldn't. Her breath wouldn't come. She tried to swallow, but something caught in her throat. She kept seeing Teagan running across their clearing: nose up, furry cap near falling off, traps clanking, Rosie jumping at his heels, eyes sparkling, tongue lolling. Laughing and jumping up the steps.

This is happening now, the voice said. *This is true. You must not look away.*

Liz blinked and looked to the clearing. The path that Modró and his bear and his dogs had made up the slope to the tree line was clear in the snow. Yes. Oh yes.

On that path lies salvation.

She'd have to wait. But she knew where to go. In her mind's eye, she saw Modró twenty paces from her, her bow taut, her arrow's fletching rough against her fingers, a hungry arrow, ready for flight. She blinked. Father leaned forward, his weight on his walking stick, his arm around Mother's back. He whispered something to her. She shook her head. He closed his eyes, dropped his stick, his huge arms wide around them all. A single tear ran down the side of his nose. Liz had never seen him cry. That tear, the light in it—the reality of it.

Liz blinked again, staring. Who were they? *Who are these people?* Then, without thinking, she dropped to her knees beside them. Not because she wanted to, but because she had to. She could not do otherwise. Mother's weeping was low and primal; the ultimate grief. Father put his huge arms around her, pulling them into one mass. Liz's eyes went cloudy at last, and she let the pain come. She put her hand on Teagan's neck, feeling cold skin, feeling death. Evan was holding onto Teagan, squeezing his hunting cloak. And Father was squeezing them all, trembling. The tear dropped onto the back of Liz's leather mitten, the sound like a single drop of rain.

53

"EVAN," FATHER BEGAN after a long while, casting about in the snow, finding his stick, grunting to his feet. He cleared his throat. "You'll stay here with Mother and prepare the wood and the . . . prepare things. Liz will help me get ready to go out after this cursed butcher—."

"No," Mother said.

She said it calmly, the word like a knife.

He stared at her. His mouth closed with a click. Then he shook his head, his gaze going dark. "Every moment we wait, that murderer flees."

"You think I don't know that?" Her eyes blazed.

"I meant that——."

"No," Mother said calmly. "You will stay here. You will help prepare his wood. You will help clean his body. You will help wrap his limbs for his final journey. And you will sing the proper songs and send him into memory, as he deserves. You, Hone. *You.*" She cleared her throat, wiped her mouth with the back of her hand. Blood smeared her cheek. Her eyes flashed cold fire. "Our time in the highlands here, this 'work' of ours here hiding away on this mountain—it's tainted our minds, Hone. We might have escaped the Silver Court's lies, we might have learned to live without it, but all this," she gestured around at the cabin and clearing, "this is a lie, too. And all this quiet, all this peace, all this pretending has made us *soft*. And it's not just you. It's me, too. *My* heart. My spirit. And *I* let it happen—Great Sisters curse me. I let us play house on the edge of the world because I loved you and because I loved

Darro, too. And because I thought it might be best for them." She gestured at Evan and Liz. "But I let it happen. I let this happen."

She stopped, placed her palm gently over the arc of Teagan's forehead, closed her eyes. After a moment, she looked up into Father's face. "This boy—*our* boy—has bought a lesson with his life, Hone. A lesson for you and me. It's simple: The time of hiding, the time of lies—is *finished*. Hear me? When we've done proper rites for our boy, you'll swear me a blood oath in front of our children. Then you'll swear it again on your blade in the ancient way. And then you'll call on the Sisters for war and you'll bring me the bleached skulls of that murderer, his bear, and his dogs. You'll bring them to mount atop a silver spike over the ashes of my child. The *ancient* way, Hone. Not the mountain way. Not the way of the wild. The way of the Tarn. *Our* way."

She stared at him. Her eyes were hard diamonds, winter's light catching a blade's edge. Father looked at her for a long moment, then nodded.

Evan stared at Liz, as if to ask: "What is all this? Who are they?"

Liz stood up, took a step away from them all, and looked

back at Evan coolly. "They're liars," she said simply, answering his unasked question.

Mother and Father looked up at her, something in her tone startling them. Evan blinked.

"They're both liars." She looked at Evan with a mixture of exhaustion, pity, and grief. "And we don't know them."

Mother looked away, understanding what she meant. Father's eyes went black. Liz stared back at him defiantly, then she said: "Let's get on with this."

54

As a FAMILY, they stacked Teagan's wood, they washed his body, and they prepared him for the pyre. They didn't speak—at least not much—and Liz said not a word, Mother pausing now and then to give them quiet directions. When all was done, they laid him to rest atop the carefully piled wood. Father lifted Rosie to his side, placed Teagan's arm around her neck, black nose against his cheek.

He's so pale, Liz thought blankly. So pale. Like it wasn't even him. Like it was Teagan and not Teagan at the same time.

At the edge of the clearing, the rest of the hounds

whimpered. Even Soldier looked upset, looking from the pyre, to Father, to Mother, and then to the pyre again. Father caught her eye and Liz stared back at him, daring him to say a word. But he didn't drop his gaze, and she recognized something in his eyes. Something dark. Something true. He nodded slightly, still looking at her, and suddenly she felt tired.

Where was her fury now?

Where was that new dark voice?

Nowhere.

Only silence.

She just felt cold and hollow and utterly alone.

55

MOTHER WENT INSIDE. After a few moments she came back out. She was wearing the same clothes, but she'd fastened a silver amulet around her neck. Liz had never seen her wear it. It was round, made of the priceless high silver, and embossed with the Dallanar Sun. In Mother's right hand, she held a huge sword. It wasn't some random piece of local iron like you might see down in the village. It was a sword unlike any Liz had seen before. It was over fourteen palms long and curved, like a saber. Its pommel, shaped like a stylized bear's head, shone with silver light. The scabbard was made of soft hide, dyed deep blue.

And then Liz realized that she *had* seen a sword like this. Although the blade was made of the high silver and was much longer, the sword was almost exactly like the saber that the Tarn's ranger had carried.

Mother held the weapon out to Father, and he didn't hesitate. He took it below the hilt, holding it like a man trained and accustomed to its use.

Mother turned to the pyre. There, she kissed Teagan's forehead. Father stepped up and kissed Teagan's scar, his lips and beard hard against his son's temple, his eyes shut tight. They stepped back and away as Evan reached up, touched Teagan's hand, kissed it, then kissed little Rosie. Liz waited for a long moment, then she did the same, kissing Teagan on his bare forehead, as she'd seen Mother do. His skin was cold under her lips.

Father held the fire by his side, a smoking pine torch. He and Mother stepped together to the foot of the pyre.

Mother began to speak, but Liz didn't know the words.

That is to say: the language Mother spoke was a language Liz had never heard, not a dialect from the village or the trade roads. It was another language entirely, a musical language that seemed to come from the sky itself—a flowing speech that sounded of distant lands, timeless poetry, and ancient commands. An eternal language, a silver language, an ancient tongue born of sorrow and love, blood and joy. Father said a few words in the tongue as well, but not many. Mother reached down, took Liz's hand, held it tightly. Father took Evan's hand. Together, Mother and Father closed their eyes, stepped forward, tilted their heads back, and sang. It was a mourning song, a song of grief. But there was something else inside it, too—something powerful and sacred, something that rose from within them, lifting them up, setting them free, committing them to a path as timeless as the stars themselves.

56

THE FIRE TOOK immediately.

It burned quicker still.

And for the rest of her life, the smell of it was something

that Liz would never forget. Acrid, moist in your nose with a hint of soil and boiling lard, but not like cooking meat for a meal: a fog of humanity to it, so thick as to almost be a taste. And under it all, this weird, sulfurous scent, tinged with a musky sweetness. The smell of war and death. It was not the last time she would smell it.

57

"Evan," Mother said later, when all was done, when the pyre had become a charred mound of ash in front of them, "I want you to go down to old man Jarlund's, see how he's doing, and tell him what's happened. Then I want you to go down to the village and find Mr. Barnabus and Mr. Fonhammer. Send word from there for Mr. Tulf, too. Tell them what's happened, tell them we're meeting here at our cabin tomorrow night to plan our hunt. Tell them that we'll need every able body they can raise, including their sons. We'll gather here a bell before sunset. We'll have meat and drink for all. Father will lay out his plan then."

"Yes, ma'am," Evan said, glancing at Liz.

"Liz." Mother looked at her. "You'll help Father get ready."

"What will you do?" Liz asked tonelessly.

"Prepare the food and supplies." Mother glanced at Father. "While you prepare the weapons."

58

"COME WITH ME." Father turned, his huge saber in hand, and walked up the cabin's front steps to the door, leaning on his walking stick.

Liz followed.

Inside, Father made a cup of strong tea from the herbs that old man Jarlund had sent, drank it off in two giant swallows, then moved to the bedroom door, his walking stick thunking the floor. He took an iron key from his vest pocket, unlocked the door, and pushed it open. Liz looked past him.

A large bed covered with furry blankets, a pair of oil lamps resting on nightstands, and there to her left: a large, beautifully-made cabinet crafted from bone-colored wood. Each cabinet door was set with its own lock, but the middle doors were different: they were twice the size of the others and were held shut by an intricate silver mechanism of impossible delicacy. Father took another key from his pocket, this one on a chain made from the high silver, fit it into the lock, turned it five times. With each turn, a distinct click sounded inside the cabinet, a slight whirring as some elaborate apparatus unfastened. He withdrew the key, put it back in his pocket, and threw the doors wide.

At the center of the cabinet, a huge suit of high silver armor rested on a wooden stand, the armor crafted in the same style as Father's saber: fluid, interlocking plates fit seamlessly together, each unit part of a flawless set, each individual piece adorned with subtle contours that enhanced the suit's sense of flow and elegance. Above the armor rested a helmet of identical material and design, open-faced, with a visor that could be swiveled down to protect the mouth and nose, a flare at its rear to protect the nape of the neck. Father's mandolin hung below the helmet, gathering dust.

Directly behind the high silver armor hung an elaborate tapestry made from some kind of silk. It looked old, but well cared for. At the center of the tapestry was a large Dallanar Sun, a formalized silver star with six radiating points and a single inverted tear at its center. At the end of each of the

Sun's points, woven into the tapestry's silk, there was a large tondo. At the center of each tondo was a life-sized portrait bust. The basic composition looked like this:

"The High Seal," Father said, noticing Liz's gaze. "Acasius's Star. The Dallanar family sigil. The royal crest to which House Hone has sworn allegiance for generations."

"House Hone?" Liz asked.

Father gave her a look, but didn't respond. Instead, he turned away, walking stick thunking the plank floor, and stepped to the armor. The war gear was clearly his, Liz realized. Who else could fit in such a massive suit of armor?

Clearly, it had been made for a bear of a man. The high silver, priceless and ancient. And hidden, all these years, in her parents' bedroom. One more lie upon hundreds.

Father looked at the armor for a long moment, then looked at the tapestry behind it. Liz pushed her braid over her shoulder. She'd seen a similar design in a book old Jarlund had shown her some time ago, and she remembered perfectly the names and positions of all the characters.

The tondo at the top of the Sun was the largest of the six; it held a likeness of the First King, Acasius Dallanar. The King was shown full-faced and gloomy, his eyes downcast. In a floating hand, he held his token: a silver cup. To Acasius's proper right, the next tondo held a portrait of the First Great Sister, Eressa the Lost. Her eyes were dark, gorgeous, and wise. Her finely-boned face was shown in profile as she gazed away from the sigil's center toward her token: a silver tear. The Second Great Sister, Alea the True, came next. Alea's was an unhappy face, her picture set at three-quarter profile. Liz could see a deep scar slashing across her left cheek. Alea looked to her left, where her token—a silver sword—filled the rest of her tondo. The portrait of Aaryn the Chronicler, the Third Great Sister, was at the bottom of the crest. Like her brother Acasius above her, her portrait was shown full-faced. Her eyes were filled with playful delight. She held her token—a silver book—in a disembodied hand; she seemed to be reciting from it, her mouth shown slightly open. Next came the Fourth Great Sister, Kora the Just. Her face was shown in three-quarter profile. Her features were thin and hard, but her gaze was kind. In a floating hand, she held her token: a set of silver scales, shown steady and in perfect equilibrium. Finally, coming all the way 'round to Acasius's left, was the Fifth Sister, Margo the Gentle. She was a happy girl with bright eyes and huge dimples. She was shown in perfect profile, her token beside her face: a silver cornucopia. Her eyes shone mysteriously.

"Here." Father cleared his throat. He reached into the cabinet, down beside his armor, and lifted a huge leather bandolier from inside. A short leather scabbard hung from it, a curved dagger sheathed within. Father unclipped the blade and drew it, high silver catching the window's sun, flashing the shadows. Father turned the blade in the light, holding it up in front of him.

"The high silver," he said. "Ancient, true, indestructible."

The dagger's pommel was a heavy, blunt lozenge. Perfect, Liz supposed, for crushing a man's skull.

Father nodded. "This weapon has been in our house since the time of Hakon, over nine hundred years past. The handle and wrap have been replaced countless times, the last by me." He frowned. "But the blade and body are the same as they ever were. Over ten thousand years old, a relic from the Founding. The most ancient times."

He slid the dagger back into the scabbard and clipped the leather catch-strap over its hilt. Then he unfastened the scabbard from the bandolier, handed the sheathed weapon to Liz. She took it.

"Fasten it beside your knife there," he said. "Test the draw and the weight when you have a moment."

Liz looked him in the eye—then held out the dagger and deliberately dropped it to the floor.

Father stared at her, then looked at the dagger where it lay, a strange mix of anger and surprise flashing across his face, quickly suppressed.

"I'll hunt Modró with you," she said. "I'll help you find him. But I'm not going to forget." She looked at the armor, the helmet, the tapestry. "This changes nothing."

He looked at her then, and the darkness in his gaze—that true darkness, that honest darkness, the darkness she recognized—shut her mouth.

He bent to his good knee with a grunt, retrieved the dagger where it lay, leaning hard on his walking stick.

"I don't expect this to change anything." He held the sheathed blade against his chest and looked her in the eye. "I do expect you to use this weapon as I've taught you—with courage and cunning against the enemies of this house. If you can't do that, if you want some time alone to pout while your brother's killer rides our land, then I'll give it to Evan."

He said this without malice, but his eyes were hard and merciless.

And true.

Liz almost looked away. But she didn't. Instead, she gazed at him for a moment, then nodded and reached for the blade, but he shook his head, holding the dagger close. His gaze was penetrating.

"I won't tell you that you should get accustomed to people dying, Liz. That this is supposed to be easy. I never got used to it. Don't want to; hope I never will. I saw many good soldiers killed during my service. More than I can count. Heroes, warriors, cowards, and fools. All types. Whether it was one of my men or many, it cut a hole through me. But I never wanted to forget. I never wanted to tuck it away. The scars we carry—in the flesh, in the soul—they're records. But when the scar comes from the death of a brother, from family, it's different. The scar becomes a testament. To friendship, to love. If the scar is deep, then so was the love. That simple. We'll both live with this 'til we die. But we must live with it." He cleared his throat. "And we must do right by his memory."

Liz's eyes narrowed. "So you care about him again now, eh? All these wise words? Couldn't spare him a drunken grunt for the Sisters know how long. Now a lecture with these fancy ideas of yours? You're a *liar*. Both of you. You don't have any right to teach me anything."

He looked at her for a moment, jaw clenched. The darkness flickered in his eyes, barely contained. But there was a touch of weariness, too.

She sensed her advantage and followed up ruthlessly. "What're you going to do? Put on your shiny armor, fix your little flask, and go back to your drink in the forest? That how you'll do right by his memory?"

He looked at her, something insane beginning to spin in his eyes.

She stared right back at him, daring him to say something, daring him to do anything.

But then he took a deep breath——and grinned at her.

It was the smile of a feral wolf.

And it was real.

He inclined his head. "You've got your Mother's wits and mettle. And my appetite for violence. And you're right to speak as you do. But you're wrong about what I can teach you."

She stared at him, chin up, defiant.

He inclined his head. "You don't know how to kill——I do."

She scoffed, but it was forced. He had her attention.

"Laugh all you like. But my skills are real. And useful. Especially to a young woman set on avenging her brother's murder, on saving the life of her stolen war bear."

That stopped her.

She blinked. Felt her hands in Narmos's thick fur. Looked into the little bear's soulful grey eyes. Saw Teagan.

Father took the opportunity to hold forth the sheathed dagger, handle first, standing straight, his posture almost ceremonial, some old military habit, she supposed, coming back to the fore.

She considered the dagger for a moment. Then she took it, looking him in the eye. He nodded, and she felt like she had won the exchange—but somehow had lost it, too. Regardless, she immediately threaded the new scabbard onto her belt, pushing it down above her horn-handled knife. She slipped the leather catch-strap off the hilt and drew the high silver blade a couple times, testing the weapon's balance and weight. It was light, diamond sharp, utterly lethal. It seemed made for her hand.

The blade felt good.

And then—in spite of her anger, in spite of her sadness—Liz smiled.

59

THE NEXT EVENING, a bell before sunset, a group of locals, village men, and other freeholders arrived at their clearing. Liz was sweeping the porch as they arrived; Mother was busy inside, getting the food together. Evan was still out, spreading the news. The twilight sky was clear and windless. The trees did not stir.

They showed up individually and in clumps, fur-clad, armed, a few rock mastiffs here and there, trickling in at first, then filling the bottom of the clearing, talking, milling around, lanterns clinking, wondering what was really going on. Most of them Liz knew. Others she'd seen around. Men of all sorts, villagers, trappers, herders, sledders, hunters, even a few old Konungur highlanders down from the upper range who used the village as their base. Evan had done a good job getting the word out.

"Hone ain't never asked me for nothing," Liz heard someone say. "Gotta be real trouble, like his boy done said," came a gruff answer. "Lost a hound a week ago, all torn up. Maybe has something to do with it? Didn't look like no wolf, tell you that."

Mr. Barnabus and his two sons, Belios and Beiro, came in on an old sled pulled by four reindeer, their hounds panting behind them. The two boys were a couple years older than Liz and had been friends of theirs a long time. Teagan and Evan used to tease her about Belios—but that seemed like years ago, now. They waved to her as they slid in, sled runners hissing the snow. Liz raised her hand in return. Mr. Tulf had hiked over from the other side of the valley on his snowshoes, long carbine slung over his shoulder, big wolf cloak the same color as his grey beard. He stood there, thumb in his belt, his face cold and blank.

Evan, old man Jarlund, and Mr. Fonhammer were the last to arrive. Fonhammer brought his son, Jurek, with him, and his two daughters, Ansa and Inari, all of them armed and rough-looking, the girls meaner than their brother, wearing hunting leathers and mountain gear. Jarlund had a thick bandage wrapped around his forearm. His eyes were grim as he talked to Evan and Fonhammer.

All told, the entire posse was a little over three dozen strong.

The front door opened and Father came out, Soldier at his heel. Liz put down her broom and stepped aside. Father didn't carry his saber. He was leaning heavily on his walking stick; it thunked against the porch planks. All the murmuring and muttering ceased. Father stepped to the edge of the porch, looked out over the crowd. Soldier sat without command at his side. In the west, the sun fell toward the far mountains. Father didn't waste any time.

"My thanks for coming out." Father inclined his head. "Means much to me and my family." His voice was deep and resonant, totally commanding. He was a big man, no doubt. But standing there like that, he seemed bigger than ever. Imposing. Huge. All eyes were on him. No one stirred. And Liz was again startled by the power of his voice. It wasn't the words, but the *way* he spoke them. There was something in his tone that itself seemed to compel belief. She could feel it pulling on her, even those first couple phrases. She realized that she somehow *wanted* to hear more. His sentences—simple, direct, and honest—came from the big mountain, no doubt. But his tenor—his power—was of another place.

"You might've heard what's happened up here from my son." Father inclined his head toward Evan, who looked back at him. Everyone nodded, the whole crowd mumbling assent. Then Father pointed to the black pile that had been Teagan's pyre. "Outlander came up here yesterday on a white bear, killed my boy and his dog. Been on my land—on all our lands, I suspect—for some time. Killed a grey bear for sport, took her paws near my northern line, left her cubs to starve. Heard from Jarlund this man's up here trying to kill a big grey. Thinks it's the 'Mountain King.' Got a grudge against the Tarn. Some kind of lunatic. Rangers been up here looking for him, too."

Murmurs. Tulf had a strange look on his face.

Father held up his hand for silence.

"This is what I want: I want your help finding him—finding him before the Tarn does. Rangers find him, they're gonna want to take him down off the mountain. Face justice down there. I say he needs to face *our* justice. Mountain justice, up here. I need your help."

He let that sink in for a moment, then continued. "Those people down there—with their finery, their fancy food, their scheming, their silly wars—they got nothing to do with us up here. And that's what this is about. Outlander comes up here and steals our property, kills our people, and they'll want to take him down there and put him in one of their jails for a while. I want to take care of him the old way. The mountain way."

They were all nodding. And Liz realized that she was nodding, too. Her hand rested upon the cross-slung pommel of her new blade. She liked how it felt, standing up here on the porch beside him, all eyes on them, ready to follow Father's command. *Ready to hunt.*

"Here's what I propose: Day after tomorrow at dawn, after we get our supplies and gear together, we break into four groups. Barnabus, Tulf, Fonhammer, and myself. We'll each take about ten or so men out in each direction, use the young ones as runners, get a couple of good sleds and some fast dogs to keep connected, keep aware. And then we hunt this man down, bring him here." He pointed at the ash pile. "Show him and his bear and his cursed dogs the mountain's justice."

"That sounds right," someone said.

Muttered assent rippled through the crowd.

"We're with you, Hone." Tulf nodded with no expression, leaning on his carbine from his place at the edge of the gathering. "Probably only take four, three guys—my guys—

with me, though." His voice was calm, utterly impassive. But there was something in his eyes Liz didn't like.

Father nodded.

"Ain't gonna let the Tarn's fools take him down there, Hone." Barnabus spat. "Are we boys?" Belios and Beiro shook their heads, puffing out their chests. Belios looked to Liz for approval. She gave him a hint of a smile for his trouble, and he nodded back at her, all manly.

"With you, Hone!" someone yelled in the back. Lots of nods and mumblings about fool outlanders and damned rangers up here poking into law-abiding people's business. "Cursed Tarn," someone muttered. But everyone was in agreement.

"Alright," Father said. "I've got some food and drink here for you all. Thought it best if we could break into those teams right here and now, get organized. About ten men per team should do it—save Tulf's crew, who he'll pick himself, eh?" Across the clearing, Tulf inclined his head.

Mother opened the cabin door. She carried out a folding table and set it against the back wall of the porch. Went back inside and brought out a clay stand and a huge pot of stew.

There were two more giant pots cooking in on the stove.

"More's coming," she said to Father. She turned to Liz. "Help me with the bowls and cups."

"Kill me some foreigner," a young voice said somewhere.

Liz nodded at the sentiment as she stepped into the cabin— but then she frowned.

Despite all of Mother and Father's impressive words, despite all the fancy talk, when you came right down to it, there didn't seem to be any real difference between "the mountain way" and "the way of the Tarn."

For both of them, justice was vengeance.

60

BUT LATER THAT night, long after the planning was done, long after all the locals had left, another group of people arrived in the clearing that made Liz reconsider the thought.

They were unusual people.

Although "unusual" might not have been the right word, Liz later considered.

Yet in that moment, it was the best she could offer.

61

"Ho there!" A mighty baritone called across the clearing, echoing across the snow. The voice was deep, grinding like boulders beneath the mountain's roots. "Ho there! In the freehold!"

Father and Mother looked up from their discussion at the kitchen table. They'd been talking about the supplies and logistics of the coming hunt. Evan had crawled up to bed a bit before, but Liz was still up, absently working with Soldier by the fire, reciting a few of his basic commands, rewarding him with scraps of cold grouse. She missed Teagan. She missed Rosie. And she missed Narmos. She kept seeing them, all of them, like they were right there in front of her, playing at the fire. Through her shirt, she touched the pendant Father had made of Narmos's weird claw.

And then that strange, deep voice came again from across the clearing. Liz and Soldier looked up. Soldier growled. Father scraped back his chair and picked up his saber, holding it sheathed below the handguard.

"Your freehold is getting busy, Hone," Mother said.

Father grunted something that was both affirmative and

a bit apologetic. He downed his tea, patted at his vest like he was looking for his flask, and stepped to the door with a lantern. He didn't take his walking stick.

"Might as well come along, Lizzy," he said, reaching for the latch. "You'll eavesdrop anyway." Out of habit, Liz looked at Mother. Mother nodded, stood, kissed Liz on the forehead, turned her back on the door, and began straightening up.

"Want to come?" Father asked Mother. He was still waiting to open the door, testing his weight on his leg, as if building his courage to walk without his stick.

"I know who it is." Mother shook her head. "And I know exactly what they want."

62

OUTSIDE, ACROSS THE clearing, a massive man wearing furs and leathers waited beside the carved prow of what looked like . . . well, a small, silver *ship*. The ship floated about a pace above the snowy ground, rope ladders dangling from its sides. Its prow was carved as the head of a roaring silver lion. Its crew, wearing royal blue uniforms, were busy roping it closer to the earth, going about their business with smart proficiency, as if it was the most normal thing in the world. Three silver-white rudders swung from the ship's stern, but they weren't really "rudders"—they were much larger, more like sails. As Liz watched, one of the crew touched something at the ship's stern and the sails immediately pleated themselves away, a paper-folding trick. Tiny glowing orbs, blue and effervescent, floated around the ship's rigging and tackle, dancing like sapphire fireflies.

A dwarf with purple skin was hammering an iron tethering spike into the snow with a mallet—CHOCK! CHOCK! CHOCK!—grumbling about something, talking to himself. Other crew members did the same elsewhere. A little blue dragon sat on the purple dwarf's shoulder. Liz blinked. The dragon's head and neck bobbed with each mallet strike, but it held its little body level and steady, not leaving the dwarf's shoulder, tiny claws sunk into the dwarf's cloak. Above the ship, bound to it by a complex web of pulleys and gears and ropes and harnesses, a zeppelin-like creature floated in the moonlight, a glowing lozenge of pulsing luminescence. Liz had seen messenger zeppelins in Korfort before, but this was something different altogether. Bigger, stranger, cooing softly, the noise like a magical flute . . . . One of the crew members was talking to the blimpy thing, loosening the straps around it, touching it gently. The zeppelin's surface was taut, but it also seemed delicate and fragile, a glowing skin of translucent wonder that carried its own light. The sapphire fireflies danced.

On the front porch, Father raised his saber in silent acknowledgement. The huge fur-clad man raised his hand in return and began crossing the clearing.

But it wasn't a man, Liz realized.

Or, if it was, it was the largest and strangest man Liz had ever seen.

While the giant man had seemed huge from across the clearing, as he approached he became larger still. *Enormous.* Fully twice Father's height and width. Not a man at all—an ogre. His head was massive, and, as he approached, he pulled off a leather cap to reveal a bald skull, careful-ly shaved. He had clean grey skin. A pair of giant goggles swung from his colossal fist. Liz swore that she could feel the ground tremble as he walked. He wore a gigantic vest of fur and leather, and a broad leather belt. A dagger that would've served an average man as a sword hung at his hip. His leather boots were huge, almost ludicrous in their size. *Who's your cobbler, sir?* Liz thought randomly, staring at the massive footprints in the snow. Behind the ogre, back by the silver ship, the purple dwarf muttered some kind of curse. The little blue dragon nodded and squeaked angrily. A slender young man of eighteen years, or thereabouts, appeared near the ship's prow, dressed in flowing robes of yellow wool. He said a couple of words to the dwarf that Liz couldn't fully hear, something about the ground being frozen. The dwarf promptly fired back something in a language Liz didn't understand. The little blue dragon hissed from his shoulder. The dwarf gave the iron tether spike a final CHOCK! with his hammer. The young man in yellow reached up and stroked the zeppelin. It pulsed brightly at his touch, its tender skin shivering.

The ogre was at their front porch now. He took a knee in front of Father, his huge boots crunching the snow. Then he bowed—low, with complete deference—and said in his deep voice: "High General."

Liz looked from the ogre to Father.

High General.

Her mouth started to open.

"Captain," Father nodded, as if receiving this most profound of salutes from the hulking creature was nothing more than his due. "Long time."

The ogre paused a moment, blinking, as if considering his words carefully. Then he inclined his head and revealed a mouth of gnarly white fangs. "Too long, my Lord." He grunted to his feet, blocking out the mountain, and glanced at Liz expectantly. Around his neck, he wore a large silver amulet. The pendant was a stylized silver sword suspended in a globe of sapphire.

Father turned and gestured to Liz. "Captain Fellen Colj of Jallow, this is my daughter, Elizabeth Hone."

The ogre paused again, blinking. Then he bowed deeply, with something like reverence. "I am honored, my Lady." His voice was deep, rumbling as if it came from a vast cave.

By some miracle, Liz remembered her manners. "The pleasure is mine, sir." She bowed.

The ogre captain paused and inclined his head. He turned slowly to look at Father. "The young lady has the look of her

Mother." Another pause. "Although quite a bit taller."

Liz stared. Father's eyes shone with pride . . . and a touch of amusement.

"Alright already," a voice muttered from behind the ogre. "He's right here. Hold on! He's right *here*! Great Sisters *save* us!" These words were followed by a happy little dragon squeak. It was the purple dwarf and his little dragon, walking in the footsteps of the giant ogre captain. And behind them came the slender man in yellow. Behind him, a smaller figure, clearly a young woman, wearing a frost-colored cloak trimmed with light grey fur. Liz couldn't see her face.

The dwarf stepped around Captain Colj, took a knee in the snow.

"High General." He bowed his head.

"Master Zar." Father nodded. Then he held out his arm to the little dragon, like summoning a hawk to its perch. "Still hanging about this old vagabond, Gregory?"

The little dragon—Gregory—squeaked, nuzzled the dwarf's ear for a moment, then jumped lightly to Father's raised forearm. He had milky yellow eyes, a marked contrast to his faded blue scales. He seemed to be missing most of his teeth; Liz could see only two. Gregory hissed, chirped, and cocked his head at Father, tasting the air with his broad tongue. Father nodded back to him, as if he was quite interested in what the little dragon was saying.

The purple dwarf, Master Zar, growled, rubbing his purple head. He was mostly bald, and shaved the remaining hair he did have. A large white tattoo—the Dallanar Sun—had been inked into the center of his forehead. "Whelp spent the entire trip complaining about the food. Spoiled brat is what he is."

"And whose fault's that?" Father grinned, stroking the little dragon's crest fondly. The dragon purred and pushed his head into Father's hand. Liz suddenly wanted to pet it—but she wasn't sure of the etiquette.

After a giant and his crew lands at your clearing in a floating silver ship, do you need permission to touch the purple dwarf's dragon?

Master Zar grunted. The dwarf was about a pace and a half tall, and about a pace wide. He wore a light cloak slung loosely over one shoulder and seemed invigorated by the cold. His skin was purple, his eyes violet and deeply set beneath bushy purple brows. He wore fingerless leather gloves and iron-shod boots. A silver clasp, shaped like a book, held his cloak.

A fat revolver of high silver hung beneath his left arm, the worn grip just visible.

"How's the knee?" Master Zar raised an eyebrow, looking at Father's right leg skeptically.

"Been worse," Father said. But from his posture, Liz could tell that he was doing everything he could to stand like his leg wasn't killing him.

Captain Colj cleared his throat, paused thoughtfully, then turned to the yellow-clad young man and the girl who had followed him. "General Hone, allow me to introduce you to our arbiter, Nivar xen Varren, of Targus. And here, our seer, Sister Darian Faer, of Anótos." As he said this, the ogre gestured formally to the slender young man and the grey-robed girl, respectively. Father nodded to both. They stepped forward and bowed before him.

The young man, Nivar, was slender, almost willowy . . . and *very* handsome. In fact, it was all Liz could do to keep from gawking. Slightly horrified, she lifted her chin and glanced past him to the glowing zeppelin. And then back. It was no use. He was just too beautiful. He wore layers of golden-yellow robes. A thick yellow cloak, hemmed with embroidered seams, graced his shoulders. Each of his long fingers was careful-ly wrapped in yellow-colored bands, leaving only his fingertips exposed. His skin was a light tan, his ears long and just slightly tapered at their tips. He had a full mouth, a small nose, and a broad forehead. His eyes were brilliantly green with yellow glints. Thick eyelashes. He might have been the best looking young man Liz had ever seen. *Certainly leaves poor Belios in the dust.* As he stepped forward to bow before Father, Liz noticed that he wore a pair of curved daggers on a slender belt, each high silver pommel inscribed with a miniature set of balancing scales.

The young woman behind him, Darian, stepped forward and pushed her hood away from her face to reveal delicate, elfin features, dark brown skin, and eyes unlike any that Liz had ever seen: fairylike and breathtaking—large, widely spaced, with irises the color of silver moons. She did not have pupils, at least none that Liz could see. On a thin chain, she wore a silver pendant the shape of an inverted tear, pierced through the point. Her white robe was heavy, the edges wrapped with thick grey sable. Liz couldn't tell her age, but felt she must be in her middle teens, at least. About the same age as Liz herself, perhaps.

Father bowed to the two youngsters, acknowledging their salutations. Still petting Gregory, he asked the robed girl, "Sister Darian, might your father be the High Seer of Anótos, Doron Faer?"

"The same, my Lord." Sister Darian inclined her head. Her voice was gentle, an otherworldly breeze. She did not blink. Her huge eyes were wide and penetrating.

Father nodded, looked up at the huge Captain Colj, then down at the stocky Master Zar. "And Arbiter Nivar here is most definitely the son of Varren xen Cenoren, the Grand Master of Assassins of House Targon."

The yellow-robed young man, Nivar, bowed deeply, but said nothing. Liz realized that she was trying to catch his eye, unconsciously. She cleared her throat and looked away. She was the daughter of a "High General," after all. She had her family pride.

Father cocked his head. "The assassins of Targus are few . . . but those we do have are sufficient." He said the words as if they had special meaning. Whatever it was, Liz didn't understand it. Again, Nivar bowed with the utmost respect.

Behind them all, on the other side of the clearing, the ship's crew had finished their work. The sapphire fireflies winked and bobbed. Freed from its tack and harness, the glowing zeppelin flickered and throbbed, an unearthly whistling fluting through the trees, a thousand different shades of silver and gold glimmering beneath its luminous skin, a lightning storm in a bottle as it floated up and away from the silver ship, orbiting the clearing, long translucent fronds of light—like tentacles or tubes—peeling away from its underside as it pulsed and swelled, tooting and singing to the mountain and woods. Then it began tugging at a treetop with its arms, pulling at small branches, shaking off the snow, pushing the branches into a small, dilating orifice—its mouth—at the front of its body.

Father had stopped petting Gregory; his eyes were grim. He looked at Captain Colj, then glanced at Master Zar. "Dorómy sends two of my oldest friends, pulls them from their homes and duties, accompanies them with the children of two of my most trusted allies. What am I to make of this?" He asked the question like he already knew the answer.

Captain Colj looked at Father for a long moment, as if carefully assessing Father's words. At last he nodded. "Lord

Dorómy will arrive tomorrow, High General. The day after, at latest. We were sent to guarantee your compliance."

Father raised an eyebrow, waiting for the rest of it. Master Zar lifted his purple arm in Gregory's direction. The little dragon flew from Father, landed on the dwarf's wrist. Master Zar stroked the dragon's faded blue crest, looked Father in the eye. "Dorómy wants your help tracking his daughter's killer, General. He wants the man. That's it." But then Zar looked away, as if uncomfortable with his own words, and rubbed the Dallanar crest on his forehead.

Father gestured to the floating zeppelin, to the silver ship, to Captain Colj and his team. "Seems a rather extravagant way to ask for an easy favor. What reason could a High Lord of Remain—the Silver King's own brother, no less—have to doubt my obedience?"

Master Zar's eyes flickered with a knowing mix of displeasure and sympathy.

Captain Colj paused, made as if to speak, then glanced at Sister Darian.

"We have seen your son's death, my Lord," Darian said, her large eyes wide. Her voice was soft and lilting, ethereal.

"High Lord Dorómy knows your pain."

But Father was already looking back at Captain Colj.

"In other words . . . ." Father's eyes flashed. "Dorómy wants Modró's head. Before I take it. He claims vengeance."

"*Justice*, my Lord General," Nivar said, looking at Father directly, his fingers steepled loosely in front of him. His voice was an easy tenor, with an accent that Liz had never heard. "As is his right and duty. Lord Dorómy will do much for the sake of peace. And while justice is more important than peace—peace is made by justice."

Master Zar scowled at Nivar's sophistry. Captain Colj inclined his head, as if giving full consideration to the young man's words.

But Father just laughed. "I won't argue philosophy with you, arbiter—I know your father too well. But I will tell you this." He gestured at the big mountain and his voice seemed to change, to deepen, to become more powerful. "Out here, things are different. Simpler. All the theorizing in the world won't change that fact. And it won't change this: Modró murdered my son, on my land, at my home. The right to justice is mine. And I *will* have it."

Captain Colj frowned. Master Zar shook his head knowingly, as if all his suspicions had been confirmed. Sister Darian stared at Father, her strange eyes seeing all.

Nivar made to speak again, but Father stopped him with a raised hand. Then he turned, looking pointedly into Sister Darian's eyes. But when he spoke, it was as if he spoke to someone else. "If you wanted full authority over such matters, you should never have given up the throne, my Lord. This is my land." He pointed at Teagan's pyre, the dark pile of ash, still not taking his eyes from Darian's. "That was my boy. And the right to 'justice'—such as it is—is just as much mine as yours. I appreciate your loss, and I'll most certainly hand the man over to you—after I'm done with him."

Darian did not respond. Her eyes were wide. It was as if she was seeing for someone else.

"We appreciate your position, High General." Nivar inclined his head, fingers steepled before his chest. "We do have our orders, however."

Father's gaze went dark. Liz knew the look well. He still stared directly into Sister Darian's eyes. "And how does High Lord Dorómy Dallanar instruct you to guarantee my 'compliance'?"

And then Father shifted his saber to his other hand.

It was a simple gesture, an unconscious one, but the effect was immediate.

Captain Colj's frown deepened and he took a single step, pivoting his huge body slightly. Master Zar sighed, held his ground, but looked away to the mountain, shaking his purple head with something like exasperation, stroking little Gregory, rubbing his forehead. Nivar cocked his head slightly and came up on the balls of his feet, wrapped hands dropping to his sides—but the blood had drained from his handsome face. Sister Darian stared back at Father, her huge silvery eyes tunneling through space and memory.

Liz was suddenly struck by a new certainty: Father scared these people.

It was true.

However big, or strong, or smart, or cunning, or strange they were, these strange visitors were nothing to him. Even with his age and his bad leg—the visitors were afraid of him. *They* were afraid of *him*. These strange people, from who knows where, were scared of a drunken trapper on the edge of the wild? *But that's not who he is.* He could kill them. He'd done it hundreds of times before. *And he's good at it.* "You don't know how to kill," Father had told her. "I do." And once again Liz realized that she didn't know him. That she'd never known him, really. She looked again at the strange visitors. The air seemed charged with threat.

Then Master Zar cleared his throat and lifted Gregory slightly. "I think maybe we should eat some dinner? He's hungry. You can argue with Dorómy about who gets to kill who when he arrives."

Little Gregory squeaked something like affirmation. Captain Colj shook his head. Nivar seemed to relax, but only a little. He seemed to be holding his breath, his entire body on edge. Sister Darian continued to stare into Father's face. Father stared back at them all, not giving an inch. His knuckles flexed around his blade's scabbard.

"May we offer you food and drink, then?" Liz said clearly, out of nowhere. She lifted her chin and pushed her blond braid over her shoulder. If there was one thing that couldn't change on the big mountain, it was hospitality. And she realized that it was her place—and her duty—to ask.

Father glanced at her sharply, then his gaze softened, something strange coming into his eyes. *Gratitude?* He nodded and sighed. "Indeed," he said to his guests. "My home will always be open to you and your families. All of you."

Master Zar shook his head and grinned; he had thick white teeth, like a donkey's. Then he glanced at Liz, his purple eyes glittering with intelligence, gave her a thankful nod. Sister Darian blinked quickly, her huge eyes refocusing, and then she smiled. Nivar looked from her to Father with undisguised relief. The ogre captain paused, cocked his head as if considering, and then grinned, showing his huge fangs. "See?" The ogre clapped the yellow-robed young man on the shoulder, nearly knocking him flat into the snow. "Nothing to worry about."

Zar turned to Gregory, stroked the little dragon's faded blue crest, and in a mushy baby-voice said: "Told you he'd remember you. And what you like to eat."

Little Gregory squeaked hoarsely and promptly nipped at Zar's fat purple finger, as if the food couldn't come fast enough.

63

LIZ WENT INTO the house to fetch tables, chairs, food, and drink. The Great Sisters themselves couldn't have devised a way to fit the mighty Colj inside their front door, much less at their kitchen table. Nivar and Darian helped. Mother had already gone to sleep; the bedroom door was shut. In the loft, Evan snored away.

They ate together outside like old friends, beneath the quiet stars. The mountain was huge and clear above them, the moon just beginning to rise. Across the way, the glowing zeppelin was settling back into its harness after eating half the clearing's treetops. Its glowing tentacles drooped straight toward the ground. Its pulsing, floating movements seemed sluggish, almost sleepy. As it settled above the silver ship, a trio of crew members murmured to it kindly, sapphire fire-flies stirring as they threw a set of light silk ropes over its front, center, and rear. *So it doesn't float away after its meal*, Liz marveled. But that wasn't right, she realized. The crew then used these ropes to hoist a set of wide, silky sheets over the thing. Tucking it in for the night. Liz smiled. With a fluting quiver, the zeppelin nestled down beneath its blankets.

The dinner conversation went entirely over her head.

They didn't discuss the dead ranger, the killer Modró, what had happened to Teagan—any of that.

Instead, Captain Colj and Master Zar spent the entire time recounting old stories with Father. Liz listened to every word, but the names, the lords, the ladies, the gossip, the battles, the allies, the enemies, the triumphs, the losses—all belonged to some other world altogether. So she just tried to keep the plates full—the little dragon, Gregory, seemed able to eat more than the ogre, Colj—to keep her mouth shut, to keep track of every detail she could, and to keep from staring at Nivar. The first three were easy.

64

"AND THEN," MASTER Zar continued, laughing, slapping his knee, rubbing his purple forehead, pointing at Father, looking from Liz, to Nivar, to Sister Darian, his purple eyes bright, "our High General here cocks his head at the castle gate—a couple thousand bolts and arrows and guns all pointed straight down at him, a dozen hellish beasts from Lábbarkos howling blood from the battlements, a great cannon aimed right at his chest, a flight of rogue angels from Tarcéron circling above it all—and says, like he was taking a stroll after brunch on Paráden: 'If it's all the same to you, gentlemen, I'd prefer to wait 'til *after* your reinforcements arrive—I'd rather not do this twice.' Bahahaha!" Master Zar pounded the table, entirely amused with himself. Little Gregory squeaked, then burped. Captain Colj paused—thought about it—then smiled with his huge fangs. Liz glanced at Nivar and Darian and realized, with some relief, that they seemed just as lost as she was.

"We must rest," Captain Colj said suddenly, his voice huge. He gave a giant yawn, mammoth fangs wide. Little Gregory immediately followed suit, his yawn accompanied by a little squeak. "There will be much work tomorrow," the ogre continued. "May we pitch camp here, High General?"

Father looked past Captain Colj, to the silver ship, to the whistling, snoring zeppelin above it. The crew had already crawled off to their bunks. The sapphire fireflies seemed to have settled. "Of course." Father nodded. "Looks like your men beat you to it."

"They've had a long couple of days," Master Zar acknowledged. Little Gregory squeaked and yawned again.

And so, without ceremony, they all said their good nights and Liz started clearing the table.

65

"You knew that giant," Liz said to Father, after the others had returned to their ship. She was finishing clean-up, moving the chairs up onto the porch. Father stood on the front step, gazing up at the big mountain. "And you knew that dwarf and his little dragon. Those others' families. They called you 'High General.'"

She knew she was stating the obvious. But she'd always been able to coax him a little, to nudge him a bit toward what she wanted. *But everything is different now.* And she had the distinct impression that all her old tricks had zero chance of working. But she really wanted to learn. In fact, she was dying to know more. So she rolled the dice. "Maybe you could tell me a story? About from back then, when you knew them? A short one?"

Father shook his head. He looked tired. It was clear that his knee was bothering him. He'd pat at his chest for his flask, then recognize the gesture, blink, rub at his mouth, then close his eyes and take a deep breath, as if dispelling a demon.

"Just a *short* story?" Liz encouraged. Father shook his head, but then he nodded suddenly, apparently changing his mind. He bent down with a grunt and sat on the front step, holding his sheathed saber between his knees, scabbard point in the snow. He looked at her, then drew a little circle in the snow crust with his weapon, marking six little points radiating from it, a little point hanging in the center. The Dallanar Sun.

"Alright." He nodded. "If you'll grab us some tea—and my walking stick—I'll finish the dishes."

Liz hurried inside, returned with his stick under her arm and two steaming cups of tea. He took the stick. She sat next to him on the stoop.

Father was looking at the moon as it rose over the big mountain. The night was so quiet, the sky thick with stars. Beautiful. And for a moment, all Liz wanted was for Teagan and Rosie and Narmos to be back. If she could have them right now, she'd never want anything else again. She blinked and saw that Father was looking down at her. She cleared her throat.

"It's late," he said, hands cradling his cup's warmth. He

didn't just look tired, Liz realized.

He looks exhausted.

"I miss him," Liz said plainly.

Father nodded.

"And I miss Narmos, too," Liz said. "I know he's just a bear—."

"No such thing as 'just a bear,' not when you're talking about a grey bear." He cleared his throat, wiped at his mouth. "I miss them, too."

They didn't say anything for a long time.

66

AFTER WHAT SEEMED like ages, she looked up at him, drawing her knees to her chest, huddling over her cup. "Can I ask a question?"

He nodded, sipped his tea. "Fire away."

Without hesitation, Liz asked: "Who's that woman down in the shed?"

Father nodded. "Her name is Giácoma Norfell. A royal member of House Dallanar. Ward and adopted daughter of Dorómy Dallanar, the High Chancellor. The adopted niece of Bellános Dallanar, the High King of Remain."

Liz's mouth opened slightly.

"That's the short answer." Father cleared his throat.

Liz nodded, shut her mouth, prayed he'd continue.

Father took another sip of tea, closed his eyes with the taste. "Lord Dorómy adopted her when he was a young man. A wound made it impossible for him to have children of his own, but that's not the reason he adopted her. He adopted her to help her, a debt to her family. He was in his early twenties then; Gia was fourteen, a little younger than you. She was the second kid Dorómy adopted, in fact. He adopted another after, too. So she has two step-brothers: Kane, her older brother, and Robert, her younger. Long tradition of that kind of thing in the high families.

"Anyway, Gia's mother had died in childbirth and Sam Norfell, her father, never remarried. He was a lieutenant in the Sixth Artillery corps; served under me, in fact. Good man. When Sam was killed on Baleen, Dorómy took Gia as his ward. He and Sam had been good friends from a number of campaigns—and Sam had saved his life on Indónok. Doró-my formally adopted Gia a couple months later, took her into the family. This was three years before his father—Dorómy's father, Balmás—got sick and abdicated the Silver Throne. The real start of all this mess." He gestured out toward the silver ship and the floating zeppelin—but Liz got the sense that there was much more to "this mess" than a dead girl and a visit from old friends.

"So, she's Lord Dorómy's daughter and High King Bellános's niece?" Liz asked, trying to make sense of all the other information, or at least to store it away for later contemplation. It was a lot to sort.

"That's right." Father carefully straightened his knee, wincing with the pain of it.

"What was she doing out here?"

"That's what Dorómy will want to know. But I think he knows already. She was doing her job. Gia had served with the Silver Legions for two years after her rites of passage, served until she turned eighteen. Then she quit and joined up with the rangers. Bellános had taken the throne by then. Your mother and I had already left Paráden for the Tarn. Good years.

"Anyway, Gia was a skillful soldier. And she loved the

service. It's the right of any high born lord or lady to bear arms for the Silver Throne, if they're able. And she'd always loved Kon. The snow and the sky and the Tarn—and she loved the Tarn's library. She was something of a loner, too. I can see why the ranger's life appealed to her. Out for months at a time. You, your bear, the boundless woods. Hunt what you want, keep the peace. A good life. A meaningful life, especially when you get sick of the cities, of the Silver Courts. So she left the Legions and became a ranger."

"That's when Gia was eighteen?" Liz asked, trying to keep it straight.

"Right." Father nodded. "Served up here in the high country ever since, or so I understand." He looked up at the big mountain. "I even saw her once, a few years ago, down in Korfort. Didn't make myself known." He sighed. "My guess here is that she was tracking this poacher and he got the drop on her, somehow. He'll pay for it now, one way or another."

Father finished his tea, set down the cup, and stabbed the snow with his scabbard. "It's not just Dorómy, either. Bellános, the Silver King, loves her, too—as if she were his own niece, his own blood. Dorómy's rage is worthy of fear, no doubt. But Bellános? Bell is smart. *Cunning.* Wouldn't be surprised if he's got his own little plans for this Modró, something terrible."

"What about us?" Liz asked.

"Us?" Father looked at her for a long moment, his eyes darkening. Then he nodded. "This is our land, Liz. Teagan was my son. I failed him, especially this last year. My eternal shame, Great Sisters curse me." He wiped at his mouth. "But I won't fail him again. Not that it makes any difference now." He closed his eyes. "Regardless, day after tomorrow, Jarlund and the rest of them will be back up here with the posse and we'll hunt him down. We'll have our justice."

"I'm going with you." She looked up at him, caught his eye, daring him to disagree. "I'm going to hunt him. And I'm going to get my bear back, if he isn't dead already."

"Yes." Father nodded. "You know the land. You have the skills." The barest hint of a smile touched his lips. "You'd go out anyway, even if I refused. Probably drag poor Evan along with you. And Narmos is still alive. Way Jarlund made it sound, Modró wants to use him as bait for his 'Mountain King.'"

Then Father picked up his walking stick, grunted, and

leaned forward to get up—then stopped himself. He wiped at his mouth. "Noticed you paying young Nivar some attention. And vice versa."

Liz blinked, blushed, cleared her throat, and looked at her furry boots. She made a waving, vague kind of gesture with her hands.

Father sat back, put his massive arm around her shoulders, and squeezed her to his side. "Seems like a good lad. His family is one of the most respected in the Realm. Known his Father since I was your age."

Liz made to speak, but he stopped her with a raised hand.

"Take one piece of advice? From your old Dad?"

She nodded, embarrassed, but somehow thirstier than ever for his words.

"Make *him* do the work, Liz. If he's not willing to fight for you, to take risks, to pay his dues, to earn your attention, your respect, then he's not worth your time." He looked up at the milky sky. "You don't know it yet, but your choices now will be as many as the stars. Infinite . . . and more. Make him—make them *all*—earn it. I'll always stand behind you, Lizzy." He squeezed her to his side.

She nodded, swallowed, tried to be strong, to find her old resentment—but instead felt tears threaten.

It took her a moment to understand why, and she blinked when the realization came.

She believed him.

67

THE MORNING SUN was just up when the front door slammed open and Evan near fell into the kitchen, tumbling over himself, giving no thought to the snow and slush he tracked into the house. Liz was upstairs in bed. They'd let her rest late, and she was grateful. It had taken her forever to finally fall asleep. Strange to wake without Teagan and Narmos beside her. No matter how hard she tried to think about something else, she kept seeing Teagan die. Kept seeing his eyes, his blood pushing between Mother's fingers. Kept imagining Narmos's little pelt spiked to some tree somewhere. The same images, over and over. Horrible. She cringed, shook her head, and tried to push the images out of her mind. Tried to turn her thoughts to everything she'd heard last night, all the new things she'd learned—and then

Evan banged into the cabin.

"There's a *dragon* in the clearing!" Evan cried, his voice breaking awkwardly. "A giant black *dragon*! With riders! Four riders! In *our* clearing!" He pointed back out the door.

Liz's rolled out of bed and stepped to the ladder.

Mother and Father were sitting at the kitchen table drinking tea. Father was holding Mother's fingers in his huge hands. Liz had heard them talking quietly as she woke. What struck her most now, however, was how totally unimpressed they seemed by Evan's news.

Evan stared at them both, his eyes near popping from his head. ". . . um." He waved his hands in the air at nothing, looked up to the loft, saw her. "I'm not kidding." He looked from Liz, to his parents, back again. Blinked. "There's a *dragon*. In the *clearing*?" He pointed back at the front door, looked at Liz, apparently puzzled that she wasn't more impressed.

Mother looked pointedly at Father. Father took a sip of his tea, wiped his mouth with the back of his hand, lifted his walking stick from the table's edge, and cleared his throat. "Here we go."

He glanced up at Liz, then looked over to Evan. "Put on some decent clothes and come on, both of you. I want to introduce you to somebody." Then he looked at Mother. "You coming?"

"I suppose I must," she said.

Father nodded. "Liz, Evan. Time to get moving."

Liz didn't have to be told twice. As she turned away from the ladder toward her dresser, she heard Evan say, with significantly less excitement: "Dwarves and ogres and some kind of floaty, glowing blob attached to a silver *ship* out there—and nobody tells me anything. And now *I'm* the only one who seems to think that a dragon—a *giant, black, enormous dragon in our front yard*—is worth mentioning."

68

THE SUN SHONE blindingly bright on freshly fallen snow as they stepped out of the cabin.

And there—sure enough, big as day—was the black dragon, just as Evan had said.

It was huge. Enormous. At least sixty paces long—maybe longer. Scales shining black like obsidian. Wings like a ship's midnight sails. Its tail was long, thickly crested, swiping lazily at the snow, pushing up huge white berms. Its head was a crenellated boulder, two enormous black horns curling forward and down, rooted deep in its massive skull. When they shut the cabin door behind them, the black monster turned and looked at them. Its eyes were molten red, smoldering volcanic pits. It wore a large, elaborate saddle on its back—more like a kind of litter—designed to seat at least half a dozen riders. From this saddle, four men descended.

No. Liz corrected herself, pushing her braid over her shoulder.

Three men—and a boy.

The boy was the first off. He was younger than her, perhaps by three or four years. He was lanky and awkward looking, even though she had to admit that he was kind of handsome, in a bookish sort of way—for a kid. In fact, the first thing Liz noticed about him was his incongruous reading spectacles, which he incessantly polished with the end of his frayed blue riding scarf. He would polish his spectacles, put them back on his nose, cross his eyes as he looked through them, then take them off and polish them again—not seeming to realize that the ratty scarf itself was the problem, covered as it was with frosty condensation from his flight. Otherwise, the boy was very well attired. His chest was protected by a fine breastplate of high silver—but the armor seemed just a touch too big for him in the torso and shoulders; correct height, but too broad. He wore stylish leather breeches dyed dark blue and trimmed with mink. Matching boots and gloves. A fur-lined cloak was thrown over his narrow shoulders, also deep blue. His hair was dark and cut short in a soldier's crop, but the haircut looked kind of strange on him, probably because of his overly large head, which seemed even larger still when compared to his thin neck. Behind his spectacles, his eyes were dark and intelligent. He had a funny little smile on his face as he looked around the clearing, taking it all in.

Father took a deep breath and leaned heavily on his walking stick. "Backs straight, chins up," he said softly. "I want you to stay on either side of me—about a pace behind me, a pace apart. Understand? Mother will follow."

Mother inclined her head, then added, "And keep your position behind Father when he stops."

Liz nodded. Evan looked at her, saw her nodding, then nodded himself.

"Alright." Father stepped off the porch and they all followed.

One of the three other men was clambering down from the dragon's elaborate saddle. At the bottom, he tripped on some tackle and nearly fell the rest of the way, brushing himself off with a flourish, as if he thought he was being watched. He looked to be in his early twenties. Like the bespectacled boy, he was finely dressed. *Maybe too finely dressed*, Liz thought. He wore maroon velvet leggings, a maroon doublet of soft-looking silk, and knee-high boots of maroon leather. A maroon riding scarf wrapped his neck and a heavy maroon cape graced his shoulders. An elaborate dagger, its pommel set with a fat burgundy stone, swung and bounced from his belt on a golden chain. He had longish blond hair that he kept brushing away from his face. His ears were wrapped in gold casings that seemed more appropriate for a merchant's wife than a soldier. As he pulled off his riding gauntlets—or tried to pull them off—Liz saw that he wore elaborate, jeweled rings beneath his gloves, one ruby on each skinny ring finger.

His gloves caught on the jewels as he tried to remove them; looked like he'd have to remove his rings to get his gloves off.

The next man was an armored, dark-haired dragon rider. The massive dragon's pilot, Liz guessed. He leapt lightly from the other side of the saddle, stepped to the front of the huge dragon, adjusted something on its harness, unclipping some slender reins, tossing them back up over the dragon's neck. He pressed his forehead to the center of the dragon's head and shut his eyes. It looked like he was whispering something to his huge mount. The dragon cocked its head slightly and closed its massive red eyes, savoring the contact. The rider wore a thick blue cloak over a breastplate of black iron. At his chest, the central plate of his armor was dramatically beveled to a V-like point. As he unwound the blue riding scarf from his neck, Liz saw a revolver of high silver slung under his left armpit. The man turned toward them. The moment he saw Mother and Father, the rider's eyes lit up.

"Erik!" Father shouted at the man, all decorum forgotten.

A huge, crazy smile broke across his face.

Mother's eyes flashed happily.

The dragon rider cocked a wry kind of grin, dark eyes shining, and stepped quickly through the snow. He stopped in front of Father and gave a formal salute, fist crossing his chest. He was tall and broad of shoulder. His movements were graceful and deliberate. A trained warrior, no doubt. He looked to be just a touch younger than Father, too. Perhaps in his later thirties. And quite handsome.

"High General." The rider grinned easily and bowed, smile lines creasing. "My Lady." He bowed to Mother. The skin around his eyes was lighter than the rest of his weathered face, calloused on the bridge of his nose. A pair of tinted riding goggles was pulled down at his throat.

Father handed Liz his walking stick, and clasped the dragon rider's forearm, pounding the man's shoulder with complete familiarity. "Five Sisters save me! It does me good to see you, Erik! And Voidbane! Great Sisters! He's bigger than ever! Should've known you two would be dragged into this."

The rider nodded, clasping Father's arm in return, looking from Father's face to Mother's. "The High Chancellor wanted to get here quickly. Our orders came from the Silver Throne itself."

"And what *time* you made! Amazing!" Father stopped, seemed to realize he was making something of a scene, then cleared his throat and tried to take a step back. "It's been too long, my friend."

The dragon rider laughed infectiously, but he didn't let go of Father's arm. "*Far* too long, High General." The rider looked into Father's eyes, his hand still on Father's shoulder, something timeless passing between them. The huge dragon, Voidbane, growled and shifted on his huge claws, black tail pushing around the snow.

"We are honored by your presence, Captain," Mother said, a gorgeous smile on her face.

"Indeed." Father nodded, smiling.

"Although the circumstances are unfortunate," the rider said. Something flickered in his smile.

"Aye." Father glanced over the rider's shoulder at the fourth man now coming down off the dragon's saddle. He frowned and shook his head. "But here, let me introduce you to my children. Elizabeth, Evan—this is Captain Erik Dyer of Dávanor. Captain of the Sundaggers. The bravest man I've ever known."

Captain Dyer bowed solemnly before them both. "I am honored to know you." He looked them in the eyes as he said this.

Liz and Evan bowed in turn.

"Jessica is well, I trust?" Mother asked.

"Never better." Captain Dyer's eyes gleamed. "We've just had another little girl. Wendi."

"*Another* girl?!" Father's smile came back, enormous and uncontrollable. "Congratulations!" He pounded Captain Dyer on the back, nearly knocking the dragon rider sprawling. Behind them all, Voidbane grunted and shook his head, tackle jingling. Across the clearing, Captain Colj, Master Zar, and the others were coming down off the silver ship, making their way toward them. Behind them, the crew seemed to be waking the zeppelin from its sleep. It tooted gently, its fluting voice greeting the morning sun. Little Gregory squeaked from Master Zar's shoulder.

"How many girls do you have, then?" Mother asked.

"Penelope is seven and my eldest, Anna, is nine."

Father shook his head wonderingly; his smile was huge.

Captain Dyer grinned back at him. Then his eyes went

serious. "We always said we wanted our children to grow up together, General."

Father looked at him for a long moment. "Yes." He nodded, his smile gone.

Mother inclined her head. "Strange how things can change."

The fourth man dropped to the snow beside Voidbane, turned, and walked toward them. The boy with the spectacles and the young man with the ruby rings turned as the man passed them, following in his wake about a pace apart, a pace behind, formal attendants.

This must be Dorómy Dallanar, Liz thought.

There could be no doubt that he cut a striking figure. He was middle-aged, tall, and broad of chest—not as tall as Father, but certainly taller than Captain Dyer. He wore a full black beard, carefully trimmed and shaped to a point at his chin. His dark hair was cut short. His eyes were widely set and seemed to shine with wisdom, power, and sorrow all together. His garb was simple: Under a thick black cloak he wore a silver-grey uniform without adornment, well-worn boots of black leather, and a broad black leather belt clasped with a simple buckle of high silver. A high silver revolver was strapped beneath his left armpit, its handle polished with use. He sported no jewelry save a flat band of high silver on his right index finger, which Liz noticed as he removed his leather riding gloves. No marks or insignia showed his status. Dark circles troubled his eyes. He did not unwind his black riding scarf from his throat.

The man stopped in front of Father and bowed formally, but not deeply. His face was strained.

"High General." His voice was deep.

"My Lord." Father bowed in return, saying nothing else.

"My Lady." The man inclined his head.

Mother bowed. "My Lord."

There was a long moment of silence.

Captain Colj, Master Zar, Nivar, and Sister Darian had all arrived from the silver ship. They stood at a respectful distance, watching the scene unfold.

The man cleared his throat. "Will you introduce me to your children?" He did not look at Liz or Evan as he said this.

"Of course, my Lord." Father bowed. "High Lord Dorómy Dallanar—Ward of the Káladar, Chancellor of the Realm—this is my daughter and son, Elizabeth and Evan Hone."

Liz took a step forward and bowed deeply and long. Evan hesitated a moment, then followed suit, copying her.

Lord Dorómy bowed to them both. "My honor," he said politely. "My attendants." He gestured behind him. "My nephew, Lord Garen Dallanar of Kon." The lanky boy in the spectacles—still looking cross-eyed through driblets of water, almost trying to look *around* the water on his spectacles—stepped forward, gave an awkward smile and a clumsy bow. "And Lord Layne Tevéss of Dávanor." The young man in maroon nodded, adjusted his blond locks, and gave an elaborate, courtly salute. Upon hearing Lord Tevéss's name, Father looked at Captain Dyer, one eyebrow raised. Captain Dyer closed his eyes briefly and shook his head with subtle exasperation, as if to say: "Don't ask me." There was something mechanical in Lord Dorómy's voice, Liz realized. As if he did this all from practiced habit. The High Lord's eyes seemed empty—haunted.

Lord Dorómy made to speak again, but he was interrupted by the young man, Lord Layne, who took another step forward and gave an even more florid bow. "I am *deeply* honored to meet the most impressive warlord of our shared history, most highly honored General Hone. And his lady, of course. My father, the great Lord Gideon Tevéss, has asked me *personally* to convey his *warmest* wishes and regards to you and your family and to express his *deepest* respect and admiration for your courage and your dedication to the Realm."

Father frowned and inclined his head toward the young man, but just barely. Mother and Lord Dorómy said nothing. Behind Lord Tevéss, Master Zar rolled his eyes. On Zar's shoulder, little Gregory spread his blue wings and squeaked with something that sounded very much like displeasure. This was immediately echoed by the huge Voidbane, whose low growl seemed to tremble the ground itself. His black tail thrashed the snow. Lord Layne stepped back to his place, looking around—apparently to make sure that everyone had paid attention to his little speech.

"I would like to see my daughter, General." Lord Dorómy looked at Father directly. "Take me to her."

"Of course, my Lord." Father nodded. "My deepest sympathies are with you, my Lord."

"As mine are with you, General." Lord Dorómy inclined his head, his eyes troubled.

Father shot Mother a quiet look, then gestured with an open hand past the house, toward the trail down to the skinning shed, inviting Lord Dorómy to walk.

Lord Dorómy made a brief sign to the dragon rider, Captain Dyer, who nodded affirmation. Then Lord Dorómy Dallanar—brother of the Silver King—followed Father into the woods.

69

THE MOMENT THEY were gone, Lord Layne turned to Liz, twisted a ruby ring on his finger, and said, "I require drink and the use of your facilities, girl. Take me there."

All of them—everyone present, even Mother—looked to her, as if gauging her reaction. Liz hesitated. The man was clearly a pompous ass, but she didn't know where she sat in the hierarchy nor what was expected of her.

So she went with what she knew: hospitality.

"Of course, my Lord." She bowed. "If you'll follow me?"

Lord Layne sniffed, brushing at his shoulders with his gloves. "Well?" he asked, nose in the air when she didn't immediately turn to leave. "Go *on*."

Mother nodded at her decorum. Liz bowed politely, tried to ignore the looks that the others gave her, and turned to lead him to the outhouse on the other side of the cabin. Then she stopped, glanced at Mother, and whispered quickly to Evan, "Ask them if they'd like a drink." And after a split second, "And if they need food for their mount."

Evan stared at her like she was speaking a foreign language, his eyes wide. "Food for their *mount?*"

"The dragon?" Liz hissed, tilting her head toward the giant Voidbane. Mother nodded.

Behind her, Lord Layne cleared his throat impatiently.

"This way, my Lord," Liz said.

As she left, she heard Evan say awkwardly, with a weird little bow and Mother's encouragement: "Can I get you some breakfast, uh, some food for your dragon? If he's hungry, sir?"

Voidbane rumbled.

"My thanks, young Lord Hone." Captain Dyer laughed easily. "He's always hungry. Worse than little Gregory here, if that's possible."

"It's not," Master Zar muttered.

70

"WHAT A CHARMING little house you have, girl," Lord Layne mused as they passed the side of the cabin, out of sight from the others, threading their way through the trees and the stacked cordwood between them. He brushed his blond locks away from his face, twisting one of his rings with the same hand that held his gloves. "So very *quaint*. I never did understand why General Hone left the service. It *is* the topic of *much* gossip, as you can probably imagine. Especially these days. What with all that is happening? The greatest tactical mind in the Realm, just *resigns* his commission . . . . No better than a commoner now—in *legal* terms, of course. He *is* respected, naturally. Especially by Taverly, Lessip, some of *those* types of people. You have heard of *them*, I am sure? No? Matters not. I have some very clever ideas as to why he left. I have shared them with my father. But to leave for this *wilderness*? Great Sisters save us. I suppose you do not even have running water in that shack, do you?" He stopped in the snow. "Where *are* you taking me?"

"The latrine, my Lord," Liz said, trying her best to keep her tone neutral. There was no way this Tevéss idiot's manner of address was appropriate. But he clearly was too stupid to grasp that fact, and Liz herself didn't understand all the dynamics well enough to counter his inane chatter. She certainly didn't want to embarrass Father or Mother in some way that she couldn't anticipate by insulting this fool—. She paused at the thought. She'd never really thought about it that way before. Embarrass the family. *House Hone.* She smiled, realizing to her surprise that she liked the sound of it.

"Why do we wait *here?*"

Liz blinked.

Hospitality, she thought, and gritted her teeth.

"We are here, my Lord." Liz turned slightly, extending her palm toward the path that led to the outhouse. "I will fetch your refreshment."

Lord Layne craned his neck down the path, looked at the outhouse, sniffed, then sighed. "I suppose it will have to do."

He made to pass her, then stopped suddenly at her side, looking down at her—he was quite a bit taller than she. There was something appraising in his gaze. He looked her up and down again, then suggestively hung a thumb in his belt buckle. Liz could smell his perfume. Like cloying flowers. She was suddenly confused—and wary.

She took a step back, in spite of herself.

He pursed his lips. "You *are* a pretty thing, are you not?"

"Thank you, my Lord." Liz nodded curtly. But immediately she was up on the balls of her feet.

"Of course, you will *never* be able to marry well. You might do for one of my lesser cousins, but that is the *best* kind of match you can hope for, surely. Hmm." He paused, then looked around. "Perhaps you would be willing to help me for a moment, girl. We are alone here, after all." He cocked his head at the thick trees, in the direction of the clearing. The others were completely out of sight. "Perhaps you might fancy a taste of truly *noble* blood? Perhaps a bit of *service*?" He put his hand on her shoulder.

"Of course, my Lord!" Liz smiled her most dazzling smile.

Lord Layne blinked as if confused, then grinned widely. His teeth were long and slightly crooked.

Then he laughed, finally understanding her, and stepped forward. "Oh, how *delightful*—!"

Liz kneed him straight between the legs, a short, chopping

blow that planted the ball of her knee straight into his groin. Layne gasped, sucked air, dropped his gloves, eyes wide. His shins buckled and then he just kind of tilted over onto the snow, collapsing in a huddle, his eyes shining.

Liz drew her high silver dagger, its smooth lethality firm in her hand, grabbed the lordling's long hair, yanked his head back, and dropped her knee straight down onto that soft spot Father had shown her, right beneath his rib cage. Layne wheezed and tried to double up, but her weight on that spot kept him pinned to the snow. Her pendant, Narmos's long black dewclaw, slipped from her shirt and dangled directly over his face, its sharp point a finger's breadth from his nose. She touched her blade to his throat. He made a weird little noise—not exactly a whine, more like a whimper—both his hands clutched between his legs, staring at her in white-eyed horror, the sharp point of Narmos's claw swinging in front of his eyes, the edge of her blade at his throat.

Liz smiled down at him, charmingly. "Out here in the 'wilderness,' my Lord, we have some 'quaint' rites that you might find interesting. During the Middlewinter festival, for example, we sacrifice the best ewe and the best ram in the village out on the Flat Rock. The ewe has her throat cut clean, there on the great stone. The ram? We take his balls first, before we let out his blood. The ancient way. Old Konungur tradition. I did it myself last year. Cut so clean and fast that the ram didn't even feel it—at least that's what old man Jarlund told me."

Layne's face had gone green.

Liz smiled, let her voice become gentle. "You touch me again—you touch *anyone* up here on the big mountain—I'll cut you." She ran her dagger point down his throat, boring her eyes into his, dagger running down his velvety doublet, past her knee, stopped at his belly, right above his belt buckle. "And I'll cut you *slow*. Do you understand, 'my Lord'? There should be no confusion between us—on so trifling a matter."

Layne nodded, but just barely. Then he shut his eyes, clenching them tight.

Liz got off him, sheathed her blade, tucked her pendant back in her shirt—then sniffed at a new stench rising from the young man's maroon pants.

"You seem to have soiled yourself, my Lord." She frowned

with mock concern. "Can I be of 'service'?"

His look was a bizarre mix of rage, misery, and shame.

"No?" She cocked her head. "Then I would wash that up with some clean snow, if I were you. Your trousers look quite expensive. Please do take your time. I'll have my brother bring you a towel in a few moments. No need for anyone else to know about this." She turned to go.

Layne's eyes narrowed and he took a breath, as if to speak.

Liz stopped, her eyebrow arched. She touched the pommel of her blade. Layne's mouth closed. She nodded. "You *mention* this to anyone—a single word—it'll be worse for you. Worse than you can imagine."

He stared at her, his glassy eyes widening, totally perplexed now, somehow believing her, yet wondering what in the Great Sisters' names could be worse than the nightmare of humiliation and bone-crunching pain that he currently suffered.

"'What could be worse?' you're wondering," Liz asked, sensing his confusion.

She pushed her blond braid over her shoulder, and looked him in the eye for a long moment, letting him think about it. Then she grinned. "I'll tell my Dad."

71

Liz WENT TO the cabin, opened the door, and stepped inside. Evan was still out front, talking to Captain Dyer and Master Zar. Little Gregory sat on her brother's shoulder, the small dragon's pale blue tail wrapped around Evan's neck.

Mother sat inside at the kitchen table, calmly drinking her tea.

"Mother?" Liz walked to the table.

"You did well," Mother said.

Liz wasn't sure what she was talking about, if she'd somehow seen what had happened with Lord Layne, or if she was commenting on her and Evan's performance in front of Lord Dorómy.

Mother looked at Liz for a long moment. Then she cocked her head at the counter. There, on a small wooden tray, two cups of fresh tea waited beside a chunk of cheese, some bread, and a small bowl of preserved olives. She cleared her throat. "Perhaps you should offer your Father and the Lord High Chancellor some refreshment? He's had a long flight." Mother's gaze glittered. "We must know what is said. Every word."

"Yes, Mother." Liz nodded, understanding her immediately. She picked up the tea.

72

As she approached the shed, Liz heard a voice inside—Lord Dorómy's voice—thick with sorrow: ". . . and a dream haunts me, Hone. *Haunts* me. I'm marching forward—on some battlefield somewhere, some grey endless field, a huge shield on my shoulder. Nothing else. Just a shield. I'm leaning into it—marching forward in the dark. And then I sense something behind me, and I look back, and I see a white shape on the ground. It's her. I can't see her, but I know it's Gia. One who I've sworn to protect has fallen. But then—in a blink—I'm marching forward again, shield back up, ready to defend once more. But again I sense something behind me. I look back. And see her again. And again." There was a break in his voice, then a low moan.

Liz stepped to the door, uncertain whether she should enter, if she should even listen. She cleared her throat uneasily, but Father was already there, opening the door for her.

Lord Dorómy stood at Gia's side, bowed over her wrapped

body, clinging to her, one hand resting on her forehead. They had unwrapped Gia's face, but the rest of her body remained tightly bundled in furs and skins, only her head and silvery blond hair showing. Her skin was white and bloodless. And beautiful. The mark of the Tarn stood out proudly on her right temple. Liz swallowed and looked at Father, raised the tray to him in a silent question. He took it without a word, touched a finger to his lips, set it down on the workbench.

Lord Dorómy cleared his throat, lifted himself up, and kissed his daughter's forehead. Then, looking down at her face, he said: "Will I ever find a way through this darkness? Will I find you there in the dark, Gia? Will you be waiting for me? Has anyone ever dared death to search, to find someone there? Did they find their love, at last?" He bowed his head and groaned. "My sun is gone. They said 'She is gone,' and the sun died. But where *are* you, dearest?" He shook his head. "If I'd never known you—Great Sisters save me—all would be well. I'd never feel *this* . . . ." He went silent, then shuddered. "It's the *never* that aches me, Gia. Never to be here with me. Never to smile at me again, never laugh, never fight, never sit with me at table, never argue . . . . All the rest of my life, never again. Only death can stop this pain of death. Only in death will I find you."

He wiped his face, took a deep breath, and turned— stopped himself at the sight of Liz, seemed to straighten unconsciously. Then he seemed to sag a bit and he smiled at her so sadly, so unselfconsciously, that the sight tore Liz's heart.

"Your Father is the very best of men." Lord Dorómy cleared his throat and looked at her, glancing at Father. His eyes were raw. "And I am sorry for your loss, young Lady."

Liz nodded silently. Father offered Lord Dorómy a cup of tea. The High Lord accepted it gratefully, took a sip, closed his eyes for a long moment, then shook his head. "Of all the places in all the Realm, she's killed on your front porch, Hone."

Father nodded grimly, tilting his head in acknowledgement.

Lord Dorómy took another sip of tea. "And you've heard that Robert, too, has been murdered?"

Father stopped short, as if shocked. Liz remembered that name. Robert was one of Lord Dorómy's other adopted children. The youngest son, if she recalled correctly from her conversation with Father.

"That news has not yet reached you?" Lord Dorómy asked.

Father frowned. He shook his head and said softly: "I had not heard, my Lord."

Lord Dorómy sipped his tea. "Three months ago. On Borádon. We don't even know what he was doing there. Not even Lessip can find out—with all his tricks and resources. We don't know who he was with. Who did it. Took me several weeks to get there. But not this time. This time, the trail is warm."

Father stepped forward and put his hand on Lord Doró-my's shoulder. "I am truly sorry, my Lord."

"It is why this Modró must come with me, Hone," Lord Dorómy said, looking Father in the eye. He smoothed his thick beard, looked hard at Father for a moment, then took another sip of his tea and turned back to Gia's body, resting his palm on her forehead. "You must see that. She was not killed in the line of duty, Hone. She was assassinated. As was Robert. They killed them. Killed them both. And most sure-ly they will try for Kane next. Kane *wants* them to try—as

you can imagine. I think they'll have a harder time with him."
Lord Dorómy gave a bitter little laugh.

"Who?" Father looked confused. "'They' *who*, my Lord? Who would dare? How can you know——?"

"I don't *know*, General." Lord Dorómy sighed, looking up at the side of the shed, the pelts' empty slit eyes staring back at him. "I *suspect*. And I'm not alone. Which is why this man, this Modró, must be brought back to the Tarn and then to Paráden——brought back *alive*, for proper questioning. These are not my orders, Hone. They come from the Silver King himself. Bellános has prepared something for Gia's killer." He paused. "In close consultation with high scholars of both the Eressan and Koran Orders, my brother has formulated an array of techniques with which he plans to extract the truth from this Modró, this thrice-damned mongrel."

Lord Dorómy turned and faced Father. "I know we feel the same pain, Hone. We've both felt it before. I am sorrier than I can say for your son. And I heard your words clearly yester-day. I understand your anger. I also know you have your own posse gathering here, mountain folk, tomorrow at dawn."

Father made to speak, but the High Lord stopped him with

a raised hand. "I will not stand in your way. Nor will those who serve me."

Father raised an eyebrow.

"But this Modró cannot be killed here, General. He *must* be brought to Bellános for questioning. Someone strikes at the very center of the royal family. Someone is murdering my children. We must know who. We must know why."

"Agreed." Father nodded, without hesitation.

Liz looked at him.

"But on one condition," Father continued.

Lord Dorómy's gaze flashed, then hardened—and for a brief moment, Liz felt the full extent of his power: vast, merciless, and terrifying. She shuddered involuntarily. Lord Dorómy tilted his head. "And what might that 'condition' be, High General?"

"Nothing easier." Father looked him in the eye. "When you're done with him, you bring him back here for execution. You let us have him after you're finished."

"And if I refuse?"

"Then the locals and I will go tomorrow morning without you. We will find him. And we will kill him ourselves. Zar and Erik will not raise arms against me, as you well know. And in all the Realm, Voidbane obeys no one but Dyer. Which leaves you Colj, your two attendants, the seer, the boy from Targus, and the ship's crew. I will have three score mountain men, at least. They all know the land—and none of them have much love for the Tarn."

Lord Dorómy looked at Father for a long moment. Then he nodded, something like admiration in his face. "Very well. Agreed."

The two men stepped forward, clasped forearms, and looked into each other's eyes.

"Agreed," Father said.

They stepped apart.

Father cocked his head toward Liz. "Can we get you something else, my Lord? Food? Drink?" He gestured at the tray of food on the workbench.

"I'd like to spend some time with Gia, if I may," Lord Dorómy said. "But I am hungry."

Father nodded. "Of course, my Lord."

Lord Dorómy looked at Father for a long moment. "These are hard circumstances, Hone. Even so, it does me good to see you. To meet your family." He looked at Liz, paused for a long moment. "I know you were disappointed with me. With us." He shook his head. "But you should know that you are missed. Bell said so himself, before I left. And he's not one to waste breath on idle words."

"I thank you, my Lord." Father inclined his head.

Lord Dorómy nodded silently, turned back to his dead daughter, looking into her face, his hand cupped lightly over her cold forehead.

73

WHILE LORD DORÓMY watched over Gia, Captain Colj, Master Zar, and the others spent the rest of the day preparing for the coming hunt. Anticipation ran high. Nothing frantic or overblown—just quiet, professional preparations. After receiving Captain Dyer's blessing and instruction, Evan had also taken on full responsibility for keeping the mighty Void-bane fed and watered. Evan's first move was to immediately secure a pair of good-sized reindeer for the dragon from Jarlund. The two beasts had gone down the monster's throat without ceremony . . . and without much chewing.

"How old are you, young Hone?" Dyer asked him later that afternoon, after Evan had finished bringing up another half dozen reindeer from old man Jarlund's.

"I turned sixteen just after Middlewinter, sir," Evan answered.

"Well." Dyer cocked his head at Voidbane, patting the huge dragon's enormous muzzle. "This big fellow doesn't take to everyone. Hardly anyone, truth be told. But he seems to like you just fine. Hmm. You're of age. Perhaps the High General would allow you come to Dávanor? We're in need of talented dragon squires who show no fear. And if Bane approves of you—which he clearly does—then you're half-way there already."

In spite of himself, Evan's mouth fell open, his eyes moving from Captain Dyer, to Voidbane, to Liz, to Dyer, and back again. "A *dragon squire?*" he asked, wide eyes filled with awe.

"Why not?" Dyer grinned. "It's not unknown for young women and men from other duchies to serve on Dávanor. With your family name, you'd be welcomed. House Dradón needs good men. And if I remember correctly, my Lord David, the High Duke of Dávanor, owes your Father a favor or two."

Evan nodded, but couldn't really manage to say anything. Voidbane rumbled hungrily, his breath steaming the cold. Evan blinked. "I guess I better feed him, then."

Captain Dyer laughed, his dark eyes sparkling, and patted Evan on the shoulder.

A few other men had come up from the village with supplies for the hunt, looking for direction from Father. They'd been taken aback at first, grumbling a bit at the silver ship, its strange crew, and the giant black dragon. But they were mountain men and could take almost anything in stride. One or two of them, Liz also learned, had served in the Silver Legions, or had relatives who had done so. Indeed, once they'd learned that their quarry would be fairly sought by all parties and that High Chancellor Dorómy Dallanar himself was not only present, but also had given his word that Modró would be returned to face the mountain's justice, most of the grumbling had ceased. (But not the gossip, which Liz could only imagine had already reached the far side of the big mountain and back.)

The foppish Lord Layne kept his distance the entire day and would turn away from her when confronted by her gaze, clumsily busying himself with some pointless task.

Both Nivar and Darian seemed to notice Layne's strange behavior, and both had rather different reactions.

"I saw what happened," Darian said, her huge eyes wide. She did not blink, her dark brown skin making her eyes seem larger still. A funny little smile touched her lips as she cocked her head. She shivered slightly in her cloak. "You were quite kind to him, if I may offer an opinion. With your rank, you were well within your rights to do as you wished. With your rank, you could have killed him there on the spot. You have a generous heart."

My rank? Liz wondered.

"Yes." Darian nodded, as if hearing her thought. "Your family could buy and sell the Tevéss clan a thousand times over, without notice—although that brainless peacock does not know it. Like swatting a gnat. Why did you spare him?"

"Didn't want to get blood on my clothes," Liz muttered.

"Sensible." Darian nodded kindly. "But still, merciful." Her eyes were wide, her voice calming. She paused and cocked her head. "Although, now that I consider, gelding an heir of House Tevéss might properly have been considered a high service to the Realm. From what I understand, they are all vain, foppish halfwits. Quite bad for royal bloodlines."

Darian said this with such calm sincerity, such matter-of-factness, that Liz laughed out loud.

"What's this all about?" Nivar asked, coming up behind them, a friendly smile on his face. He looked ravishing in his yellow robes. He barely seemed to imprint the snow as he walked. His green eyes glittered, yellow sparks flashing in the winter sun.

Liz blushed, then cringed inwardly at the fact that she'd blushed at all.

Darian stepped smoothly into the pause in the conversation, expertly covering Liz's embarrassment, threading her small arm through Liz's elbow with gentle familiarity. "Lady Hone and I were just discussing the strengths and weaknesses of House Tevéss. We are both quite certain that Lord Layne will have some trouble finding a proper match. We are equally sure that that fact might be in the best interests of the health and well-being of the Silver Kingdom as a whole."

"Ah." Nivar nodded sagely, his mouth going mock serious. "Its dynastic planning we're onto this morning, eh?" He looked at Liz, smiled, then paused, gesturing at Voidbane, the silver ship, the floating zeppelin, everyone. "There's not one fellow in this clearing worthy to clean your worst pair of boots, my Lady."

Liz only had one pair of boots——but alright. She felt the blush rise again.

"Just so." Darian nodded, a brilliant smile lighting her face.

Nivar blinked, then cleared his throat awkwardly. "Not that I would ever presume to state the obvious, of course."

And that's when Liz realized that *he* was the one who was blushing.

74

LATER THAT EVENING, with the sky turning purple and the mountain snow glowing red with the fading sun, Liz carried a small bowl of fresh stew, some tea, some warm bread, and a napkin on a tray down to the skinning shed. Lord Dorómy had been up once or twice during the day. But after completing whatever task had occupied him, he'd immediately returned to the cold and to his daughter's vigil. At the shed's door, Liz knocked respectfully and stepped back a bit. Somewhere, a winter crow cawed.

"Come," Lord Dorómy said.

She opened the door and stepped inside. Lord Dorómy sat on a stool beside his daughter. He looked up at her when she entered. Liz said not a word, but rather raised the steaming tray to show her purpose, set it down on the workbench, bowed, and turned to go.

"She was your age when I took her in. Did you know that? You're fourteen, are you not?"

"Fifteen, my Lord." Liz turned back to him, kept her eyes down, and bowed.

Lord Dorómy nodded. "I'm sure you've heard this before, but you very much have the look of your Mother." There was a long pause. Liz looked up. He was smiling sadly, looking at Gia. He looked drained and haggard. "The same face and hair. You're much taller. I hear that you know well these woods and lands. That you're an accomplished archer?"

Liz inclined her head at the compliment, pushed her braid over her shoulder, but did not answer.

"I don't blame your Father for stepping away from us. I'm sure he's told you why. I don't blame him. And now," he put his hand on the bundled corpse of his daughter, "maybe he was right all along."

Liz had no idea what Lord Dorómy was talking about or why Father had left royal service—she herself had just found out that he'd *been* in royal service to begin with—but her curiosity burned hotter than ever. So she nodded. "My Father is rarely wrong."

The dark circles beneath Lord Dorómy's eyes were pronounced. "Too true." He smiled ruefully.

"But he holds responsible only himself for his decision to leave," Liz added, lamely fishing for more information.

"That sounds like him," Lord Dorómy said. He closed his eyes for a long moment, then sighed. "He was always the realist. Although now, I wonder. Perhaps he's more of an idealist than he'd care to admit?"

Liz said nothing.

Lord Dorómy nodded. "When my father, Balmás, took ill—this was almost twenty years ago, mind you—your father was one of the first commanders of the Silver Legions to insist that I step forward to the Silver Throne. Maybe he was the first?" He paused. "Hone had little respect for my father in the first place, I'm afraid. Not that I can wholly blame him. Balmás was always feeble; Hone never had tolerance for the weak."

He closed his eyes. "I agreed with him, at first. The throne was mine, by rights. And this point was echoed by others. After all, I was the firstborn son. 'Of course, it should be you!' they said. Or: 'There can be no other choice, my Lord.'"

Lord Dorómy shook his head cynically. "Sycophants, most of them, alas. But a few true men, too. Like your father. Realist or idealist . . . . Either way, your father was right, after a fashion: there was no other choice. At least none that he or the others could see."

He paused and looked at his daughter's bloodless face. Then he murmured, almost to himself, his voice heavy with exhaustion: "The Silver Throne is often said to be the seat from which all the Remain is ruled. 'Tis only part true. The Silver Throne also rules the one who sits it."

He cleared his throat, looked back at Liz, and let out a deep sigh. "And yet, I had no ambition to rule and I was unmarried and I couldn't have children. And Balmás yet lived. My brother Bellános is only two years my junior. And he's a far more accomplished politician and diplomat than I could ever be. I'll be the first to admit that. They call him the 'Silver Fox' with good reason." He smiled, then frowned. "And that same year, mere weeks before we met with Balmás and his advisors to discuss the succession, Adara—my sister-in-law, Bellános's wonderful wife—gave birth to a son. Their first-born. Thomas. And everything changed."

He glanced back at Gia, her lifeless face cold in the waning light. "Oh, how quickly my adopted sons and daughter— all three of them the children of dear friends, more family than anything else—how quickly they became the subject of 'serious conversation.' It was as if they'd never been known before. Whispers. Gossip. The Silver Courts are rife with such scheming, the likes of which you can't imagine. 'How will the royal dynasty be best preserved upon Lord Dorómy's death?' 'Will Lord Dorómy's adopted children complicate the succession down the line?' 'How can the stability of the Silver Throne *best* be preserved?' And more. Hitherto, Bellá-nos and I had always ignored this idle talk. You must. You'll drive yourself mad. Listening to these rich, simpering liars, brains so poisoned with wealth and idleness their mouths seem to run on their own accord. Many a monarch has taken a seat at the table of power, only to be eaten by the rumors of fools. And besides, there had always been factions in the Silver Courts, in the High Council of Lords, factions who had sought to make us rivals for their own purposes—even from when we were children. Such are the hazards of monarchy. How Bell and I infuriated them."

He closed his eyes and paused for a long moment. "But after Thomas's birth—and with our father Balmás sick and near the edge of death—things changed, and we realized that a decision *had* to be made. And that *we* had to be the ones to make it. Just the two of us. Brother and brother. With complete trust and agreement."

He opened his eyes, his gaze sought hers. "Our urge as a people, as a race, to 'choose sides,' to demonize others, to search out—to create—war, is strong. It takes twice the strength and ten times the discipline to resist this impulse. But Bellános and I—we *knew* that simple truth. And that knowledge was the source of our power.

"It was my idea to step aside for my brother, to yield the

Silver Throne. But it didn't feel like I was giving anything up. It felt like I was lifting a weight from my shoulders by granting something to another part of my soul. Bell and I, we've always loved each other. And he remains not only my brother, but also my dearest friend and confidant. But that's not why we chose as we did. Nor was it Bell's new son—important as my nephew Thomas was, healthy and strong, nobly born of a good marriage—to whom the throne and crown could be justly passed upon Bellános's death. Rather, we agreed quite simply that Bellános would make a better king. A *wiser* king. Of course, our father disagreed, slave as he was to his own weakness—the lies born of greed, the easy habits of war. But he was dead within the year, so it mattered not."

Lord Dorómy stood, took the tray of food from the workbench, sat back down beside his daughter's corpse. The tea steamed in the cold. He dipped his bread into the stew mechanically, took a bite, his eyes brightening at the taste. He blinked, looked into his bowl, then raised the bowl at Liz. "This is good food. My gratitude to you and your Mother. I hope you'll pass my thanks to her."

"Your servant, my Lord." Liz nodded politely, but her brain spun with his words.

One fact in particular kept coming 'round, centering in her mind. *You are a part of this, Liz.* The world he described— the Silver Courts, Paráden (wherever that was), the Silver Legions, even the Tarn—all of it was *her* world now, even though she'd never known it.

"And war was the real issue," Lord Dorómy said. He wiped his mouth with his napkin. "I know that now. War and lies and their servants. I'm a soldier. My brother is a scholar. It's been like that since we were children. I remember once . . . . This was so long ago. We were here on Kon. At the Tarn. I must've been eleven or twelve, Bellános nine or ten. One of our older cousins, Tollón, he kept giving Bell a hard time." He smiled sadly. "Bellános was awkward back then, you must understand, very much like my nephew Garen. Just like him, really. Could barely tie his shoes, so involved was he with his books and scrolls and maps and libraries. And Tollón, he just wouldn't leave him be."

Lord Dorómy shook his head. "My solution to Tollón's abuse? 'Easy,' I told Bell. 'I'll go pound the snot out of the idiot and we'll be done with it.' Something along those lines, eh? But Bell, he wouldn't have it. He had to win him over *his* way. And it worked, Great Sisters save me. In a couple of months, the big fool was following Bellános around like a puppy on a string. Turns out, Bell found something out, some nasty tidbit about Tollón's mother, used it as a lever. But he never told me what it was. Ever. Even when I asked him, brother to brother, tucked in our bed in the deep of the night, no one else to hear. Bell just shook his head. 'I swore to Tollón, promised him that I'd not tell a soul,' he'd say. And by the Great Sisters, he wouldn't tell me."

Lord Dorómy smiled ruefully. "He's not just smart, you see? He's true to his word, always. He's *good*. And that's what my pathetic father and his cronies couldn't tolerate. It's what they *still* can't tolerate. They had always liked me, you see. I was easy. A blunt instrument. 'Point Dorómy on his way, he'll get the job done.' And that's true, to be sure. I have a talent for war. But Bellános? Bellános has a talent for *peace*. And that is infinitely rarer. The most precious and fragile thing there is. Any fool can name an enemy, stoke the fires to burn a world. Only the strangest and greatest of kings can hold the nightmare of war at bay." He looked into the face of his dead daughter, set his food aside, and closed his eyes. "Clearly, I am not that kind of king." He swallowed. "Because when I see my dead children, all I want is vengeance. To kill until I can't lift an arm. *I* am the weak one."

He was quiet for a long time, his eyes closed.

Outside in the fading light, the snow grouse took up their twilight call.

Liz said nothing.

When Lord Dorómy spoke again, his voice was thick. He did not open his eyes. "Your father never trusted Bellá-nos. But most of that's because your father is a professional soldier, like me. Bellános, on the other hand, is a profession-al scholar, a professional politician. Hone and I spent years together in the field, when we were young men. Years of fighting together creates a different kind of family. If you've never been there, it's hard to describe. Beyond brotherhood, really. A kind of intimacy that death somehow makes. The things shared in a cold ditch somewhere, huddled around an iron helmet used for a cooking pot, thinking any moment the enemy might come with his thousands to grind you and your brothers and sisters into mud—those times open a man's heart in a way no other thing can. Your father loves me. And I love him. Which is why he was furious when I gave the throne to Bellános. To your father's eyes, even now, Bellános is a false king. Not because Bell is wicked, or cruel, or stupid, or incompetent, or undeserving. But simply because Bellános is not me. And then there was what happened between your Dad's brother Darro and Balmás—the accident with Teagan. Again, not Bellános's fault. But after Balmás was dead, your father and mother left anyway."

Liz nodded knowingly. Even though she knew nothing.

Lord Dorómy opened his eyes. "I'll sleep down here tonight, young Lady Hone. If you would tell your parents?" He placed his hand on the wrapped corpse next to him. "Keep her company, one last night."

Liz bowed.

"My thanks, for the meal." He held the tray out to her.

"Your servant, my Lord." Liz bowed, stepping forward.

He looked at her as she took it. "I *am* sorry for your loss, young Lady Hone. There is nothing worse. But we'll make it right. On that, you have my word."

Liz looked him in the eye, saluted as she had seen the other soldiers do, fist across her chest. Then she took the tray, turned to the door, and left.

75

THAT NIGHT, TUCKED into the sleeping loft, exhausted and exhilarated for the hunt and almost too tired to sleep, Liz dreamed.

A bizarre nightmare—but it didn't start as such.

She was a bird, perched high on a silver rafter, looking down into a kind of workshop.

No.

Not a workshop.

A factory. A factory filled with silver machines. The machines looked like presses of some sort—like something you'd see in a great city's forge. The silver machines whispered and rumbled as they opened and shut, opened and shut—silver-hot steam hissing from glowing mouths. Giant silver cogs turning on silver tubes—open and shut, open and shut—the machines' noise a continuous clunking. A silver light glowed everywhere, but softly. The pipes, the gears, the floors, the walls, the machines themselves—all glowed with silver radiance.

Dozens of little girls tended the silver machines. The girls wore silver boots and stepped with small, careful steps. They wore silver gloves on their hands, silver nets on their heads, and silver masks over their mouths. They were children, all of them—and strangely young. Not even ten years old. Some even younger.

The work must be protected.

A little girl placed something into a silver machine and pulled a lever. The machine hissed and clumped shut. When it opened, a steaming silver tear rested in its center. The tear was hot, silver-white, and smooth. The girl took the tear from the machine and turned to Liz, holding it up to her with both hands, as if wanting her to take it. Liz reached for it with her silver gloves—but as she took it, the tear slipped through her hands and shattered—CRASH!—on the floor. A black, chitinous thing curled there amidst the broken shards, its shadowy feathers sharp, obsidian carapace splitting apart like a swollen insect, clicking, as the dark thing shook itself sliding toward a grate in the silver floor where it dropped into the black.

A moment passed.

Another.

Then, somewhere below, a massive door crashed open and a sound echoed up from the deep.

It was the sound of rotten hooves pounding on ancient iron.

The sound of rage and despair.

The sound of the men that worked the other machines— the machines far below.

The tear's creature had set them free.

Gripped by fear, Liz turned to run, to fly, but the silver doors crashed open in front of her and a gang of black-cloaked men flooded into the factory. Their robes were oily shrouds. Black gore dripped from their sleeves. Their hands weren't hands. They were old vulture claws, joints moldy with age. And the worst was their faces: like soft grey eggs. Mouths toothless slits. Flickering black tongues. They didn't have eyes. The egg faces reflected no light.

A faceless man grabbed Liz by the wrist, lifted a jagged dagger, stabbed her in the chest, dropped her dead to the silver floor.

Liz looked down, saw her own blood swell.

But it wasn't blood.

It was silver.

Liquid silver.

When she touched her hands to it, her fingers came away dripping and luminous, palms covered in silvery bile.

The work must be protected.

All around her, the egg-faced men held the other workers down, ripped the silver masks from their faces, and cut into their throats, their legs, their arms. But, again, there was no blood. The girls did not bleed. Instead, liquid silver poured from wounds, flowed, dribbling and spraying bright over the silver machines, while the faceless men hacked and howled, their oily shrouds rustling like the feathers of rotten birds.

There was another sound.

It was Liz herself.

She was screaming.

The other workers took up the cry.

More tears shattered. More black things crawled and hissed into the darkness beneath. More hooves pounded up from below—BANG! BANG! More killing. More faceless men, their smooth egg heads bobbing and nodding as they broke again through the silver doors, mouths hissing open to reveal empty, gummy holes as they pulled the little workers from their machines.

And still, Liz bled.

She bled, but she did not die.

Another tear shattered to the floor. But this time, instead of a black insect, a crow leapt from the shards and landed on the silver machine above her body, shook its dark feathers, and looked down at her, black eyes glittering.

When they saw the crow, the egg-faced men stopped, their claws frozen in time.

The crow cocked its head at Liz, then flew to the silver beam from which she had first observed the scene. The crow looked down at her, its beady eyes gleaming, intelligent. The men tracked the crow as it flew, their heads moving as one, as if their eyeless faces could see. They gathered together, craning their necks up toward it, their oily clothes stinking of burnt hair and ancient ice. As the crow watched them, the eyeless egg faces nodded and the slit mouths gibbered.

Again, the crow's eyes found hers.

"You may choose," it cawed in its weird crow voice, a

voice blended from a thousand different throats.

Choose what?

"Who lives, of course." The crow cocked its head, its jewel eyes black and shiny. "And, who dies."

Liz looked at her horrible silver wounds.

But I'm dead already.

The crow tutted. "But *I* can show you the way."

As one, silently, the egg-faced men turned and looked down at her. Their talons flexed, cracking with age.

Then one of them whispered, lisping: ". . . we thirst . . . ."

". . . *all* of us . . . ," the others answered in unison.

Grey worm tongues flitted at the corners of a hundred toothless mouths.

They edged closer to her, huddling, towering over her.

Liz tried to move, but she was frozen in place, as if her silver blood had suddenly congealed, locking her to the floor.

Then a rotting man dropped something to the floor beside her face.

It was a little body.

It was Narmos.

No, it was Teagan.

And now it was Evan.

Now Mother.

And then it was Father.

Yes.

"You may choose," the crow repeated.

A strange, tiny version of Father seemed to coalesce before her eyes.

A child. A baby. Father as a little boy.

Or what was left of him.

He'd been hacked to pieces, his limbs cut to ribbons. His little knee was a mottled purple mass, puffy and veiny, a cleft of scar tissue running raw and puckered above the knee cap. And the smell was horrible. His little toes——she could see his tiny toenails.

Liz shut her eyes.

But she still saw him.

Around her, the faceless men became more agitated, jittering, heads tilting, waiting on her, toothless mouths open, waiting . . . waiting . . . waiting on her choice.

Casually, one of the faceless men toed the little body at her, its egg head cocked, as if asking a question.

Finally, through the clenched teeth of her mind, Liz snarled: *I'll kill you all. All of you!*

A vast sigh, and the black egg heads began to hiss, to crack open. Other things—darker things—crawled from within, clawing through fractured shells. A wicked flash of scale and feather, the dark edges of black swords.

The crow cawed, its strange voice somehow familiar, sounding from countless throats: "And so you have chosen."

76

"Liz!" Evan hissed, shaking her. "Liz! Wake up! Something's wrong! Something's happening!"

Liz jerked awake shivering, freezing with night sweat.

"What?!" She muttered, foggy, the dream still fresh in her mind.

A strange sound stopped her.

It was horrible.

A high, fluting scream, airy and hollow, like steam in a kettle, sobbing, breathless.

Evan was still shaking her.

But the light in the loft's tiny window wasn't daylight.

It was firelight.

The mountain was on fire.

No. Not a fire.

Torchlight, from the clearing. So bright as to light the dark with a dread orange glow.

And still that horrible screaming, whistling through the trees.

Downstairs, below the loft in the kitchen, the sound of armor and weapons being fitted, buckles and snaps clicking.

Then Father's voice: ". . . looks like a couple hundred men. Saw Tulf with the bastard, standing right next to him, there with him and his bear. All of them Konungur highlanders, geared for war. A dozen war bears. Ballistae, too. And they've got a couple big cages. Covered up. A little surprise for us from somewhere, I suppose."

"They're here for Dorómy," Mother said. Her voice was calm.

"No doubt."

"Gia?" Mother asked. "Bait?"

Father grunted. "To catch a king, threaten his blood."

"Pretty elaborate plan."

"Indeed," Father agreed. "And well executed. They knew

what to do to bring him here."

"What Dorómy said about Robert's death. Is he right? Does someone hunt his children? What is this?"

"The beginning."

"Of what?"

There was no response, just another grunt, a series of metallic jingles, then a weird deep chuckle. "Cursed thing."

Outside, the eerie screaming went higher still, the airy tooting shrill and dreadful.

"You barely fit," Mother fussed. "Can you even move?"

"Well enough." The creak of leather straps. "Give me a couple leaves of that? For the pain?"

Liz heard a small case open and shut. Father's affirmative grunt. "That should hold me for as long as this takes."

"I would certainly hope so."

Father chuckled. "If you can protect Voidbane, get him and Erik airborne, this whole thing is over before it's begun."

"As you wish, High General." Mother's tone was strange. Then, after a moment, she said, "You've missed this."

Another deep chuckle.

"Maybe I have, too," Mother said.

Father grunted, then: "Liz. Evan. Come down here, please."

They peeked over the ladder.

Father stood below them. He was clad in his war gear, the light from the fire flickering red in the curves and arcs of his silver armor. It did seem tight on him, but only a touch. There could be no doubt that his appearance was imposing. He held his huge saber loosely in one hand. A high silver revolver hung from his hip. A long dagger was slung across his breastplate, its pommel marked with a blunt blue stone. His hand axe was sheathed in a holster at the back of his belt, the little silver leaf on its handle shining. His eyes glowed like coals, his face was strangely flushed. Mother stood beside him, fiddling with a strap at his back. Soldier sat alert at his side. The rest of the dogs huddled in their kennel, eyes wide, tracking Father's every move, ears perked at the strange, horrible shrieking.

And then the terrible noise went quiet, as if cut off by a razor.

Liz and Evan looked at each other, scared and wondering. They turned to Father.

He'd cocked his head at the silence. "Soldier, you'll protect the house. Stay." The big mastiff blinked. Then Father glanced at Mother. She nodded. Father looked up at Liz and Evan, his eyes bright and deadly. "Get your weapons."

77

FATHER OPENED THE door and stepped onto the front porch. Liz and Evan followed, holding their bows strung and ready. In addition, they each carried two blades sheathed across their chests, and full quivers on their backs. Mother was there too, behind them. She wasn't armed. At least she didn't seem to be. Instead, she wore an unadorned tiara of high silver, like a simple crown. She'd taken it from an ornate box in the cabinet in the bedroom. There was a kind of crest in the middle, at the center of her brow, and two curls circling back behind her ears. On each of her thumbs, she wore a plain ring of high silver crafted in a similar style.

Father wasn't limping. Liz's hands were cold. Her heart hammered in her chest. They walked out onto the porch.

Their clearing was surrounded by a small army.

At least two hundred men, probably more.

Most of them carried torches. The snow flickered, glowing orange.

Fur-clad men, armed with spears and lances and bows. Several of them carried rare, expensive carbines. There were at least a dozen war bears that Liz could count, huge and menacing, grunting in the snow, their breath pluming the air, their riders armed and alert. The bears didn't wear armor, but instead were wrapped in traditional Konungur war gear: furs and skulls and leathers. The riders carried lances with white pennants hanging from their iron tips, a spidery symbol painted on them that Liz had never seen before. She did recognize a few faces of highlanders who'd been at their clearing the day prior, but the vast majority were strangers.

Behind this army, the enchanted silver ship had been knocked onto its side, the strange zeppelin above it slack and quivering, airless, caught in the branches of a great fir tree, its soft hide scorched with fire, punctured by arrows and bullet holes, a black projectile that looked like a gigantic crossbow bolt pinning it to a tree. The poor thing still made its strange hooting noises, wretched and horrible, but softer now, as if it could scream no longer. Rage blossomed in Liz's mind, replacing her fear, the sight of the injured creature infuriating. She took a deep breath, quelled both fear and rage, sought her true enemy.

There!

Beside the knocked-over ship, Tom Modró sat atop his huge albino bear. He wore his black-horned helmet and looked at them with narrow eyes, his scarred face distorted by torchlight and shadow. Liz didn't see his dogs. But there was a tiny cage strapped to the back of his white war bear, something small and furry crammed into it, silver-grey fur smashed painfully between iron bars. Mr. Tulf stood next to Modró, leaning against his long carbine in his wolf cloak, a blank look on his face, his hair braided in the old Konungur fashion. Behind Tulf and Modró, right at the tree line, half a dozen strange machines waited, pointed down into the bowl of the clearing. They looked like giant crossbows, each loaded with a huge bolt. Behind this line of machines, there were four tarp-covered cages. The cages rattled every so often, a weird grunting coming from within.

Captain Dyer, Captain Colj, Master Zar and little

Gregory, Nivar, Darian, Lord Garen, Lord Layne, and the ship's crew stood near the cabin, in front of Voidbane, waiting for Father's command. Their faces were grim, but they didn't look afraid. They looked angry and impatient. Liz wondered at their strange discipline, their commitment to Father, first as their host and now as their leader. Liz didn't see Lord Dorómy. Master Zar grinned, his purple eyes twinkling. Liz watched as he stroked the white Dallanar Sun on his forehead, said something to little Gregory. The tiny dragon squeaked, turned his yellow eyes toward the enemy, and hissed his anger, showing them his two remaining fangs. Young Lord Garen was holding an oddly shaped vial up to the torchlight, shaking it, ticking the side with his fingernail, frowning as he tried to inspect whatever the vial contained. Voidbane's tail moved slowly back and forth in the snow, piling up great white berms. Captain Dyer was whispering to the giant dragon, clearly trying to keep him calm—or something like calm. The dragon rider must have sensed Liz's gaze, because he looked up at her, smiled, then nodded—one soldier to another. Liz nodded back, and as she did so something rose in her mind, like a tidal wave of fire, building at the base of her skull, coming up, hungry for release. Darian looked up at her as if sensing her thoughts, then stepped toward the porch. Her silvery eyes were wide, unblinking. She smiled at Liz, then turned and looked up at Father.

"High General." She saluted.

He nodded. "Sister Darian."

Darian withdrew a high silver tiara from a leather case at her side, kind of like the one that Mother wore, but slightly smaller. In two hands, she raised the tiara to Father, offering it to him. It seemed to grow in her hands. There was a question in her eyes.

Father shook his head and moved aside.

"Give it to Liz," Mother said, looking at Darian. "You can keep an eye on her." Father raised an eyebrow at this, then nodded.

Darian inclined her head, stepped past Father and placed the tiara on Liz's brow. A soft, cool tingle settled across her forehead. Liz touched the high silver tiara. It seemed somehow fixed to her skin. It wasn't uncomfortable, but she couldn't move it. She looked to Darian questioningly.

"I will be with you in battle," Darian said simply, as if this explanation was all that was required. Her huge eyes seemed larger than ever. She stepped past Liz and the rest of the family, walked through the front door into the cabin, and closed the door behind her.

Across the clearing, Modró was saying something to the army, something in the old Konungur language, his big white bear shifting from paw to paw as he spoke. Liz didn't understand a word, but Father and Mother listened intently.

"Father?" Liz asked.

She was still afraid, she realized. And angry.

But she was calm, too. Strangely so.

There were hundreds of them.

But it didn't matter.

I will show you the way.

"Father?" she asked again.

"Don't worry," Mother said, squeezing her shoulder. Then she leaned forward and kissed Liz on the forehead, right below the high silver tiara.

Father looked out over the clearing. His eyes were bright.

Modró had stopped talking.

Something like a smile touched Father's lips. Still looking

out over the enemy he said: "Sometimes you fight, Liz. It's that simple. And no amount of waiting or doubting will change it. What counts, when the time comes, is that you go fearlessly, with total commitment, with your whole heart. Every warrior feels fear. But to our enemies? To our enemies—however many, however dark—we are pure fury. Silver fury. And *they* are the ones who shall tremble."

Out of nowhere, nearby, the winter crow cawed. It was close, almost directly above them. Without thinking, Liz spun, blond braid whipping 'round, spotted the crow on the dead branch of a spruce tree, drew an arrow, nocked it, and shot the bird straight through the body, spiking its feathery breast to the tree. It fluttered once, gurgled hoarsely—its beady black eyes shining with something like surprise—and died.

"Crow in winter." Liz shrugged, wiped her nose on the back of her sleeve. "Bad luck."

Father looked at her for a moment, then leaned back and laughed. The sound was huge and resounded across the clearing, against the mountain. He pulled Liz roughly to his side, kissed the top of her head. "You're your father's daughter."

Then, chuckling, he adjusted the revolver at his hip, hitched up the axe at his belt, and stepped off the porch into the torchlight, his saber held loosely in one hand.

Together, as a family, they followed.

78

FATHER WALKED PAST Voidbane and the others. As he passed, Father gave Captain Dyer a not-so-subtle look. Dyer nodded. Voidbane growled, his power vast, indomitable, and barely contained. Zar's grin widened at the dragon's noise. Little Gregory hissed ferociously. Father stopped about a quarter of the way into the clearing, looked out over the surrounding army. The torchlight flickered in his eyes. Evan and Liz were right behind him, as was Mother. She held her palms together formally, as if in prayer, the two rings on her thumbs just touching. She calmly inspected the gathered army, utterly composed. When Father spoke, his voice was deep and resonant, in perfect control. Liz felt its power.

"Glad to see you're back, stranger." He cocked his head at Modró. "Saves me the trouble."

Modró said nothing. Beside him, Mr. Tulf's face was a

stoic's mask. None of the other men moved. The torchlight wavered in the wind.

"And what about you, Tulf?" Father looked at the highlander. "You sign up with this foreigner? This killer? Stand beside the man who murdered my son?"

Tulf's eyes flickered. Then he spat in the snow and said, "This got nothing to do with you or your boy, Hone. We're here for justice. Hand over the Silver King's brother, we'll be on our way."

"Nothing to do with me?" Father laughed, something truly frightening flashing in his eyes. "You're in my clearing, at my home. And that thrice-cursed dog murdered my child. I'd say I've got a little something to do with this."

Tulf shook his head. "Sorry for your loss. But this's been a long time coming—and you know it. Time we took back some of our rights up here, properly. Opportunity for us to open parley on some of the old treaties. Bigger than you or me, Hone. Like I say: Sorry for your loss. But we ain't gonna bend knee no more without some proper respect for our ways up here."

Father looked him in the eye. "You think you'll get what

you want taking a guest from my home? Standing with the man who killed my boy?"

"This is our *land*, Hone," Tulf said. "Ours. They ain't got no right to tell us what to do with what's ours."

Mutters of agreement from the gathered crowd. The torchlight glimmered in hundreds of angry eyes.

"That liar tell you that?" Father asked, lifting his chin at Modró. "That dog make you think his cause was yours? He say the right words? Words he knows your people want to hear? He's not even from the mountain."

"Neither are you, Hone." Tulf shook his head. "And *I* speak for these men. Just me. Hand the High Lord over and we'll be on our way. Don't want trouble with you and yours."

"'Don't want trouble.'" Father laughed. He gestured with an armored palm at the assembled men, their bears, their war machines, the covered cages behind them. "You bring an army onto my land and you 'don't want trouble'? Never figured you for a fool, Tulf."

"Hand him over and we'll be on our—."

"I'll do you one better." Father cut him off. His smile was feral. "Throw down your arms, lead this band of peasants off my property, turn that murdering cur and his bear over to me now, and I'll let you live. Can't promise what state you'll be in, but you'll live. On that you have my word."

A murmur of laughter sounded 'round the clearing—cut short.

As one, the torches lifted, the heads turned, looking past Father, toward the cabin.

Liz looked around.

High Lord Dorómy Dallanar—High Chancellor of Remain, brother of the Silver King—stood there at the edge of the clearing. His black cloak was wrapped around him, like he was cold. He held a dark sword before him, the blade's black tip resting in the snow. It was unlike any sword that Liz had ever seen. A huge black blade, wide and long, but not shiny. Flat black. Lightless. Like a shard of dead night, shapes seeming to move within it, to swirl somehow, cloudy eddies of dark barely contained by its edges.

We thirst . . . all of us.

A strange voice. A woman's voice. The words blending and warping together as if whispered from a hundred mouths. To Liz, the voice seemed to come from the dark sword itself.

Somehow familiar. She looked around. Nobody else seemed to hear it.

Lord Dorómy looked up at the gathered host, the hundreds of men and their bears and war machines. Then his exhausted eyes seemed to flare, growing strong with dark light, that darkness that lives between stars.

"Come," the High Lord of Remain said simply.

"Shoot him!" someone cried from back in the trees, a young voice, tinged with hysteria. "We have them twenty to one! Just *shoot* them!"

"No!" Tulf cried hoarsely. "That's not—."

But it was too late.

A synchronized *CHUNK!* and the war machines fired together. Their black bolts lanced toward Voidbane's chest, penetrating instead a field of radiant silver mist that flowered into being, the bolts dissolving into splinters with a soft hiss as they passed through it. Mother's head and hands alight with silver fire, her palms out, rings blazing, the silvery field swelling around them, the enemy's next volley of arrows and carbine fire phasing to dust as it passed through her sorcery. A sky-rending roar, and Voidbane leapt to the air. He did not flap or run into flight—he literally sprang straight into the heavens, Captain Dyer on his back, the great dragon's primal thunder shaking the mountain peaks. The enemy was shouting now, churning with activity, disarray, Tulf and Modró trying to coordinate the mass of undisciplined amateurs. The mechanisms of the great bolt-throwers ratcheted, their crews working the machines like demons. Colj, Zar, Nivar, and the ship's crew shouted together, coming up behind Father now, weapons at the ready. The great ogre captain held a giant shield in one hand, a huge war axe of high silver in the other. Zar carried something that looked like a carbine, but fatter, its bore wide enough to swallow a fist, a weird silver jug-like thing attached to its rear. Little Gregory hissed encouragement from the dwarf's shoulder, pale yellow eyes flashing in the torchlight. Nivar and Layne were there, too. Nivar had his daggers out; his face was earnest. Layne hung back a little, but carried a broadsword that he appeared to know how to use. The lordling seemed to have been charged with protecting young Lord Garen who—seemingly oblivious to anything else at all—kept holding his weird vial up to the torchlight, shaking it harder now, frowning and muttering with frustration.

"Charge!" Tulf cried, his face livid with rage and confusion. "Charge! We have them! *We have them!*" But his voice
sounded desperate. Then he barked some words in the old
Konungur tongue and the entire army bucked, stuttered,
then shouted as one, lifting their torches and weapons, starting to run——to run right at her, white pennants streaming,
torches like burning comets, over two hundred men, a dozen
war bears coming straight at her.

And Liz froze.

Locked in place.

Then Father touched her shoulder, and their eyes
connected.

"Fearless," he said.

And it was as if the word *became* her.

Without another thought, she took a knee, smoothly drew
her bow, felt the arrow's fletching brush her cheek——loosed.
Her arrow caught Tulf right below the jaw, burst blood from
his lips, tilted his head back. He crumpled to his knees, limp
hands dropping his gun as he fell to the snow.

"See!" Father roared, laughing, war lust swelling. "Girl can hit a copper sun at fifty paces!"

He threw his scabbard from his saber and leapt in front of her, straight into the teeth of the coming army, his blade a silver scythe reaping autumn wheat, the enemy falling before him, blood hissing, missiles and weapons vanishing to sand the moment they entered Mother's protective mist. Evan knelt at Liz's side, and together they loosed arrows as fast as they could draw, their missiles taking a deadly toll. And then Lord Dorómy, Colj, Zar, Nivar, and the rest of the crew were at Father's side—and *they* were charging. Lord Dorómy's black sword moaned for blood, a hungry fiend, its pommel a black egg, huge blade sweeping some- how through five bodies at once, a tongue of night flame, blood fanning gouts over white snow, soaking fur and man and beast. Master Zar held his strange weapon against his hip, cranked a brass lever, pounded on it, cursed, and then spurting silver-white fire belched from its muzzle, a rope of sizzling flame that spawned screams of agony wherever it touched. Liz loosed another arrow, caught her target in the heart, down. And then Voidbane dropped like a meteor into the enemy's rear, silver-white fire blasting between his huge fangs—black neck stretched forward, eyes clamped shut—fury roaring from his mouth. Two thirds of Modró's army and most of his war bears vanished, melted to slag by the searing funnel of silver-white fire. The stench of burning flesh was raw, potent in her nostrils. "The smell . . . ," Evan muttered. Liz grimaced, loosed another arrow, and killed. On Voidbane's back, Captain Dyer stood high in his saddle, standing upright in his harness, working the mechanism of a long silver carbine, one eye clamped shut, aiming, dropping men in their tracks with horrible efficiency—crack-down, crack-down, crack-down, crack-down—man and dragon leaping back to the skies with a roar that seemed to shake the very earth itself. With a grunt, Colj cut a fur-decked man in half with his great axe, from crown to crotch, splitting him open like a hissing gourd, swung his shield sideways, blasted half a dozen men backwards. The three remaining bear riders whose mounts could still run turned and scattered for the woods. Others turned to run. Liz and Evan shot them as they fled. Liz was terrified, elated. She was screaming. No words, just screaming and shooting. Directly in front of her, Father, Lord Dorómy, Nivar, and the rest of the crew fought side by side, swamped in the enemy's midst, Nivar's twin blades flashing like moon on water, fine lines of blood painting the snow with a calligraphy as old as time itself, Lord Dorómy's dark blade spilling and drinking gore. Every now and again, Father would kill his man, look around, check on her and Evan, then draw his revolver, shoot some enemy on the other side of the battlefield before turning back to it. *CHUNK!* Another volley from the war machines vaporized against Mother's silver haze.

Liz.

The tiara at her forehead went warm, a cool voice whispering in the front of her mind.

Darian's voice?

Yes, it whispered. *I am here. I can see him. Modró. He's doing something.*

Liz looked around, trying to see through the churning battle, the chaos.

He is there, up at the tree line. Beside that big cage.

There!

Modró was still mounted atop his white war bear. He was struggling to open one of the covered cages without dismounting. Father hacked a man's head off, the helmet and face seeming to hang in time above the fray as Master Zar unloaded again with his weird flame weapon, its eerie fire splashing and sizzling into the enemy, freakish screams flooding their midst. Little Gregory squeaked approvingly. Nivar danced between at least a dozen men, took their biggest down with a peeling slash across the throat, yellow robes spinning, then was hit hard on the back of his head, blindsided, went down. Like twin lions, Lord Dorómy and Father leapt to his aid.

Stay focused, Darian's voice came. *He's doing something.*

The cage fell open. Modró ripped the tarp away.

Beside Lord Garen, Lord Tevéss shrieked and pointed: "Monsters! They have fiends! Some kind of . . . !"

It was a freak from nightmares. Big. Almost as big as Colj. No real head, four notched arms like scimitars, three muscly legs, a tripod of corpse flesh glistening, eyes everywhere, milky cataracts peeling open, looking this way and that, finally seeing Lord Dorómy there beside Father as they fought to protect the fallen Nivar. The monster charged straight at Lord Dorómy, its four weird shoulders cocked back, muscly legs churning, blade-arms dragging the snow, plowing through its allies as it charged its prey. Liz shot three arrows at the freaky thing, watched them bounce off its grey hide—no damage. And she was running out of arrows.

"Look sharp there, Dor," Father tilted his head at the weird monster, shooting two men—CRACK! CRACK!—stabbing his saber into the snow, reloading his revolver with the smooth ease of habit. Lord Dorómy turned, saw the monster, then ran straight at the thing, leaping directly into the beast's path, his black sword burning cold flame. The beast lunged for the High Lord, its four arms slicing together as if it would cut him into quarters, but Dorómy rolled beneath the flashing blade-arms, came up, and drove the black blade straight through the thing's middle, ripping the sword out its top, clear ichor spraying skyward. The monster dropped lifelessly at his feet.

Up by the tree line, Modró ducked behind a thicket, came out on its other side. Liz saw an opening, aimed, ducked a thrown spear, loosed her arrow—but she was off and her arrow hit Modró's war bear in the back leg, right above the knee; a bad wound. The bear roared in pain and Modró jerked at its reins, yanking on the iron ring in the old bear's sensitive nose, forcing it toward the next cage. Liz winced, cursed her aim. The bear roared once more, turned away, limping. Voidbane landed near where Nivar had fallen, massive tail sweeping the enemy clear, silver-white fire blasting flesh from bone, charred corpses hurled back into piles of smoking ruin. Most of the enemy was running now, and Captain Dyer butchered them as they fled, their white pennants trampled in the snow, the dragon rider's deadly aim punching gory holes as they ran for the safety of the woods. Colj had a fur-clad highlander by the ankle, threw him across the clearing, the man spinning through the sky like a bizarre pinwheel, crashing broken into a group of his fellows. Master Zar laughed out loud, shouted something that Liz couldn't hear. Little Gregory hissed with glee.

He is releasing the other beasts, Darian's voice came. *The monsters are distractions. He tries to divert us, to get away.*

Back at the tree line, Modró had opened the other three cages. The blade-armed tripod-things quivered a moment, their multitudinous eyes peeling open, then all three of them charged straight at Lord Dorómy.

Modró had disappeared.

He is back in the trees, moving up that narrow path, toward the ridge. I can see him . . . I can still see him. He is trying to escape.

Behind Liz, young Lord Garen cried with happy delight. "Ha-ha! Finally!" Liz looked back. The young lord adjusted his spectacles, held the vial he'd been messing with triumphantly over his head. Something silver moved inside it. Lord Layne leaned to Lord Garen's ear, pointed at the huge blade-armed creatures charging Lord Dorómy. Lord Garen nodded, ran forward, and threw the vial. The thing flew overhead, crystal curves catching the firelight, and shattered on the lead monster, disgorging what looked like thousands of tiny silver beetles. They swarmed over the monster as it ran, sinking into its pale skin, burrowing into its eyes, its strange mouth, muscly legs, its flesh turning metallic, the color of bright lead, arms stiffening, stopping—then it leapt madly forward toward Lord Dorómy, stopped, whirled 'round like a spinning top, and jumped back toward the other two attacking creatures, blade arms whirling, cutting the legs out from under its fellows, proceeding to dice them into neat little cubes like a demented chef, snow spattering with clear fluid.

Lord Garen laughed and pointed. "See, Uncle! I *told* you it would work!"

Lord Dorómy shook his head with what looked like exasperation, and was promptly tackled by three tough-looking highlanders that came in from the side. Father and the others rushed to his aid and the last remnants of the army piled into the fray.

He is running. Darian's voice again, whispering in the center of Liz's mind. *He is about a hundred paces back in the woods, running up that path, toward the ridge. I can see him. His bear is slowing. You must tell your Father.*

But Father and the rest of them were completely embroiled in the final melee. Liz turned, ducked as a fur-clad highlander swung the butt of his carbine at her, dropped to the snow, drew her high silver dagger, trimmed his hamstring behind the knee, and dashed past his screams, past the last pockets of battle, toward the woods. Voidbane and Captain Dyer were at the tree line now, burning the forest down, tossing the bolt-throwing machines and their crews every which way, smashed pieces scattering against burning trees. A man's leg dangled from the corner of the dragon's mouth. Captain

Dyer worked his silver carbine with lethal precision. Void-bane crushed a highlander under his claw, the great dragon's triumphant roar filling Liz's heart with a kind of hot zeal as she raced between the trees, up the path, fast as a snow leopard.

Even over the packed snow, Modró's trail was clear. The blood from his war bear's wound and the beast's giant prints made the way impossible to lose. And the murderer seemed to be leaving gear and equipment behind him as he ran, lightening his load for flight. A pair of saddlebags thrown haphazardly against a tree, a cluster of traps tossed in a snow bank—and there in the center of the path, a small iron cage with a little ball of silver fur crammed into it.

"Narmos!" Liz cried, dropping to her knees, fumbling for the latch. "Narmos!"

The cage opened easily and she pulled the little bear out, yanking off her gloves, placing her palm on his small chest, right next to his furry white blaze. The splint on his leg was missing and his back paws had been wired together so that he couldn't walk, the twine cutting deep into his fur and skin. Liz cut the wire with her dagger, massaged his little legs, got the blood flowing. Narmos's huge grey eyes opened and he blinked up at her sleepily, stretched hard, and gave a giant yawn, his pink tongue curling. He didn't seem hurt, but it was also clear that Modró hadn't been feeding him. Then he looked over Liz's shoulder, up the ridge. His nostrils flared. A little growl rose in his chest.

I think Modró heard you, Darian's voice came.

Liz stopped in her tracks.

"Where is he?" Liz swallowed, looked around. She was completely alone up here. And she didn't know if Darian could hear her. She glanced up the ridge, scanning the shadows. Then, not knowing why, she put two fingers on either side of the high silver tiara, at her temples. It was cold to the touch—but still warm on her brow.

"Where is he?" she asked again.

Darian's voice came. *He has stopped up top there, on the ridge above you. One hundred paces up the path—almost out of my range. He is off his bear. Outside a tent. He is not moving . . . still not moving. It looks like he is thinking. His bear is limping. Now he is trying to pull the arrow out of the bear's knee. His bear is badly hurt. He might have to go on foot. You should back out, Liz. They are all but finished down here. Nivar is injured. Captain Dyer and*

Voidbane are hunting stragglers. Come back.

Sensible advice, Liz thought. She turned and started down the way she had come.

Modró's dogs.

There was something new in her tone.

"What?" Liz asked, her scalp prickling.

His dogs. He has unchained them. He is . . . . He is giving his dogs something.

Liz's blood froze. Above her, the forest was icy and dark. Below, Voidbane's fires still burned. Somewhere, down there in the clearing, a man screamed like a child, begging for mercy.

He is making his dogs drink something . . . . Come back. Please come back.

Liz nodded. She calmly picked up Narmos, slung the bear cub on her hip, and started walking back down the path. Scared, but not panicked. Not hurrying. Walking carefully, so as not to trip. *Slow is smooth and smooth is fast.*

Narmos looked up at her and blinked his grey eyes. Liz kissed him on the furry forehead. "You might not have had dinner in a while, but you're getting fat."

The dogs. Darian's voice, calm in her mind. *They are coming. He is coming with them. They are coming right at you.*

Through the trees above her, a deep, wicked baying. Something thrashing up in the underbrush, an evil, rabid snarl, snapping twigs and branches. Then a hunting horn sounded, its moaning cry low and baleful.

Run! Darian cried.

But Liz stopped in her tracks.

There was no point running.

Liz knew rock mastiffs.

And she knew the snowy trail.

She couldn't outrun them, even if she tried. It was impossible. And climbing a tree would do nothing against Modró's carbine.

Father's words came to her again, unbidden: "Sometimes you fight. It's that simple. And no amount of waiting or doubting will change it."

She swallowed, sat Narmos down beside her, reached for her quiver—only to discover that a mere handful of arrows remained.

Five, to be precise.

Five arrows. Five mastiffs. One giant war bear. One murdering lunatic. The math didn't work.

Doesn't matter.

She pulled the arrows from her quiver, pushing the five arrowheads point first into the snow, their black fletching within easy reach.

A deeper grunting came behind the dogs, the old white war bear's lopsided, shuffling charge.

The hunting horn sounded again, closer, practically on top of her.

From down in the clearing, through the trees, Liz just barely heard Evan's voice, indistinct, then Father's distant shout: "Liz?"

Narmos growled.

Father, again in the distance, louder through the trees: "Liz?!"

She heard Mother shout something.

"Stay behind me," Liz muttered absently, shoving the little bear back. He tried to grab onto her arm with his paws, pull her away. "Knock it off," she muttered.

The sounds were getting louder, the throaty growl of

Modró's dogs deep and savage.

Below her, far away in the clearing, Darian cried out, her voice high and clear, shouting words that Liz couldn't understand.

She sounds so far away.

It was as if the young seer's voice came from the other side of the world.

And then things started to slow down.

From below, Father's voice was a bear's roar: "LIZ? LIZ!" Then: "Erik! THERE!"

Voidbane blasted overhead, setting the treetops alight. But the forest itself was too dense for him to penetrate. Cinders dropped from the heights. The snapping-pop of burning pine, hissing sap, the entire scene lit with hellish orange light.

Things went slower still.

A burning piece of ash floated slowly past her face, strangely beautiful. A crash in the undergrowth, right there in front of her now, breaking branches, the pack coming like a wave.

Narmos growled again, but it was more like that weird little roar of his than a growl, a strange noise, not exactly loud—but quite ferocious.

And then he waddled out in front of her, his little growl rumbling in his chest, standing up on his rear paws, dropping back to the ground, his silver head swaying this way and that, a war bear already, a part of his soul.

"Get back." She grabbed one of his back paws, pinched it hard, but he snarled viciously at her, pulled away, standing up on his wobbly legs, nose waving back and forth, his growl steady now, getting louder. He dropped to all fours and gave a little roar. A challenge. Burning branches fell from above.

And then the lead mastiff came crashing through the trees, blasting onto the path in front of them, skidded momentarily to a stop, its panting tongue raw and inflamed. Its eyes were red coals, fangs white and vampiric, something rotten, slimy, coating its muzzle and jowls, black acid dripping in the snow.

And then little Narmos charged.

"No!" Liz screamed.

But it was too late.

The little bear charged straight up the path, his hips off-center from his shoulders, his little silver tail hanging down behind, head tilted to the side, that angry little growl of his low and steady, his breath steaming in the cold. The mastiff roared and went straight for him. Liz blinked. Dropped to one knee. Drew. Loosed. Her form was fluid and perfect, the action more than habit—a part of her. Her arrow took the monster in the throat, lodged there, the infected beast collapsing forward, plowing snow. She nocked her next arrow, drew, waited on her target. Two mastiffs came through the trees side by side, leapt onto the path, claws scrabbling ice as they charged, flying together over their fallen leader, red jaws wide—and Liz shot one through the chest, but the other dog hit Narmos head-on, the two animals going down in a thrashing ball of claw and fang. Liz stepped up, drew her high silver blade, stabbed the hellhound in the back of the neck—once, twice, three times—hot blood spraying, little Narmos pulling himself up to his feet, covered in blood, his bad back leg injured now, bleeding, trying to stand, wobbling, trying to get out in front of her, turning to protect her—and then the next two mastiffs came from nowhere and hit him together, knocking him back over her arrows, the snaps of shafts breaking, dog fangs flashing, shaking him, hunting for his soft belly—but Narmos had one of the mastiffs by the throat, his eyes clamped shut, bleeding, hanging on for all he was worth. Liz leapt into the middle of it, stabbing at anything that wasn't bear, finding a mastiff's head, slamming her silver blade into its ear, turning back to Narmos, cutting the last dog's throat straight to its spine, her high silver blade diamond sharp, the little bear bloody and weak from his wounds.

And then Modró and his war bear broke through the snowy brush onto the trail above them, just a dozen paces away, the old bear's red eyes raw with pain and rage, its back leg dragging behind it, red on his white fur, the murderer aiming his carbine at Liz's face, one eye squeezed shut along the barrel, the burning forest shining red in his eyes, ready to put her down.

And once again, little Narmos charged.

Bleeding and wounded, the little bear had somehow managed to get back on all fours and now ran slowly up the path at the giant bear and its rider—not growling anymore, his mangled back leg dragging uselessly behind him— hobbling, but still charging all the same, still trying to get in front of her, still trying to protect her.

Evil blossomed in Modró's pale eyes.

Slowly—for show—he adjusted his aim, carefully sighting along his weapon, the carbine's barrel a deadly hole dropping toward Narmos. The white bear looked at the charging cub, his old red eyes sad with deep knowledge.

"No!" Liz leapt to her feet, threw her dagger at him—but it didn't even come close, Modró slowly aiming once again, savoring the moment.

"Me!" Liz screamed. "Here! You thrice-cursed coward! *Me!*" Waving her arms, running forward up the path now.

Modró's rifle stopped moving.

Narmos was still charging.

Modró's angle was perfect.

He couldn't miss.

Above them, a tree branch scorched by dragon fire cracked.

Liz cast around, looked to the arrows buried behind her in the fire-lit snow.

There was one left, half buried, unbroken.

Liz dove for it.

Modró fired at Narmos.

But somehow, the poacher *missed*—the white bear lurching suddenly to the side, ruining his aim, the discharge dreadfully loud, Narmos's right ear blasting away in a bloody spray of tattered flesh and silver-grey fur, still wobbling toward the great white bear and his rider, almost there now.

Liz had her arrow.

"Cursed beast!" Modró screamed maniacally, pale eyes rolling mad, his face a twisting mask of insanity and rage, savagely jerking the reins, ripping the iron ring from the bear's nose, leveling his gun at the back of his own bear's skull, chambering another round. Narmos was still charging up the path, the old war bear watching him come, a strange acceptance in his old red eyes.

"Great Sisters, guide my way," Liz whispered as she nocked, drew, and loosed.

Her arrow took Tom Modró in the left eye, the black fletching filling the socket as the point punched out the back of his skull, his head knocked back, his other eye staring wide into the burning treetops as he coughed backwards, teeth open, leaning now, then falling from his saddle to the snow. The old white bear immediately sat down on his big rump in a drift, looked at Liz, blinked, lifting his weight off his injured knee. Blood ran freely down his white fur. It didn't want to fight. Narmos was there now in front of the giant bear, bleeding, but trying to bite and claw at the massive beast's front paw with zero effect. The old white bear looked at the cub, sniffed at him curiously, looked back again up at Liz. The torn nostril cartilage where his nose ring had been was ragged and tender. Liz looked back into his ancient red eyes, something passed between them, and they knew each other. "I am tired and hurt and hungry," his eyes said. "I am no threat to you, your bear, or your people."

And then Father was at her side, crushing her to his chest, saying her name over and over again, kissing the top of her head, the rest of them coming up beside them, weapons drawn, looking around at the bodies, the blood, the carnage.

"Kill that thing." Liz heard Mother command, saw her finger aimed at the old bear.

Liz made to push away from Father. Colj and Zar stepped forward, their weapons held ready. Everyone else was there, too—Lord Dorómy, Lord Garen, Lord Layne, a number of the ship's crew—everyone except Darian and Nivar. Liz looked again at the old war bear, saw the knowledge and resignation flicker in his huge red eyes. He did not move as the ogre and dwarf approached. At his feet, in the bloody snow, Narmos still wrestled with the great bear's giant paw, doing his best to gnaw it, but doing no harm, the bear cub nearly collapsing from his own wounds. Dorómy stared at Modró's body, a strange mixture of satisfaction and rage and terrible disappointment twisting his face, the black blade hissing in his hand. A few of the others were looking at him now, tensely.

Mustering everything she had, Liz pushed away from Father, stood as tall as she could, and cried: "*Hold*! I claim the life of that animal as my fair battle prize! *Hold I say*! By right of combat and victory, that war bear is *mine*!"

She did not speak as a girl from a log cabin on the edge of the wild, nor as a huntress of the big mountain. She spoke as a high lady of Remain, as her father's daughter, as a young woman whose authority traced its roots in law, custom, and force to the beginnings of the Silver Kingdom itself.

And they felt her power, her words stopping them in their tracks, all of them—Colj, Zar, Lord Layne, Lord Garen, Evan, Mother, little Narmos, even Father and High Lord Dorómy, the latter blinking as if waking from some dark dream, his black sword softly moaning at his side.

"That bear is mine," Liz repeated, turning to look at Father and Mother, the rest of them, her chin high, indomitable.

Mother looked at her for a long moment, then inclined her head in agreement. Father's face was blood-splattered, but his eyes were clear, filled with pride.

Liz looked him in the eye. "He is mine, Father."

He returned her gaze, nodded. "He is yours."

79

WHEN OLD MAN Jarlund, Mr. Barnabus, Mr. Fonhammer, and the rest of the locals arrived the next morning, they found a rather unexpected state of affairs at the Hone family's clearing. The sky was clear and blue, the sun glittering hard on the high white of the mountain.

Jarlund squinted at Father, toeing over a bloody Konungur battle standard, looking around at the clearing, the fire, the remains, the blood. Jarlund's face was bruised and yellow, his wounded forearm slung across his chest. He glanced past Father, at the giant white war bear being tended by young Lord Garen on the front porch. Little Gregory was perched on Lord Garen's shoulder, the little blue dragon overseeing the procedure. Soldier sat calmly at Lord Garen's side, surveying his domain. The prodigy pushed his spectacles back up onto his nose as he rambled ceaselessly about the innumerable properties of the various herbs he was using, tapping the massive bear on its huge, furry shoulder when its attention strayed, almost like he was talking to a distracted student rather than a wounded war beast. Master Zar and Captain Dyer sat on a pair of stumps beside the porch, the purple dwarf laughing at something, both of them smoking their pipes as they drank their morning tea. Across the way, Mother, Captain Colj, and the crew were busy making repairs to the silver ship and its zeppelin, tenderly smoothing the poor creature's body in the sun, cleaning its wounds, anointing its burns with a silver balm. Near the center of the clearing, the mighty Voidbane sat amidst a pile of bones, smacking and crunching, his black scales gleaming as Evan clambered all over him, polishing and cleaning. Every so often, when Evan hit a spot behind his horns or wings, the big dragon would close his eyes with pleasure. When the locals approached, Voidbane glared at them hungrily.

"Ah." Jarlund cleared his throat. "Looks like you've had

guests."

Father shrugged and leaned hard against his walking stick. "Hospitality still means something in this house."

Mother and Liz served them tea before Father sent them on their way.

80

FATHER HAD RE-SPLINTED Narmos's back leg and Lord Garen had given the little bear some special medicine for the ear he'd lost. "Won't grow back, I'm afraid." Lord Garen had frowned. "But this will help it heal quickly. You'll want to clean it twice a day." Liz had nodded. The young lord had then turned his full attention back to the giant white bear and the silver ship's zeppelin. The zeppelin's name was Ooma, Liz had learned. "This will take a while," Garen told Captain Colj and Master Zar.

"Stay as long as you like," Father told them.

Nivar had been knocked unconscious during the battle, but he was feeling better now, his head wrapped in thick white gauze. In the evenings, he and Darian and Evan and Liz would stroll the edge of the clearing, side by side, laughing and telling stories while the grown-ups feasted near the cabin.

"I have heard many amazing things about the Hone estates on Egáton, Liz." Darian smiled, her huge silver eyes and brown skin radiant in the rising moon. "My father says they boast some of the most extensive and most beautifully kept grounds in the duchy."

"My parents say the same." Nivar nodded.

Sometimes Nivar's hand would brush against Liz's as they walked, but she couldn't tell if it was on purpose or not, and it was driving her crazy. He always seemed to make a point of being next to her when they set out. And afterwards, when they talked by the fire, the yellow sparks in his green eyes would dance with a music all their own.

"Perhaps we could visit?" Darian continued. "Next time you are there? I would love to visit. I do not mean to be rude, but I have never been."

Liz grinned. "Me either."

Evan, munching an apple he'd gotten from one of the ship's crew, asked: "Where's 'Egáton'?"

For some reason, the question struck them all as crazy funny, and they laughed until their stomachs ached.

81

"I'M GOING TO Dávanor," Evan told Liz later the next night, whispering up in the sleeping loft. Narmos was tucked in under the covers between them, his splint sticking into her side, the dressing on his missing ear freshly changed. Below them, the fire glowed low and warm. Soldier's tail thumped on the rug. Outside, Liz could hear Father and Lord Dorómy talking softly on the porch. They'd been out there for hours.

"Captain Dyer says that I can do it," Evan continued. "I'm older than a normal dragon squire would be, but he says if I work hard it won't matter and that he'll find me a position in a High House there. Because of our family name. Won't be an issue, he says." He paused. "I'm going to ride dragons in the service of the Silver King."

"Evan Hone." Liz smiled. "Dragon rider of Dávanor."

"Yes!" He beamed. "And I'm gonna spend my first year with Voidbane, he says."

"What do Mother and Father say?" Liz asked.

"Do I need their permission?"

"No." Liz shook her head. "But you might want their blessing."

Evan paused, considering. Then he nodded. "Probably right. Hmm. What about you?"

"What about me?"

"'What about me?' she says! Well? Where will *you* go? And don't tell me you haven't thought about it! We're rich! Nivar was telling me that Mother is one of the wealthiest landowners in the entire Kingdom. And she's a famous 'war mage.' I don't know what that means exactly yet, but you saw some of it during the battle. And Father—he's *important*. He knows the Silver King! He's rich, too. And renowned. We can do whatever we want!"

Liz rubbed Narmos's belly, his thick fur soft between her fingers. "I want to stay up here for a while, I think. Think about things . . . . Be here for a while with Narmos. Get him fixed up. And I want to learn about his training. Father knows all about war bears, how they fight, how you train them. There's so much to learn. Too much."

"Come *on*! You don't want to *see* everything? It's huge! Nivar says there are over a hundred duchies. Different *worlds*, Lizzy! All connected, but totally different! You can learn whatever you want!"

Liz considered for a moment. Then she nodded. "If that's true, then I'd probably want to start here, at home. Train Narmos. Maybe serve as a ranger, if they'll have me. Figure out what *this* place is really about first."

"Not me! Heck no. I'm going out there." He waved at the ceiling. "Everywhere. On my dragon. I'm gonna fly everywhere I can. I'm gonna see it all."

Liz had to admit that his dream sounded superb. But she barely knew what she would find down the line past Korfort, much less farther down. And that was one road. Toward one town. On one mountain. On one world. The scale of her new reality was vast—almost beyond imagination. Scary, exhilarating, incredible, wonderful, all at once.

She stroked Narmos's fur for a long moment, then asked: "You ever wonder why they never told us? You ever wonder what we'd be doing right now—right this moment—if we hadn't found her dead on the mountain?"

Evan shook his head, but the question gave him pause.

Liz kissed Narmos on the nose. He promptly licked the spot where she'd kissed him, his black nose shiny.

Liz shook her head. "Teagan would be alive. There'd be

no Narmos. No dragons. No ogres. No kings. No riches. No nothing. And tomorrow, we'd be out checking the lines, and then again every day, stretching the fur, doing it all over again and again. I'd probably marry some local guy, some guy like Belios. You'd marry some local girl. Build a couple more cabins here on the clearing. And that would be that. The whole cycle, just over and over again."

"But that's not how it is, Lizzy."

"That's my point. If Gia hadn't died up here, if they hadn't come for her, we might never have known any of this. We might never have known who we really were. We might never have known that the Silver Kingdom is real."

82

THE NEXT MORNING, Lord Dorómy, Lord Garen, Lord Layne, and Captain Dyer brought Gia's body up from the skinning shed. They did it without ceremony, without words, strapping her wrapped body carefully to the gunner's shelf at the rear of Voidbane's large saddle. They then said their farewells all around, Lord Layne doing his absolute best to be courteous and superior and apologetic all at the same time. (Which was no small feat, Liz realized.) Lord Garen had given Liz some instructions on the care of the old albino bear, along with a leather case filled with various herbs and tonics. "And under no circumstances should you ever touch that purple one unless he absolutely will *not* go to sleep," Lord Garen had said, pushing his spectacles up on his nose.

Captain Dyer and Father had been working out the details of Evan's move to Dávanor. Her brother would finish the trapping season up here on the big mountain, then they'd all go by zeppelin down to the Tarn, from whence they'd travel to Dávanor as a family for a long visit to get Evan settled. Liz had to admit it: She was tired, she was still a little shocked, she was still a bit overwhelmed—but she couldn't wait.

Lord Dorómy was the last to mount up, but before he did so, he stood in front of them as they waited on the front porch, his fingers laced before him. There was no trace of the black sword.

"Once more, I am in your debt, High General," he said formally. "And yours, my Lady."

"Not at all, my Lord." Father bowed, leaning hard on his walking stick. Mother inclined her head, her arm laced

438

through Father's huge elbow.

"I will send word after I've conferred with Bellános and Lessip. There's much yet to discuss. To understand."

Mother and Father bowed. Their eyes were happy, but serious, too.

"And you, young Lord Hone?" Lord Dorómy turned to Evan. "I understand you will soon be counted among the squires of Dávanor?"

Evan bowed, still a bit awkward, then crossed his chest with his fist. "Truth and honor, my Lord!"

"Ancient words." Lord Dorómy smiled. "And true. Katherine the Second explained it thus: 'For this reason the dragon riders of Dávanor are rightly feared throughout the Realm: Nothing is more terrifying than a warrior willing to die for his word.' The Silver Legions are in need of strong, righteous fighters, young Lord Hone. I wish you all good luck and success."

Evan bowed and saluted once more.

Lord Dorómy turned to Liz, reached into his cloak, and took out a small leather bag, like a finger bag in which you might carry a few coins in your pocket. He looked at it for a long moment, cleared his throat, squeezed the bag, then handed it to Liz. "A small token of my thanks and esteem, young Lady Hone. If we can ever be of service, consider it done. In this I speak for my brother as well, High Lord Bellá-nos Dallanar, the Silver King, Overlord of the Realm, the High King of Remain."

Liz took the bag and bowed deeply.

Lord Dorómy nodded to them once more, turned, walked to Voidbane, and mounted with his fellows. Captain Dyer gave Father a final nod, then touched the great black dragon's side. With a muscly grunt and a blast of wind, Voidbane leapt to the sky.

Liz felt the bag, knew instantly what was inside, turned it open into her palm until they fell into her hand: two earrings, dark blue sapphires held in the silver grip of dragon claws, the details of each scale perfectly captured by the artist's skill.

"A royal gift," Mother said, resting her hand on one of her shoulders.

"Indeed." Father nodded, putting his hand on the other.

Liz looked back up, out to the sky and the big mountain, but the mighty dragon and those he carried were already gone.

83

THE STRANGE ZEPPELIN, Ooma, tooted in her harness, humming her flashing colors, her translucent skin pulsing happily as Captain Colj lifted the last crate of supplies over the silver ship's gunwales. The sky was pure blue, not a cloud in sight, the sun shining warmth that hinted at spring's coming.

The big white war bear was sleeping on the front porch, covered from head to tail in snoring hounds. Even Soldier had gotten in on the action, lying stretched out against the great bear's side. The old bear's wound was healing nicely. Each morning, he and Father would take careful walks around the clearing, limping, leaning on each other, two veterans enjoying the peace and quiet of sunrise. Mother had carefully stitched the tear in the big bear's red-brown nose, whispering softly to the old beast as her elegant hand sewed with silver thread. And then, in the evening, Father would bring out his mandolin and sing the giant bear softly to sleep as Mother watched fondly from the doorway. Father had yet to come up with a new name for the big fellow, but he was working on it. Liz could tell that Father still itched for his flask, but between the herbs from old man Jarlund and some vials Mother had received from Lord Garen, he was clearly feeling better.

"Got a long way to go," he'd say to Mother sheepishly. She'd pull him down to her and kiss his forehead.

On the deck of the silver ship, Darian, Zar, Nivar, and little Gregory were already aboard, looking down at Liz and the rest of her family, laughing and waving, making promises to write, to see each other again soon. Below them, squinting up into the sun, little Narmos slung on her hip, Liz was both sad and happy to see them go. On one hand, she felt that she'd known them her whole life, as if they were the friends that she'd always been meant to have. On the other hand, she was just plain tired of company. She smiled at the thought. It was a great problem to have.

Colj heaved himself up onto the silver ship, the entire thing listing to one side, everyone on board laughing, holding onto the rigging, trying to help the great ogre to his feet.

Master Zar grinned, rubbed the Dallanar Sun on his purple forehead, looked at Colj. "Our big friend here needs a very specific seat, as you can tell. Ogre-sized. Dead center there, right in the middle."

"I shall fetch it, Master Zar!" a crewman cried and scuttled off. Little Gregory squeaked and Colj shrugged his huge shoulders. The rest of the ship's crew made ready to depart.

"Thought Zar was joking." Father grinned, leaning hard on his walking stick as two crewmen brought out a massive chair and set it in the center, amidships. Evan laughed. At Father's side, Mother stood up on her tippy-toes, held onto Father's thick arm, pulled him down, and kissed him on the cheek. His eyes sparkled.

"Rigging, ready?" a petty officer cried.

"Rigging ready, sir!" a crew of voices answered.

"Promise again you will write, Liz!" Darian cried, waving.

"I will!" Liz waved. "Tonight!"

"And me, too?" Nivar asked, smiling, holding his yellow robes close to his heart, the sunlight catching the sparks in his green eyes.

"Yes!" Liz cried, her face going warm.

"Sails, ready?" the petty officer cried again.

"Sails ready, sir!" the crew answered.

The sail-like fins on the back of the ship opened up, silver and smooth, like unfolding magic. Above the silver ship, Ooma tooted and seemed to grow, the lights within her shining and twinkling, her strange mouth opening and closing, opening and closing, sapphire fireflies dancing, the harness 'round her great body stretching softly 'round her swelling girth.

"Launch!" the officer cried.

"Launching, sir!"

The boat began to ascend, softly, very slowly, noiselessly.

Darian said something to Nivar, elbowed him in the side. Nivar nodded and cried, "Oh yes!"

He reached into his yellow robes and tossed something to Liz.

It was a yellow envelope, sealed with golden wax. Something was written on the front.

It fluttered awkwardly in the air, wobbling down, and Father caught it before she could, reaching up above her head. Father gave Nivar a long, pointed look before he handed the evelope over to Liz. Nivar bowed very deeply, his face going red. Mother patted Father's shoulder.

Liz set Narmos down in the snow, took the envelope in both hands, and read the inscription. It was simple, just her address, but it was written in a flowing, magical script that seemed to glow on the page:

High Lady Elizabeth Hone

In the Care of Mr. Otto Jarlund and / or Gen. Branten Hone

Aaryn's Cry, Over-the-Trange

The Grand Duchy of Kon

She looked up at Nivar, his face just a bit smaller now, and pushed her braid over her shoulder.

"What is this?" she cried.

Nivar grinned and waved. "I thought I would beat you to it! Now *you* owe *me* one! "

Darian clapped her hands and laughed. Somewhere Master Zar said something and little Gregory squeaked a reply.

Liz smiled, waved one last time, then put her hand over her eyes and watched them sail away until they were nothing but a sliver mote in the sky.

"I'm hungry," Evan said, turning to the cabin.

"That makes two of us." Father patted his stomach.

Mother squeezed Liz's shoulder. Father kissed her on the top of the head. Narmos had attached himself to Father's good leg, both his paws wrapped around his knee.

"Shall we?" Father asked. He touched Liz on the shoulder.

She looked up at him, holding her letter before her, eager to open it.

He glanced at the letter, nodded, and smiled gently. "Take your time."

He turned away and walked with the family toward the cabin, little Narmos out in front of them now, doing that weird lopsided run in the snow, his missing ear—which he didn't seem to miss—making him more adorable than ever. Mother leaned against Father, his huge arm around her shoulder. Evan was babbling nonstop about dragons, and Dávanor, and dragons.

Liz looked to the sky once more, caught the last wink of that silver star in the blue, opened her letter, and began to read.

EPILOGUE

HIGH GENERAL CORLEN Lessip lifted his pocket watch on its silver chain, glanced at it, smoothed his thumb over its crystal face, then slipped it back into a silk pocket.

Almost time.

Lessip nodded to himself, turned from the center of the throne room, and gazed out the tall windows.

It was a spectacular view.

Down over the golden coast, out over the Sea of the Sun, out toward that misty distance where shore and ocean joined. Impossibly far below him, the surf washed silently onto the long beach, wave after wave, a marching succession of white lines etched on an eternity of gold. White gulls wheeled, turned, held, tilted, then angled away at speed, pushed by the wind. To the west, the sun had begun its gilded descent, hovering a palm's breadth above the scintillating sea.

It was a potent and seductive perspective, Lessip had to admit.

High above it all. The patterns and the relationships perfectly clear. Everything logical, understandable.

Potent because the view was the unmistakable product of power; nowhere in the Realm could a man enjoy a vantage such as that afforded by the Káladar's great throne room, the Hall of the Silver King. Seductive because the clarity which the view seemed to offer was false—a lie.

Because it's too high.

Too far above everything. At this elevation, it was impossible to see the details. Impossible to see the truth. And that was the material point.

Because nothing is clear.

Lessip frowned.

Today had proved that fact. Proved it beyond all doubt.

It was quite simple, really: Lessip didn't understand what had happened to Gia—and to Dorómy—on Kon.

Not at all.

Oh, he understood the basics, to a certain extent. Gia had been killed. High Chancellor Dorómy—with the help of Branten Hone, of all people—had killed her killer. But Lessip didn't understand how these things had happened. And he most certainly didn't understand *why*. The powers and the players and the motivations behind the whole scenario were entirely unknown to him. They were, therefore, inherently problematic. *And, thus, dangerous.* While Lessip hoped that his coming appointment would illuminate the matter, that rendezvous itself presented its own kind of peril.

Lessip turned back to the throne room.

He stood near the rear wall of the Hall of the Silver King, the eastern wall of the high throne room of the mighty fortress of Káladar. The chamber was a soaring, vaulted space of mounting buttresses, endless glass, and golden-white marble, its great windows facing north, south, and west, looking out over the Sea of the Sun, its marble floor shining like glass, buffed smooth by countless servants and the passing millennia.

At the western side of the throne room, at the front of the hall, a bustling, rainbow-colored crowd of nobles, counselors, generals, delegates, and envoys gathered around the Silver Throne. Now these people, Lessip could understand.

Too well, perhaps.

The courtiers were there to be seen by the others, to be seen by the High Chancellor, to be seen by the Silver King, to offer their perspectives on recent events, to suggest what they might mean, to listen to other suggestions of the same sort, to ascertain how all of it might affect their houses, their agendas, their alliances, their plans, their families, and their worlds—and so on, and so on.

Lessip smiled to himself.

On one hand, the entire scenario—the crowd, the jostling, the noise, the whispers, the nods, the glances, the machinations, the reek of fifty different perfumes from fifty different duchies—all of it was quite typical. The nature of high courts everywhere.

On the other hand, this was the Silver Court, the High Court of Remain, home to a unique pair of royal brothers. The Silver Fox. The Iron Lion. High Lords Bellános and Dorómy Dallanar, the two most powerful men in the Realm. It was only natural that their smallest gestures—their shortest sentences, their most careless glances—would become the subject of the throng's scrutiny, study, and speculation.

But today is different.

Indeed, for the last bell and a half, Lessip had listened to Dorómy Dallanar, one of his oldest friends, tell an extraordinary tale, a narrative that seemed, from Lessip's perspective, far more suspicious and far more troubling than the brothers Dallanar were making it appear. Of course, it was the second time Lessip had heard the story that day—Doró-my had told him the tale privately that morning—but the details had not changed. Dorómy's adopted daughter, Gia, had been murdered. Dorómy and his entourage had been attacked. Dorómy had killed the aggressor and his allies with the help of High General Branten Hone, an exile upon whose land the entire situation had conveniently unfolded.

Lessip shook his head.

Too many coincidences.

Too much luck. Too much risk.

Too many unanswered questions.

Lord Dorómy had just finished his story, and the crowd had just begun to shuffle and murmur: speculations, doubts, congratulations, advice. Behind it all, to the west, behind the Silver Throne itself, the sun shone warm as it edged toward the glittering horizon.

Lessip turned away and stepped toward the chamber's back wall. The wall was hung with a row of large oval mirrors, each held in an identical frame of ancient high silver. Lessip paused in front of the last mirror on the left, as if checking his appearance. As he did so, he used the mirror to look behind him, to see if he was observed—and he was, of course.

Toromon Jor of Hakonar was staring right at him.

So Lessip put on a little show, adjusted his outfit, primped a bit. Lessip was short, rotund—and wonderfully dressed. He wore a gorgeous jacket of Eulorian silk, a grey doublet, and matching silk pants, all cut in the latest courtly style. His shoes were to die for. He touched his dark red hair, smoothing it at his temples, adjusted the small golden hoops he wore in his ears, fiddled with the gems he wore on his chubby fingers—a fine ruby on each pinky, blood-red garnets on each thumb. He was clean shaven, save a small patch of red hair below his plump lower lip.

Nothing to see here, Jor.

Nothing at all.

Lessip smoothed his little beard with a flourish, pinching the hair together with thumb and index finger, his pinky ring flashing. Just a round little man, a courtier with a penchant for high fashion.

Finally, Jor looked away.

The moment he did so, Lessip touched the hidden stud on

the mirror's frame and stepped directly into his reflection, his skin tingling as he passed through the ancient portal. The throne room's noise ceased.

Lessip nodded. He was certain that Jor hadn't seen him enter. And when the ever-suspicious High Lord of Hakonar looked up again, Lessip would simply be gone.

Lessip now stood on the landing of a narrow stone staircase. It was pitch black. He didn't move for a moment, giving his eyes time to adjust, then reached into his vest's inner pocket and pulled forth a small velvet bag. From this bag, he withdrew a crystal vial. The vial was filled with blood moss from Eureok. Lessip shook the vial twice, making the moss glow red. He shook it one more time, held it overhead, then used the bloody glow to light his way down the staircase. It was a tight fit—cramped, to say the least—but the Káladar was riddled with such passages, especially in the deeper parts of the great citadel; hidden rooms, secret chambers, narrow tunnels, scores of winding, circuitous passages known to but a few, four hundred generations of building, demolition, re-building, the guts of the great citadel more like a rat's warren than a high seat of empire. *And Sisters save me, it's a tight squeeze here!* More than once, as he descended, Lessip found both sides of his waist scraping against the cool stone walls.

The perfect place for an ambush.

No way to turn around.

After a few moments of descent, Lessip stepped off the stairs into a large storage room. The room held various accoutrements for the Great Hall above, all the things needed for audiences: flags for various state holidays, piles of different colored rugs to match, incense burners, row upon row of stacked chairs, banners for most of the Realm's ruling houses, braziers and lamps from all over the Remain—Bellános had this clever habit of honoring visiting nobility at state dinners by lighting the occasion with lamps made on their own worlds—all packed alongside countless wardrobes of various sizes filled with livery, long forgotten gifts, cleaning supplies, random decorations, candelabra, draperies, and more.

Lessip crossed to the back of the room and stopped in front of a thick, fireproof door. There, he slipped the vial of blood moss into his pocket and waited in the dark for a moment, head cocked, ears alert.

He heard nothing.

If someone followed, they made no sound.

Lessip took the vial from his pocket, opened the little door, stepped inside, and quietly shut the door behind him. The narrow closet was an extra storage magazine for the throne room's lamp oil. Five large pithoi, all lined in a row, filled the space. Lessip grunted and squeezed himself past each of the giant oil pots, ducked down, and felt for the hidden catch at the base of the closet's rear wall.

There it is.

Click!

The bottom half of the wall swung open on smooth hinges. Lessip ducked, pushed himself through the tiny opening, and sealed the secret door behind him.

It took Lessip another half a bell of meandering and back-tracking through the maze of passages—back up a small flight of steps, through another hidden portal, four rights, then a left, then a right, down another flight of hidden stairs—before he arrived at his meeting place: an ancient, dead-end hallway, the opening of which had been walled up during the reign of Kyla the Pale—or had it been during the rule of Tarlen the Finder? He couldn't remember. Lessip entered the place by climbing over a broken foundation pier, through a big hole knocked in the wall's side. A few large stones lay scattered in the dust below him, their edges caked with crumbling mortar. Lessip clambered over and held up his vial, the red light throwing weird shadows over the scene.

Nothing.

Nobody.

He pulled his silver watch from his pocket, looked at it. He was on time—.

And then one of the shadows moved.

A crow shadow, up there in the corner, atop a broken stone, its beak long and sharp, feathers shiny black. The crow cocked its head at Lessip, beady black eyes gleaming in the vial's bloody light.

"Greetings," Lessip said, with a slight bow.

Then the crow flowed off its stone, pooling into two dark shapes, the shapes rising from the dusty floor, becoming large, billowing up like black fog, taking human form in a swirl of smoke, shadowy feathers falling from arms and fingers, tendrils of mist circling and gathering into coils and loops of hooded robes. One of the shapes was tall. The other was tiny, like a child. The tall one carried a sword of black metal, holding the blade beneath the hilt, its shoulder sagging with the weapon's weight, as if the blade were too heavy to bear. Its face was hidden in a deep cowl, but its hands were black claws, fingers like skeletal talons. The tiny one threw back his hood to reveal a childlike face: completely bald, eyes heavily lidded, the color of glass, his skin almost white, like an albino's. A black stone—about the size of a robin's egg—was set into the center of his forehead amidst a cluster of purple veins. The stone reflected no light, and the veins seemed to radiate from it, pushing back over the little man's tiny skull. A band of black ink was tattooed vertically beneath his bottom lip, running down his chin and disappearing beneath his jaw, down his throat. The little man had a soft overbite. He bowed and raised his hand in formal greeting.

"High General Lessip," the little man said, stepping forward. When he spoke, his voice was high and lisping, like a child's. Under the bloody light of Lessip's red vial, the little creature's face, the dark stone in his skull, his robed companion, all seemed more disturbing than ever. When the little man smiled, his tiny teeth glittered. His gaunt protector followed him, dragging its dark sword behind.

"Sles." Lessip nodded. He brushed himself off casually, adjusting his clothing. As always, Lessip carried high silver daggers strapped to each of his forearms. For further protection, his boot tips contained spring-loaded blades coated with a fast-acting Zelorian poison. Beneath his finery, he wore his father's ancient vest of high silver mail. Lessip feared neither the voidling nor his fiend, nor any of their derelict kind—not in the slightest.

But that's no reason not to be careful.

"How can we be of service, my Lord?" Sles asked, lisping. "We were puzzled by your summons. Your message said it was urgent?"

"Indeed."

Sles looked at him, cocked his head slightly, but said nothing. Beside him, his companion was almost motionless. Just a slow rising and falling of gaunt shoulders, nothing more. Still, Sles said nothing.

"I have need of information." Lessip cleared his throat. "Something has happened on Kon. Have your people heard anything? I would like to propose a trade, if you have something. Some news. Perhaps as we've done in the past?"

But the little man was already shaking his head, as if with remorse. "Alas, High General," the little man lisped. "Our agent was killed on Kon some days ago. An interesting coincidence, to be sure. But our intelligence is worthless. We do not wish to dishonor our past arrangements—our trust—by offering to you rumors. Our relationship, it is too valuable."

But Lessip's mind was whirling.

At least one of Sles's people had been there.

They *had* been watching.

That information itself went a long way to confirm Lessip's darker suspicions. But who had killed the voidling's spy? And how? The darklings' powers of disguise were legendary to those who knew them. (And mythical to those who did not.) Had Dorómy, or one of his men—young Lord Garen, perhaps?—somehow identified Sles's operative? Killed him for reasons unknown? Reasons that Dorómy had not already shared? Lessip knew that Dorómy had no patience with the strange, hooded wanderers . . . but even so, it seemed unlikely that the High Chancellor would have failed to mention such an important detail.

But if it was true, if Dorómy had intentionally kept the informa-tion from him——.

Lessip blinked. Sles was staring at him, his eyes strangely colorless, touching the black stone in his forehead with child fingers. The little man did not speak.

"Perhaps you could share with me what you *do* have?" Lessip set the red vial down beside him, leaning it against a chunk of ancient mortar. "Allow me to judge its worth?"

"As you wish." Sles bowed, a strange smile on his face. Beside him, the robed fiend grunted, shifting from side to side. Sles reached up and took the thing's taloned claw, holding it the way you might see a child hold the hand of its parent. "But we worry we shall disappoint you."

"No need for that," Lessip said.

Sles paused for a moment, cocked his head as if listening, then nodded, lisping. "We will give you what we have. On one condition."

"What might that be?"

"That you receive it as a gift. We have so little to offer. We want nothing in return."

"Agreed."

"Very well." Sles cocked his head. "We believe that Giácoma Norfell was assassinated by Lord Tomas Modró of Farák. We believe that the assassin's true target was the High Chancellor, High Lord Dorómy Dallanar. We believe that Modró coordinated with local Konungur rebels in an unsuccessful attempt to murder Lord Dorómy and his entourage. The assassin and his key allies were then killed before they could be interrogated. We believe that Modró was hired by Lord Dorómy's brother, High King Bellános Dallanar."

Impossible! Lessip's mind screamed.

But he gave no hint of his reaction; he'd been in the game far too long for that.

Instead, Lessip cocked an eyebrow and said nothing.

"As we said." Sles shook his head regretfully. "It is all we have. Pieced together—all but useless. You have doubtless reached the same conclusions without us. Our agent was killed before she could report the full details, confirmations. We have nothing but a skeleton of possibilities. Our apologies, High General."

But they were not "possibilities."

Quite the contrary.

They are realities.

Indeed, the majority of Sles's details matched Dorómy's account word for word.

But that last line, those last words, were—quite literally—impossible.

Bellános hired Modró?

Out of the question.

Bellános had loved Gia as his own family, as his own niece. Bellános had prepared something horrible for Modró upon his capture. After hearing of Gia's death, Bellános had immediately ordered Paráden's High Gate opened to both Dávanor and Kon, had instantly ordered war dragons from House Dradón to be conscripted to speed Dorómy and his men to the Konish highlands, had called up a full battalion of the Silver Legions to follow by air. . . .

Sles was lying.

He *had* to be lying.

But why?

It was certainly possible that Dorómy had been Modró's true target—Dorómy thought so himself.

But that Bellános had paid an assassin to murder his own

niece, in order to trap and kill his own brother?

Impossible.

The Dallanar brothers were inseparable. Indeed, these last months, they'd been closer than ever, spending even more time in closed conference and discussion. When they'd learned about Gia, Bellános had moved heaven and earth to help Dorómy and his people reach Kon quickly.

Sles was lying.

Of course, it was quite likely that Modró had capitalized on local unrest to make his play for Dorómy and his men, that he had hired or encouraged local provocateurs. Such things were a constant threat.

But that Bellános had hired a professional agitator to ignite local factions to kill his brother and his brother's entourage?

Absurd.

Bellános's son had been there, for the Great Sisters' sake!

Young Lord Garen himself had *been* there, as a part of Dorómy's entourage.

Bellános would kill his own beloved son so that he could kill his beloved brother? All while stirring up potential rebellion in one of the Realm's most important duchies?

Nonsense.

Sles *was* lying.

And lying badly, at that.

But already, something dark itched at the back of Lessip's mind.

Why does he lie?

"We see that we have disappointed you, High General." Sles frowned. "Again, our apologies."

"Why are you lying?" Lessip turned to face them both. The question came from some lower part of Lessip's brain— perhaps the fastest part. And he hadn't stopped it. Sometimes he could talk quicker than he could think, and he'd learned to let it ride, let his instincts push an asset, see what gave, see where the pulled thread went.

Sles bowed, brushed his fingers over the black stone in his skull. "As we said," the small man lisped. "It is what we *believe* to be true. Nothing more. We have never lied to you, High General."

That stopped him.

Because it was true, as far as Lessip knew.

But now—just as quickly—that fact itself seemed suspect.

What is Sles up to here? What game does he play?

Lessip *knew* the voidling was lying. Indeed, the proper iden-
tification of lies—and disguises, and plans, and lies within
lies, and spies, and secrets, and covert actions, and lies about
lies—formed an important part of Lessip's daily duties, part
of the delicate work assigned to him by High King Bellános
and High Chancellor Dorómy. *The Silver Fox. The Iron Lion.*
The royal brothers. The two most powerful men in all the
Remain. The two rocks upon whose relationship the stability
of the entire Realm rested . . . .

"And we never shall lie to you," Sles continued. "What
reason could we have?"

Lessip frowned.

Because this was a lie, too.

He knew that.

Even now, Sles was lying to him. Lying to him about never
lying to him. Some details of the voidling's story might be
true—almost certainly were true.

But the motive for the lie?

And yet . . . .

Sles smiled at him, touched the black stone in his skull, his tiny teeth glittering in the bloody light. At the little man's side, the black fiend panted in its cowl.

"The truth is strong, is it not, High General?" Sles asked. "Powerful. Like an infection—an infection you cannot kill. Once inside, it spreads. Becomes stronger. Becomes a part of you. The more you learn, the more you want to know. Truth builds upon truth. Facts, histories, information—you can never have too much. And the more truth you have, the more powerful you become, the more *right* you feel. As students of your people's long and admirable history, we have always appreciated humanity's regard for the truth. Your strength and wisdom and honor are legend. You never settle for easy answers. You never settle for deceit. You never hide in the darkness. Always the truth—the truth and its light. It is your greatest strength. Is that not so, High General? Or do I lie?"

APPENDIX 1

The Duchies of Remain
as Recorded by Susan Dallanar

High Lady Susan Dallanar composed the following list of the Realm's fiefdoms in the Third Year of Dorómy III, Founding Year 12,040. At that time, she was four years old. Lady Susan's roster is a succinct account of the Kingdom's constituent duchies. Her record consists of a catalogue of the Remain's worlds in alphabetical order, organized by founding Great Sister. (All names are given in the Kingdom's Common Tongue rather than the duchy's local dialect.) Each entry begins with a brief description of the character and/or the notable features of the named principality. This is followed by the year in which the duchy was annexed (its so-called "Founding Year"), the number of High Gates known to have been established on the world, and the name of the duchy's current ruling family. The colors and sigil of the current High House are also included. (While the illustrations printed here are based on Lady Susan's original drawings, they have been adjusted and cross-checked to precisely reflect the specifics of each duchy's coat of arms.) The world of Paráden is not included. As the Remain's Founding World, humanity's First Home, and the royal seat of Acasius Dallanar, it is the only world known to have been inhabited before the Five Sisters began their Great Expedition. Five High Gates were established on Paráden in F.Y. 1, by Acasius Dallanar. These five High Gates are the only Gates known to have been created by the Great King.

— Nordo Ness, Chief Librarian of the Tarn
Fourth Year of Dorómy III, F.Y. 12,040

The First Great Sister, Eressa the Lost
53 worlds recovered

Amágos

A world of vile pits, stench, and decay; violent hills and castles of iron.
Founding Year: 11; two High Gates.
Ruling House: Gokór.
Color and Sigil: A scimitar of bronze on a split field *(par fess embattled)* of red and black.

Anis

A world of frost with three moons of fire; the toughest soldiers in the Realm.
Founding Year: 21; one High Gate.
Ruling House: Kellson.
Color and Sigil: Three red discs on a field of pale silver.

Anótos

A world of dreams, dreamers, and magic; soundless, mystical, and enchanted.
Founding Year: unknown; one High Gate.
Ruling House: Wanten.
Color and Sigil: A silver crescent over a lavender mountain on a field of deep purple.

Asarnór

A world of clean, green waters and seas; glass cliffs, diamond shores, and scintillating coasts.
Founding Year: 12; two High Gates.
Ruling House: Moráldan.
Color and Sigil: A jumping, silver fish on a split field *(per fess engrailed)* of lime green and aqua blue.

Árcdoth

A world rich in gold, silver, and copper; productive mines and cunning engineers.
Founding Year: 5; three High Gates.
Ruling House: Dérenno.
Color and Sigil: A golden miner's pick on a split field *(party per pale)* of dark brown and dark tan.

Atlósios

An unsoiled world of green plains, vast trees, and windy steppes; home of the tree shamans.
Founding Year: 9; two High Gates.
Ruling House: Barnard.
Color and Sigil: A silver tree of many branches on a field of high green.

Batládea

A night world of thieves and assassins, bathed in perpetual twilight.
Founding Year: 27; three High Gates.
Ruling House: Torg.
Color and Sigil: A silver bull's skull on a black field.

Callón

A world of foggy swamps; low sad hills.
Founding Year: 1; one High Gate.
Ruling House: Veticar.
Color and Sigil: Two copper snakes entwined on a split field *(party per pale)* of sad green and melancholy lime.

Cathanósa

A world of turbulent storms; lightning fields of sparks and chaos.
Founding Year: Unknown; one High Gate.
Ruling House: None (Contested).
Color and Sigil: None. At least four "high houses" currently claim dominion of Cathanósa.

Colodóx

A near dead world; a ruined husk of blighted misery and sorrow.
Founding Year: Unknown; one High Gate.
Ruling House: Landown (Contested by Jahoryn).
Color and Sigil: A white disc crossed by a black sword on a field of red.

Danarcion

A world of orange and brown sunsets; the merchant's nest and trading center of the Realm.
Founding Year: 11; four High Gates.
Ruling House: Tacir.
Color and Sigil: A crescent harp of gold on a field of brilliant orange.

Dunsáor

A flooded world with eternal seas and oceans; home of the sea folk and their kin.
Founding Year: 22; one High Gate.
Ruling House: Garosh.
Color and Sigil: A silver sea-beast with eight tentacles on a field of deep blue.

Exarkiha

A world with deserts of obsidian sand; sharpest blades in the Kingdom.
Founding Year: 26; two High Gates.
Ruling House: Saan.
Color and Sigil: Crossed silver daggers on a split field *(party per fess)* of black and emerald green.

Ebum

A world of madmen, fanatics, and criminals; low, whispering hills; silent, cold mountains.
Founding Year: Unknown; one High Gate
Ruling House: None (Contested).
Color and Sigil: None. At least six "high houses" currently claim dominion of Ebum.

Egáton

The largest and most bountiful world in the Realm; a farmer's paradise.
Founding Year: 15; three High Gates.
Ruling House: Nelleron.
Color and Sigil: Crossed pitchforks in gold on a field of light green.

Egókontos

A world with ageless mountains of iron and granite; the most ancient forges in the Realm.
Founding Year: 4; two High Gates.
Ruling House: Von.
Color and Sigil: A jet black hammer on a field of pale grey.

Ekor

A frozen, barren rock inhabited almost entirely underground; home of the tunnel men.
Founding Year: Unknown; one High Gate.
Ruling House: None (Contested).
Color and Sigil: None. At least three "high houses" currently claim dominion of Ekor.

Escódon

A luminal world of eternal twilight; second only to Anótos with regards to the arcane.
Founding Year: Unknown; one High Gate.
Ruling House: Porró.
Color and Sigil: A silver quarter moon and two stars on a field of pale lavender.

Espónyo

A world with cavaliers and ladies; the best drink in the Kingdom.
Founding Year: 7; two High Gates.
Ruling House: Dontaigne.
Color and Sigil: Crossed golden rapiers on a split field *(party per fess)* of crimson and white.

Elágios

A world of song, dance, and merriment; the musician's haven; a world of eternal sunshine.
Founding Year: 15; two High Gates.
Ruling House: Zappata.
Color and Sigil: A lyre of white on a split field *(party per bend)* of dark orange and dark yellow.

Eupóseol

A merry world, with primitive shores of crystal and gold.
Founding Year: 16; one High Gate.
Ruling House: Lan.
Color and Sigil: A golden fish on a split field *(party per pale)* of white and green.

Eureok

A world with black seas, blood red moons, and vast, blank continents.
Founding Year: Unknown; one High Gate.
Ruling House: None (Contested).
Color and Sigil: None. At least eight "high houses" currently claim dominion of Eureok.

Evalok

A world of wind storms and typhoons; a tropical maelstrom.
Founding Year: Unknown.
Ruling House: Liau (Contested by Tak).
Color and Sigil: A black crane over a black mountain on a field of blood red.

Farámor

A world of vast, grey oceans and huge, grey skies; clever sailors and navigators; best boat builders in the Realm.
Founding Year: Unknown; two High Gates.
Ruling House: Hannér.
Color and Sigil: A grey kraken on a field of black.

Gellátek

A dying world near the Kingdom's edge; supposedly visited by the Voidfolk.
Founding Year: Unknown; one High Gate.
Ruling House: None (Contested).
Color and Sigil: None. At least two "high houses" currently claim dominion of Gellátek.

Golladós

The frozen moon of a massive gas giant; vicious; last world to be reclaimed in the Founding War.
Founding Year: Unknown; one High Gate.
Ruling House: Svonsorn.
Color and Sigil: a white bear on a split field (party per bend sinister) of black and grey.

Gunorica

A world of huge, flat hills; huge, broad men; some of the best infantry in the Realm.
Founding Year: 17; two High Gates.
Ruling House: Yordán.
Color and Sigil: A dark brown war hammer on a split field *(party per pale)* of tan and crimson.

Hakonar

A world of savage, brutal cliffs and mountains; relentless, ruthless, and cunning.
Founding Year: 14; two High Gates.
Ruling House: Jor.
Color and Sigil: A double-bladed axe of blood red, lined with silver, on a field of black.

Helvanthíos

The high sky land of the floating folk; rainbow dawns and polychromatic seas.
Founding Year: 13; one High Gate.
Ruling House: Holte.
Color and Sigil: A silver falcon *(rampant)* on a field of high blue.

Indónok

A world of razor blade storms; uninhabitable save the mountains at the southern pole.
Founding Year: Unknown.
Ruling House: None (Contested).
Color and Sigil: None. At least three "high houses" currently claim dominion of Indónok.

Itáteos

The smaller library world; second only to Genonea for the size of its collections.
Founding Year: 4; four High Gates.
Ruling House: Cuon Sach.
Color and Sigil: A copper chalice on a field of brown.

Jaga

The world of the snake lords – and their pets; pale green sunsets; eternal marshes.
Founding Year: 14; two High Gates.
Ruling House: Soness.
Color and Sigil: A coiled silver serpent on a split field *(party per bend)* of pale and emerald green.

Jun

A world of burning, dry, red sands; an untamable wasteland governed by violence.
Founding Year: 20; two High Gates.
Ruling House: None (Contested).
Color and Sigil: None. At least eight "high houses" currently claim dominion of Jun.

Lábbarkos

A world of strange animals, melted mountains, and ashen fields.
Founding Year: Unknown; one High Gate.
Ruling House: Vyre.
Color and Sigil: A black wolf on a field of dead grey.

Lythéntor

The mercenary world; a land of professional soldiers, scouts, spies, and saboteurs.
Founding Year: 6; three High Gates.
Ruling House: Rorvik.
Color and Sigil: A blood red, spiked mace on a field of white.

Marsinion

The land of eternal war; also known as "Acasius's Folly."
Founding Year: 2; seven High Gates.
Ruling House: None (Contested).
Color and Sigil: None. At least nineteen "high houses" currently claim dominion of Marsinion.

Mercal

A world of death, graves, tombs, and dark scholarship; rumored alliances with the Voidfolk.
Founding Year: Unknown; one High Gate.
Ruling House: Fando Myre.
Color and Sigil: A skull crowned in red on a field of black and mustard *(per saltire)*.

Nelor

A world of green, soft fields; high harvests; honorable customs; "Acasius's Rest."
Founding Year: 15; one High Gate.
Ruling House: Nellerman.
Color and Sigil: A white lion *(passant regardant)* on a field of high green.

Norága

A world with a sky of a thousand colors; the nursery of stars and suns. Once bred dragons.
Founding Year: 7; two High Gates.
Ruling House: Mong.
Color and Sigil: A golden dragon *(rampant regardant)* on a split field *(party per pale)* of red and purple.

Olóros

A world of pure white ice; blinding skies; frozen tundras and steppes.
Founding Year: Unknown; one High Gate.
Ruling House: Ty (Contested by Tuk).
Color and Sigil: Crossed black axes on a split field *(party per fess)* of grey and white.

Peléa

A world of hard warriors and sly slavers; steel grey skies and blood feuds.
Founding Year: 6; two High Gates.
Ruling House: Lessip.
Colors and Sigil: Crossed, curved falcions in silver on a field of iron grey.

Somákos

A world of liars, thieves, and assassins; violet skies and sunsets; four moons.
Founding Year: Unknown; one High Gate.
Ruling House: Bostrok.
Color and Sigil: A straight, black dagger on a field of bruise purple and black *(quarterly)*.

Swozox

A world with dark caverns of glowing stones and skies with dark moons.
Founding Year: 4; two High Gates.
Ruling House: Mordán.
Color and Sigil: A crescent in silver on a field of dark purple.

Tarcéron

The world of the flying cities; winged men of white and gold and copper.
Founding Year: 9; two High Gates.
Ruling House: Clarán.
Color and Sigil: Acasius's Star in deep gold on a field of pale ivory.

Terelag

A world with high brown grasses and deep, eternal fields; endless plains and rolling hills.
Founding Year: 3; one High Gate.
Ruling House: Xiang.
Color and Sigil: A golden stag *(rampant)* on a field of light brown.

Terótan

A word with twelve weird moons; bizarre, dark creatures unlike anywhere else in the Realm.
Founding Year: Unknown.
Ruling House: None (Contested).
Color and Sigil: None. At least three "high houses" currently claim dominion of Terótan.

Tóvonok

A small red moon, like a demon's eye; some of the cruelest soldiers in the Realm.
Founding Year: Unknown; one High Gate.
Ruling House: Xath (Contested by Modán).
Color and Sigil: A blind red eye on a solid field of midnight black.

Ugásur

A world of eternal forests; high cities of the trees; home of the tree folk.
Founding Year: 3; one High Gate; sister world to Ugátria.
Ruling House: Sur.
Color and Sigil: An oak of black on a field of silver.

Ugátria

A world with low hills; grey plains; dreary and primitive, but full of undiscovered secrets.
Founding Year: 3; one High Gate.
Ruling House: Gatron.
Color and Sigil: A silver-grey sun with seven rays on a field of black.

Ursobór

A massive and dark world; giant brown sun; ancient warrior traditions.
Founding Year: 12; one High Gate.
Ruling House: Anor.
Color and Sigil: A disc of deep brown, crossed with two blades in white, on a field of tan.

Wasondí

A world with caravans of spice, bronze, and sand; pale green moons.
Founding Year: 6; four High Gates.
Ruling House: Faraní.
Color and Sigil: Two green discs over a bronze griffin *(rampant regardant)* on a field of tan.

Wenevron

A world of ashy darkness; painfully grey and bloody.
Founding Year: 10; one High Gate.
Ruling House: Shakán.
Color and Sigil: A double headed lion in red *(rampant)* on a field of dark grey.

Zeloros

A burning world on the farthest edge of the Void.
Founding Year: Unknown.
Ruling House: None (Contested).
Color and Sigil: None. At least three "high houses" currently claim dominion of Zeloros.

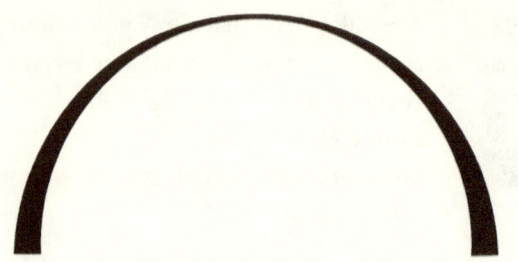

The Second Great Sister, Alea the True

22 worlds recovered

Akrivor

A world of nightmare skies and demons, blood red suns, and warrior clans.
Founding Year: 7; one High Gate.
Ruling House: Tallyn.
Color and Sigil: A hawk's head in black over a disk of red, on a field of dark grey.

Albotos

A world with cool waves and sunny islands; an idyllic haven for hedonists and philosophers.
Founding Year: 12; two High Gates.
Ruling House: Bonón Tor.
Color and Sigil: A dark blue sea turtle on a field of silver.

Amá

A world of grey wastes; tough, melancholy, and dire; home of the beast men.
Founding Year: 40; two High Gates.
Ruling House: Konter (Contested by Dor).
Color and Sigil: A grey lion's head on a field of brooding black.

484

Amótros

A world with friendly hills, blue flowers, and a huge, silver moon.
Founding Year: 8; one High Gate.
Ruling House: Hylor.
Color and Sigil: A silver circle on a split field *(party per bend)* of light blue and deep blue.

Anortion

A world of hard edges and broad, pale mountains; great hunters, trackers, and scouts.
Founding Year: 21; one High Gate.
Ruling House: Maeleon.
Color and Sigil: A black boar on a split field *(party per pale)* of white and grey.

Anor

A world of iron hills and strong, stocky, broad trees; home of the purple dwarves.
Founding Year: 14; one High Gate.
Ruling House: Nor.
Color and Sigil: A broad plain tree in iron grey against a field of deep purple.

Asada

A world of smiling clouds and skies; a sandy, open world of merchant princes and traders.
Founding Year: 25; one High Gate.
Ruling House: Asanar.
Color and Sigil: A radiant, silver star on a field of brilliant, light green.

Básadon

A world with a wide archipelago; teal seas and shores; great beasts of the lurking deep.
Founding Year: 37; one High Gate.
Ruling House: Kerek.
Color and Sigil: A copper octopus on a split field *(party per fess engrailed)* of teal and dark green.

Brotunaeon

A world of volcanic chaos and lava flows like the veins of a molten giant.
Founding Year: 7; one High Gate.
Ruling House: Lorno.
Color and Sigil: A black mountain peak crossed by a double tipped spear on a field of orange.

Corícea

A world of honor and principle; fine cities and towers; the finest steel in the Kingdom.
Founding Year: 38; one High Gate.
Ruling House: Reneé.
Color and Sigil: A high silver tower on a field of clean, radiant blue.

Dalíos

The most tragic world in the realm, haunted by memories of lost loves and dreams.
Founding Year: 42; one High Gate.
Ruling House: Dalían.
Color and Sigil: A circle of braided black and silver on a field of blue.

Dalonás

A world with lonely, pale shores; seven pearl moons, also inhabited; intricate politics.
Founding Year: 39; two High Gates.
Ruling House: Han (Contested by Tros).
Color and Sigil: Seven circles of silver over a mountain of gold on a field of pale blue.

Ebavia

A world of fierce warrior women; fertile plains, fields, and streams.
Founding Year: 40; one High Gate.
Ruling House: Bavian.
Color and Sigil: Five crossed war spears in red on a field of dark blue.

486

Eborium

A world of underwater cities, island ports, and deep coral islands of glass.
Founding Year: 7; one High Gate.
Ruling House: Ebor.
Color and Sigil: Acasius's Star on a split field *(party per pale)* of deep blue and healthy green.

Ephak

A world with wide clouds of pink and gold; seas of grass; home of the roc riders.
Founding Year: 10; two High Gates.
Ruling House: Phak (Contested by Lenow).
Color and Sigil: A falcon *(rampant)* in silver over a field of ruby pink.

Ferragias

A world with a mother-of-pearl moon; towers of light and diamond. Once bred dragons.
Founding Year: 23; two High Gates.
Ruling House: Jang.
Color and Sigil: A silver dragon *(passant)* crossing a silver crescent on a field of mother-of pearl.

Genonea

The world of scholars, philosophers, historians, and poets; eternal, grand libraries.
Founding Year: 22; two High Gates.
Ruling House: Scolum.
Color and Sigil: The ancient letter "A" in silver on a field of high blue.

Okógon

The land of the giants; vast mountains, deep rivers, and ancient seas.
Founding Year: 40; two High Gates.
Ruling House: Gorók.
Color and Sigil: A war hammer in silver on a split field *(party per pale)* of high white and blue.

Panávion

The Realm's only truly divided world; lavender skies and cities; land of the eternal men.
Founding Year: 15; two High Gates.
Ruling Houses: Jyran and Kylon; contested since the Founding.
Colors and Sigils:
House di Jyre – A circular silver shield on a field of high blue.
House di Kylo – A golden, double-bladed battle axe on a field of blood red.

Spárunok

A world of grunting beasts and brutal villages; a freakish, primordial hell.
Founding Year: 6; one High Gate.
Ruling House: None (Contested).
Color and Sigil: None. At least six "high houses" currently claim dominion of Spárunok.

Teládon

A world of high blue glaciers; deep, clean rivers and pure mirrored lakes.
Founding Year: 5; one High Gate.
Ruling House: Serán.
Color and Sigil: Acasius's Star in white on a field of glacial blue.

Yor

A raspy, harsh, barren, and hot world.
Founding Year: 10; one High Gate.
Ruling House: Krodan.
Color and Sigil: Twin, curved daggers in black, crossed on a split field *(party per fess)* of burnt orange and blood red.

The Third Great Sister, Aaryn the Chronicler

14 worlds recovered

Abúcia

A world with rich soils, strong men and women, and dark, bountiful earth.
Founding Year: 10; one High Gate.
Ruling House: Ción.
Color and Sigil: An ox in white *(passant)* on a split field *(party per pale)* of brown and tan.

Dávanor

A world with high, white peaks, stony vales, and eternal forests; home of the dragon riders.
Founding Year: 21; two High Gates.
Ruling House: Dradón (Contested by Fel).
Color and Sigil: A roaring white dragon *(rampant)* on a sky blue field.

Dorn

A world with huge mountains, tan fields; strong and implacable; home of the iron dwarves.
Founding Year: 10; two High Gates.
Ruling House: Beln.
Color and Sigil: A broad mountain of deep brown on a field of tan.

Ethené

A world of healing lakes and trees; gentle farms and plains.
Founding Year: 23; two High Gates.
Ruling House: Benford.
Color and Sigil: A silver plow on a field of gentle blue.

Farák

A world of wailing winds and frozen rains; merciless and unforgiving.
Founding Year: 22; one High Gate.
Ruling House: Nyr.
Color and Sigil: A silver lightning bolt across a split field *(party per fess)* of bruise blue and black.

Gelánen

A world with great rivers, green grasses; clean, bountiful, and pure.
Founding Year: 17; one High Gate.
Ruling House: Julane.
Color and Sigil: A braided circle of white on a field of high green.

Horizon

A world with fine sands; wind farms; silk trade and unsurpassed hospitality.
Founding Year: 13; two High Gates.
Ruling House: Dallanar.
Color and Sigil: Acasius's Star in silver on a split field *(party per fess)* of high blue and golden yellow.

Ibittion

A world of madmen and lunatic moons; longest continuous High dynasty in the Realm.
Founding Year: 28; one High Gate.
Ruling House: Goylen.
Color and Sigil: Four crescents *(white, blue, silver, and grey)* on a field of black.

Jallow

A hard and honest world; deep lakes and rivers; mighty mountains; home of the ogres.
Founding Year: 31; one High Gate.
Ruling House: Dallanar.
Color and Sigil: Acasius's Star in silver on a split field *(party per pale)* of high blue and deep brown.

Kon

A world with icy seas; snowy forests and mountains; a world of perpetual winter.
Founding Year: 9; one High Gate.
Ruling House: Dallanar.
Color and Sigil: Acasius's Star in silver on a field of high blue.

Pénulen

A world of gritty dust and yellow hills; low valleys of shame and hauntings.
Founding Year: 32; one High Gate.
Ruling House: Len.
Color and Sigil: A dog *(rampant)* on a field of dusty, burnt yellow.

Póntokos

The home of the star sailors; a world with rainbow river boats and prismatic sunsets.
Founding Year: 12; three High Gates.
Ruling House: Evenór.
Color and Sigil: A golden boat on a split field *(tierced per pall)* of red, orange, and purple.

Rigel

A world with platinum sands and lakes; fish of silver and gold and copper.
Founding Year: 33; one High Gate.
Ruling House: Ruge (Vymon).
Color and Sigil: Acasius's Star in brilliant white on a field of dark blue.

Sparáton

A world of stern hills and fortresses; pale, cruel warriors of the most lethal cunning.
Founding Year: 36; one High Gate.
Ruling House: Stenegard.
Color and Sigil: Two crossed scimitars of silver against a field of pale grey.

Utarcton

The Kingdom's prison world; a baked husk; completely subterranean.
Founding Year: 9; one High Gate.
Ruling House: Konnór.
Color and Sigil: A flat black key on a field of pale, lifeless silver.

The Fourth Great Sister, Kora the Just

9 worlds recovered

Aradan

A world of soft hills and fields; flowers of silver, yellow, orange, and pink.
Founding Year: 15; five High Gates.
Ruling House: Aradak.
Color and Sigil: Acasius's Star in white on a split field *(party per fess)* of deep pink and gold.

Borádon

A world of violent caves; underground lairs of the deepest and strangest dark.
Founding Year: 27; one High Gate.
Ruling House: Rondan.
Color and Sigil: A battle axe in black on a split field *(tierced per pall)* of purple, red, and green.

Bentór

A world with eternal stonewood forests; towering jade peaks.
Founding Year: 13; one High Gate.
Ruling House: Kentón.
Color and Sigil: A green serpent wrapped around a silver mountain on a field of light green.

493

Kesst

A world of high waves; blue-green skies; eternal breezes; timeless sunsets.
Founding Year: 26; two High Gates.
Ruling House: Ruge (John).
Color and Sigil: Acasius's Star in silver on a split field *(party per fess)* of cobalt and white.

Nordán

A beautiful, azure world with an ocean-white moon and castles of cloud.
Founding Year: 16; two High Gates.
Ruling House: Dallanar (Dorómy).
Color and Sigil: Acasius's Star in ice white on a field of dark blue.

Nod

A world of black, wet jungles and weird, moaning cliffs; undoubtedly haunted.
Founding Year: 29; one High Gate.
Ruling House: None (Contested).
Color and Sigil: None. At least three "high houses" currently claim dominion of Nod.

Sodemar

A world of decayed cityscapes and skeletal, dark castles long since destroyed.
Founding Year: 26; one High Gate.
Ruling House: Sode.
Color and Sigil: A black tower against a split field *(party per pale)* of grey and red.

Selánon

A world of dread ice; deadly blue-grey glaciers and giant war-bears.
Founding Year: 14; two High Gates.
Ruling House: Jellenyr.
Color and Sigil: A giant silver bear *(rampant)* on a field of ice blue.

Weron

A world with high towers of air, color, grace, and clarity.

Founding Year: 30; one High Gate.

Ruling House: Weron.

Color and Sigil: A blue spear on a split field *(party per pale)* of high yellow and high white.

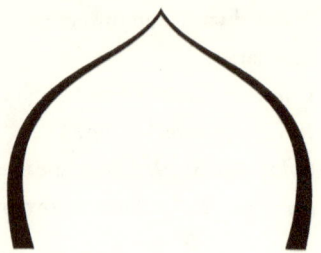

The Fifth Great Sister, Margot the Gentle

5 worlds recovered

Baleen

A world of dusty plateaus, faded trees, and leeched soil; all but barren.
Founding Year: 45; one High Gate.
Ruling House: Jomónoz.
Color and Sigil: A barren, lifeless tree in black on a field of dead grey.

Dayáden

A bountiful world with honey farms, cheerful winds, and sweet clover.
Founding Year: 16; three High Gates.
Ruling House: Dayon.
Color and Sigil: Acasius's Star over a field of sweet green.

Escena

The land of eternal night; inhabitable only at the northern-most pole.
Founding Year: 27; one High Gate.
Ruling House: None (Contested).
Color and Sigil: None. At least three "high houses" currently claim dominion of Escena.

Jenysyn

A rainy world; blue-grey; high cliffs; home of the best horse cavalry in the Realm.

Founding Year: 33; one High Gate.

Ruling House: Tworn.

Color and Sigil: A silver horse *(rampant)* against a rain cloud of grey on a field of high blue.

Targus

A world with nine quick, golden moons; skillful and sharp; home of the Guild of Assassins.

Founding Year: 19; one High Gate.

Ruling House: Targon.

Color and Sigil: A crescent of deep gold on a field of dead white.

APPENDIX 2

The Canon of Tarn and the Dallanar Kings

The Canon of Tarn—also called The Tarn's Canon and, less commonly, The Silver Book—is an epic prose work begun by the Third Great Sister, Aaryn Dallanar ("The Chronicler") during the Second Year of Alea the First (F.Y. 29). The descendants of Aaryn, and many others, continue the composition of the Canon to the present day.

The original copy of the Silver Book is located on the world of Kon, in the central library of the fortress of Tarn. It has been protected there (with two brief interruptions) since its inception. There are five other "primary copies" of the Canon—all endowed with unique properties. Three thousand and twelve other "official manuscript copies" of the Canon are known. Many of these copies are housed on the worlds of Kon, Genonea, Itáteos, and Paráden. Countless other printed copies, of various quality, are available throughout the Kingdom. At present, the Canon consists of 128 main entries (one for every Dallanar monarch) and well over ten thousand appendices that treat various heroes, villains, mercenaries, warlords, merchant-princes, healers, adepts, explorers, brigands, poets, and scholars. Also included in the appendices are stories that pertain to notable events in which otherwise unknown characters play prominent, if brief, roles.

The Canon is the founding literary monument of the Silver Kingdom. It has been considered a work of history, an epic poem, and a historiographic treatise. It is all of these and more. Throughout the Realm, the Canon is regarded as the foundation of a liberal education in both the practical and scholarly sense. To "know one's Canon" is a mark not only of basic literacy but also of cultural and historical fluency.

At its core, the Canon is a history of the Kingdom of Remain, beginning with the creation of the Realm by Acasius Dallanar and his five Great Sisters and continuing to the present moment. The Silver Book is constantly being updated, copied, and transcribed. It is a living, breathing document. The work is not precisely chronological (especially when the magical "primary copies" are "consulted") but, even in those instances, there is a clear sense of movement through time. While the organization of the work is bound to the reigns of the Dallanar monarchs, the Canon's sustaining theme is that of the Silver Kingdom itself. This is important to remember, since some scholars continue to claim that the Canon is nothing more than Dallanar propaganda. This debate need not be treated with much seriousness here. (Indeed, the Canon's accounts of Christopher I "The War Bringer," Christopher II "The Cursed," Simon I "The Silver-Hand," Michael I "The Peacemaker," and—above all—Hakon I "The Terrible," are so unflattering as to make any notion of royal interference in the Silver Book's composition near impossible.) The Canon does include accounts of the Dallanar monarchs, but those are hardly the full measure of its contents. Indeed, if there must be one, then the true protagonist of the Tarn's Canon is not the Dallanar family, but rather the Eternal Kingdom itself.

The Canon is divided into three parts: the heroic, the historical, and the contemporary ages. I have treated the debates regarding the nature and origins of these divisions at length in my *Introduction to the Study of the Canon of Tarn*. Although some controversy remains, it is almost certain that these divisions were created in the second year of Hakon I, by Hakon's Chief Librarian, Kator Xu. Academic opinion is divided on the reasons for Xu's move, but most scholars now believe (as do

I) that it was an attempt to mark Hakon's reign as the end of an era. In at least one sense, then, the Canon's organization is entirely arbitrary.

Two final notes on the List of Dallanar Kings, below:

First, Founding Year designations are given here for convenience only. In educated parlance, the dates in question are known exclusively by the names of the ruling monarch. Thus, Founding Year 10,315 (F.Y. 10,315) would be called "The Third Year of Michael I." This convention was dictated by the practice of Great Sister Aaryn; it has been adhered to here.

Second, following the murder of the Fifth Great Sister, Margot I, in the Third Year of Her Reign (Founding Year 45), all Dallanar rulers until Hakon the Terrible belonged to the House of Alea. Following Hakon's Purge, all Dallanar rulers belonged to the House of Aaryn. Since all ruling families, on all one hundred and four of the Kingdom's worlds, are of "Dallanar" descent, only those High Dallanar belonging to the ruling House of Aaryn now employ the Dallanar family name.

– Nordo Ness, Chief Librarian of the Tarn
Third Year of Dorómy III, F.Y. 12,040

The Dallanar Kings

The Heroic Age

The Founding – The Founding Monarchs

       Acasius I "The Great" or "The Great One" (01-27)

       Alea I "The Cruel" (27-42)

       Margot I "The Generous" (42-55)

       Garen I (55-67)

       Julia I (67-79/80)

       Adara I "The Kind" (79/80-101)

The Founding War – The Warrior Monarchs

       Christopher I "The War Bringer" (101-102)

       Poder I "Poder Jarlen" also "The Invincible" (102-109)

       Bellános I (109-110)

       Katherine I (110-112)

       Terence I (112-113/4)

       Dorómy I (113/4-120)

       James I (120-129)

       Jessica I "The Trickster" (129-131)

       Samuel I (131-133)

       Diégan I (133-167)

         – The First Peace –

       Emily I (167)

       Jordun I (167-169)

       Kelian I (169)

       Julia II (169-171/2)

       Korlen I (171/2-173)

       Katherine II "The Scholar Queen" (173-191)

         – The Second Peace –

       Jon I (191-192)

Derek I (192-193)
Margot II "The Strong" (193-195)
Samuel II (195)
Christopher II "The Cursed" also "The Blight" (196)
— Dawn of the Plague Years —

The Plague Years (196 - 10,211)
Also known as the "10,000 Year War."

The Restoration — The Avenging Monarchs
Marden I (10,211)
Jason I (10,211)
Peter I (10,211)
Heath I (10,212-10,213)
Samuel III (10,213-10,216)
Kelian I (10,216-10,218/19)
William I (10,118/19-10,222)
Jane I (10,222)
Daniel I (10,222-10,217)
Simon I "The Silver Hand" (10,217-10,245)
Jon II (10,245-10,266/7)
Peter II (10,266/7-10,278)
Margaret I (10,278-10,282)
Derek II (10,282-10,284)
Kendal I (10,284-10,289)
Jeremy I (10,289-10,298)
Hugo I (10,298)
— The Siege of Paráden —
George I (10,298)
Korlen II (10,298)
Gregg I (10,298)
Richard I (10,298)

Karen I (10,298)

Julia III "The Siegebreaker" (10,298-10,300)

Falmon I (10,300-10,301)

Susan I "The Silver Whore" (10,301-10,312/13)

Michael I "The Peacemaker" (10,312/13-10,349)

       – The Final Peace –

Peter III (10,349-10,367)

Katherine III (10,367-10,401)

Hugo II (10,401-10,433)

George II (10,433-10,458/9)

Doldon I "The Eternal" (10,458/9-10,519)

The Historical Age

Délen I (10,519-10,522)

Délen II (10,522-10,568)

Fen I "The Silver Dog" (10,568-10,590)

Samuel IV (10,590-10,604)

Susan II (10,604-10,616/7)

Filip I (10,616/7-10,643)

Peter IV "The Just" (10,643-10,699)

David I (10,699-10,717)

James II (10,717-10,726)

Marden II (10,726-10,744)

David II (10,744-10,825)

Alea II "The Virgin Queen" (10,825-10,868)

Terence II (10,868-10,874)

Roger I (10,874-10,901)

Kendal II (10,901-10,916)

Mikal I (10,916-10,924)

Xavier I (10,924-10,943)

Órtha I "The Explorer" (10,943-10,975/6)

James III (10,975/6-11,003)

Fen II (11,003-11,012)

Vymon I (11,012-11,045)

Tomas I (11,045-11,046)

Marcus I (11,046-11,058)

Peter V (11,058-11,069)

Deborah I (11,069-11,081)

Heather I (11,081-11,085)

Acasius II (11,085-11,110)

The Contemporary Age

Hakon I "The Terrible" (11,100-11,132)

    – Hakon's Purge –

Michael II (11,132-11,146)

Dorómy II (11,146-11,158)

Jessica II (11,158-11,190)

Roger II (11,190-11,208)

Elizabeth I (11,208-11,222)

Kyla I "The Pale" (11,222-11,270)

Króan I (11,270-11,271)

David II (11,271-11,301)

Charles I (11,301-11,345)

Filip II "The Wandering King" (11,345-11,402)

Roger III (11,402-11,431)

Andrew I (11,431-11,467)

Peter IV (11,467-11,489)

Xavier II (11,489-11,520)

Hakon II "The Beast" (11,520)

James IV (11,520-11,534)

Délen III (11,534-11,572)

Sophia II (11,572-11,604)

Derek III (11,604-11,616)

Marcus II (11,616-11,660)

Marcus III (11,660-11,663)

Hugo III (11,663-11,687)

Susan III (11,687-11,706)

Tarlen I "The Finder" (11,706-11,770)

Garen II (11,770-11,794)

Orlen I (11,794-11,809)

Hana I (11,809-11,832/33)

Sophia III "The Deceiver" (11,832/33-11,840)

Sabella I (11,840-11,845)

Michael III (11,845-11,867)

Susan IV (11,867-11,884)

Filip III (11,884-11,905)

David IV "The Lonesome" (11,905-11,910)

Marden III "The Silver Shield" (11,910-11,913)

Timothy I (11,913-11,923)

Poder II (11,923)

Peter V (11,923-11,925)

Dana I "The Caregiver" (11,925-11,948)

Adara II (11,948-11,972)

Tomas II (11,972-11,996)

Balmás I "The Frail" (11,996-12,014)

Bellános III "The Silver Fox" (12,014-12,034)

Dorómy III "The Iron Lion" (12,034 – present [12,040])

ACKNOWLEDGEMENTS

This project was funded in part by a grant from the Lake Region Arts Council and the McKnight Foundation.

Deepest thanks are due Christopher P., Eric N., Erika J., Erin H.K., Erin M., Heidi G., Jaimin W., Jason W., Jen H., Jen K., Kari W., Mark E., Nikoli F., Nina M., Robert K., Tamara W., and Zach F. for their generosity, criticism, support, encouragement, and faith. High Ladies and Lords of Remain, the Kingdom and its peoples salute you.

A special debt is owed an elite squad of bear riders who reviewed an early version of this book: Aubrie G., Gentry N., Lindsey H., Maya R., and Thomas W. Let it be known throughout the Realm: The next generation of war bears is blessed with riders of the highest quality—sharp, loyal, and fierce.

Finally, the Kingdom of Remain would not exist without the love and friendship of the following warriors and poets: Anna S., Aurora M., Brian J., Cady M., Chunlin Y., Darcie D., Eugene L., Jesse H., Kan L., Kelsey D., Kristin L., Liz N., Lucia X., Mari H., Matt C., Nataly S., Olga P., Roger S., Ruth S., Tianhua X., Tom M., Travis K., Vanessa H., William S., and Zoey S. As usual, I have not the words—so again, I borrowed these: Πάς γοῦν ποιητής γίγνεται οὗ ἂν ἀγάπη ἅψηται.

ABOUT THE AUTHOR

Peter Valerianos Fane served in the Silver Legion's artillery corps for over forty years, rising to the rank of Peer Colonel under High Lords Bellános and Dorómy Dallanar. His most well-known actions took place on Colodóx, Batládea, and Ebum—all in the service of the High House of Remain. In retirement, Colonel Fane spends the majority of his time on the great library world of Genonea, where he lectures on military theory, ancient Davanórian war poetry, and moral philosophy. He winters at his clan's hereditary estate on Egáton with his wife, his family, and a small flock of messenger dragons.

The Silver Kingdom awaits your thoughts regarding the latest tale from the Canon of Tarn. Indeed, Colonel Fane dispatches messenger dragons weekly to retrieve the latest reviews from Amazon and Goodreads, which he then archives along with other material from the Canon. So don't be shy—let your voice be heard. For the Remain!